Praise for Janet Dawson

"In recent years women private eyes have become big business, as anyone who's been following the fortunes of Sue Grafton and Sara Paretsky can attest. Thanks to their success, the way has been opened for many other women to write mysteries uniquely their own. A fine example is Janet Dawson."
The Denver Post

"Dawson keeps suspense and interest at high pitch."
Publishers Weekly

"Janet Dawson's new kid on the block, Jeri Howard, another Californian, is a kindred spirit of Dashiell Hammett's Continental Op character."
USA Weekend

"A welcome addition to this tough genre."
The New York Times Book Review

Also by Janet Dawson
Published by Fawcett Books:

KINDRED CRIMES

TILL THE OLD MEN DIE

Janet Dawson

FAWCETT CREST • NEW YORK

A Fawcett Crest Book
Published by Ballantine Books
Copyright © 1993 by Janet Dawson

Library of Congress Catalog Card Number: 92-97252

ISBN 0-449-22133-4

Manufactured in the United States of America

First Edition: April 1993

For Clarissa

Acknowledgments

Salamat po to Leonora Ballar and Benito Aquino for fiesta invitations and translations. I also wish to thank Special Agent Mike Smirnoff, Immigration and Naturalization Service; Lt. Mike Sims, Homicide Section, Oakland Police Department; Lynne Houghton, private investigator, for legwork lessons; Fran Boyle, for her help; and Susan Dunlap, Susan Lowe, Michael Mabes, Fred Isaac, and Bonnie Isaac for readthroughs and suggestions. And many thanks to my agent, Charlotte Sheedy, for her support.

Prologue

RAIN BLEW INTO HIS FACE AS THE MAN WALKED through the double glass doors of the building, leaving the warm light of the corridor for the wet darkness of the sidewalk. The rain had been a fine mist when he entered this building more than an hour ago. Now drops fell steadily as the wind buffeted him. He shivered and paused long enough to button the tan raincoat around his short, wiry body, tying the belt at the waist. As he started walking again, he turned up the coat's collar, wishing he'd brought a hat or an umbrella.

Behind him the double doors opened again. Footsteps joined him on the wet pavement as he neared the busy downtown intersection, but he didn't hear them. Their sound was drowned out by the other sounds that punctuated the night, growl of cars and buzz of people, bells and whistles and shouts, distant sirens, and above all the moan and patter of wind and rain.

He walked quickly toward the parking garage where he'd left his car, past glittering store windows and neon signs blurred by the rain, sharing the sidewalk with shoppers and derelicts and people out on the town, sampling the many sorrows and pleasures the city had to offer. By the time he reached the garage, his thick black hair, threaded with silver, was also beaded with rain. Under the concrete shelter he shook his head once or twice and the droplets flew.

One set of doors was just closing as he reached the bank of three elevators, so he waited for another elevator to descend, alone at first, then joined by a young man who kept playing with the zipper of his shiny blue cotton jacket. The two remaining elevators reached street level at the same time. The man in the tan raincoat stepped into the car on the right. The man in the blue jacket joined him, hands moving to the control panel. "What floor you goin' to?" he asked.

"Seven."

"Lucky seven it is," the younger man said, punching the button. "Same as me." As the elevator door closed, he stared out at the third figure, a dark-haired man who had just stepped into view, head bowed, hands stuck deep into the pockets of his black topcoat.

As the elevator rose, the younger man played again with the front of his jacket, running the zipper up and down. The older man ignored him, staring fixedly at the vertical line where the elevator doors came together. On seven, the older man stepped from the elevator into the wide, dimly lit arena full of vehicles. His was in the far corner. He walked toward it, his footsteps echoing on the concrete floor. He stepped between two parked cars, unfastening his tan raincoat, reaching for the car keys in the pocket of his gray slacks. Behind him he heard a soft *bing* as another elevator door opened on this floor.

He paused in the space where the snouts of two cars met, the key ring in his hand now, sorting the keys by touch, familiar with their shapes. Suddenly a hand seized his arm, spinning him around, slamming him back against the hood of a parked car, then yanking him upright. He dropped his car keys and drew in a shocked lungful of air as he saw two faces, one contorted, one cold.

One mouth sneered above a black topcoat, spat out a few words, and moved toward him. Then the black topcoat slipped behind him and two hands seized him, pinning his arms to his sides. In front of him the shiny metal teeth of a zipper opened and closed and opened again, while above them another mouth grinned like a death's head. The hands at the end of the two blue sleeves left the zipper tongue and invaded his clothing, picking and plucking at his tan raincoat and the tweed jacket he wore beneath it. The hands drew out his wallet, a pen, a handkerchief, and a forgotten grocery list.

He struggled and opened his mouth to scream, but the hand that held his wallet flew at his face, smacking him hard across his mouth and nose. He tasted blood as the other mouth moved against his hair and the other set of hands pulled his arms farther back.

In front of him one hand shoved the wallet into one pocket of the blue jacket and invaded his clothing again, this time pulling out a long brown plastic rectangle. The younger man held it up with a sharp hiss. The man in the black topcoat released the pinioned arms, seized the unexpected object, and fumbled with it. As he forced it open, two cylinders fell into his hands and he tossed them away. One tumbled under a parked car, while the other rolled just beyond the fallen key ring.

"Where is it?" one mouth snarled above the black topcoat. He struck the other man again and again. A streak of blood from his victim's streaming nose stained one white cuff at the end of one black sleeve. "Where is it?" His demand gained no response. He seized the older man's arms again and barked an order. His blue-jacketed companion stopped playing with his zipper and drew something from his pocket, something that seemed alive, glittering as it moved, like a snake about to strike.

Pain knifed into the older man once, twice, three times, pain burning-hot and liquid, like the blood that spurted, then seeped, slowly soaking his tweed jacket and tan raincoat. The second pair of hands released him, and he slumped to his knees in front of the parked car. He reached for the grille and tried to rise to his feet, but he couldn't get his body to obey. He fell forward, embracing the cold concrete floor, his nose filled with the stink of gas and oil and some new odor that must be his own blood.

Above him the two mouths conferred in urgent whispers, while four hands turned him onto his back and searched his clothes again. The blue jacket seemed to float high above him, while the black topcoat loomed at his side. Everything around him seemed fuzzy, but with a brief flash of clarity he saw the crimson smear on the white cuff.

Their voices sounded far away, as did their footsteps when they finally left him. He smiled up at the burned-out light fixture and managed to roll over onto his side, eyes blurring as he looked at tires and the undersides of cars. He saw his keys lying nearby, and one of the silver and black cylinders, but he couldn't quite reach them. He was so cold he felt numb. And tired. So tired that all he wanted was sleep.

"I keep seeing it," my father said after the first nightmare. "Imagining how it must have happened."

"Try not to think about it," I told him. A totally inadequate response, but what else can one say?

My father sat up in bed, illuminated by a pool of light from the lamp on his nightstand, and ran a hand through his thinning hair. He had a haunted, troubled look in his eyes, an expression I'd never seen before. I would have done anything to take it away. Unfortunately I couldn't remove the source of the look, that incident that my father referred to as "it."

Later I could guess how it must have happened, because I'd read the police report and talked to the investigating officer. And my father kept seeing it in the dreams that interrupted his sleep and seeped into his waking hours, drawing lines on his face and smudging shadows under his eyes. After the funeral he tried not to think about it, with the assistance of warm milk or sleeping pills. Soon he didn't have nightmares anymore.

Or if he did, he didn't tell me.

One

THE WOMAN WITH THE SCAR ON HER CHIN HAD costumed herself for the role of a widow. Her wardrobe included a black silk dress, stylish and expensive, accented by a circular gold brooch and a chic little hat with a veil, anchored to her smooth black chignon by a wicked-looking hatpin. A wide gold band adorned the third finger of her left hand. The manicured fingers of her right hand clutched a single sheet of paper.

Unfortunately for her, she had failed the audition. That's why her brown eyes glared beneath the plucked brows and jade eye shadow, and her full lips, sleek with coral lipstick, twisted with anger. That's why, on this warm Monday morning in May, she stood in the middle of the History Department office of California State University at Hayward, swearing at my father and Dr. Isabel Kovaleski in a mixture of Tagalog and English. I don't understand Tagalog, but the venom behind the words was unmistakable. As for the English, I hadn't heard language that colorful since the last time I visited the Alameda County Jail.

The woman's tirade cut through class-break chatter and caused heads to turn in the corridor, where I stood next to the bulletin board. Professors in nearby offices appeared in their doorways, looking for the source of the racket. I fingered a notice about spring-quarter finals and watched the drama in the office, mentally taking notes.

She was Filipina, her English good but accented, her voice throaty, almost guttural. Height five three, I guessed, weight about one ten, and I put her age as mid- to late thirties. I had noticed the scar right away, a thread of white along her left jawline, perhaps three or four inches long. It could have been caused by any number of things, but my first thought was that someone had struck her. Otherwise she looked prosperous and well kept, with a certain hard-eyed, calculating edge, and a high-handed attitude that told me she was used to getting her own way. Maybe that's why she was now angry enough to swear at the people she was trying to convince. She'd gone to a lot of trouble, but no one was buying her act.

She had been waving that sheet of paper under Dr. Kovaleski's nose. Now she shoved it into her black leather clutch purse, whirled, and marched out of the office, pushing past me without a glance. Her high heels staccatoed the linoleum as she headed for the stairwell. I followed her.

Outside Meiklejohn Hall, she plowed a path through crowds of students like a battleship at full steam, moving up the hillside steps toward the campus bookstore. Before reaching the store, she turned right and crossed the street to a parking lot, where a white Thunderbird with California plates straddled the line between two spaces. She unlocked the door, hurled the purse onto the passenger seat, and slid in behind the wheel. The engine roared and she backed the car out with a jerk, narrowly missing a couple of students. One of them yelled something at her. She responded with the raised middle digit of her left hand and gunned the engine. The Thunderbird squealed down a row of cars and exited the parking lot at an entrance.

I wrote down the Thunderbird's license number, then retraced my steps to Meiklejohn Hall. When I got back upstairs, Dr. Kovaleski was seated at her desk, a frown on her face and her fingers beating a tattoo on her desk blotter. My father, Dr. Timothy Howard, occupied one of the two chairs opposite her.

"What do you think, Jeri?" Dad asked, crossing one long leg over the other.

"Tell me again how all this started," I said, taking the other chair. Dad had given me bare bones on the phone the previous night, but I wanted to add some flesh to the skeleton.

"She says her name is Dolores Cruz Manibusan," Dr. Kovaleski said in her mittel-European accent. "She appeared quite suddenly Friday morning, demanding to see the head of the department. I'm acting chair, so I asked if I could help her. She announced that she was Dr. Manibusan's widow and she wanted his papers. That was the word she used—papers. I explained that Dr. Manibusan's office had been cleared out by his next of kin. She became quite angry and shouted at me. She said *she* was his next of kin and she'd be back today."

"Dr. Manibusan was murdered in January. This is the first week in May. It's been almost four months. Where," I wondered, "has the grieving widow been all this time?"

"Indeed." Isabel Kovaleski's voice was as dry as the grass on the hills surrounding the campus.

I looked at my father, searching for signs of that haunted expression he wore earlier this year. When he called me last night he'd sounded upset. Now his eyes were troubled, a frown etched his face below his thinning red-brown hair, and his lips were drawn into a thin line. I hoped this mystery woman with her off-the-wall claim wouldn't bring back the nightmares that came with the murder of Dr. Lito Manibusan.

He and Dad had been good friends as well as colleagues, both history professors at Cal State. Dad's specialty is American history, particularly the trans-Mississippi West, while Dr. Manibusan's expertise focused on Asia. In fact, he'd been on his way to a conference on that subject, at the University of Hawaii, when he was killed.

The last time Dad saw Dr. Manibusan alive was around six-thirty on a Friday evening in January. Rain fell on the city as my father drove over the Bay Bridge to San Francisco to meet some friends for dinner and a play at the Curran Theater. Dad parked his car on the seventh floor of the Sutter-Stockton garage, near Union Square. As he walked toward the elevator, putting on his raincoat, someone called his name.

"I was surprised to see him," Dad told me later. "I thought he was on his way to Honolulu."

The professor smiled and told Dad he planned to have dinner that evening with his brother-in-law in Daly City, south of San Francisco. He would spend the night there, then on Saturday morning catch a flight from San Francisco International. As they stepped onto the elevator and pressed the button for the street level, my father asked why his friend was in San Francisco. Dr. Manibusan said he had a stop to make first. Unfortunately, he didn't say where or why. He seemed to be in a hurry, Dad recalled, moving aside the cuff of his tweed sport jacket to check the watch on his left wrist. He carried a tan raincoat over one arm, and as the elevator descended, he put it on.

Dad was meeting his friends at the China Moon on Post Street near Mason, so he and Dr. Manibusan left the parking garage and walked quickly through the rain to the corner of Post and Powell, two blocks away. As they parted with a few words about seeing each other at work the following week, Dr. Manibusan raised his hand and waved good-bye, silhouetted against the lights of Union Square, hazy through the misting rain, with a clanging cable car as background music as it headed up Powell Street.

Dad didn't give the chance meeting another thought as he had dinner and went to the theater. After the performance he and his friends stopped at David's Deli on Geary, for coffee and pastry. It must have been about eleven-thirty when he returned to the parking garage, tossed his raincoat into the backseat, and got into his car. He backed the car halfway out of the slot, then stopped abruptly when he saw a crumpled figure in a tan raincoat lying on its right side with its back to my father, in a pool of what looked like oil.

"It never occurred to me that he was dead," Dad said several hours into Saturday morning. We were at the San Francisco Hall of Justice, and his green eyes brimming with shock in his white, distraught face, hands shaking as he held a paper cup of bad coffee. "I thought it was some poor street person who came in out of the rain and fell asleep between the cars. Or that somebody slipped in the oil and fell down. I think I said something, hey or hello. Then I leaned over and touched the shoulder. The body shifted and I saw the face. My God, it was Lito. He had blood all over his face. His eyes were open, just staring up at me."

My father cried out and backed away from the corpse. He told me later his hands felt as though they were burning. He turned away, saw a young couple walking toward their car, and called to them in a strangled voice. The man found a phone and summoned the police, while his wife stayed with Dad, whose heart was pounding, as he had trouble taking air into his tight chest. When the police arrived and Dad calmed down a bit he asked the woman to call his daughter in Oakland. That's how I wound up talking my way through a San Francisco police line in the early hours that Saturday morning.

I knew about the nightmares because I spent the next few nights with Dad at his condo in Castro Valley. The first time he cried out in the early hours before dawn, I roused myself from the daybed in the second bedroom and padded across the hallway to Dad's room. He turned on his bedside lamp and ran a hand over his face, assuring me that it was nothing.

"You had a bad dream." I touched his shoulder, wanting to banish ghosts.

"I keep seeing it," my father said. "Imagining how it must have happened."

"Try not to think about it." The words sounded foolish even as I spoke, but I didn't know what else to say. Dad sat up, propping himself against a pillow, and ran a hand through his hair. He seemed embarrassed, as though a sixtyish college professor wasn't allowed to have bad dreams after finding the body of a friend.

It's okay, Dad, I told him. Remember all those nights you came to my rescue? When I was a kid, the wind often blew the bare branches of a tree against my bedroom window, an odd rattling sound that sent shivers up my spine as I watched the moon shining through the curtains onto my patterned wallpaper, creating shadows that seemed to take on life. The tapping noise and the shifting light summoned the ghosts and ghoulies who crept out of my closet or slithered from under my bed. When I cried out in the night, it was usually Dad who turned on the light and sat by my bed until the specters went back into hiding.

Now it was my turn to sit by the bed and watch my father slip back into uneasy sleep. I leaned over and kissed the top of his head, where his red-brown hair was thinning, feeling protective, as though I were the parent and he the child. He's such a gentle, scholarly, sometimes unworldly soul who believes the best about people until he is convinced otherwise. As a private investigator, I've seen a lot more of the ugly side of life and people. That doesn't mean I'm used to it. But it doesn't shock me the way the sight of Lito Manibusan's corpse shocked my father.

He kept having dreams, and for the next few days he talked about Dr. Manibusan's murder, the way people do when they're trying to work something out of their system. He and his colleagues at Cal State attended the funeral that next week, held on the day the professor would have returned from Hawaii. Then Dad didn't talk about it at all. He had participated in the public rituals of grief, and now it was time to put away the feelings and get on with life. A very grown-up thing to do. It's how we cope with death and other tragedies.

But things like murder have a way of creeping out of the closet, like my long-ago ghosts. Now, as I sat here in Dr. Kovaleski's office, I saw a hint of the lines and shadows I'd seen on my father's face that weekend four months before, when he found Dr. Manibusan's body. I feared that for him the woman claiming to be his friend's widow brought with her the old nightmares.

"It's all so very odd," Isabel Kovaleski was saying. I tore my eyes away from Dad and turned my attention to her.

"Odd doesn't quite describe it," I said. "With the right combination of guts, bravado, and timing, she just might have pulled it off. Guts and bravado she may have, but her timing—'' I shook my head.

"Nevertheless," Dr. Kovaleski said, "we really must look into this incident. I've talked it over with Dean Cleary, and he agrees. Lito's personnel file listed a nephew as his next of kin, a Mr. Alejandro Tongco of Union City. I met him at the funeral, but I must say I don't remember what he looks like. He and another man—a brother, I think—came to the department the week after the funeral. They donated all of Lito's books to the university, packed everything else into boxes, and took it all away. More important, the money from Dr. Manibusan's pension plan was distributed to the beneficiaries he listed. If this woman really is the surviving spouse, and does have a legitimate claim, we need to be certain. We should locate Mr. Tongco as soon as possible. Perhaps he can shed some light on the situation. But I tried to call him at the number listed in Lito's personnel file and I got a recording saying the phone had been disconnected."

"So you want me to find him," I said. "That shouldn't be too difficult. I don't buy this mystery woman's story at all. If she really is Mrs. Manibusan, why hasn't she sicced a lawyer onto the university? That would be the logical thing to do. No, she's after something, and I don't think it's a slice of Dr. Manibusan's pension. Whatever she wants must be in the professor's files. She thinks she can get it by posing as his widow." I turned to my father. "You told me someone was seen prowling around your office last Wednesday. Could it have been this woman?"

"I don't know," Dad said. "I didn't see her, but Nancy Calderon did."

Nancy Calderon was a clerical worker, a part-timer who was working that day. Summoned from the departmental office a few doors down, she repeated her story. While Dad was briefly away from his office last Wednesday afternoon, Nancy glanced through his open door and saw a woman rummaging through the stuff on my father's perpetually untidy desk. The woman mumbled something about a research paper and made a hasty departure. "She was in her thirties,"

Nancy guessed, "Asian or Latino. Her hair was tied up in a red kerchief, but of course I could see her bangs. They were black. Couldn't see her eyes, though. She was wearing dark glasses."

"Interesting," I said. "Did she look at all like the woman who was just here?"

"It's hard to say. The woman I saw was short, but she was wearing baggy blue sweatpants and a big T-shirt, not dressed up like the lady who was here today."

"This is a commuter campus," Dad pointed out, "with all sorts of people attending classes. But she was definitely not one of my students. Not in any of the classes I have this quarter."

Dr. Kovaleski sighed. "I wouldn't have given the incident much thought, but the following night someone tried to break into the History Department office. Then on Friday, Dolores Cruz appeared."

"Tell me about the attempted break-in." There wasn't much to tell. On Thursday, as evening classes ended and the students dispersed, a professor leaving his office at Meiklejohn Hall looked down the corridor and spotted someone trying to open the door to the History Department office, across the hall from Dad's cubicle. Challenged, the intruder bolted for the nearest stairwell.

"Man or woman?" I asked.

"Couldn't tell. We've been having a crime wave on campus," Isabel Kovaleski explained. "Robberies and assaults. Purses stolen at the library, offices burglarized. A math professor was mugged last week after a late class. So I don't know if these incidents here are separate or part of the whole. You should talk to the director of the campus Public Safety Department."

"I will. It would help me if you'd talk to other members of the staff, to see if anything else has happened that might focus on Dad or Dr. Manibusan—phone calls, other unexplained visitors. As for Dolores Cruz, did you get a good look at that piece of paper?" I asked Dr. Kovaleski.

She shook her head. "Not really. She never let it out of

her hand. She claims it's a marriage certificate, that they were married in Manila last August.''

"The hell of it is, Lito did go to Manila last August," Dad said. "That surprised me. He'd been planning to spend the break between summer and fall quarters in the central valley, interviewing Filipino immigrants for his book. Then he dropped by one night, gave me his extra key, said he had to go to Manila instead, and would I water the plants and take in the mail. He was gone two weeks, back in early September in time for fall quarter. I don't know why he went to the Philippines. Research, I assume. And he still had family back there. But getting married—'' Dad shook his head. "It's out of character. If Lito had married, he would have told someone. He'd have changed the beneficiaries on his pension, because he took care of things like that. Besides, he was so broken up after his wife died of cancer, I just can't see him getting married again, let alone so suddenly."

Behind her desk Isabel looked troubled. "I don't know, Jeri. Perhaps we're making too much of this because of the way Lito died. It could be nothing, merely a nuisance."

"Maybe," I said, but I didn't think so. I remembered the calculating brown eyes in the angry face. Dolores Cruz hadn't been able to get what she was after by posing as Dr. Manibusan's widow. But most plotters have contingency plans. The woman reminded me of a sleek and scrappy terrier with a bone in its mouth. Whatever she was looking for, I had a feeling she wouldn't quit worrying the bone until she found what she sought. "The nephew cleared out the professor's office, and probably the professor's house as well. So Alejandro Tongco has all the professor's personal effects."

"Not all," Dad said with an embarrassed frown. Dr. Kovaleski and I looked at him, surprised. "I have something. Or I thought I did. I didn't even remember it until after I talked to you last night, Jeri. But I looked everywhere, my office at home, my office here at the university. I can't find it."

"Can't find what?" Isabel Kovaleski and I asked simultaneously.

"A brown envelope, five by seven inches, addressed to me here at Cal State." Dad sketched a shape in the air and told us he'd received the envelope in the mail five days after Lito Manibusan's murder, on the day of the funeral. When he opened it, the first thing he pulled out was a brief note from the professor, asking Dad to keep the envelope in a safe place.

"I was about to leave for his funeral. You can imagine how I felt," my father said, running a hand through his hair. "It was eerie. I was so upset, I didn't even look to see what else was in the envelope. I just closed the flap and tossed it aside. Now I can't remember where I put it."

"You stashed it in a safe place," I commented, teasing him a bit. It wasn't the first time Dad had gone into absentminded professor mode and misplaced something.

"Or put it in Lito's office," Isabel added. "Maybe it got packed up with the rest of his things."

"Could be." I stood up to leave. "In that case, it might still be in Dr. Manibusan's files. When I locate Mr. Tongco, maybe I'll find the envelope as well."

Two

WHEN I LEFT MEIKLEJOHN HALL I TOOK WITH ME a recent issue of a history journal containing an article written by the late Dr. Lito Manibusan, his last published work according to Dad. My father had also unearthed a photograph of his friend, a color snapshot taken last year at some History Department function. In it, a compact Asian man looked unsmilingly into the camera, his dark brown eyes intense and serious. He had been near my father's age, with a few wrinkles around his eyes and his short black hair threaded with silver. The professor held a glass of wine in his right hand, but he didn't look as though he was enjoying himself. Dad said the photograph was taken right after Mrs. Manibusan died.

I had met the professor, of course, since he and Dad were such good friends. I thought the snapshot was a good likeness of the man I remembered. The only time I'd seen Dr. Manibusan smile was while his wife, Sara, was still alive. I had met her, too, a short, round-faced woman whose gentle humor contrasted with her husband's more sober mien. They had no children, and together the two of them seemed to be such a perfectly matched pair that I understood why her death sent the professor into a long black tunnel of grief and isolation. That made it all the more bizarre that Dr. Manibusan would suddenly get married last August—to the unlikely Dolores Cruz—and then not tell anyone.

The university's Department of Public Safety was located in the basement of the campus library. I gave my card to the patrolman on duty and asked to see the director. He picked up a phone and punched in a number, talking briefly to the party on the other end of the line. A moment later an interior door opened and Cal State's head cop favored me with a penetrating gaze and an economical greeting. "Jeri Howard? I'm Chief Martini."

She didn't offer her hand. Instead, she pulled her door wider and motioned me inside. As I stepped past her into the windowless office, I gave her a quick once-over, guessing she was in her late thirties. She was a couple of inches shorter than my five feet eight inches, looking trim in her crisply tailored uniform. She had straight black brows over brown eyes, high cheekbones, and a long, prominent nose. Her black hair, silver at the temples, was combed straight back from her face and tucked behind her ears, where tiny gold balls decorated each lobe. The only ring she wore was a plain gold wedding band.

At the front of her orderly desk I saw a large ornate pen-holder decorated with the globe and eagle insignia of the United States Marine Corps. The brass plate was inscribed to Master Sergeant Elaine A. Martini on the occasion of her retirement from the Corps, five years ago. Next to the phone was an eight by ten color photograph in a silver frame, showing Martini looking somewhat softer than she did now, in a blue knit dress and a smile, standing with a dark, broad-shouldered man in a Marine Corps warrant officer's uniform. She and the man stood behind two teenagers, a boy and girl who looked like amalgams of their parents. Based on the ages of the kids and her Marine Corps retirement date, I revised my estimate of Elaine Martini's age upward.

"Good-looking kids," I said.

"Thanks. Have a seat, Miss Howard."

I took a chair and she sat down as well, lacing her fingers together on the surface of her desk as she regarded me with those direct brown eyes. "Dean Cleary tells me the History Department has retained you," she said in her low, no-nonsense voice. I sensed that she didn't particularly like the idea of having an investigator on her turf. "I gather it has something to do with a woman claiming to be Dr. Manibusan's heir.''

"Yes, it does. I'm sure the university has procedures for handling such claims. For now I'm simply going to locate Dr. Manibusan's nephew, since he's no longer at the address listed in the university records. I stopped by because I wanted you to know I was in your jurisdiction. But I am curious about the attempted break-in at the History Department and the woman who was seen in Dr. Howard's office. Possibly that person was the same woman who showed up today. Her name is Dolores Cruz, by the way.''

"Maybe. But she sounds like a crank to me. I'll check to see if we have a student registered under the name Dolores Cruz. I take it you want to look at the reports on both incidents.'' She let me read the paperwork, a bit reluctantly, I thought. But someone, probably Dean Cleary, had told her to cooperate, so she did. There wasn't much in either report, though, beyond what Dad and Dr. Kovaleski had told me.

I gave her the license plate number of the Thunderbird Dolores Cruz had been driving, just in case it had come to the attention of the campus police. "The way this woman drives,'' I told Martini, "she must have some tickets.''

After leaving the Cal State Department of Public Safety, I retrieved my car and drove down the hill to the flatland, through Hayward to the Nimitz Freeway. I headed north along the east shore of San Francisco Bay, past San Lorenzo and San Leandro to downtown Oakland. In the foyer of the Franklin Street building where I have a third-floor office, I encountered my friend Cassie Taylor, stylish as usual in one of her lawyer uniforms, a blue linen suit and high-heeled pumps.

"How do you walk in those things?'' I asked. "It's six blocks to the courthouse.''

"That's why I'm not taking the stairs.'' She punched the button and we waited for the elevator to lumber its way down to the first floor. I'd been reading the first page of Dr. Manibusan's article, a scholarly study on crime and Filipino immigrants. "I know someone from the Philippines,'' Cassie said, glancing at the title as the elevator arrived. We stepped aside while it emptied of occupants, then got in. Cassie pushed the button for the third floor. "A photographer, Felice Navarro. She's a member of our East Bay professional women's group. The one I've been trying to get you to join."

Cassie had cajoled me into attending a few of the group's monthly luncheons. I'm a professional, but as a private investigator I feel little in common with the doctors, lawyers, and corporate types in suits and briefcases who make up a majority of the group. Still, it's a good place to make contacts. At the meetings I had attended, I handed out my business card and as a result got several cases from women attorneys who wanted to hire a woman investigator.

When we arrived on the third floor, Cassie headed for the front suite of offices occupied by the law firm of Alwin, Taylor, and Chao. My own office was opposite the elevator, a long, narrow room with J. HOWARD INVESTIGATIONS lettered in gold on the wooden door. Once inside, I set the history journal and photo on my desk and walked to the back of the office to open my lone window. It looks out at the flat roof of the building next door and, beyond that, the steel girders of a new building going up several blocks away, an indicator of Oakland's much-promised urban renaissance. The new construction blocked what used to be a view of the freeway. If I were on a higher floor, I might have been able to see a sliver of water, the estuary separating Oakland from the island city of Alameda. The window and the water's proximity at least gave me some light and the hope of a breeze on this hot day.

I unfastened the top button of my striped cotton shirt and stood for a moment, watching the heat simmer off the surrounding buildings. It was early May and northern California was heading into another summer of drought, the winter snowpack below normal and the rains of March and April insufficient to fill the reservoirs and meet the needs of the growing Bay Area population. So we were back to water rationing and mandatory cutbacks, short showers and bricks in toilet tanks.

In the back corner of my office a square wooden table holds my coffee maker and various other supplies. Tucked under the table is a little refrigerator. Now I opened it and took out a bottle of mineral water, running the chilly glass over my perspiring forehead. I twisted off the metal cap and took a swallow. Moving back to my desk, I checked the messages on the answering machine. One call was from an insurance adjuster who frequently hired me to investigate claims. The remaining calls were from people I didn't know—prospective clients, I hoped.

I'm a sole practitioner of the private investigator's craft, and every bit of income is welcome. I've done fairly well on my own, but it hasn't been as steady as the years when I worked as a legal secretary and paralegal for an Oakland law firm, or during my five years as an investigator for the Errol Seville Agency before Errol had his heart attack and retired to Carmel. But I like being my own boss, and my clientele keeps growing, mostly insurance and prelitigation work referred by satisfied clients and by friends like Cassie.

I returned the calls, setting up appointments with two prospective clients, both for the next day. The insurance adjuster had an errand that meant spending a good chunk of the afternoon digging through records in the Contra Costa County Courthouse in Martinez. I ate lunch, the remains of yesterday's turkey sandwich, and finished my mineral water, tossing the empty bottle into the recycling box I kept under the table.

It used to be a lot easier to obtain someone's address from the Department of Motor Vehicles. But in the interest of protecting the privacy of Jeri Howard, citizen, the state of California has made life more difficult for Jeri Howard, investigator. Now I had to be judicious and selective about prevailing on my contact at the DMV, since I didn't want to get him fired, thereby losing him altogether. But all I had on Dolores Cruz was the license plate of the white Thunderbird she'd been driving. So I called the clerk at the DMV and he groused about it, but finally agreed to run a check on the number.

"It'll take a couple of days," he said grumpily. "Don't call me, I'll call you."

I already had a file of sorts on the Manibusan murder. It contained a copy of the police report and several newspaper clippings. The media, print and broadcast, had played up the irony of Dad finding his colleague's body. I read through the police report.

Dr. Manibusan's death looked like a robbery, a particularly vicious one, since the professor had been struck several times in the face, hard enough to bloody his nose. His wallet was missing and had never turned up. I looked over the list of items the police had found in the vicinity. Dr. Manibusan's key ring, a ballpoint pen, a white linen handkerchief, a crumpled scrap of blue paper containing a penciled grocery list, and a couple of AA batteries, one under a car, the other next to the key ring. The battery closest to Dr. Manibusan's body had a smeared partial fingerprint that wasn't the professor's, nor did it match any on file in the fingerprint computer used by the San Francisco Police Department.

I set the report aside, recalling a conversation with Inspector Cobb, the investigating officer. He theorized two assailants, one holding Dr. Manibusan's arms, while the other stabbed the professor, because there was no indication the dead man had tried to shield himself or deflect the assault with his arms or hands. On the other hand, the professor could have been attacked suddenly, swiftly, with no chance to fight back. Either way, he'd bled to death from three deep stab wounds near the heart.

I picked up the phone and called SFPD, finding Cobb at his desk. Had there been any progress in the four-month-old investigation? There hadn't, which didn't surprise me. Despite a much-publicized plea for witnesses and information, the police had neither. Most cops will tell you if they don't have a suspect in their sights within forty-eight hours of a murder, the perpetrator's trail rapidly grows cold and stale.

I made a few notes about today's visit to Cal State Hayward and stuck them into the folder, returning it to the filing cabinet. Finding out what Dolores Cruz was up to would have to wait until I had a lead on her address.

Then, two nights later, someone broke into Dad's town house.

Three

THAT EVENING I WAS SPRAWLED ON THE SOFA IN A pair of baggy green sweats with a hole in one knee. After dinner I'd popped a tape of *The Maltese Falcon* into the VCR and settled in, my head propped on pillows at one end of the sofa and my bare feet resting on the arm at the other end. My fat cat, Abigail, joined me, kneading my stomach with her paws before giving herself a thorough wash. Finally she finished her ablutions, curled up, and went to sleep while I watched Hammett's tale unfold. I had just gotten to the part where Bogie tells Mary Astor, "I hope they don't hang you, precious . . ." when the phone rang. Grumbling, I hit the pause button on the VCR remote, dislodged the cat, and shuffled off to the kitchen to pick up the receiver in midpeal. Abigail muttered cat imprecations as she followed me, hoping for food in place of a lap. When I heard my father's terse report, I put on a pair of shoes and grabbed my car keys.

It took me about twenty minutes to drive south on Interstate 580, through Oakland and San Leandro to Castro Valley, exiting at Crow Canyon Road. I climbed into the hills, then took a left at the intersection anchored by a convenience store, heading up the street where Dad lived. It's a hilly residential area with single-family homes mixed in with condos and apartments, east of Castro Valley proper, with some woods and open space nearby. Dad lives in the third of three buildings, each with four units arrayed in a line up the hill's slope, backing up to a ravine. Between each building a drive leads to the carports behind. Dad's two-story town house is the last unit in the uppermost building, with twenty yards of trees and shrubs between the end of the property and a split-level house farther up the hill.

A patrol car was pulling away from the curb as I parked. My father met me at the door, accompanied by his next-door neighbor Harold, a retired navy chief petty officer.

"What happened?" I asked.

"I have a class from six to nine," Dad said. "I got home about nine-thirty and the police were here. Harold called them. He saw somebody in the house and he knew it wasn't me."

"I know his schedule." Harold was a burly man with a light tenor voice that sounded out of place coming from a man with his bulldog face. "Besides, his car wasn't in the carport. I was out on my patio, looked up, and the light was on in the back bedroom—"

"My office," Dad said.

"That's right," Harold continued. "The blinds were open and I saw somebody moving around. I knew it wasn't Tim, because he's tall. This guy was short, with dark hair."

"What time was this?" I asked Harold.

"About nine."

I looked from Harold to Dad. "Did the cops have an idea how the intruder got in?"

"Picked the lock on the patio door," Dad said. "The patrolman who just left said it looked pretty slick, like whoever it was knew what he was doing. He was gone when the police got here."

"Was anything taken?"

"Nothing down here, as far as I can tell." Dad swept his hand toward the living room, and I saw that his stereo system was still intact, though cabinet doors had been opened to reveal LPs and CDs. Drawers in the built-in storage cabinet between the kitchen and dining room had been pulled open and the contents of several dumped on the floor. The television and VCR hadn't been touched, though, nor had Dad's collection of Indian pottery, resting in the cabinet where he stored his treasures. Some of those pots were far more valuable than the electronic gadgets.

"Some stuff was rearranged in my bedroom," Dad said, "and the office is a mess."

"Let's take a look."

We went upstairs, with Harold tagging along, to the smaller of the two bedrooms. Along one wall was the daybed, with a trundle bed underneath, for company. Opposite that was a desk and a four-drawer filing cabinet. Bookshelves filled the other two walls. Most of Dad's files and books were at the university, but he had quite a few at home, too.

The office was indeed a mess. All four drawers of the filing cabinet had been opened. Manila file folders were strewn on the desk, the floor, and the daybed. Books were shoved around on the shelves as though the intruder had been looking for something hidden behind the volumes.

"I'm surprised he didn't take the computer," Harold said, pointing to Dad's new portable system resting on one end of the desk. I wasn't. My best guess was that whoever broke into Dad's town house was after the envelope Dr. Manibusan had mailed to Dad before he died.

Back downstairs I examined the lock on the sliding glass door. The town house had a patio enclosed by a tall redwood fence running the width of the unit, with about twelve feet between the glass door and the gate leading to the carport. The gate locked and Dad usually secured it, but it was open when he and the police arrived, indicating the intruder had taken that route.

Harold decided it was time he went home. While he and Dad were at the front door, I went to the kitchen and picked up the receiver of the wall phone. I unscrewed the mouthpiece. Nothing there that shouldn't be there. There was a second phone upstairs in Dad's bedroom. No bug there either, but that didn't mean there wasn't an electronic device somewhere in the town house.

"Jeri, where are you?"

"Up here." I came down the stairs. "Walk me to my car."

I had parked the Toyota directly in front of Dad's town house. Once we were outside, I turned to my father. "Get another lock for that sliding glass door. The one you've got is too easy to open."

"I will."

"What's your schedule tomorrow?" I asked him.

"I have a nine o'clock class and I'm at the university until about six. Why?"

"Give me your extra key. I'm coming back to sweep for electronic devices."

He looked stunned. "You think he planted a bug?"

"I don't know. Maybe I'm being paranoid. But there's no harm in being careful. These days he might even have planted a virus in your computer. That's out of my league, but I can certainly have a friend of mine sweep for bugs. In the meantime, stay off the phone, or watch what you say when you're talking. When you put your office back together, see if you can determine whether anything is missing."

Dad took his key ring from his pocket, removed his second house key, and handed it to me. "We've been saying he, but it might just have well been a woman. It's that envelope Lito sent me, right?"

I fingered the key. "Offhand, I can't think of any other reason for tonight's break-in. Especially since someone was prowling around your office at the university last week. Does anyone besides you, me, and Dr. Kovaleski know about the envelope?"

Dad shook his head. "No. I haven't mentioned it to a soul. I wish I could remember what I did with it."

"Look again, here and at the university. I'll find Dr. Manibusan's nephew and see if the envelope is somewhere in the files he took out of the professor's office."

Dad voiced the question that had been on both our minds. "Do you think it was this Cruz woman?"

"I don't know. She's short with dark hair. She's looking for something that belonged to the professor. And a woman with dark hair was seen in your office last week. Question is, how did she—or whoever—know that Dr. Manibusan sent you the envelope?''

I went home to a night of interrupted sleep. It wasn't just that I was concerned about Dad. Abigail spent most of the night hunting and killing her yellow mouse, a cat toy made of crocheted lemon-colored yarn, its ears and tail frayed and fuzzed, its black felt eyes long gone. And I had only myself to blame.

My motive in purchasing the mouse was Abigail's welfare. She's a ten-year-old indoor cat who spends her days sleeping and eating. As a result, she's too fat and I get lectured about it every time I take her to the vet. I tried some of that low-cal cat food. She looked at me like I was on drugs. So I mixed the low-cal stuff with the regular kibble. With unerring accuracy she ate the regular stuff and left the rest, giving me a haughty stare that asked who was trying to fool whom. Exercise, I thought, but how to move Abigail's silver and brown bulk off the dining room table, a favorite snooze spot, especially when she has a whole basket of cat toys she ignores.

But the yellow mouse evidently caught my cat's fancy as much as it caught mine, with unexpected results. She played with it constantly, tossing it up in the air, pouncing on it, kicking it with her hind legs while she chewed on it. She discovered some long-buried cat memory of being a jungle hunter. Each night she carried the yarn mouse in her mouth, yowling deep in her throat like a mountain lion as she stalked through the apartment, usually at three A.M. That morning I awakened to find the chewed and dilapidated mouse sharing my pillow.

''I ought to take this thing away from you,'' I threatened. But she was enjoying it so much. I hadn't seen her so frisky since she was a kitten. I brushed the mouse to the floor as I got up. Abigail followed it, landing with a thump. She preceded me through the living room to the kitchen, where I fed her before making coffee.

After a bowl of cereal and a quick glance through the morning paper, I picked up the phone and called Levi Zotowska. I met Levi several years before while I was an investigator with the Seville Agency. He was a big, solid man in his forties whose blond hair was fading to silver. It was long and silky and he wore it in a ponytail. Levi was from the coal country of eastern Pennsylvania, but he left it long ago, in spirit as well as body. He came to UC Berkeley as a freshman and embraced the sixties like a lover. He still lived in Berkeley, in a brown-shingled house north of the campus, with his wife, Nell, and four stair-step kids with the same cornsilk hair. His passion is electronics and he owns a shop on Telegraph Avenue, around the corner from People's Park, where in another lifetime he'd been teargassed and arrested.

"Jeri, you just get better-looking," he said as he climbed out of his van parked in front of Dad's town house. He gathered me into a bruising bear hug.

"Don't let Nell hear you say that."

"She wouldn't mind. We haven't seen you in a while. Come over for dinner. Nell will make her famous carrot cake."

"You shouldn't tempt me like that," I said. Nell's famous carrot cake has cream-cheese frosting an inch thick. If I ate at the Zotowskas every day, I'd be as big as a bear myself.

"So what's the gig?" Levi asked.

"Somebody broke into Dad's town house last night. I want to know if he—or she—left any calling cards."

Levi got his equipment out of the van. As we went up the walk, I dug out the extra key Dad had given me the night before and unlocked the front door. It was eight-thirty, and Dad was already on his way to the university. Levi started his electronic sweep upstairs in the office, then moved slowly from room to room. He didn't find anything on the second floor, and his sweep of the ground level yielded nothing.

"Clean," he reported, standing in the middle of the living room.

I frowned and shook my head. "I'm sorry to drag you all the way down here, Levi. I guess I am being paranoid."

"No, you're being cautious. Somebody breaks into your old man's place and trashes his office, you got to take precautions. Besides, I don't mind." Levi gathered up his electronic gizmos. Locking the door behind us, I walked him to his van. "Come see us," he called as he drove off.

I headed south to the university. At Meiklejohn Hall I plinked a quarter into the jar in the History Department lounge and helped myself to a mugful of bitter black coffee, sipping it while I waited for my father to finish his first class. When he was free I joined him in his book-lined office.

"Did you find anything?" he asked, red-brown eyebrows drawn together.

"No. Levi swept the whole place. It's clean."

"When I got to work I told Isabel about the break-in. Turns out someone—a woman—called here yesterday, asking for my home address. Unfortunately she got it from a grad student working in the office."

"Wonderful," I said. "Where is said grad student?"

We crossed the hall to Isabel Kovaleski's office and she summoned the student. He was a skinny guy with pale brown hair and a wispy mustache that didn't succeed in making him appear any older than he was, which was probably early twenties. As I quizzed him in Isabel's office, he looked as though he expected me to rip the buttons off his plaid shirt, burn his thesis, and drum him out of the master's program.

"I know I shouldn't have done it," he said, stumbling over the words, "but she said she was calling from a furniture store about Dr. Howard's order and the salesman wrote down the address wrong and the delivery truck was on its way and if she didn't get the address, she'd have to reschedule the delivery for next week. And Dr. Howard wasn't in his office so—"

"Never mind that," I interrupted. "What did her voice sound like? Was it pitched high or low? Did she have an accent? Any speech quirks or impediments?"

He screwed up his face and concentrated for a long moment, stroking his almost nonexistent mustache. "It was on the high end, you know. Kind of light and breathy. And she did have an accent. Not really heavy, but not your basic midwestern English either."

I traded looks with Dad and Dr. Kovaleski, recalling Dolores Cruz's voice as low in timbre. The grad student brightened suddenly and held up a finger. "She said 'ax' instead of 'ask.' She said she hated to 'ax,' but she had to have Dr. Howard's address."

"Well, that's something," I said. What, I wasn't sure. After obtaining Dad's address, anyone with a map of Castro Valley could locate the town house. And if Dolores Cruz had been hanging around the university, she would know my father's schedule—it was on a card posted outside his office door. But I didn't think the woman who called yesterday was Dolores Cruz. Which left me with the intriguing prospect that more than one person might be looking for Dr. Manibusan's envelope.

Four

WHEN I GOT TO MY OFFICE IN OAKLAND, I CALLED
my contact at the Department of Motor Vehicles. On Monday he'd told me it would take a couple of days to run the
plate number on the car Dolores Cruz had been driving. But
the break-in at my father's town house had increased the
urgency of the situation. In answering my request, he added
a new question.

The white Thunderbird belonged to one Charles B. Randall, who lived at an address on Lakeside Avenue near Seventeenth Street. Who was he, I wondered, and how did he
fit into the picture? Did Dolores Cruz live at that address?
Maybe she was renting the place from Randall. If that was
the case, it was odd that she also had the use of his car.

I walked the few blocks to the Alameda County Courthouse, a multistoried white building looming near the eastern
shore of downtown Oakland's Lake Merritt. Dolores Cruz—
or Manibusan—was not doing business in Alameda County
under either name. Nor was she registered to vote. Charles
Randall was, as a Republican. Alejandro Tongco, Dr. Manibusan's nephew, had chosen the Democrats, but the registration affidavit showed the address in Union City I already
had, the one he'd apparently left. I went across the street to
the county administration building to check the assessor's
records. Dolores Cruz didn't own any property in Alameda
County. Charles Randall owned a unit in a condominium
complex called the Parkside Towers, at the Lakeside Avenue
address on his DMV records.

The Union City house owned by Alejandro and Nina

Tongco had been sold in February, the month after Dr. Manibusan's murder. I wrote down the name of the current owner and transaction document number, then went back to the courthouse, this time to the recorder's office. This is why they call it legwork, I told myself, waiting for the green light at the corner of Oak and Fourteenth. I found the real estate documents on microfilm. They provided no forwarding address, but they did contain the names of the real estate agents and title companies who had handled the transaction. Surely someone could tell me where to find Mr. Tongco.

As I unlocked the door to my office, my phone was ringing. It was Dan Greenlow, an attorney and a regular client. "Kyle didn't show up for the deposition," he said glumly.

I swore under my breath. Kyle was an affable, easygoing construction worker from Pinole. He had witnessed an auto accident involving Dan Greenlow's client, the defendant in a personal injury case. At Dan's request I had located and interviewed Kyle, whose information was favorable to the defendant. The plaintiff's attorney wanted to depose Kyle, who evidently didn't understand that failing to respond to a deposition subpoena means you're in contempt. Now the plaintiff's counsel could ask the court to issue a bench warrant for Kyle. More important, as far as Dan was concerned, the other attorney was threatening to ask that Kyle's testimony be excluded from the trial. The deposition had been rescheduled. Now Dan pleaded with me to find Kyle one more time and explain the situation to him.

"I've already explained it to him. Words of one syllable, even. Maybe you ought to get a bench warrant. Spending the night in jail might get Kyle's attention."

"I don't want to turn him into a hostile witness," Dan said. "I need him to win this case. Just find him, Jeri. Escort him to the damned deposition if you have to. I'll pay your usual, plus a bonus."

Nothing like the promise of extra money to appeal to my baser needs, like paying rent. I set out in search of the reluctant witness. Kyle's union local couldn't, or wouldn't, tell me where to find him, so I went to the construction site in

Richmond where I had first located him. No luck there, so I tried his apartment in Pinole, farther north on Interstate 80. A neighbor told me she thought he'd mentioned a job on a commercial building in Antioch, out in eastern Contra Costa County. I drove inland on State Highway 4 and checked several construction sites. No Kyle, but I found someone who told me he was working in Tracy.

Halfway to Stockton, I grumbled to myself. Hell, more than halfway. I cut through the Delta region where the San Joaquin and Sacramento rivers flow together toward San Francisco Bay, driving through rich cropland bisected by canals. After going through Brentwood I consulted my map and headed southeast on a country road until I hit Tracy, located at the north of a rough triangle formed where Interstates 5 and 580 meet in the central valley. Tracy and other towns out here were growing fast, due to the astronomical housing prices in the Bay Area. You could still buy a three-bedroom house at a reasonable cost in Tracy or Manteca or Modesto—if you were willing to accept a commute that kept you on the road two to three hours a day.

It was midafternoon when I finally ran Kyle to ground, east of Tracy, where tract houses were gobbling up acres of farmland. "I can't take time off this job," he protested as I backed him into a corner. After spending hours driving from construction site to construction site in my non-air-conditioned Toyota, I was not in a particularly forgiving mood. I explained the situation to him again, in words of one syllable, and told him he would be at the rescheduled deposition later this month or he'd answer to me as well as the lawyers. I hoped his testimony was worth it. I couldn't imagine him being a good witness. He had the attention span of a rock.

I headed back to the Bay Area on Interstate 580, my Toyota climbing the eastern slope of Altamont Pass, where energy-generating windmills lined the ridges on either side of the freeway, blades whirling in the constant wind. The rolling hills looked like old velvet fading from green to brown, a testament to the dry year.

At Pleasanton I took the Interstate 680 exit south toward Fremont and San Jose. As long as I was out this way, I might as well swing by the address in Union City where Dr. Manibusan's nephew had lived. It had been only three months since Alejandro Tongco's house was sold. Maybe the current owner or the neighbors would know where I could find him. I left the freeway at Niles Canyon Road, headed west. When I reached Mission Boulevard in Fremont I angled north toward Union City. The town was hemmed by the Bay and the hills to the east, one of a series of suburban communities between Oakland and San Jose, threading the shoreline like beads on a string. I located the house in a subdivision off DeCoto Road, one of many similar one-story stucco homes with picture windows and postage-stamp front porches. The name on the mailbox read Carroll. A young woman answered the door, blond hair caught back in a ponytail and a baby riding her hip.

"Mr. and Mrs. Tongco?" she said. "We didn't have any dealings with them directly, just with the real estate people. They must have left a forwarding address with the post office, because we haven't gotten any of their mail."

She gave me the name of the realty company, which I already had from the documents at the courthouse. I thanked her and stepped off the front porch, assessing my chances of finding anyone in this neighborhood who remembered the Tongcos. It was past three in the afternoon. My stomach reminded me that it had been a long time since this morning's cereal and coffee. I thought seriously about heading back to DeCoto Road to search for a fast-food joint where I could get a dose of grease and salt. Then I could hit the post office in search of Alejandro Tongco's forwarding address and try to locate the real estate agent who sold the house.

"You look lost, hon," a voice said, interrupting my reverie as I stood on the sidewalk. A large woman in bright purple slacks and a pink and green flowered shirt stood before me. I could have sworn she had blue hair, but maybe it was the sun playing tricks on my eyes. She held a red leather leash. At the other end of the leash was a brown and white barrel-shaped terrier who had detected the presence of cat hair on my blue slacks and was now giving me a thorough sniff-over.

"I'm looking for the Tongcos, but they've moved."

"Why, shoot, hon, they split up sometime last year." The terrier sneezed and sat down abruptly. The lady in the pink and green shirt put one hand on her hip and continued. "She went home to Mama and he stayed in the house till it was sold. I don't know where he is now. I'll bet his aunt does, though."

"You know his aunt?" Hope glimmered as I asked the question.

"We're both in the garden club. She lives right here in the neighborhood." She waved her right hand in a direction that could have encompassed all points south and gave me more specific directions. "Couple of streets that way, and then turn left. The house is kind of an off-white color, in the middle of the block, on the right, with lots of flowers. She just does so well with her roses."

"Thanks." I blessed my luck and the blue-haired lady as she tugged on the leash. She and the terrier moved on down the sidewalk. Two blocks, then left, and I started looking for the house with lots of flowers. It was a cream stucco with brown trim, and it stood out from its neighbors. Despite the drought that threatened the whole Bay Area, someone was giving the garden water and plenty of care. The sidewalk leading up to the porch was bordered with frothy white alyssum and red verbena. Ground-hugging purple and yellow pansies and a riot of petunias rimmed the front porch, which was decorated with ceramic pots filled with bright red geraniums. The roses in the beds along the house were indeed spectacular, in all colors ranging from lavender to yellow to deep red. Their hot, sweet scent carried on the warm air as bees buzzed around their velvety petals.

I stepped onto the low front porch and rang the bell. A moment later the door opened. A tiny brown woman looked out at me. "Yes?"

"I'm looking for Alejandro Tongco. I understand you're his aunt."

She frowned. Then she tossed a single word over her shoulder. "Medy!" For a long moment she scrutinized me with her bright black eyes. Then the door opened wider and a second pair of black eyes joined the first. Standing side by side, the two women looked like twins, both small and slender, streaks of gray in their short black hair, dressed in slacks, shirts, and sandals.

"Hinahanap niyasi Alejandro," the first woman told the second. For a long moment they inspected me through the screen door. "What do you want with Alejandro?" the other woman said in accented English.

"My name is Jeri Howard. I'm a private investigator." I took one of my business cards from my purse and held it out. "I need to talk to Mr. Tongco about his uncle, Dr. Lito Manibusan."

The first woman unlatched the screen door and opened it, reaching for my card. They consulted each other in quick-fire Tagalog, then nodded to me. "You come in."

I stepped into a living room with white walls and teak furniture. Asparagus ferns hung from the ceiling. African violets and coleus stood in ranks on plant stands and atop the shelves holding the television set and stereo. I felt as though I were in a tropical forest. I fingered a fern with envy. Why couldn't I get my plants to thrive this well?

"Please sit down," the first woman said. "I'm Josefa Luna. This is my sister, Medy Pangalinan."

A yellow cat dozed on the floral print cushions of the sofa. Josefa Luna nudged it to the floor, where it wound itself through my legs before strolling toward the kitchen. I took one of the chairs grouped around the sofa. To my right I saw a high square table that held a crucifix carved from a dark, satiny wood, standing upright with a rosary draping its base. On the wall above the crucifix hung a small oil painting of a Madonna and Child. A rosary lay on the table's surface.

"Are you also related to Dr. Manibusan?" I asked.

Mrs. Luna shook her head as she and Mrs. Pangalinan

settled on the sofa. "No. My sister-in-law—Alejandro's mother—was Lito's sister. Why do you want to talk to Alejandro?"

"It's a confidential matter. Where can I find him?"

"He and Nina got a divorce," Medy Pangalinan said, radiating Catholic disapproval at her nephew's marital breakup. "Alejandro went to a special school at North Island."

"North Island? The navy base down in San Diego? So he's in the military."

"Lieutenant commander, U.S. Navy," Josefa said proudly.

"I'd appreciate it if you'd give me his address and phone number in San Diego."

"The school was only two months. He's back at Alameda now." Josefa got up and disappeared down a hallway, returning with a loose-leaf address book. She lay it on the coffee table and opened it to the T's. Judging from the crossed-out addresses, the navy had moved Alejandro Tongco around quite a bit. I saw addresses in the Bay Area, San Diego, Guam, the Philippines, Japan, and Hawaii. Two current addresses and phone numbers were listed, the operations office at the Naval Air Station, located on Alameda's West End, and Tongco's apartment on Shoreline Drive in the same city.

I copied the information and refused Mrs. Luna's offer of tea. She and Mrs. Pangalinan were avidly curious about my visit, but I wasn't about to be plied with hot liquids. I thanked the two ladies and left Union City for Oakland.

The Parkside Towers proved to be a high-rise building on Lakeside Avenue near Seventeenth Street, across from Lake Merritt in downtown Oakland. From my parking place on the opposite curb I counted ten stories, looking up at wide balconies and lots of glass. Expensive, I thought, getting out of my car for a closer look. Which unit belonged to Charles Randall?

A short, curved driveway ran past the front door. Through the plate glass windows I saw a counter staffed by a man wearing a khaki shirt and a name tag, no doubt a security guard. Directly behind him was a bank of mailboxes. I'd have to get inside, past the guard, to check the names on the mailboxes to see whether Dolores Cruz was in fact living there. Beyond the wall with the mailboxes I saw a short corridor with two elevators on the right and another door at the end, probably leading to the parking garage. To confirm this, I strolled up the two-lane drive that ran between the high-rise and its neighboring building. The garage appeared to take up most of the ground floor. Its only entrance consisted of side-by-side metal gates with a free-standing apparatus between them, the kind where the driver of a car inserts an electronic card to open the gate.

I walked back toward Lakeside Avenue. In the small half-circle of grass between the sidewalk and the curved driveway I saw a hanging real estate sign listing a two-bedroom condo for sale. When I returned to my car I jotted down the real estate firm's name and phone number. With a guard stationed at the entrance, posing as a condo buyer might be my best chance to get inside the building.

I sat outside the high-rise for a while, watching a BMW enter the garage and a Mercedes exit, counting the seconds the metal gates remained open. I didn't see the white Thunderbird Dolores Cruz had been driving.

Back in my office I ate an apple to quell my rumbling stomach as I took the messages off my answering machine. I pitched the core into my wastebasket and picked up the phone. Dan Greenlow was relieved to hear that Kyle had been located and leaned on. I returned several phone calls, then I called Alejandro Tongco's work number at the Naval Air Station in Alameda. The petty officer who answered the phone told me the lieutenant commander was out, so I left my name and number.

When I called the real estate company listed on the sign at the Parkside Towers and said I wanted to take a look at the condo that was for sale, the agent eagerly described such amenities as a Jacuzzi, fireplace, and formal dining room, and assured me the place was a steal at the astronomical price she quoted. And of course if I didn't like this unit, she had some other properties in a similar price range. In between the gush she probed for information about my yearly income and how much cash I could come up with for a down payment. I put her off with some vague talk about investments and set up an appointment to look at the condo the following day.

A steal, I thought grimly, hanging up the phone and contemplating my future as a perpetual renter. Buying wasn't an option, not in this lifetime, and certainly not for a self-employed private investigator.

Five

ALEJANDRO TONGCO HADN'T RETURNED MY CALL by the time I left my office at six. I tried his home number and got no answer, then drove to Alameda, the town where I grew up. It's an elongated island located across the estuary from Oakland, a pleasant city with a small-town feel, with lots of wide, tree-lined streets and big Victorian houses. The area called South Shore has a long beach on San Francisco Bay, and Tongco's Shoreline Drive address was an apartment building near the intersection where Willow Street ends at the beach. The path between the shore and the street was crowded with a changing stream of people—runners in shorts, walkers in sweat suits, and bicyclists in skintight spandex shorts and helmets. I saw clumps of kids wading in the chilly bay water as gentle waves lapped the sand where a few souls stretched, catching the late afternoon sun as it inched its way westward down a blue sky. In the distance the San Francisco skyline looked like the Emerald City.

I parked on Willow and walked back to Shoreline. The apartment building was a two-story L-shaped white stucco with open walkways. Tongco's apartment was on the second floor at the end of the L. As I climbed the stairs I heard rock music blaring from another apartment and smelled barbecue sauce burning on someone's grill. At Tongco's door I knocked and waited.

The man who opened the door had been out running. He wore a pair of skimpy blue shorts that displayed his sinewy thighs. A short gold T-shirt with U.S.N. in blue letters covered his upper chest but bared his flat stomach. He carried a white towel draped over his left shoulder, using one end to blot the sweat from his lean, dark face. Long-lashed brown eyes moved over my body, then rested on my face as he waited for me to speak.

"I'm looking for Alejandro Tongco."

"You found him." A smile lifted the corners of his mouth. "Who are you?"

"Jeri Howard. I called your office earlier."

"I wondered what that was about."

"Your uncle. Lito Manibusan."

The smile vanished, replaced by a narrow-eyed, assessing stare. "What about my uncle?"

"May I come in and talk with you, Mr. Tongco?"

"Only if you call me Alex."

He held the door wide and motioned me into his living room. To my right, a set of sliding glass doors opened onto a balcony facing the beach. I saw a couple of white metal chairs on either side of a matching round table, and a small barbecue grill standing in one corner. The kitchen was to my left, separated from the living room by a counter. Beyond it I saw a dining alcove with a round table and four chairs.

Alex Tongco shut the door. He was about five ten, moving with easy grace in his Adidas running shoes. Late thirties, I guessed, noting the glint of silver in his close-cropped black hair. He walked to the counter and leaned against it, crossing his arms in front of him.

"Who are you?" he asked. "And what's this all about?"

"I'm a private investigator," I told him, handing him one of my cards. "My father, Dr. Timothy Howard, teaches history at Cal State in Hayward. He and your uncle were friends. He's the one who found Dr. Manibusan's body."

"Howard . . ." He examined my card, holding it with long, tapered fingers. "I remember. We met at Lito's funeral."

"After your uncle died, you packed up all the files in his office. Are they in storage? I'd like to take a look at them."

Tongco smiled again, an ironic quirk of his mouth. He set my card on the counter and went into the kitchen, where he took a glass from a cabinet. Filling it from the faucet, he drank the water down, looking at me over the rim of the glass. "Why do you want to see my uncle's files?"

"Dr. Manibusan sent my father an envelope. Dad can't find it. He thinks it may be with the things from your uncle's office."

Tongco put the glass in the sink and rejoined me in the living room. I wanted to know the reason for the smile that played on his lips, but he was taking his own time letting me in on the joke.

"You're the second person this week," he said finally, "who wants to look at my uncle's files. Considering that Lito has been dead since January, I find this very interesting."

So did I. "Was it a woman?"

"A man named Edward Villegas. He says he's a writer who met my uncle last year, while Lito was working on an article." Good cover, I thought. Difficult to verify. "Why did you ask if it was a woman?"

"Several days ago a woman named Dolores Cruz showed up at Cal State Hayward. She claims she's your uncle's widow."

"Bullshit," Alex Tongco said, his black eyebrows drawing together over his dark eyes.

"She has what appears to be a marriage certificate. She says they were married in Manila last August."

"It's still bullshit. Lito wouldn't have married anyone after Sara died. If he did, why didn't he tell the family? I'm the executor of his will. And the pension stuff from the university, he would have changed the beneficiaries. He took care of things like that."

"That's what my father said."

"Did somebody hire you? Somebody at the university?"

"I was hired to find you. Now that I have, I'd like to look through Dr. Manibusan's files. Where are they?"

"In storage." He pulled the towel off his shoulder and twisted it in his hands. Perspiration still glistened on his smooth brown skin. "I'm going to take a shower. Then we can talk about it over dinner."

I thought about the leftovers in my refrigerator and the apple that served as my belated lunch. Dinner sounded good to me. Besides, the man was attractive—and not very forthcoming. He headed for the bedroom. A moment later I heard water running in the bathroom. With one ear focused on that sound, I gave Alex Tongco's apartment a quick once-over.

Everything looked new. Maybe his ex-wife got all the furniture in the recent divorce. The sofa and matching chair were oak with beige cushions, separated by an end table that matched the coffee table. They faced the wall opposite the front door, which was dominated by an entertainment center holding a large-screen television set, a VCR, and a high-tech stereo sound system. The bottom shelf of the center held an assortment of record albums, compact discs, and videotapes. I looked at some of the titles and smiled. Our tastes were similar—jazz and Humphrey Bogart.

The door to the bedroom was open. I could still hear water running, so I peered in and saw a queen-size platform bed covered with a dark blue comforter. A rowing machine sat on the floor at the foot of the bed.

I crossed the living room to the desk and bookshelf that stood next to the front door. The bookshelf held a mixed bag of titles, including military history and paperback copies of Herman Wouk's novels. Tongco also had several books on the Philippines, including a hard-cover edition of *In Our Image* by Stanley Karnow. I pulled the Karnow book off the shelf and leafed through it. It looked new, with a bookmark from Black Oak Books in Berkeley stuck into a section dealing with the ongoing Communist insurgency in the Philippines, the New People's Army.

I put the book back on the shelf and picked up the scarred black leather briefcase leaning against the leg of the desk. Shut tight, the case had a combination lock. The afternoon mail, junk and a couple of bills, had been left unopened at the base of the desk lamp. Underneath I found a copy of the *Philippine News*, published in south San Francisco, a weekly newspaper proclaiming itself as the largest Filipino-American newspaper. On the wall above the desk hung two framed certificates, the first a diploma from Auburn University in Alabama, granting Alejandro S. Tongco a degree in aeronautical engineering, the second commissioning him as an ensign in the United States Navy.

I heard the water go off in the next room. By the time Alex walked out of the bedroom, dressed in a pair of gray slacks and a yellow pullover, I was standing on the balcony, looking out at the beach.

"Mexican food?" he asked.

"Love it."

He drove a bright red Mazda Miata convertible, a two-seater built so low to the ground that every time he went over a bump I could feel it in my tailbone. We went to Chevy's at Mariner Square, on the Alameda side of the estuary, a loud, echoing place with a view of downtown Oakland and the waterfront.

"Find out anything interesting?" Alex said after we'd ordered a platter of beef and chicken fajitas. His brown eyes looked amused as he poured a bottle of Corona beer into a tall, frosted mug.

I picked up my margarita and sipped the icy concoction. "What do you mean?"

"You tossed my living room, didn't you? I would expect a private investigator to make use of the time I was in the shower."

"*Tossed* is an overstatement. I looked around." I set down my drink and willed myself to ignore the basket of tortilla chips in the center of the table. I always eat too many of the damn things.

"What can you tell me about myself?"

"You have ten Humphrey Bogart movies on videotape and you listen to Miles Davis. You like to read Herman Wouk and John Toland. Judging by your age and the dates on your diploma and commissioning certificates, I'd say you're a mustang, an ex-enlisted man who got his degree and went to Officer Candidate School."

"Very good," Alex said with a laugh.

"How did you end up at Auburn? That's a long way from any oceans."

"I was commissioned through NESEP—the Navy Enlisted Scientific Education Program. The navy sent me to Auburn to get my degree and gave me some gold bars to go with it."

"How long have you been in the service?"

"Eighteen years. I joined when I was twenty. I'd worked and had a year of college, but I wanted to do something else. I was an aviation machinist's mate. Now I'm a lieutenant commander." He fixed me with a mocking gaze. "Since I haven't had the opportunity to check out your living room, you have to tell me about yourself. Where is your living room, by the way?"

"In Oakland, over by Lake Merritt. I share it with a cat named Abigail." The waitress brought our dinner. I took a fresh flour tortilla from the basket in the middle of the table and filled it with grilled chicken and salsa.

"What did you study in college?" Alex asked, piling a tortilla with beef and beans.

"History." He looked up at me and grinned. "Don't laugh. I can always teach."

"How did a history major get into the private-eye business?"

"I was a legal assistant. Then I worked as an investigator with a man who had his own agency. When he retired, I went into business for myself."

"Investigating is a long way from history."

"Not really. I prefer to think of it as the study of late-twentieth-century human behavior. Tell me about your uncle."

"Ah, business intrudes." Alex was quiet for a moment, concentrating on a mouthful of fajita. He took a swallow of beer and wiped his mouth with a napkin. "He was my favorite uncle."

"On your mother's side, according to your aunt Josie and aunt Medy."

"So that's how you found me," Alex said with a smile,

reaching for the basket of tortillas. As he talked, he built himself another fajita.

He told me Lito was born in a town called San Ygnacio, in Pampanga Province, northeast of Manila on the island of Luzon. The professor's father was a teacher who died at the end of World War II and the family moved to Manila shortly thereafter. Lito was educated at the University of the Philippines in Manila, where he met his wife, Sara. He obtained his doctorate in history at the University of California at Berkeley and returned to the Philippines to teach. Like many Filipinos, the Manibusans became increasingly disenchanted with the reign of Ferdinand and Imelda and took steps to immigrate to the United States, leaving the Philippines less than a year after Marcos declared martial law in 1972.

I knew Sara Manibusan had succumbed to breast cancer two years ago. My father told me that his friend had been devastated by the loss, and I myself had seen the change her death wrought. Now Alex confirmed this. "They were married sixteen years," he said. "No children. She had a couple of miscarriages. Lito was devoted to her. He took a leave of absence when she had the mastectomy and went through chemotherapy, just to be with her. When she died, he was inconsolable."

"So it doesn't make sense that he'd suddenly marry again," I said.

Alex dismissed the idea with an abrupt wave of his hand. "Hell, after Sara died he was married to his work. He didn't even go out with women. His social life was his university friends. And family, of course. He and I saw each other fairly often. Sara's brother, Pete Pascal, lives in Daly City. He owns a stationery store." He paused to finish his fajita. "You say this woman has a marriage certificate. It must be a forgery."

"I didn't get a good look at it. Nobody did. I suspect that was intentional on her part." The waitress stopped by our table and Alex ordered another round of drinks. I filled another tortilla with chicken. "My father says Dr. Manibusan's trip to the Philippines last summer was unexpected."

Alex nodded. "I thought he was going to do some research in the valley, down near Fresno and Madera. He was writing a book about Filipíno immigrants. Then Lito called me a couple of days before he left and told me he had to go to Manila and San Fernando, the capital of Pampanga Province. And he said he might go to San Ygnacio."

"Do you still have relatives there?"

Alex shrugged. "Some cousins. I remember visiting them when I was very young."

"Were you born in the Philippines?"

"You ask a lot of questions, don't you?"

"It's an occupational trait."

"Yes. I was born in Cavite. It's a province south of Manila. We moved to the States when I was fourteen."

"Tell me about the Manibusan family."

"I don't know much about the Manibusans other than what I've already told you," Alex said abruptly. "I can't help you there."

I had a feeling he was lying. I looked at him across the table. His eyes turned opaque and his lean face became guarded as he picked up his beer mug. He stared over my shoulder at the estuary, where the reflected lights of downtown Oakland shimmered on the water.

"Any idea why Dr. Manibusan was in San Francisco the night he was killed?" I asked.

The tension on his face eased as he shook his head. "No. I knew he was going to that conference in Hawaii and he was supposed to have dinner with the Pascals in Daly City. He was flying out of San Francisco International. Pete Pascal called me late Friday night. He said Lito never showed up at his place and did I know where he was. Of course, by that time he was dead." He stopped, grim-faced at the memory.

"It doesn't make sense that Lito would go to San Francisco first. From where he lived in Castro Valley he would have taken the San Mateo Bridge to the Peninsula, not the Bay Bridge. To get to Daly City he'd take 101 north, then 380 to 280. That way he'd be against the afternoon commute. I can't see him going through San Francisco. He didn't like that traffic. On a Friday rush hour it would have been worse than usual. Besides, he wasn't supposed to be at Pete's until eight, and your father saw him in the garage about six-thirty. So Lito must have gone to San Francisco for a reason. But I'm damned if I know what it was.'' He shook his head. ''Do you think this business of the files has something to do with Lito's murder?''

''I don't know what to think at this point. I just want to check all the angles. This man who's interested in your uncle's files—Edward Villegas—when did he contact you?''

''Monday, two days ago. He called me at my office. I told him I was busy and I'd get back to him. So far I haven't.''

''Do you still have his number?'' Alex nodded and reached for his wallet, taking out a yellow message slip with Villegas's name and number scrawled in black ink. I made a note of the number, planning to check the local criss-cross directories to see if I could obtain an address to go with it. ''Are you up to playing a game of cat and mouse?'' I asked.

''With you,'' Alex said, a smile playing at his mouth, ''or with Edward Villegas?''

I ignored the suggestion in his smile and kept my voice businesslike. ''Call Villegas back. Set up a meeting as soon as possible. Lunch, at the Rusty Scupper on the Oakland Embarcadero. When you get there, ask for a table by the window. I can see the dining room clearly from the bar.''

''So you don't think he's a writer?''

''No more than I think Dolores Cruz is your uncle's widow. And I need to look at the professor's files to see if I can find the envelope he sent my father.''

''You're welcome to them. I have no idea what's there. I got rid of the furniture, but everything else in Lito's office and house got tossed into boxes and hauled to the storage facility. Just say when, and I'll meet you there.''

''Tomorrow afternoon?''

''Four o'clock,'' Alex agreed. ''It's in San Leandro, on Doolittle Drive, between Davis and Marina. I'll call Villegas first thing in the morning to see if I can arrange a meeting.''

We both reached for the check and finally compromised

by splitting it. Back at Alex's apartment he invited me up for a nightcap, but I demurred. Alejandro Tongco was an interesting man, I thought as I drove back to Oakland. No, *interesting* didn't cover it. He was charming, sexy—and still not very forthcoming. He was helpful up to a point, mainly because he was as curious as I was about Dolores Cruz, Edward Villegas, and their interest in his late uncle's files. But Alex Tongco had closed up abruptly when I asked questions about the Manibusans, claiming he didn't know much about that side of his family.

I can't help you there, he'd said. Can't or won't? Alejandro Tongco didn't want to talk about his Manibusan relatives, which made me all the more curious to find out why.

Six

MARGARITAS ALWAYS LEAVE ME WITH A COTTON mouth and a dragged-through-a-knothole feeling. Not exactly hung over, just dicey. It was a quarter to six in the morning and the light coming through my bedroom window had a grayish cast to it. I lay sprawled on my back in my double bed, my body wanting more sleep. Business and Abigail made such a notion impossible.

At least the margaritas had made me unaware of Abigail's nocturnal peregrinations with the yellow mouse. That morning she'd left the mouse on the floor next to the bed and parked her solid tabby body on my stomach, where she sat staring down at my face, willing me to get up and feed her. I stared back at her and she stretched one paw forward to rest lightly on my cheek. If I ignored her too long, she would put her claws out and make the reminder more pointed.

An hour later I was parked on Lakeside Avenue opposite the Parkside Towers, sipping coffee from a thermos and nibbling on a cheese Danish I'd picked up at the Merritt Bakery. The front section of that morning's Oakland *Tribune* was spread out on the Toyota's dashboard. I glanced at it periodically, keeping one eye on the driveway leading to the building's garage. The guard was at his post on the front door, but so far I hadn't seen anyone enter or exit the building. To my right, down a grassy slope, was the asphalt path circling Lake Merritt, busy with early-morning joggers making the three-and-a-half-mile circuit. I tried not to let myself get distracted by the array of sculpted male rear ends and muscled legs, but when I'm on a stakeout, sometimes my attention wanders.

Another hour crawled by. I finished reading the newspaper and consumed the second Danish. Several cars had pulled out of the Parkside Towers garage, none of them the white Thunderbird, none of them driven by Dolores Cruz. I'd been singing to myself and drinking coffee, hoping that the caffeine and Rodgers and Hammerstein would keep me awake. In this fashion I had drained the thermos and worked my way through the score of *South Pacific*. The trouble with drinking coffee on a stakeout is that eventually I need to empty my bladder. Then it becomes a contest to see how long I can hold out.

I reached into my paper sack of provisions and pulled out an orange. As I began peeling it, I cleared my throat and launched into an encore of ''Some Enchanted Evening.'' I was warbling ''Once you have found her, never let her go,'' when the white Thunderbird drove out of the garage across the street, Dolores Cruz at the wheel.

I tossed the orange and a handful of peel onto the passenger seat and started my Toyota. My quarry made a running stop at the curb and turned left, pulling out into traffic. I edged into place two cars behind her. I followed her around the curve of Lake Merritt, where Lakeside Drive becomes Harrison Street. She cut to the right across two lanes and made the right turn onto Grand Avenue, accelerating as she hopped from lane to lane. I kept up with her and zoomed through a yellow light at MacArthur Boulevard so I wouldn't lose her. Just past the intersection of Mandana Boulevard and Grand Avenue she took an abrupt right into a driveway. I pulled into a parking space a few yards back and waited.

When the Thunderbird didn't appear again, I got out of my car and walked toward the driveway. As I reached it, I saw that the narrow lane led to a parking area behind a one-story strip of businesses. I walked cautiously along the drive to the parking area. The Thunderbird straddled a white line, hogging two parking places. Dolly was nowhere in sight. I retraced my steps to the front sidewalk. The first business in the shopping strip was an insurance agency. Next to it was a beauty salon. The third door had a sign over it reading MA-BUHAY TRAVEL.

Mabuhay is the only Tagalog word I know, a word of greeting, like "hello" or "welcome." In this case it welcomed the traveler to the exotic, faraway islands of the Philippines, illustrated by a window full of large color posters of jungle-covered mountains looming over turquoise water, sandy beaches, and palm trees. A collection of travel books and brochures decorated the window ledge.

The travel agency was closed. A sign on the door listed the hours as ten to six, and it was just past nine. I peered through the window at the desks and computer terminals visible in the dim light. Then I saw someone move at the rear of the office. A light switched on, and Dolores Cruz walked toward a desk, the skirt of her red and yellow dress swirling around her. She carried a red straw handbag which she set on the desk, fumbling inside as she picked up the telephone. I backed away from the window and headed for my car.

According to the business name records on file at the Alameda County Courthouse, Mabuhay Travel was owned by Arthur and Perlita Randall, who lived at an address in Daly City. It was an easy bet that the Charles Randall who owned the condo where Dolly lived and the car she drove was related in some way to Arthur Randall. I just had to find the connection.

A computer consultant named George has an office next door to mine. He offered advice and recommendations when I bought my own computer equipment, and I pick his brain when necessary. He subscribes to an array of data bases, something I can't afford to do. When I need information, he digs it out and bills me for his services. Trouble is, he keeps odd hours, and this morning he wasn't in. I'd have to catch him later. In the meantime I had other resources. I requested a credit check on Dolores Cruz and all three of the Randalls, as well as a Dun and Bradstreet report on Mabuhay Travel.

Locking my office, I went next door to the law firm of

Alwin, Taylor, and Chao. Since Cassie Taylor and I are good friends, the partners and I have mutually beneficial arrangements. In return for use of their copy and facsimile machines, I buy supplies. In exchange for my investigative services at a reduced rate, I get case referrals and the chance to pick lawyers' brains when I need answers to questions.

I waved at the receptionist. Behind her, one of the firm's two legal secretaries was wrinkling her face in concentration as she stared at her computer screen, her fingers flying over the keyboard. Bill Alwin's door was closed, which meant he was with a client or in court. Cassie's office was unoccupied. I found Mike Chao in the book-lined hallway, flipping through the pages of a volume of *West's Annotated California Codes*. He was the law firm's resident expert on immigration law.

"How would I get some information out of the Immigration and Naturalization Service?" I asked him.

"With a crowbar." He grinned. "Those government bureaucrats are tight-mouthed. Besides, there are Privacy Act considerations. Violating the Privacy Act is a felony with big penalties. Working on a case?"

I nodded. "I want to check on someone's immigration status."

"Officially, your best bet is to contact the district director of the INS. Of course, that doesn't mean you'll get a reply. Even if you do, you might not get any information. And it will take a while."

"And unofficially?"

Mike shrugged. "I can ask around, very discreetly. Give me the name. But I really can't promise anything."

"I understand. Thanks." I followed him to his office and told him what I knew about Dolores Cruz. Whether or not she had married Dr. Manibusan in Manila last August, she had to have entered the United States on some kind of visa, legal or otherwise.

When I returned to my office, there was a message on my answering machine from Alex Tongco, asking me to call him back as soon as possible. "I've set up a lunch date with

Edward Villegas,'' he told me when I got through to him at the Naval Air Station. ''Noon today, the Rusty Scupper.''

''I'll be there.'' I finished up some paperwork and left the office, planning a stop at the Oakland post office before going to the restaurant. Outside my building I saw Cassie walking toward me. It was another warm day, the sun bouncing off the pavement, but she looked cool in her beige linen suit. Someone was with her, a small-boned woman in a jade green jump suit, with straight black hair brushing her collar and a large red nylon camera bag slung over one shoulder.

''Hi, Jeri.'' Cassie waved at me and I stopped. ''This is my friend from the East Bay Women's Network, Felice Navarro. Felice, this is Jeri Howard. She's a private investigator.''

''Private eye? That's great.'' A topaz ring in a chunky gold setting glittered as Felice Navarro stuck out her right hand. She was in her late twenties, with a wide, enthusiastic smile and an accent flavoring her words. ''I'm doing a photo series on women in nontraditional jobs. Will you let me follow you around for a couple of days while you're working?''

''Most of what I do isn't particularly photogenic,'' I said, thinking of this morning's stakeout.

''Oh, but it sounds so fascinating,'' Felice said. ''How did you make such a career choice? Was your father a policeman?''

''No, he's a history professor at Cal State. I was a paralegal for a while, in the same law firm where Cassie worked before she went to law school. Then I went to work for a local investigator. After he retired, I went into business for myself.''

''Call me, and let's talk about it.'' Felice reached into her camera bag for her business card, and I gave her one of mine. Then she looked at her watch. ''I wonder where Rick is. He was supposed to pick me up. I'm shooting a job for my brother, down at the Oakland waterfront.''

''Imports, right?'' Cassie added.

''Yes. From the Philippines and other Asian countries. He has a warehouse south of Market in San Francisco, plus two shops, one near Union Square and one at the Stanford Mall in Palo Alto. Now he's thinking of expanding to this side of the Bay.''

"There are three import shops down there already," I commented. The Port of Oakland owns a lot of land along the estuary shore at Jack London Square. Development is proceeding at a brisk pace. Each time I visit the area I'm struck by the changes. I didn't think the area could support another import shop, but Felice shrugged.

"I know. But everything Rick Navarro touches turns to gold. He's quite the entrepreneur. Like father, like son." She grinned as she spoke, but the words had an undertone of sarcasm.

At that moment a sleek black Jaguar pulled up to the curb beside us. Felice waved at the driver, a dark-haired man talking on a car phone. Finishing his call, he cut the engine, got out, and approached us. "Cassie, Jeri," Felice said, "this is my brother Rick."

Rick Navarro was handsome in a rough-hewn way, about five feet eight with a powerfully built body that moved easily in an expensive gray suit. A diamond stickpin glittered in his red striped tie. He smiled—white, even teeth in a square dark face—and shook my hand and Cassie's as Felice completed the introductions. He was closer to my own age of thirty-three, perhaps older.

"Are you an attorney, too?" he asked me.

"No, a private investigator."

"An unusual career for a woman. I suppose my sister has already buttonholed you about this photo series of hers."

"Yes, she has." I glanced at my watch. "I'll say good-bye now. I have a lunch date. It was nice meeting both of you."

"Call me," Felice said. She turned to her brother. "Speaking of lunch, you *are* going to feed me after I take these pictures for you. At Scott's. I'm going to order the most expensive thing on the menu."

It was now a quarter to twelve, not enough time to stop at the post office. I drove directly to the Rusty Scupper on the

Oakland Embarcadero. Like many of the restaurants lining the waterfront, the Scupper was built on pilings over the estuary, with an outdoor deck. It shared a parking lot with a small marina full of sailboats, and a condominium-office complex that included a yacht broker's office. Inside, I took a seat at the far end of the bar, facing the dining room with its long expanse of window looking out at the water, where a pelican dived for its lunch. I ordered a bottle of Calistoga mineral water and the fried mozzarella sticks and waited.

Alex arrived on the stroke of noon, resplendent in a summer khaki uniform with the gold oak leaves of a lieutenant commander on his collar and an impressive collection of ribbons pinned above his left breast pocket. He scanned the bar area, giving no indication that he'd seen me. He spoke briefly to the hostess, then stepped to one side. A few minutes later a dark-haired man in slacks and a blue jacket walked in and introduced himself to Alex. The hostess escorted the two men to a table near the window. As they walked past me, I glanced at Edward Villegas. Early thirties, I guessed, with Asian features and a muscular body. He looked self-assured and friendly. Could be a writer, I thought, as he claimed. But what does a writer look like?

When they reached the table, Alex took the chair facing away from me, so I had a clear view of Villegas's face. I ordered another Calistoga while the two men talked and ate lunch. It looked like Villegas was doing most of the talking, smiling and using his hands for emphasis. In fact, he was constantly in motion, as though he couldn't sit still. I wondered how Alex was faring. I sipped my drink and glanced out at the shimmering water on the estuary, keeping one eye on the table as a long barge went by, pushed by an impossibly small tugboat.

Finally the waiter brought the check and Villegas quickly reached for it. I slipped off my stool and made my way around the bar to the door, timing my exit so that I walked outside just as Alex and Villegas shook hands and parted. Alex walked off to the left, toward his bright red convertible. Villegas moved down the sidewalk that ran next to the blue-roofed condominium complex, headed in the same direction where I'd parked my car. I followed several paces behind him. He paused outside the yacht broker's office to fire up a cigarette. I slowed my step, rummaging in my purse as though I couldn't locate my keys. Then he moved again, walking briskly past my Toyota. Villegas unlocked a gray Nissan sedan, fairly new, several parking slots down the row. I cut between two parked cars and crossed behind the gray car as he started it, getting a good look at the California license plate. As soon as he backed out of the slot and drove toward the street, I wrote down the number.

Back in my office I called the Oakland Police Department. When the operator came on the line, I asked to be connected with Sergeant Walters in Records. I spent a moment or two on hold, looking at a spiderweb high in the right-hand corner of my ceiling. Then the sergeant picked up the call.

"Hey, Angie, it's Jeri Howard."

"Haven't heard from you in a while," she said, her big voice raspy from too many cigarettes. "What's up?"

"I'd like to find out if someone has a police record. Can you help me?"

"Sure. What's the name?"

"Edward Villegas." I spelled it for her and gave her a description of Villegas as well as the license number of the Nissan he was driving.

Angie hummed tunelessly as I talked, as she always did when she was taking notes. "Okay. I'll see what shakes out. Might take a couple of days."

"It's not a priority. Thanks, Angie. I'll owe you."

"Damn straight. Come down to the Warehouse some night and buy me a drink."

It was time to head for the Parkside Towers, to keep my appointment with the real estate agent. But first I had to dress for the part. I have several changes of clothing stashed at the rear of my office, and now I put on a suit of brown herring-bone tweed and an ivory blouse with a bow at the neck, left over from my days as a paralegal. It took me several attempts to tie the bow. I was out of practice. I put on a pair of low-heeled pumps and combed my short auburn hair back from my face. Then I brushed green eyeshadow onto my eyelids. A swipe of lipstick completed my transformation into upscale yup.

I was early for the appointment with the real estate agent, early on purpose. Waiting in the lobby of the Parkside Towers gave me time to look around and chat with the security guard, a sharp-eyed silver-haired man with a name tag reading O. Barnwell. Barnwell looked fit and had ex-cop stamped all over him. He was informative, but only up to a point, as he presided over his domain from a counter just to the left of the front door. The phone rang and the guard picked it up, giving me the opportunity to stroll to the wall behind him and check the names on the mailboxes. Dolores Cruz wasn't listed, but Charles Randall lived in Unit 803.

The real estate agent arrived, apologizing for being late, even though she wasn't. Her name was Estelle. She was in her forties, a birdlike woman with a helmet of dyed platinum hair. She carried a brown leather case in her right hand. Her left hand fluttered like a wing as she talked, and her beaklike nose twitched at the prospect of a hefty commission.

"I am extremely concerned about security," I told Estelle and Barnwell, jumping right into my prospective-buyer routine.

"State-of-the-art," Estelle trilled, not missing a beat as she opened the leather case and took out a fistful of brochures. Residents were issued electronic cards that opened the front door and the garage doors. Estelle took out a map of the building, and Barnwell obligingly pointed out all the doors, adding that the alarm system was tied in directly with the Oakland Police Department. There was a guard on duty twenty-four hours a day, and he assured me the Parkside Towers had never had an incident, either in the building or on the grounds, as long as he had been in charge. He implied there wouldn't be, either.

As Barnwell talked, I took lots of notes. When he was finished with his spiel, I thanked him and let Estelle shepherd me to the elevator. We waited as a tanned, white-haired couple stepped off the car, then we climbed aboard and Estelle hit the button for the tenth floor, where the available unit was located. On the way up, Estelle inquired about my job status and finances. I didn't tell her about my checking account and IRA down at Wells Fargo, but I did mention that I worked for a law firm here in Oakland, which isn't entirely untrue. As a private investigator, I do a lot of prelitigation work for several local law firms, large and small. If Estelle wanted to believe I was an attorney, I'd let her.

"How many units are there on each floor?" I asked as the elevator doors opened.

"Ten," Estelle said. "Four on either side and one on each end. The penthouse has only six units." She opened a brochure. "This shows the layout of each floor."

I studied the floor plan as she led me down the hall. It looked like the numbering started at the elevators and ran clockwise around the elongated rectangle. That meant that Dolly lived three doors to the left of the elevator, on the lake side of the eighth floor. The brochure showed stairways located on both ends of the building, between the third and fourth units and the eighth and ninth units.

Estelle unlocked the door to 1005, the two-bedroom condo she wanted to sell me. The door was solid rather than hollow-core. It had a peephole, a spring lock, and a dead bolt that opened with a key outside and an ornate latch on the inside. I asked Estelle if each unit had a similar door.

"Oh, yes, this is standard," she said. "Unless individual owners have added other types of locks."

We stepped into a tiled entryway. On the wall next to the door was a telephone intercom, a link to the guard. Estelle gave me a tour of the empty condo, extolling its virtues, while I consulted the brochure to see if this floor plan matched 803, Dolly's unit. It was similar, though not exactly the same. I opened the sliding glass door leading to the balcony, which gave me a view of downtown Oakland and the San Francisco skyline across the Bay. While Estelle pointed out the roominess of the outdoor storage closet, I leaned over the balcony rail, wondering how easy it would be to get from one balcony to another. Spy-novel stuff, I thought, shaking my head at an image of Jeri Howard, girl detective, dangling from a rope.

I asked to see the parking garage. We took the elevator down to the first floor and stepped through the security door. It looked like every other parking garage I'd been in, with lines and numbers painted on the concrete surface. It appeared one of the electronic security cards was required to open the door from the garage to the lobby as well, probably the same one that lifted the metal garage gate.

I dawdled along, noting the location of the garbage Dumpsters in the back corner, listening to Estelle's sales pitch, until I got what I came for. A Lincoln Continental stopped outside the metal entrance gate and the driver inserted his electronic card into the apparatus on the driver's side. The gate moved slowly upward until it paralleled the low ceiling, and the Lincoln drove into the garage, heading for its parking slot. I counted the seconds until the gate dropped back into place. Plenty of time to dart into the garage before the gate closed, I thought, just in case one had to get in away from the watchful eye of O. Barnwell, security guard.

The driver of the Lincoln, an older man in golf clothes, got out of the car and moved to the trunk. He took out a set of clubs and carried them to the security door that led to the elevator. He used his electronic card to open the door, which he held for Estelle and me.

"I didn't realize it was so late," I said, consulting my watch and moving across the lobby to the front door. I thanked Estelle for showing me the condo and escaped back to my office.

Seven

THE STORAGE FACILITY ON DOOLITTLE DRIVE IN San Leandro covered several acres, row after row of connected two-story sheds surrounded by a high chain-link fence. Access was a matter of signing in and out on a sheet in the office, under the disinterested eye of the young woman at the counter.

Alex Tongco and I had agreed to meet at four that afternoon. I was on time, but Alex wasn't. I waited in my car, parked near the office door. Fifteen minutes went by, then half an hour. The sign on the office door said the place closed at six, and I knew going through the boxes would take a while. Irritated, I decided he wasn't coming. Then I saw Alex's sporty red Mazda pull into the parking lot. I got out, locked the door, and walked over to join him.

"You're late," I said.

"Sorry. Had a busy day." He smiled coolly and indicated his stained T-shirt and faded blue jeans. "I stopped at home to change."

He signed in at the office, then led the way through the gate, where he shouldered one of the stepladders that leaned against the outside wall.

"Tell me about Edward Villegas," I said as we walked about fifty yards south of the office. "Is he Filipino?"

"*Pinoy?* Definitely. American-born, though. He doesn't have an accent." We turned left into a row of storage sheds. "I asked him about his credentials. He claims he's done some features for the *Philippine News*. He says he met my uncle last year, while Lito was researching an article about

Asian immigrants and crime. Villegas says he'd liked to expand Lito's research into a book.''

It was a plausible explanation. Maybe Villegas really was a writer. The article he'd mentioned was the one in the history journal Dad had loaned me, published after Dr. Manibusan's death. But Villegas's interest in the professor's files came right on the heels of Dolores Cruz's appearance at the university, and that made me suspicious. A call to the *Philippine News* should tell me whether anyone on the newspaper's staff had heard of him.

''I told Villegas I'd think about it,'' Alex said. ''Do I just keep playing him along?''

''For the time being. Let me know if he contacts you again.''

The storage units at the end of the row were small units with regular doors, while those in the middle had garage-type doors. Alex stopped in front of one of these. I held the ladder while he unlocked the padlock, slipped it from its coupling, and lifted the door.

The shed was about the size of a one-car garage. It was stacked floor-to-ceiling with cardboard boxes, with just enough clearance at the top for the bare light bulb that provided the only illumination. Between the stacked boxes were several narrow rows, wide enough for one person to slip in sideways. I touched the nearest box, labeled FILING CABINET in thick black letters, and my hand came away dusty.

''Do you know what you're looking for?'' Alex asked.

''A brown envelope, five by seven inches, mailed by your uncle to my dad. I don't know what's in it or whether it's mixed in with all the stuff. All I know is Dad can't find it, and I have a hunch it's important. I guess we'll have to look through all these boxes, and maybe haul some of them to my office. As long as I'm doing this, I'd like to look through the professor's files, to see what he was working on when he died.'' I shook my head at the contents of the storage unit. ''This is going to be grimy work.''

He laughed. ''That's why I went home to change.''

''Are all these boxes labeled?''

"Some are, some aren't."

I sighed. "We can eliminate books, furnishings, knick-knacks. Is there any order to all of this stuff?"

"Only that some of it is from the university and the rest from Lito's house. I packed the things from the university. My brother Carlos helped me at the house. We were in a hurry, so we weren't too organized."

"You didn't tell me you had a brother."

He favored me with a slow smile. "There's a lot I haven't told you."

Alex climbed the ladder and handed boxes down to me. Most of them had the name of the room the contents had occupied in Dr. Manibusan's house, such as kitchen, bathroom, bedroom, and living room. We stacked these boxes to the right of the storeroom entrance. On the left we piled a smaller collection of cartons, labeled OFFICE and BOOKS. His uncle's home had been full of books, Alex recalled, and he didn't remember whether any books had been mixed in with the files.

"I'd like to borrow your book," I told Alex, lifting the lid on a box.

"Book? Which one?"

"The Karnow book. *In Our Image.*"

"Doing a quick study on Philippine history?"

"I'm not completely ignorant. After all, I was a history major. I know there's more to it than Ferdinand Marcos, and Commodore Dewey in Manila Bay."

" 'You may fire when ready, Gridley,' " Alex said sardonically, quoting Dewey's famous order. He lifted a box down from a stack and pulled off the lid.

I saw something stuck between the file folders of the box I was looking through and pulled it out. No luck on the envelope front. It was a paperback dictionary, English and Tagalog. "Tagalog is the official language, right?" I asked Alex, waving the book.

Alex nodded as he fanned through the file folders in the box, glancing at the labels. "English is commonly used, though. There are so many different ethnic groups and dialects. The Philippines is made up of more than seven thousand islands, about two thousand of them inhabited. Try to make one cohesive country out of such a mixture.''

I pulled back the flaps of a box and ran my hand slowly along the tops of the folders, reading the words printed in black ink. Insurance, credit card receipts, utility bills. I shut the box and pushed it to the right, then eliminated a second carton, containing the professor's tax records. We had gradually whittled the boxes from Dr. Manibusan's house down to six containing papers and files. It looked like the boxes from the university were at the back of the storage unit.

"We know your uncle wrote that article about Filipino immigrants and crime. What other subjects was he interested in?" I mopped a trickle of sweat from my face with the bottom of my T-shirt.

"The whole immigrant experience," Alex said, pushing another box aside. Our joint effort looking through the boxes was loosening Alex's tongue, and I was hoping to obtain a clearer picture of the Manibusans. "And anything to do with World War Two. Lito was very young when the Japanese invaded, but he remembered the occupation vividly. Food shortages and how badly the soldiers treated the people. The town where he was born was close to the route of the Bataan Death March. It was a bad time. My mother doesn't like to talk about it. But Lito talked about his father, Carlos, quite a bit. I think it was because of the way he died."

"Was he killed in the fighting?" I asked.

"Shot by some Japanese stragglers at the end of the war," Alex said grimly, "during the liberation of Luzon. He was a teacher, not a farmer. Lito said he'd been something of an agitator for land reform during the thirties. That made him more visible, I guess."

I lifted the lid off another box. "How did he become a teacher?"

"While the Philippines were a colony, after the Spanish-American War and up through the thirties, American teachers used to come over like missionaries, educating their 'little brown brothers.' That's why the literacy level in the Philippines is higher than it is in other Asian countries. So Carlos taught kids to read and write in a little one-room school in San Ygnacio.''

''You said you'd been there once.''

''Yeah. I was just a kid, eight or nine. We went up there for a funeral, my mother's great-aunt or something.''

''You're not sure if she was your mother's aunt?''

''Compadrazgo.'' The word rolled off his tongue. ''It's a kinship system, with roots back to the days when the Philippines belonged to Spain. It means a Filipino has blood relatives all the way down to fourth cousins, plus your godparents and all of their kin are considered part of the family. When I was growing up in Cavite, it seemed like everyone on the coast was a relative of some sort. It was kind of bewildering.''

''Tell me about San Ygnacio.''

''Not much to tell,'' he said with a laugh. ''A dusty little town off the main road, surrounded by sugar cane fields, looking like all the other little towns in the central plains. If my grandmother hadn't left after the war, maybe I'd be there, cutting cane. I'd much rather be where I am.''

''Dad told me Dr. Manibusan came to the States after Marcos declared martial law,'' I said, rooting around in another box.

''Yes, in 1973, about six months after the martial law declaration,'' Alex said as he turned to another stack of boxes. ''Lito saw what was going on in the late sixties and early seventies, and started working on visas several years before. It's tough to get into this country legally. Takes a long, long time. That's why there are so many illegals. Sometimes the wait is as long as twenty years, unless you're immediate family, like a parent or a spouse or an unmarried kid. Sara's brother came over years ago, and he's a naturalized citizen. Siblings are fifth preference, so ordinarily Lito and Sara would have had to wait quite a while. But Lito had a doctorate from Cal Berkeley and a job offer at Cal State Hayward. That moved him up to third preference—skilled labor. It shortened the time.''

"What about your family? You said last night at dinner that you came to the States when you were fourteen."

"Intracompany transfer. My father had applied for a visa years before. He worked for a company in Manila that opened a subsidiary here in California, and they transferred him here. Dad's brother was living in San Jose too. Then I joined the navy. That helped get permanent-resident status. Now we're all citizens."

"I'd like to talk to Sara's brother," I said, sitting on a box. "The one in Daly City."

"Pete Pascal? I have his address and phone number at home. I'll call you."

I stood up and set to work again, losing track of time until an employee of the storage facility wheeled by on a bicycle and told us the place was closing in fifteen minutes. By then Alex and I had unearthed the boxes from the university and were stacking the cartons I didn't need back inside the unit. There was no sign of the envelope. I was beginning to doubt the damn thing existed. I was coated with dust and could feel sweat beading on my face. Muscles in my back, legs, and arms ached, payment for all this exertion. Closing my eyes, I lusted after a long, hot shower.

"Are you going to haul this stuff back to your office?" Alex asked.

"That's what I had in mind." I opened my eyes. "Unless you have some objection. That way I can look through them more carefully. If I can't find the envelope, maybe I can find something else that will give me an idea what your uncle was working on when he died."

"Will all these boxes fit in your car?"

"I think so." I mentally measured the hatchback of my Toyota. "It'll be tight, though."

We put the rest of the cartons back in the storeroom, then walked to the parking lot to get my car. We managed to load ten of the twelve boxes into the Toyota. Alex wedged the remaining two boxes into his Mazda. He returned the stepladder, signed out of the storage facility, and followed me as I drove to Oakland. Fred, the security guard at my office building, told me there was a handcart down in the basement. I fetched it, then Alex and I unloaded the boxes and hauled them up to my office, stacking them along one wall. When we were done, I glanced at my watch. It was nearly eight. I'd had no dinner and I was bone-tired.

Alex's Mazda was parked behind my Toyota in the loading zone in front of the building. It wasn't quite dark yet, but the streetlights were on. The evening fog had come in, cooling the air. A breeze funneled between the buildings on Franklin Street. It had a wet chill I could feel through my filthy T-shirt.

"Thanks for the help," I said. "If I find anything, I'll let you know."

"It's early." Alex stood close. I caught the tangy scent of male sweat. "We have time for dinner."

I shook my head. "It's been a long day, Alex. Hot shower, cool sheets."

"Sounds even better." His eyes sparkled. "Am I invited?"

"Not tonight."

"I don't usually like to take a rain check." He leaned forward and kissed me, taking his time, his hips pressing mine against the Toyota, his arms circling my waist. I closed my eyes and enjoyed the warm sensation that crept over me, banishing the chill of the night air. One of Alex's hands moved to the back of my neck, ruffling my hair. The other slipped under my shirt and caressed my back.

"Tell me something," I murmured as his hand moved upward, toying with the fastener of my bra.

"What?" His lips tickled my ear.

"Why did your wife divorce you?"

He stopped kissing me and placed his hands on my shoulders, looking at me with opaque brown eyes. "What makes you think my wife divorced me?"

"Just a hunch."

He didn't say anything for a moment. The corners of his mouth twitched. "I had an affair with someone."

"That's what I thought. You move fast."

"I don't like to waste time. Besides, you seem to be enjoying it," he said. He tilted his head and kissed me again.

He was right. I did enjoy it. My skin flushed and my nerve endings tingled. I reached up and moved his hands from my shoulders, disengaging my mouth from his.

"I have to go."

I fished my car keys from my bag. He caught my hands, stalling me. "Ever been to a Filipino fiesta?" he asked.

"No. Do they have good food?"

He laughed. "The best. There's a fiesta Saturday in Fremont. Come with me."

Saturday, I thought, tilting my head to one side as I studied his face. I needed to do laundry and clean my apartment. "I'd love to. What time?"

"I'll pick you up at ten. Tell me where."

I gave him my address. "What should I wear?"

"Clothes would be appropriate." A teasing note crept into his voice.

"Thanks, Alex. That's very helpful."

"Casual is fine."

He kissed me again, this time a friendly peck on my grimy forehead, and climbed into his red convertible. I got into my own car and started the engine. So the laundry pile got higher and I could write my name in the dust on the bookshelves. Attending a Filipino fiesta sounded like more fun than household chores. Besides, I hadn't been on a date in ages, and I'd worked the past two weekends.

As I unlocked the front door of my apartment, Abigail came running, her tail upright and twitching. She had a huffy look on her face, the one she gets when I've been away from home too much. She set up a chorus of plaintive meows designed to push all my pet-owner guilt buttons and spur me to fill the food bowl. It always works. I headed straight for the kitchen and opened a can of cat food. Then I knelt and scratched her between the ears as she ate. She purred and I knew I was forgiven—this time.

I foraged in the refrigerator and made myself a salad for dinner, augmenting it with crumbled feta cheese and some sesame crackers. Then I took my hot shower, feeling my muscles relax under the steaming spray, turning the water off between soaping and rinsing in deference to the drought. In my oversized T-shirt I went to bed, my head filled with deliciously erotic thoughts of Alex Tongco.

Eight

I ARRIVED AT MY OFFICE EARLY FRIDAY MORNING
and made a large pot of coffee. When I had a mug within
reach, I hauled one of Dr. Lito Manibusan's cartons down
from the tower of boxes Alex Tongco and I had stacked along
the wall the previous night. So far Dad had been unable to
locate the mysterious envelope at home or in his Cal State
office. I surmised that in the aftermath of the professor's murder Dad stuck it somewhere in Dr. Manibusan's office and it
had been packed away when Alex and his brother emptied
that space. Surely it had to be somewhere in one of these
boxes. I removed the lid from the first carton and pulled out
several file folders.

Dr. Manibusan had no doubt organized his files in a logical fashion, but after his death the Tongco brothers were
more interested in getting their uncle's stuff packed in boxes
than in maintaining any kind of order. As I sifted through
the folders, I noted the labels and the array of subjects. In
one box I didn't see anything related to the professor's research about crime and Asian immigrants, or the book he'd
been writing on Filipino immigrants. I stuck my hand down
between each folder and around the inner sides of the box,
feeling for the envelope. No luck.

I cracked open another carton. The professor had certainly
been a clipper, saving articles from newspapers and magazines and journals. He and his scissors were particularly active during the years when the Marcos regime toppled under
the weight of its own corruption and the housewife in the
yellow dress, Corazon Aquino, swept into her unlikely ten-

ure as president. Manibusan had files on Cory, on her assassinated husband, Benigno Aquino, on Defense Minister Juan Ponce Enrile, and other notables. Besides the writings of others, the professor kept a record of his own work on an array of subjects—published articles, final copies, final drafts, and notes.

When I was a kid I constantly got sidetracked while looking up words in the dictionary. Other words caught my eye and I would read page after page of definitions, my imagination so captured by all those intriguing words and exotic meanings that I'd forget my original purpose. That's what happened now as I delved into Dr. Manibusan's files. The historian took over from the detective. I sat cross-legged on the floor, reached for a folder, opened it, and began to read, fascinated by this private self-paced seminar on the Philippines.

Lito Manibusan's interest in his native land was vast and all-encompassing, extending from the precolonial Philippines through three hundred years of Spanish rule, to the United States' hegemony dating from 1898, when Admiral Dewey sailed into Manila Bay and began the Pacific phase of the Spanish-American War, to commonwealth status in the 1930s, World War II, and, finally, independence in 1946. File after file related stories of rebellion, revolution, and war—Rizal against the Spanish in the nineteenth century, Aguinaldo against the Americans after the Spanish-American War, social unrest in the thirties, the Huks against the United States after World War II, and the current insurgencies of the New People's Army and the Muslim separatists in Mindanao. There was much here about World War II and the Japanese occupation, including files on partisans, POWs, and collaborators. Names of people and places leapt out at me—MacArthur and Wainwright, Quezon and Roxas, Leyte and Lingayan gulfs, Bataan and Corregidor.

I was on my second cup of coffee when the phone rang. I looked up, startled. It was past eight. I had been immersed in the professor's files for over an hour, sitting cross-legged on the floor at the back of my office. My answering machine kicked in, but when I heard Alex's voice, I scrambled to my feet and grabbed the phone.

"I'm here," I said, switching off the machine.

"I've got phone numbers and addresses for Pete Pascal, both home and work," he told me, repeating the information slowly while I wrote it down. After Alex hung up I called Pascal at his home in Daly City and he agreed to meet me before he opened his stationery store at ten. Before leaving my office I tidied up, replacing the professor's files in the carton I'd been searching. Then I unplugged the coffeepot and left.

According to a series of articles I'd read recently in one of the San Francisco papers, the Filipino-American community is the fastest-growing Asian minority group in California, and Daly City is northern California's Little Manila. I found this easy to believe as Pete Pascal and I sat at a table in a bakery a few doors down from Pascal's store. I heard as much Tagalog as I did English, and the faces around me were predominantly Asian.

Pascal was a gray-haired man with a stocky figure clothed in blue slacks and a pin-striped shirt. I'd met Sara Manibusan only a few times before her death, so if there was a family resemblance, I didn't recall it.

Pascal stirred cream into his coffee. In a precise voice with barely a trace of an accent, he confirmed what I already knew about his late brother-in-law's plans that January night Dr. Manibusan was murdered.

"We expected Lito at eight. My store is open until seven on Friday nights, so that gave my wife and me plenty of time to close up and get dinner started. When he didn't show up, we were concerned, of course. We wondered if he'd changed his plans. But if that was the case, it wasn't like him not to call and let us know." He took a bite of his pastry, washing it down with coffee before he continued.

"I phoned his place in Castro Valley around ten, but there was no answer. Then I called Alex. He didn't know anything. The police notified him early Saturday morning, and he called me to break the news." He shook his head slowly. "What a shock. And your poor father, finding Lito's body like that. He seemed so upset when I met him at the funeral.''

"Yes, he was. He and Dr. Manibusan were good friends." I sipped my coffee, asking Pascal for some background information on the Manibusans.

"Sara was my youngest sister," he said. "When I came to the States in the early sixties, she was engaged to Lito. They met at the university in Manila, before Lito came over to Berkeley for his doctorate. They corresponded, and when Lito returned to the Philippines, they were married. Lito taught at the university and Sara gave piano lessons in their home. I know they hoped to have children, but it didn't happen."

"What made them decide to come to the United States?"

Before answering, Pascal poked at his pastry with his fork, then lifted his eyes to mine. "Do you know anything about Philippine history?" he asked finally.

"A bit."

"My native land has a troubled past." He shrugged, his mouth moving into a wry smile. "It has a troubled present, too. Back in the sixties, when Lito began teaching, things were pretty bad. Marcos was elected in 1965, and he was going to fix everything. Instead, the situation got worse. In the countryside the Communist insurgents and the Muslim separatists were getting stronger. The economy was in a shambles and there was corruption in the government. By the early seventies people were protesting. Things got violent. You can't imagine what Manila was like."

"So Lito and Sara decided to leave?"

"Yes," Pascal said. "As things deteriorated, they made up their minds to leave the Philippines and come to America. They were at the Plaza Miranda in August 1971 for a Liberal Party rálly when a number of bombs went off. Several people were killed, and more than a hundred injured, including some of Lito's students. Lito was a Liberal Party supporter and he greatly admired Benigno Aquino. Then Marcos declared martial law in September 1972 and Ninoy was arrested. We were all relieved that Sara and Lito were able to leave shortly after that.''

"What did they have to do to get a visa?''

"It takes a long time," Pascal said with a shake of his head. "By then I was a naturalized citizen. And so was Lito's older sister, Alex's mother. My immediate family members, like my wife, my mother, and my children, I brought them over right away. But for a brother or a sister, this takes much longer. The wait can be fifteen, twenty years now. It's no wonder so many people come in"—he looked around and lowered his voice—"illegally.''

"Does that happen often?''

Pascal nodded. "Very much. There are people who marry Americans, like tourists, or servicemen from the American bases, to get a spouse visa in order to enter the United States. Others come over on tourist or student visas and just stay. Once here, they buy phony green cards. I hear there's a big trade in forged documents. As a businessman, I have to be careful, because if I hire an illegal alien, INS comes after me and slaps me with employer sanctions.''

"But the Manibusans didn't have to do that. Alex told me that Lito had some kind of skilled labor preference.''

"Preference three. He used his connections from his graduate student days at Berkeley. It took several years, but when he and Sara came over in 1973, Lito had a job waiting for him at Cal State in Hayward. He really enjoyed teaching there. Everything was going so well. Sara and Lito became citizens, they bought their place in Castro Valley.''

"Then Sara was diagnosed with breast cancer.''

He nodded, his expression saddened. "Yes. It was a tragedy. She found this lump, and six months later she was gone. Lito was . . . desolate.''

"Do you think it likely that he would marry again?''

"Lito?'' Pascal's eyebrows shot up. "Get married? But he didn't.''

"There's a chance that he did, on that trip to the Philippines last summer," I said without mentioning Dolores Cruz and her claim of marriage to Lito Manibusan.

For a moment Pascal looked shocked at the idea. Then his face turned thoughtful. "If he married again, this is news to me. I can't claim to know what was going on in his mind. After Sara died, he kept to himself. We didn't see him as frequently, though he was always invited to family gatherings. He was a fine man, a professor, handsome and in good health. Any woman would have been proud to marry Lito. But I don't think he wanted to go out with women, let alone marry again. If he suddenly got married on his trip to the Philippines, that was an impulsive thing to do." Pascal moved his head slowly from side to side. "I must tell you, Miss Howard, my brother-in-law was not an impulsive man."

Based on my own brief and casual acquaintance, I didn't think Lito Manibusan was an impulsive man either. It was completely out of character for that quiet, professorial widower to suddenly marry a woman in Manila on his last trip to the Philippines, and then, as Alex pointed out, not tell anyone about it. Dolores Cruz's claim was such an obvious scam, transparent as cellophane. Yet she must have thought it the only way she could gain access to the professor's files. The stakes were no doubt high.

"When was the last time you spoke with Lito?" I asked Pascal.

"Thursday, the day before he died. He called to confirm our dinner plans for Friday night."

"He said nothing to you about going to San Francisco before coming to Daly City? Some sort of appointment or errand he had to do first?"

Pascal shook his head. "Nothing at all."

"Think back to other conversations you had with him, between the time he returned from the Philippines last summer and his death in January. Anything special come to mind?"

Pascal finished his pastry and leaned over the table, lowering his voice. "Politics. Always politics."

"Why is that?"

"Right before Lito went to the Philippines last summer, there was another coup attempt against Corazon Aquino, one of many since the revolution, I'm sorry to say. Lito and I talked about that a great deal when he returned, and about the mood of people back home in Manila. We didn't agree on a lot of things. I think this is normal whenever two Filipinos talk politics."

"Even two American citizens?" I asked him.

"We have feet in both worlds," Pascal said with a shake of his head. "Everyone has an opinion, or two, or three. And we are more than willing to tell you about it. Sometimes it even leads to violence. You've heard about those men in Seattle?"

I nodded. Pascal was referring to two Filipinos convicted of murdering an anti-Marcos labor leader in Washington State. That case had the unsavory odor of death squads, something Americans didn't like to think could happen in the United States. But it was right here in Daly City that Chinese-American journalist Henry Liu had been gunned down in his own driveway by Taiwanese gangsters allegedly working for the government in Taipei.

"Here we have the same divisions and factions that they do back in the Philippines," Pascal was saying. "Lito was very much a supporter of Aquino. Others, like Hector Guzman, for example, make no secret of their pro-Marcos leanings."

"Even though Marcos is dead? And who's Hector Guzman?"

"Imelda and her children are very much alive. Hector Guzman is a real estate tycoon here in Daly City. Very rich, very influential. Bong-Bong stayed with him the last time he was in the Bay Area," Pascal said, referring to Marcos's son by his nickname.

"What do you know about the Manibusan family?" I asked.

"They lived for many years in San Ygnacio," Pascal said. "That's a town near Lubao in the southern part of Pampanga Province. It's mostly flat, with sugar cane and rice fields as far as you can see. Lito's grandfather—and mine—was *mestizo*, a little bit of *Indio*, Spanish, Chinese. He fought with

Aguinaldo against the Americans in the Philippine Insurrection, after the islands were liberated from Spain. When the *insurrectos* were defeated, he settled in San Ygnacio and owned a little store.''

Pascal stopped to sip his coffee, then continued. ''Carlos, Lito's father, was educated by the Americans and he became a teacher also. From what Lito told me, Carlos was something of a radical in the thirties, when conditions were so bad for the peasants. It got him in trouble with some of the big landowners in that part of the province.'' Pascal shook his head. ''You see, Miss Howard, for all those democratic principles the Americans brought with them, the power and the wealth in the Philippines has always rested with those who own the land.''

''Then came the war,'' I said.

''Ah, yes. It's ironic, really. Carlos Manibusan lived to see the Americans liberate the Philippines, only to be murdered by Japanese stragglers. That's when Mrs. Manibusan left San Ygnacio and moved to Manila to live with her sister. Manila was nearly destroyed during the liberation, but it came back to life quickly. Mrs. Manibusan was dead by the time I met the family, through my sister's engagement to Lito. I understand she was a formidable old woman. She supported herself as a seamstress and managed to send all four of her children to college. Lito, Concepcion, Javier, and Alex's mother, Maria.''

''Javier?'' I looked across the table at Pascal. This was the first time anyone had mentioned the name. ''Javier Manibusan?''

''Lito's older brother. Alex didn't mention him?'' I shook my head. ''Javier went to seminary to be a priest, but he was never ordained. He got involved in left-wing politics and liberation theology. The last I heard he was organizing sugar plantation workers in the Central Plains.''

A dangerous occupation, I thought. Men in power do not give up their power easily. That is as true in the Philippines as it is anywhere else. I remembered the book at Alex's apartment, with a marker stuck in the section about the New People's Army. Perhaps Alex's interest in the insurgency went beyond current affairs into the realm of the personal.

I thanked Pascal for his time and left the bakery. As I drove toward San Francisco, I reflected that there was much I didn't know about the Philippines, or the culture of the people who were immigrating to my corner of northern California in ever-increasing numbers. What I knew was what I read in the newspaper, which focused infrequently on events in the Philippines and how they reverberated through the Filipino-American community in the Bay Area. What I read or heard in the media was filtered through an American perspective. For more than twenty years the Philippines meant the rule of Ferdinand and Imelda Marcos. First the Marcos regime had been viewed as progressive, stable, democratic, and, most important, anti-Communist. Then it became increasingly evident that Ferdinand and Imelda were Lord and Lady Misrule, and the purported "showcase of democracy" was a shaky house of cards propped up by lies, self-interest, and billions of dollars in American aid. And the Filipinos, back in the archipelago as here in the States, were loyal or in the opposition camp or simply looking out for their own interests.

From what I read, only the players had changed since the 1986 "people power" sweep that brought Corazon Aquino to the presidency. Now Cory's hold on power was tenuous as she contended with coup attempts, the acrimonious debate over American military bases on Philippine soil, a rebellious military, and a disintegrating economy. And, of course, agrarian reform, always promised and never accomplished, the never-ending issue of who owns land and who labors on it. Add to that not one, but two insurgencies—Communist and Muslim—and you have a volatile cocktail. Politics is a quagmire, whether in the United States or in the Philippines.

Before crossing the Bay Bridge to Oakland, I stopped at San Francisco's Hall of Justice, hoping to talk with Inspector Cobb, one of the homicide detectives handling the still-open Manibusan case. He was in, a short, stocky guy with receding brown curls made all the more unruly by his constant habit of running his left hand through his remaining hair. Most of the cops I see look tired and overworked, and Cobb was no exception. He reiterated what he'd told me on the phone a few days earlier. No leads on the Manibusan case—the investigation was at a dead end. Appeals for witnesses remained unanswered, though SFPD had the usual gang of cranks and nuts confessing to the murder. The only person who reported seeing Dr. Manibusan alive and in San Francisco that rainy January night was my own father.

Cobb listened with interest as I described the events of the past few days. He assured me that despite media interest in Dad, the only information concerning him that had been officially released was that Dr. Timothy Howard was a professor at Cal State Hayward and a Castro Valley resident. "Let me know if you turn up a lead," Cobb said as I left his office. "I'm fresh out."

Nine

GEORGE, MY COMPUTER-CONSULTANT NEIGHBOR, was in his own cubicle when I returned to my office, so I walked down the hall to talk with him. He doesn't fit the stereotypical profile of computer nerd. He's tall and rangy, his skin burned to a permanent nut-brown by the sun. He spends his weekends in hiking boots tramping up Mount Tamalpais or Mount Diablo in the Bay Area, or heading off to the Sierra Nevada to camp and hike. In fact, he was finishing up a project so he could hit the road for a long weekend in Yosemite, his tabernacle.

I stood under a poster of Ansel Adams's famous photograph of Half Dome and asked him to search various data bases for information on Mabuhay Travel and Dolores Cruz, as well as Charles, Arthur, and Perlita Randall. "See if you can find anything on an Edward Villegas," I added.

"I'll do it when I get back on Monday," he said, tossing a lock of sandy hair back from his face with one hand as the other sped over a keyboard. His pale blue eyes were intent on the computer screen before him.

Angie Walters at OPD had not yet called me with any information about Villegas. Back in my own office I checked the criss-cross directory for Daly City. The phone number Edward Villegas had given Alex was an address on Serramonte Boulevard. Further checking revealed that the address was that of a restaurant called the Manila Galleon. Odd, I thought. I picked up the phone and called the *Philippine News*, verifying what I suspected. No one there had ever heard of a free-lance writer named Edward Villegas.

As I hung up the phone, I glanced at Dr. Manibusan's boxes looming like the Great Wall of China, hoping I'd get back to my search for the professor's envelope—or anything else that might indicate what the professor had been working on at the time of his murder.

I checked the messages on my answering machine, returned several phone calls, then switched on the computer. I updated the Manibusan file by making notes on my conversations with Pete Pascal and Inspector Cobb. As I was printing out the pages, the phone rang. I picked it up and heard a familiar voice. It was Sid Vernon, my ex-husband, a big man with golden tomcat eyes and an Oakland Police Department detective's shield. Our divorce had been painful; most divorces are. But the passage of time helped and we were trying to be friends.

"Hi, Sid. What's up?"

"How about lunch?"

"Sure." I consulted my watch. It was nearly twelve. "Now?"

"Yeah. Meet me at Ratto's."

I left my office on Franklin Street and walked toward the Old Oakland development that fronted Broadway between Eighth and Tenth. The buildings are some of the oldest in the city, recently rehabbed and slowly filling with tenants. On Fridays Ninth Street is closed off between Broadway and Clay for a farmers market. This weekly event draws a large crowd of shoppers, especially when the weather's good and the produce plentiful. It was early in the season, but the street was full of people lured by the warm May sunshine, seductive colors, and the array of fruits and vegetables—and the desire to taste the flavors of this particular slice of urban life.

As I crossed Broadway I saw a line of wide-eyed Chinese preschoolers on a midday adventure, each with one tiny hand clasping a long, thick rope, this lifeline held at both ends by teachers. Farther down Ninth Street I heard a lilting melody, looked for and found the Peruvian street musicians playing guitar and pipes. Near them an elderly black man leaned on his cane, enjoying the music, his purchases in a canvas bag at his feet.

I waited for the light at Washington Street, with a group of women in business suits and sneakers, lunchtime refugees from the nearby office buildings. Then I crossed the street, past the stall where the Hmong woman, from Southeast Asia by way of Modesto, sold her exquisitely sewn handicrafts.

Ratto's International Grocery anchors the corner of Washington and Ninth, and it has been an Oakland tradition since the turn of the century. I had never realized there were so many different kinds of beans until I saw them at Ratto's, displayed in bushel baskets on the wooden floor of the grocery, a culinary wonderland with tall shelves holding cooking utensils, implements, spices, vinegars, and other items to tempt the adventurous cook. Ropes of garlic festoon the light fixture over the deli case, full of fat wheels of Brie, wedges of Greek Kefalograviera and Italian Cacciocavallo, blocks of Marbier and Asiago and English Stilton rich with blue lines, the names rolling off the tongue as redolent and flavorful as the cheeses themselves. Every time I go to Ratto's I see one I haven't tried before, and one day I'm going to taste my way from one end of the counter to the other.

Next door to the grocery is a big room with plain wooden floors, a counter, tables covered with red and white oilcloth, and mismatched chairs. In this utilitarian space Ratto's offers a bill of fare that includes salads, sandwiches made to order, and plates of pasta with tomato or pesto sauce, one of Oakland's best lunchtime bargains. That's why the line of customers was already out the door.

I saw Sid standing to one side of the door, next to a poster advertising Ratto's regular Friday-night dinner of pasta enlivened by opera. He's a tall, broad-shouldered man with slim hips and curly blond hair. I'm a tall woman, but Sid always seems to tower over me. I greeted him with a wave. We know each other too well to shake hands, and we've been divorced for too short a time to exchange kisses.

"You look great," I said, surveying him as we joined the

line. He always did. Despite everything, I still felt a physical
attraction to him.

"So do you."

"How's the shoulder?" I asked. He assured me it was
fine, good as new. Sid had just gone back to work in April
after taking a bullet, the result of a case I'd been working on
last March. The line inched forward, into the grocery, past
all those baskets of beans. I did my usual survey of the deli
case and spotted a cheese called grana padano. I'd never
heard of that one, I thought, promising myself a taste. As
Sid and I moved slowly toward the doorway leading to the
lunchroom, we traded news about our respective families.
Sid's seventeen-year-old daughter, Vicki, the product of his
first marriage, lives in southern California. Worried about
his gunshot wound, she had visited him on her spring break.
I asked Sid about his sister in Sacramento and he inquired
about my brother in Sonoma. His parents are dead, and mine
are divorced, with Dad here and Mother living in Monterey.

Despite the family news report, Sid seemed preoccupied,
as though something was on his mind. Once through the
doorway, we grabbed something to drink from the refriger-
ated case on the left, got our trays and pasta, and paid for
lunch. We helped ourselves to napkins, cutlery, glasses, and
ice, all arrayed on sideboards at the rear of the room. I turned
and scanned the sea of tables. Most were occupied, but I
spotted two empty places at one end of a big table near the
front window. Sid and I set our trays down, ignoring the two
corporate types next to us.

"I need to talk with you," he said, pouring his soft drink
over ice.

"Am I having lunch with Sid, or with Sergeant Vernon?"
He didn't answer. I stirred my pasta with my fork, making
sure pesto and parmesan were liberally distributed. "Okay,
what is it?"

"You asked Angie Walters in Records to check to see if
someone has a record."

"Yes, I did." I broke off a corner of my French bread and
mopped up some pesto. "Look, I know she's not supposed

to do that. I don't want to get her into trouble. I withdraw the request, okay?'' He didn't say anything. ''Isn't that why you wanted to talk to me?''

''Not exactly,'' Sid said around a mouthful of pasta.

My eyebrows quirked as I reached for my mineral water. ''Just what exactly does 'not exactly' mean?''

''What are you up to, Jeri?''

''I'm working on a case. I hit the jackpot with Edward Villegas, right?''

''This guy is no prize. His name is Eduardo Cesar Villegas—also known as Eddie the Knife.''

''Eddie the Knife,'' I repeated, leaning back in my chair. The sobriquet conjured up several images, most notably that of Dr. Lito Manibusan stabbed to death in the Sutter-Stockton garage. ''He likes to play with blades.''

''Eddie doesn't play. He's slick, with a nasty reputation. A couple of felony arrests for assault, charges dropped on both of them, probably because of pressure on the victims. He was a suspect in a homicide over in San Francisco three years ago, questioned but never charged. Insufficient evidence. He's connected. Asian crime syndicates have been moving into the Bay Area in a big way over the past few years. Chinese, Japanese, Vietnamese. And Filipino. Eddie's been operating on the other side of the Bay, San Francisco, the Peninsula.''

''But not Oakland, or not until lately,'' I guessed. ''How did you know I'd asked Angie to check his record? That was between her and me.''

''When Eddie's name came up, I just happened to be in Records, and so was Sergeant Gonsalves. He works in Theft. Villegas's name rang a bell with him because of his connections. Gonsalves is working a case right now involving auto heists over at the Port of Oakland. I guess some of the major players are Filipino. So Gonsalves pinned Angie down, asking her why she was running a check on Villegas. Angie had to tell him. Gonsalves read her the riot act. I cooled Gonsalves down some, and told Angie not to do it again.'' Sid cocked his head to one side and gave me the lecture in a stern voice. "And I'm telling you not to do it again. Records is not supposed to be a place you plug into every time you need the scoop. Got that?"

"Of course. I don't want Angie to lose her job." I'd have to call her and apologize. Damn, it was getting hard to obtain information. I hated to lose Angie as a source. I stared down at my plate as though I were reading tea leaves instead of looking at pesto, digesting what Sid had told me about Villegas. Was there a connection between Eddie the Knife and Dolores Cruz, both trying to get their hands on Lito Manibusan's files? Were they working together? Or did the two of them have conflicting interests?

"Don't step on Gonsalves's toes," Sid was saying. "He's a real hardass, and he's got no use for private investigators."

"I'm quaking in my loafers," I said, unimpressed.

"Don't get prickly on me, Jeri."

"This is not prickly. You've seen me prickly, and you know the difference. Did Gonsalves ask you to warn me off?"

Sid shook his head. "No. I'm doing this on my own. I don't want you mixing it up with Gonsalves, or stepping into the middle of an ongoing Oakland Police Department investigation."

"Thanks for the tip, Sid. I'll try to stay off Gonsalves's toes, but I have an investigation of my own to conduct."

Sid gave me an exasperated look. "If Gonsalves comes after you, don't say I didn't warn you."

"Only if you promise not to gloat."

We finished lunch and went outside. I watched Sid stride briskly down Washington toward Oakland Police Headquarters, two blocks away, then I turned and went back into Ratto's for a pint of frozen pesto, a half pound of Bulgarian feta, and a wedge of that grana padano. Then I headed back into the farmers market crowd, where I treated myself to dessert, a saucer-size chocolate chip cookie. I strolled along Ninth Street as I ate it, allowing myself to be seduced by purveyors of strawberries, greens, and baked goods. By the time I got back to my office I was laden with produce and a loaf of pumpernickel-raisin bread.

I stashed my purchases in my office refrigerator and called Angie Walters to say I was sorry for getting her into hot water. Fortunately she didn't seem too upset about the situation, informing me that she could handle "that piss-ant Gonsalves." My second call was to Inspector Cobb at SFPD. I suggested he compare the partial print on the battery found at the scene of Lito Manibusan's murder with those of one Eduardo Villegas, known as Eddie the Knife.

I had a one-thirty appointment with an attorney in Berkeley, so I locked up and headed for the lot where I parked my car. On the way back to Oakland later that afternoon I detoured to Grand Avenue, parking outside Mabuhay Travel. I sat for a moment, looking past the Philippine travel posters into the front office. I didn't see Dolly Cruz. Only one of the desks was occupied, the front one on my left. A slender black woman with oversize glasses talked on the telephone and punched the keys of the computer terminal in front of her.

I waited for half an hour. Then I saw the Thunderbird pull into the driveway that led to the parking lot behind the building. I got out of my car and walked to the window of Mabuhay Travel, observing Dolores Cruz as she strolled into the agency through the door at the rear, carrying an Emporium shopping bag. The woman with the oversize glasses was off the phone now. The anger on her face was unmistakable as she turned from her computer and glared at Dolly. Through the plate glass window I watched their mouths. The pantomime left me with the feeling that Ms. Cruz and her officemate didn't quite get along.

I interrupted the sharp exchange in mid-word as I opened the door and walked into Mabuhay Travel. Both women turned to me, wiping all traces of argument from their faces, both smiling as Dolly set the shopping bag on the floor behind her desk. The phone rang as I moved toward Dolly's desk. "Get that, Belinda," Dolly ordered. Belinda picked up the phone, looking as though she'd like to do something else with the receiver besides talk into it.

"May I help you?" Dolores Cruz said in her throaty, accented voice, flashing me a smile that extended only as far as her lips. She wore red today, a sleeveless number with a neckline cut for a generous view of her cleavage. Jewelry winked and glittered from her ears, neck, and fingers. But I didn't see the wedding band she had worn the other day at the university, when she was posing as Dr. Manibusan's widow.

"Yes." I stood in front of her desk. The surface was littered with papers, and I quickly glanced at the disarray, looking for anything interesting. "I'm considering a trip to the Philippines, and I'd like some information."

"Well, I can certainly help you. I'm from the Philippines. Ask away." She said "ask," not "ax," I noticed. So she wasn't the woman who had called Cal State to request Dad's home address, unless the mispronunciation had been a deliberate attempt to disguise her voice.

"I'd like to travel in August," I told her. "Spend some time in Manila, then visit the countryside."

"I have just the tour for you," she said.

I put Dolly through her travel-agent paces, learning all about Manila and other favored tourist spots, getting fare quotes and airline timetables and a handful of travel literature. Behind my prospective-tourist questions I probed for information about Dolly, where she'd lived in the Philippines and when she'd arrived in the United States, but all I learned was that she had lived in Manila. While Dolly was looking up something on the computer screen, I glanced across the room at Belinda, who was helping another customer. I decided my next visit to Mabuhay Travel would be during Dolly's extended lunch hour. No doubt Belinda could give me an earful.

When I returned to my office, I tossed the Philippine travel information on the bookshelf behind my desk. It was past four and there were no messages on my answering machine, so I decided to continue my search through Dr. Manibusan's boxes. I was lifting a carton down from the stack, when I was interrupted.

He had a sallow, pock-marked face, dark hair, and brown eyes that flashed me a poisonous look at the same time he flashed his Oakland Police Department detective's shield. "Sergeant Gonsalves," I said. He didn't waste any time.

"You know who I am?"

"Yes, I do. Have a seat, Sergeant."

"I'll stand."

"Suit yourself." I sat down on my chair, leaned back, and looked him over. He was in his thirties, medium height and build in his brown suit, and he wouldn't be bad-looking if he'd lose the frown that seemed to have permanently soured his face. "Did you want something, Sergeant?"

"You've been looking for information on Eddie Villegas," he said, a challenge in his voice. "Why?"

"I'm working on a case. His name came up."

Gonsalves pushed an exasperated noise through his clenched teeth and looked at me as though I were the most recent dirtbag in a whole day full of dirtbags. "Who's your client?" he demanded.

"Sergeant Gonsalves," I said politely, "you know I don't have to tell you that."

He put both hands on the surface of my desk and leaned over me, his eyes narrowing. "Let me tell you this, lady. You're stepping in the middle of my investigation. My investigation gets loused up, I'll kick your butt from here to Tahoe."

I dropped the temperature of my voice from cold to icy. "You're a real charmer, Gonsalves. Drop the macho act. I'm not going to spoil your party. I'm just making a few inquiries. Besides, I could be in a position to help you out."

Gonsalves's laugh was derisive. "I don't need any help from some jerk PI."

"So forget I offered." I stood up, feeling an overwhelming urge to smack the jerk cop in the face. "And get the hell out of my office."

Ten

SATURDAY MORNING I STOOD IN MY UNDERWEAR, ironing a pair of blue slacks and a flowered shirt, when the buzzer sounded in the living room. Quickly I pulled on the clothes, buttoning and zipping as I walked barefooted to the front window. Alex Tongco stood at the security gate in front of my small apartment complex. He was fifteen minutes early. I think he did it on purpose to fluster me. At my age, I'm not easily flustered, but Alex seemed to have a talent for upsetting my equilibrium.

I buzzed him through the gate. He crossed the courtyard toward my front door, carrying a book in his left hand. He wore a short-sleeve blue shirt tucked into a pair of khaki pants, Top-Siders on his feet. I opened the door to greet him.

"You're early."

He grinned and surveyed me with a leisurely gaze. "You've done your buttons wrong. Need some help?"

I looked down and saw that he was right. "I can manage. Would you like some coffee?"

He shook his head and handed me the book. "Here you are. Stanley Karnow. Not light reading, but well worth the effort."

"Thanks for the loan."

Abigail had abandoned the yellow mouse this morning and now sprawled on the back of the sofa, pinned by a sunbeam. Alex sat down and held out his hand. The cat opened her green eyes and sniffed delicately at his outstretched fingers. She decided he was all right and commenced a purr. Alex stroked her gently between the ears, then moved his fingers under her chin. Abigail tilted her head upward to get the full benefit of all this attention, cranking her purr up several notches.

I retreated to my bedroom, unplugged the iron, and re-buttoned my shirt correctly, tucking it into the waistband of my slacks. I slipped on a pair of sandals and some earrings and reached for my purse.

"Tell me about the fiesta," I said as we walked back across the courtyard to the street where he'd parked his Mazda. "What's the occasion?"

"The Fiesta of San Isidro Labrador. People from Cavite Province get together every year, socialize, eat, and dance. My aunts will be there. It starts with a Mass and a procession of flowers. After the Mass there's a *karakol.*"

"What's a *karakol*?"

Alex shrugged. "It's a procession, a celebration. You'll see."

He drove through Oakland to the Nimitz Freeway and pointed his red convertible south. Half an hour later we parked on a tree-lined street in a Fremont neighborhood and walked a block to the Veterans Memorial Hall. Clusters of people stood outside the Spanish-style building, talking and laughing, while children darted in and out of the building. As we approached, a group of men gathered on the steps turned and greeted Alex in Tagalog, punctuating their words with slaps on his back.

Alex introduced me. Despite their friendliness, I felt out of place, the only Caucasian in view. As we moved through the crowd of people into the foyer of the building, a woman handed me a bunch of white daisies. Beyond her in the main hall of the building I saw a line of people laying flowers at the feet of a statue of the Virgin resting on a palanquin. To the left was a larger palanquin, also with a statue. This must be Saint Isidro, I guessed, studying the features molded in plaster. On the back wall I saw two flags, one the Stars and Stripes, the other a banner with wide horizontal bands of red and blue meeting at a white triangle on the left, with a golden sunburst at the triangle's center. This must be the flag of the Republic of the Philippines.

Rows of folding chairs lined the wooden floor of the main hall. It was noisy, full of people ranging from youngsters in short pants or pinafores to the old ones, white-headed and bent with years. Conversations in English and Tagalog swirled around me, bouncing off the walls. Teenage boys in jeans and T-shirts flirted with their female counterparts, decked out in the latest high school fashions. The younger men and women were dressed casually, like Alex and me, or more formally in suits or dresses.

In front of me I saw a toddler riding his father's shoulders, towering about the crowd in the hall. He was using Dad's ears as handles, making varooming noises as he steered. I laughed aloud, then looked down as someone bumped into me. Staring up at me I saw the huge brown eyes of a little girl, about six, wearing a frilly pink dress and white patent leather shoes, her straight black hair fastened with two pink barrettes. I smiled and handed her my daisies. She took the flowers from me solemnly, then smiled like sunlight breaking through a cloud. She said something I couldn't hear and disappeared into the crowd.

Many of the older people—and some of the younger ones, too—wore the Filipino dress I remembered seeing in newspaper photographs of Ferdinand and Imelda Marcos. For the men the attire was lightweight short-sleeve shirts, many with embroidery down the front, worn outside the trousers. Alex told me the shirts were called barongs, and there was a more formal long-sleeve version. "That's a barong tagalog," he said, pointing toward one man whose white shirt was open at the neck. "Sometimes they're made of banana or pineapple leaves, even coconut or hemp."

The women swirled around in ankle-length butterfly-sleeve dresses in pastel colors that trumpeted spring. Time-hardened old men stood along the walls, pinching cigarettes between their fingers. Carrying rosaries and flowers for the Virgin in their gnarled fingers, the old women looked frail, but they weren't. What faces they had, a collision of

Asian and Latin gene pools simmered together in the thousands of islands, large and small, that made up the Philippines.

"I see my aunts," Alex said over the din. He took my elbow and steered me toward the front of the hall. I spotted Josefa Luna and Medy Pangalinan standing at the end of one row of chairs to the left of the altar, both in butterfly-sleeve dresses. Again, they looked like twins, Josefa in yellow and Medy in pink. Alex barely had time to greet them, when the priest entered. He was a short man with a broad, dark face, resplendent in his vestments. There was one seat left at the end of the row. Josefa and Medy urged me to sit down. Alex remained standing, leaning against the wall.

The priest's eyes fell on me briefly, then he began the Mass, saying that he would conduct it in English since there were people in the crowd who did not speak Tagalog. I felt more conspicuous than ever. I listened and watched the people around me as the priest told the story of the Tower of Babel. Even in the Philippines, he said, people from Cavite have trouble understanding people from Ilocos Norte or the Visayans because of the many dialects. He praised traditional Filipino values as being one with Catholic values. I caught Medy's sidelong glance at Alex, whose face was still and unreadable, and recalled her disapproving comment about his divorce. The hymns were in Tagalog. The celebrants, young and old and mostly women, lined up for Communion. Alex remained standing at the wall. I watched the others in my row, including Josefa and Medy, pass single file to the center aisle. After taking the wafer and wine, they circled to the outer aisles and I stepped aside to let them return to their seats.

When the celebrants were seated again, the priest raised his hands and began a long prayer for "our country, the Philippines, and our country, the United States." As I looked around the room, I recalled Pete Pascal's comment about Filipino-Americans having feet in both worlds, struggling to maintain their own culture while assimilating into the stew that is America.

Suddenly the Mass was over. All around me, people folded metal chairs and stacked them against the wall, clearing the hardwood floor of the hall. Alex and I hauled chairs to the sidelines, and I lost sight of his aunts. Near the front door of the hall a group of men took out instruments and became a brass band. Their first notes cacophonous, they soon broke into a bouncy three-quarter time. Men slid poles through holders on either side of the palanquins holding statues of the Virgin and the saint, then hoisted the poles to their shoulders. As the band oompahed an exuberant rhythm, the people in the hall began to dance. Some held hands as they shuffled in time to the music. Others took partners and waltzed.

"The *karakol*," Alex said, shouting over the music. He seized my hand and led me into the mass of people snaking around the hall. The men carrying the palanquins moved slowly in a counterclockwise direction, preceded by others waving red and white flags, all of them dancing past the brass band. I saw the little boy, still perched on his father's shoulders, arms waving in time to the music. Another father held his small daughter in his arms as he whirled around the room. Mothers danced with their arms around their older children. The old women who looked so solemn during the Mass threw off the slow dignity of age and waltzed with their grandsons.

A leathery old man wearing a cream-colored barong tagalog stopped in front of me, bowed, and took my hand. We joined a circle of dancers that included the priest, still in his vestments. One, two, three—one, two, three—the music echoed off the walls, and suddenly I wanted to take that trip I'd discussed with Dolores Cruz the previous day at Mabuhay Travel. I wanted to ride through Manila in a colorful jeepney, climb to the terraced rice fields at Banaue, and walk along a sandy beach on the Philippine Sea.

I smiled at my elderly partner and he smiled back, head inclined in a courtly bow. I saw Alex waltzing with his aunts, first Josefa, then Medy, his dark face animated by laughter. Then he claimed me as his partner, twirling me away from the circle and into his arms.

"Having fun?" he asked, his mouth close to my ear and

his arm wound tightly around me. His other hand covered mine as it rested on his shoulder. I enjoyed the pressure of his body against mine.

"Yes," I said with a grin.

As we waltzed around the room in the throng of dancers, I saw the flash of a camera strobe several times in rapid succession. Behind the camera was Felice Navarro in a purple jump suit with a lemon yellow belt and matching espadrilles on her feet, the red camera bag riding her shoulder as it had been the day I'd met her and her brother. She spotted me and waved, a friendly smile on her face. Then she saw who I was dancing with and looked startled, startled enough to make me wonder how she knew Alex Tongco.

The *karakol* ended, the brass band replaced by sixties rock from someone's CD player. People began queuing up on the opposite side of the hall, where a wide doorway led to a corridor and the dining hall beyond. Alex kept his arms around my waist for a moment, taking the opportunity to nuzzle my neck. Then his aunts appeared with an older couple in tow. "Well, *butete*," the old man said, greeting Alex with a slap on the back. "When you gonna make admiral?"

Alex laughed, and the conversation continued in a mixture of English, Spanish, and Tagalog. I walked slowly around the room, watching faces, searching for Felice Navarro with her camera, but I didn't see her. Instead, I saw her brother Rick a few paces in front of me, looking dapper in dark slacks and a crisp white barong that bared his muscular forearms. He stood with his hand resting lightly on the waist of a strikingly beautiful woman. She wore a clinging mauve silk dress with a neckline that set off her creamy complexion and the strand of pearls around her neck. Matching pearls were displayed in her ears. Her long dark hair was swept up into a knot at the nape of her neck. She pushed an escaping strand away from her face, and I saw a huge diamond on her left hand, several carats of glitter surrounded by pearls and smaller diamonds. It looked as though she needed another ring on her right hand just for balance, but it was bare.

"Miss Howard," Rick Navarro said when I appeared in

front of him. "Delighted to see you again. Let me introduce my fiancée, Nina Agoncillo."

"Jeri Howard," I said, offering my hand. The beautiful Miss Agoncillo had smooth, cool skin and an enigmatic smile. "I'm looking for Felice. I saw her a moment ago, but now I've lost her."

Rick Navarro laughed. "She'll turn up. Just look for the flash. Miss Howard's a private investigator, Nina." Nina smiled and nodded, murmuring something polite and disinterested. "What are you doing at the fiesta of San Isidro Labrador? Investigating our Filipino culture?"

"Purely a social occasion. I'm here with a friend." I scanned the room, and my eyes located Alex, still talking with his aunts and the elderly couple. When our eyes met, he smiled and excused himself, heading quickly in my direction. Then he saw whom I was with, and his face closed up abruptly. The air around me became charged with electricity. Of course, I thought, recalling the second name on the Tongcos' real estate transaction as well as Aunt Medy's earlier comment about Alex's divorce. It appeared the former Nina Tongco didn't intend to wait long before marrying again.

Alex greeted Rick and Nina with chill courtesy. Then the four of us jumped as a flash went off in our faces, a strobe propelled by Felice, armed with her camera and a determined smile. "I see your aunts," Felice said cheerfully, looking at Alex. "Is your mother here?"

Alex shook his head. "She's in Manila, visiting Aunt Concepcion."

"And your uncle Javier?" Rick posed the question with a smile, but I sensed that it was a barb aimed at Alex, as was the way he took possession of Nina Agoncillo's hand.

Alex responded with a question of his own. "Your father?" He directed his clipped words to Felice, but it was Rick who answered.

"He flew in from Manila this week. He's doing very well."

"I'm not surprised," Alex said, an undercurrent in his voice. "Max always lands on his feet."

Josefa and Medy joined us, their butterfly dresses and

chatter quickly altering the mood as they greeted Nina with affection, reflecting the younger woman's status as a former family member. As they admired her engagement ring, I heard Nina tell the two aunts that she was living with her brother Sal in San Francisco until her wedding to Rick in August.

We had been drifting toward the corridor that led to the dining hall and the feast. "Line up, line up, plenty of food," Medy urged, sounding like my Italian grandmother down in Monterey. Felice swirled off in another direction, camera at the ready, while Rick and Nina, hand in hand, joined the queue. Alex looked as though he wanted to escape. He headed for the front door, out onto the steps, and I followed him.

"You don't like Rick Navarro." I leaned against the railing and studied Alex's face. "And it's got nothing to do with your ex-wife."

"Why do you say that?"

"I make my living observing people and drawing conclusions. You've known him a while, and you don't like him. Any particular reason?"

"You think you've got me all figured out," Alex challenged me.

I shook my head. "No. I don't know who you are at all. You give me only bits and pieces of information, whenever you choose. I know you have a mother, a brother, and an Aunt Concepcion in Manila. You never mentioned Uncle Javier. I had to find out about him from Pete Pascal. Why should Rick Navarro make a point of inquiring about him?" He didn't answer. "If you won't talk about the Manibusans, tell me about Rick Navarro. Is he a citizen?"

"No. He came over about about three years ago, on a trader visa. He lives in his father's big house in Pacific Heights and runs his father's big import business."

"That would be Max. Max Navarro. I've heard that name before." I tried to recall where I'd heard or read it. Alex wasn't helping. Instead, he favored me with a sideways glance. Then I remembered. "Something to do with Marcos."

"Everything to do with Marcos." Alex's voice was quiet, and he looked out at the street.

"Maximiliano Navarro," I said. "He switched sides, like Enrile and Ramos."

I pulled a face from my memory bank, the same square, pugnacious face as that of Rick Navarro, only older, moving across my television screen several years before, when Ferdinand Marcos's corrupt martial law regime tottered and finally disintegrated in the face of Corazon Aquino and "people power." Cory had help, though. Defense Minister Juan Ponce Enrile, one of the architects of martial law, and Fidel Ramos, head of the Philippine Constabulary, saw fedup Filipinos in the streets of Manila and shifted their allegiance from the dictator to the housewife. Others followed their lead, including a wealthy businessman named Maximiliano Navarro.

"So Rick and Felice have a famous father," I said.

Alex nodded. "And an older brother back in the Philippines. Max Junior. Everyone calls him Jun. Jun runs the big sugar plantation. That's where the family money comes from, but Max diversified. He's involved in all sorts of things— banking, electronics, imports. Rick runs the import business here in the Bay Area."

"Why did you say Max always lands on his feet?"

"They call him *Pusa*, the cat. He was a big Marcos supporter all through the martial law years. Then in 1985, when he saw which way the wind was blowing, he suddenly discovered a lot of affection for Corazon Aquino. He sailed through the revolution, all right. Now that everyone's blaming Cory for not solving a century's worth of problems in a few years, Max is about to jump into politics. He's got a lot of money and so do his friends, like Hector Guzman over in Daly City. Max just acquired a second wife with all the right connections. My guess is he's going to run for president, along with Enrile, Cojuanco, and Laurel. The same old faces, the same old fights."

"So the turmoil continues?"

"It'll never be over," Alex said, shaking his head. "Not till the old men die. Maybe not even then."

"Such cynicism," I commented.

"When it comes to Filipino politics, cynicism is the only logical response." He favored me with a sardonic smile and took my hand. "I can think of better things to do than talk politics. Let's get in line or we won't get any food."

Alex's willingness to talk about the Navarros seemed limited to the male members of the family. He hadn't mentioned Felice, and it was no oversight. He didn't want to talk about her. Had there been something between them?

The queue leading to the kitchen was shorter now, and the hall was full of people eating from paper plates. When we finally reached the kitchen, the line split, leading to a bank of tables. I saw two roast pigs, apples in their mouths, maraschino cherries and circles of pineapple where their eyes had been. The table was laden with platters of boiled shrimp and barbecued chicken as well.

"What is all this stuff? All I know from Filipino food is *pancit* and *lumpia*."

He laughed, handing me a plate as he swept one hand toward the roast pigs. "*Lechon*, otherwise known as pork, in many different varieties. *Tocino* is spiced pork and that's *lechon kawali*, which is deep fried. This is *pancit palabok*, noodles with garlic sauce, and *pancit sotanghon*, noodles with vegetables. That's *ensaymada*, a sweet bread with a filling. And here's all the *lumpia* you can eat."

We piled our plates high with everything, including *lumpia*, the Filipino egg rolls I love. Alex led the way out the side door, plate in one hand and two bottles of dark San Miguel beer dangling from the other. We found a spot on the grass and sat cross-legged, eating as we talked.

"What did that old man call you? *Butete?*"

"It's a nickname," he said. "That's what people called me when I was a kid."

"What does it mean?"

He looked pained. "Tadpole."

I choked down a laugh with my beer. "Have you turned into a frog?"

"*Palaka?* No, a frog prince." His brown eyes smoldered, and I felt my skin tingle. "Kiss me and find out what happens."

"Tell me about your mother and your brother," I said, spearing a piece of the savory roast pork. "And Aunt Concepcion in Manila."

He took a mouthful of *pancit*, chewed, and washed it down with beer. "My mother is a widow. My father died of a heart attack five years ago. Mama lives here in Fremont, not far from my brother Carlos. He works for one of those computer outfits over in the Silicon Valley. He's the good Filipino son." He said this last with a wry smile. "Married to a good Catholic wife, with three beautiful children, a house in the suburbs, a great job. All the things I'm not."

"You're the navy officer. Don't the gold stripes on your sleeve count for anything?"

"Ah, yes, but I haven't provided Mama with any grandchildren she can brag about when she goes to see Aunt Connie in Manila."

I pulled the last shreds of barbecued chicken from a drumstick and reached for a napkin to wipe the sauce from my hands. "My mother frequently tosses me barbs on that very subject. My brother is the one with the wife and two kids. He teaches up in Sonoma."

"Teaching runs in the family, then." Alex twirled *pancit* onto his fork. "Mine, too, with Lito and my grandfather Carlos."

"And my grandfather on the Howard side. Grandma Jerusha was an actress for a while. In Hollywood in the twenties. She died a few years ago. My other grandmother is still alive, down in Monterey with my mother."

"Your parents are divorced?"

"Yes. Mom owns a restaurant in Monterey called Café Marie." I leaned back, feeling stuffed and drowsy.

He dipped his last *lumpia* into a puddle of sauce and took a bite. "Any luck finding the missing envelope?"

"Not so far. I just started looking through the boxes yesterday."

"What about that guy Villegas, the one who wants Lito's files?"

I told Alex what I'd learned about Eddie the Knife. "We know your uncle was working on an article about Asian immigrants and crime. So did Eddie. The professor must have encountered Eddie when he was researching the article."

"He was interviewing a lot of people last summer and fall for his book," Alex pointed out. "The one about *manongs.*"

"Manongs?"

He gestured with his chin, and I turned to look at a trio of elderly men sitting in the sun, talking among themselves. "The first generation of immigrants, like those old men. They came over before World War Two and worked in the cities as busboys and janitors, or as cheap farm labor all over California. Worked hard all their lives and had to deal with a lot of racism and restrictive immigration laws. There weren't that many Filipino women here. Some of them married outside the culture, but most of them are old single men living in hotels. Places like the International Hotel in San Francisco. You remember that?"

I nodded. The ugly incident had been a media circus. The International Hotel once stood near San Francisco's Chinatown, full of elderly Asian men like those Alex described, alone, with no families, spending the sum of their remaining days in its inexpensive rooms. In the late seventies some corporation wanted to tear down the International and build something else, so the old men had been messily and painfully evicted, dispersed to other cheap hotels in other marginal neighborhoods. The International Hotel was bulldozed into oblivion. The irony was that nothing had been built in its place. Instead of homes, however meager, there was now a large gravel-filled hole.

"He came to this fiesta last year," Alex was saying, "with a tape recorder, interviewing the old men. Maybe you'll find his notes and transcripts when you go through those boxes. Lito was interested in all kinds of history. That's important, for people like us, for someone to tell our story." His wave encompassed the old men as well as a group of children playing on the lawn.

"We helped build America, too, but you wouldn't know it to look in most history books. You're white, Jeri. You don't know what it's like. All the time I went to school I never saw a picture in those books that looked like me. And I never read a word about Filipinos, unless the book was talking about World War Two."

"Maybe I do understand," I said, thinking about all the history books that didn't say much about women. "I hope things are changing. Was your uncle also interested in family history?"

Alex looked at me and shrugged. "I told you I don't know about the Manibusans, not much more than I told you the other night."

"You didn't tell me anything the other night, except that the Manibusans came from San Ygnacio and that they left after World War Two. I learned more from Pete Pascal. Tell me about your uncle Javier."

Alex's face tightened and his eyes became opaque. He didn't like talking about this other Manibusan uncle. Yesterday Pascal had mentioned that Javier was organizing sugar workers. Did his politics make this mysterious uncle the black sheep of the Manibusan clan? "He's a couple of years older than Lito." Alex's words came slowly, reluctantly. "He was going to be a priest, but he got into radical politics instead."

"How radical?" I asked. "Are we talking about nonviolent demonstrations? Or is he toting a gun somewhere in the mountains?"

Alex didn't answer right away, and when he did, his voice was flat and cold. "I wouldn't be at all surprised." He crumpled a napkin, tossed it onto his empty plate, and stood up. "Let's get out of here."

We went back inside the hall to say good-bye to Aunt Josefa and Aunt Medy. As we approached the two old ladies, I saw Felice Navarro's purple jump suit, her face hidden by her camera. She seemed to be watching us through her lens.

Then she moved the camera away from her face and stared past me at Alex with a frown that raised my curiosity level. Alex looked up and saw Felice, then quickly glanced away as his aunts enveloped him in hugs and admonitions, as though they wouldn't see him again for years. Felice hid her face behind the camera again.

When we finally left the hall, Alex's mood had darkened. On the drive back to Oakland he popped a tape into the cassette player, turning the volume just high enough to make conversation difficult. By the time we reached my apartment, his former good humor had returned. He walked me to my door, then put both hands at my waist and drew me close.

"Going to invite me in?"

"No. I have things to do. Like laundry and housework."

He smiled and kissed me, at first gently, then with more urgency. "I can think of better ways to pass the time."

His mouth was creating all sorts of pleasurable sensations, but I placed my hands on his chest and pushed him away. "I had a great time at the fiesta, Alex. But let's keep it on a friendly level, shall we?"

"What do you mean?" he asked, all innocence.

"Ever since we met you've been trying to get me into bed."

He acknowledged my words with a wicked grin. "Am I getting any closer to success?"

"You expect me to answer that?"

Alex shook his head. "No. Let's keep a little mystery in the equation. It's more fun that way."

Eleven

SUNDAY WAS DAD'S BIRTHDAY. THE DEATH OF LITO Manibusan and its repercussions were forgotten in the pleasure of a family get-together. Dad picked me up that morning and we drove to Sonoma to spend the day with my brother Brian and his family. Brian had marinated chicken overnight in his special barbecue sauce and fired up the backyard grill. He put the chicken on to cook shortly after Dad and I arrived. Soon the aroma wafted onto the patio and set my gastric juices roiling. The kids—five-year-old Todd and three-year-old Amy—claimed Grandpa and dragged him off to show him various treasures. I poured myself a glass of wine and went to the kitchen, where my sister-in-law, Sheila, was chopping vegetables for a salad. She assigned me the task of making garlic bread, and I set to work at one end of the counter.

Dad and Brian are both teachers, so over dinner they dissected the state of education in California while I talked about small businesses with Sheila. She's a weaver who works at home, selling her products in shops in Sonoma and Glen Ellen. Today she was excited about a deal she had closed the day before, placing some of her textiles in a gallery in Santa Rosa. After a while we cleared the dishes off the picnic table and Sheila brought out Dad's birthday cake, a tall chocolate concoction that looked as though it had a million calories and tasted so good, every one of them was worth it.

While we lingered over cake and coffee, my mother called from Monterey to wish Dad a happy birthday. Despite my parents' divorce several years ago, a shock to my brother and me, Tim and Marie Howard remained friends. After all, they had thirty years and two children to tie them together. Dad passed the cordless phone to the two grandkids, then it went from hand to hand.

When my turn came, Mother asked when I was coming to Monterey to see her and the extensive network of Doyle and Ravella relatives who proliferate on the central coast. I put her off with vague promises and phrases about a busy schedule. Dad occasionally went down to Monterey to see Mother, who was so occupied running her restaurant that she didn't come to the Bay Area often. Brian and his family visited her more frequently, but he and Mother meshed well, while I was closer to Dad. She and I hadn't really gotten along since I hit puberty and I resented her walking out on Dad. That's why my visits to Monterey are infrequent and short.

It was early evening when Dad and I drove back to Oakland, fighting the end-of-the-weekend traffic on Interstate 80. I felt sleepy with too much food and not enough exercise. After Dad left my apartment I took a brisk walk around Lake Merritt, which gave me my second wind and the desire to spend some uninterrupted time at my office, resuming my search through the professor's papers. I had managed to look through two cartons on Friday. Now I lifted another from the stack and removed the lid.

Yesterday's conversation with Alex was fresh in my mind, so the first folder that caught my eye was the one labeled MANONGS. I pulled it from the box and examined its contents, finding the transcripts of the interviews the professor had conducted at last year's fiesta. I read through them, discovering what it was like to toil in the fields of the Salinas or San Joaquin valleys, harvesting lettuce, cauliflower, or winter peas.

I pulled out one folder labeled FILIPINO/U.S. MILITARY and read about the long history of Filipinos joining American military services. Like blacks and Latinos, they had been shunted into steward ratings, finally being allowed to move into other job specialities. Reading it, I understood what it meant to Alex to have the gold oak leaves of a lieutenant commander on his collar.

In the next carton I found a large accordion file stuffed with information about Maximiliano Navarro and his family. I pulled out papers and clippings and began to read. The businessman was older than the professor, but they were from the same province, Pampanga, where the Navarro family owned a sugar plantation near San Fernando, the provincial capital. Navarro's father, Rufino, had been accused of collaborating with the Japanese during the occupation, but evidently these charges had not been proven, for I saw nothing else in the file that indicated the elder Navarro was ever prosecuted. His son Maximiliano, on the other hand, had fought the invaders as a partisan and been hailed as a war hero. In the postwar years, as a young, brash entrepreneur, Maximiliano Navarro rapidly expanded the family's sugar plantation and built a business empire that included rice and copra production as well as sugar, mining interests in the mountainous north, and the businesses Alex had mentioned during yesterday's conversation.

As I read through the collection of newspaper clippings and magazine articles, I came upon a photo of Maximiliano Navarro with both his sons, Rick and Jun, noting the strong resemblance between Rick and his father. From what Felice had said the other day about her brother Rick and the success of his import business, I suspected that there was more than a physical resemblance between the two men.

I didn't see any such physical echo in Felice. Perhaps she looked like her mother, who, according to one magazine piece about Navarro, had committed suicide a few years ago after a long and debilitating illness. None of the articles mentioned Felice, as though the daughter didn't count. There was a magazine profile of Jun, who looked sleepy-eyed and prosperous, with photos taken at the living quarters on the sugar plantation near San Fernando. Rick had a more lean and hungry look in the photos that accompanied an article from a California business magazine. The feature talked about

Rick's management of Pacific Rim Imports, and described him as a worthy successor to his father's business empire.

Curious, I thought, that Dr. Manibusan would keep such an extensive file on the Navarros. Did he have a personal interest? Perhaps not. In the next carton I opened, I found even larger files on several other Filipino families, more powerful and certainly more well known, like the Aquinos, the Cojuancos, the Laurels, and, of course, the Marcoses.

My office window had darkened from blue sky to black night and my legs had stiffened in their cross-legged position. I stretched them out in front of me, massaging calves and thighs, and looked up, surprised to see that it was well past nine o'clock. I stood up, yawned, and stretched, then began straightening the mess I had made, preparing to go home. As I picked up one folder, something fell out, an old composition notebook with a faded black cover. It was an odd size, about six by eight inches, bound at one side, and it was sealed in a plastic freezer bag. It must have been quite old, for the edges of the pages were yellowed. Inside the front cover I saw "Carlos Teodoro Manibusan" printed in block letters, and the date January 1, 1919.

I leafed through the first few pages. The writing was in blue ink, grown faint with age, and the words mostly Tagalog, though here and there I saw English phrases, mathematical exercises, and that old standby, a diagramed sentence. A school notebook belonging to the professor's father, I guessed, a historical curiosity as well as a link to the past, lovingly preserved. I slipped it back into its protective bag and sealed it.

As I stacked files back into boxes, another file caught my eye, labeled simply CORRESPONDENCE. Cradling it in one arm, I opened it and riffled through the sheets of paper. No envelope here, just letters from fellow historians and universities about seminars and articles. I saw several sheets clipped together, the top with the letterhead of the United States Army. It was a letter to Dr. Manibusan, responding to his inquiry about a Lieutenant O. M. Cardiff. Cardiff left active service in November 1945. The most recent address available for Cardiff was on California Street, in San Francisco's Richmond district.

A yellow Post-it note was stuck to the side of the letter, covered with the black scrawls I now recognized as Dr. Manibusan's handwriting. It read ''M. Harold Beddoes, SF, June 1946. Check hospitals, assns.'' My curiosity piqued, I removed the paper clip and found two letters from Dr. Manibusan to the army, requesting information on Lieutenant Cardiff, who had evidently served in the Philippines during World War II. Who was Cardiff, or, for that matter, M. Harold Beddoes? Why was the professor interested in them? Sources for one of his articles, perhaps. ''Check hospitals, assns.'' could mean that one or both of them was in the medical profession. I looked through the correspondence file carefully, but could find no further mention of Cardiff or Beddoes.

On Monday I drove up to Mendocino County on another case, spending the night in Ukiah. I interviewed two witnesses in a civil lawsuit and located some documents at the courthouse, returning to Oakland late Tuesday afternoon. I wrote my report and delivered it to my client, along with photocopies of the pertinent documents. Back in my office I took the messages off my answering machine. One of them was from Inspector Cobb at SFPD. Eddie Villegas's prints were most certainly on file, but they weren't on the AA battery found at the scene of Dr. Manibusan's murder. Too bad, I thought. Eddie was such a promising suspect. I wasn't yet ready to rule him out.

I sifted through the mail that had piled up in my absence. In that stack I found the Dun & Bradstreet report I had requested on Mabuhay Travel. I pushed the rest of the mail aside and leaned back in my chair, perusing the two-page report. The information in a D&B is provided by the company itself, so the report doesn't as a rule include anything the company's principals don't want on the public record. Still, the sheets in my hand gave me some basic information on Mabuhay Travel's finances, operations, and history, as well as some background on the Randalls.

Mabuhay Travel had been incorporated in California seven years ago. Arthur Franklin Randall and Perlita Cruz Randall were listed as partners and they employed eight people at two locations, in Daly City and Oakland. I looked with interest at Perlita Randall's middle name. Were she and Dolores Cruz related? Sisters, perhaps? Arthur was eighteen years older than his wife, and he'd been in the navy for thirty years. I guessed that he and Perlita had met and married while he was stationed in the Philippines, most likely at the naval base at Subic Bay.

I went next door to see if George had returned from his weekend with nature. I found him in the same position I'd left him, fingers on keyboard and eyes on screen. "How was Yosemite?" I asked him.

He looked up with a rapt expression in his blue eyes. "The most beautiful place on earth. I feel renewed."

"Good. Did you come up with anything on that information check I asked you to do?"

"Yeah." He swiveled away from his computer terminal and reached for a small stack of printouts in a rattan basket. "Mostly routine. I don't know whether any of it will be helpful."

"Thanks. What do I owe you?"

He waved me away. "I'll stick a bill in your mail slot."

Back in my office I sifted through the reports George had gleaned from his search of computer data bases. The information on Arthur and Perlita Randall told me little more than the Dun & Bradstreet report had. The white Thunderbird Dolores Cruz was driving belonged to Charles Randall and had been purchased two years earlier with a loan from the federal credit union at Naval Air Station Alameda. That would indicate that Charles was in the navy, or a civil service employee. The name Cruz had come up several times in the computer printouts, but none of these Cruzes was Dolores. The same was true of Eduardo Villegas.

I picked up the phone and called Alex Tongco at the air

station. After assuring him I'd had a great time at the fiesta on Saturday, I got to the point. "I need a favor. Information on a guy named Charles Randall. I don't know whether he's military or civilian, but I think he works at Alameda."

"Any idea which command?" Alex asked. "There are half a dozen shore facilities here, as well as several ships."

"Sorry, I don't. I'm playing a hunch. All I have to go on is a loan from the credit union on base."

"Does this have something to do with my uncle?"

"I think so. Dolores Cruz is living in Randall's condo and driving his car."

"I'll see what I can do. I know a chief over at the military personnel office."

I stashed the computer printouts in the Cal State file and locked it in the filing cabinet. Then I went home to my cat, who harangued me for being gone for two days, despite the fact that I'd left her plenty of food and water.

On Wednesday morning I drove to Daly City and located Mabuhay Travel on Mission Street a few blocks off Interstate 280, next to a mom-and-pop grocery store with a steady midmorning flow of customers. A car pulled away from a space opposite the travel agency and I quickly claimed it, feeding a few coins into the meter. Then I crossed the street to the grocery store, where I bought a cup of coffee and a copy of the *Philippine News*.

Newspaper under my arm, I strolled to the travel agency, where I peered in the window and pretended to be interested in its display of travel posters. Through the glass I saw a bulky gray-haired Caucasian man on the phone. At a desk next to him a diminutive Filipino woman punched a computer keyboard. She looked up and spoke to an elderly man and woman perched on chairs in front of her desk, then turned her attention back to the screen. Arthur and Perlita Randall, I decided, looking for a resemblance between Perlita and Dolores Cruz.

I returned to my car and settled into the driver's seat, one eye on the travel agency as I sipped the strong coffee and leafed through the newspaper. First I read a story about an immigration scam in Los Angeles, involving forged visas and a crooked employee at the U.S. Embassy in Manila, then several stories concerning the ongoing and seemingly never-ending cycle of political unrest and natural disasters in the Philippines. I saw as many news items about the Philippines as there were about the Filipino community here in the United States.

Feet in both worlds, I thought, recalling once again Pete Pascal's words and the priest's prayer at Saturday's fiesta. That dichotomy was reflected here in newsprint. On the one hand, I saw concerns about immigration and assimilation, racism and defining the Filipino version of the American dream, right here in the Bay Area. On the other hand, the ghost of Ferdinand Marcos hovered over everything, like a vulture sitting on a tombstone, while Imelda fluttered hand-kerchiefs and eyelashes, making her incredible pronounce-ments as she sought to hold on to power and fortune. Power, too, was the dance in Manila, where politicians played mu-sical candidates, jockeying for position in the contest to suc-ceed Corazon Aquino, who had survived yet another of the many coup attempts directed at unseating her. As I read, I felt as though Manila were five miles away instead of a day's journey by air.

Half an hour passed. After the elderly couple departed, they were replaced by a young woman pushing a stroller, a toddler in tow, then a businessman in a dark suit, carrying a briefcase. Finally there was a lull in business. Time to intro-duce myself. I got out of my car and fed more coins into the parking meter.

A bell above the door tinkled as I walked into Mabuhay Travel. The Randalls were at their respective desks, both of them on the telephone. I didn't see any other employees. Perlita was all smiles and business as she arranged for the customer on the other end of the wire to spend a fabulous week in Maui.

Arthur held his telephone receiver in his right hand and a slim black cigar in his left, its pungent smoke permeating the room. He ignored me and kept talking to someone he referred to as "old buddy." Though he had retired from the navy, Arthur still had the regulation haircut, a short-back-and-sides iron gray crew cut over his pugnacious slab of a face. His heavy-lidded eyes, a watery blue, glanced at me briefly, then dismissed me. He was more interested in reliving old times with Old Buddy.

I sat down next to a low table spread with travel brochures, slick, colorful folders exhorting me to visit the exotic capitals of the Orient, seducing me with the charms of Manila, Hong Kong, Bangkok, and Singapore. Finally Arthur made a date to go deep-sea fishing with Old Buddy and hung up the phone. He leaned back in his chair, grinning at me like a shark approaching lunch, and said, "What can we do for you, little lady?"

I stood up and walked close to the desk, forcing him to look up at my five feet eight inches. "You have an employee named Dolores Cruz. She lives in a condominium owned by your brother Charles, and she drives his white Thunderbird."

Arthur's iron gray eyebrows came together, and he frowned. "What about it?"

"How long has Dolores Cruz been in the United States?" I asked conversationally. "And how did she get here?"

"Damnation." Arthur slammed one thick hand on his desk blotter. Perlita looked up, startled, then she smiled uncertainly and continued her end of the telephone conversation, booking the Hawaiian vacation. Arthur narrowed his eyes and looked a bit less confident than he had a moment ago. "Who are you? Why are you asking? Are you from Immigration?"

The mention of Immigration had a definite effect on Perlita Randall. She paled and twitched, as though something were biting her on the ankle and she wanted to scratch, but not in public. She stared at me with anxious brown eyes over the phone receiver, then looked away.

"What's your connection with Dolores Cruz, other than the work relationship?" I asked Arthur.

"Hell, the woman works for me, that's all."

"Do all your employees get a new car to drive, and an expensive address? That's quite a benefit package, Mr. Randall. I think Dolores Cruz must be a special case. Is she a relative of Mrs. Randall's? Her sister, perhaps?"

Judging from the way Perlita squirmed in her chair, I was close to the mark. So far Perlita hadn't said a word. Her husband was doing all the talking, and I had the feeling that was the norm. Arthur looked nervous. I didn't blame him, given the fines imposed for hiring illegal immigrants. "That's none of your business," he blustered. "Who the hell are you? Why are you asking all these questions?"

I handed him one of my business cards. He tromboned his hand out and squinted at it, seeking a hidden meaning behind the black words engraved on white stock. He looked up at me skeptically, still convinced I was an agent of the Immigration and Naturalization Service. "J. Howard Investigations? What are you, some kind of snooper?"

"Private investigator is the usual term, Mr. Randall."

Perlita finally got off the phone. Now she sat very still in her chair, her hands folded on her desk, looking at me the way a cornered mouse looks at a cat.

"Dolores Cruz is illegal, and you helped her get here. My guess is that she's Perlita's sister. Your brother Charles is either military or civil service and he's out of the area for a while, so you gave Dolores a job, a place to live, and the keys to his car." I was speculating, but the frightened look on Perlita Randall's face told me I'd hit the mark. "You're already in pretty deep. Deeper than you think. Dolores Cruz is involved in something I'm investigating. She's in a lot of trouble, and so are you."

"I don't know what you're talking about," Arthur said with bravado that didn't extend to the look in his eyes.

I turned and fixed Perlita with a stare. "What about you, Mrs. Randall?" Perlita stammered something I couldn't quite hear as Arthur pushed back his chair and stood, his bulk towering over me.

"I don't know what you're up to, coming in here, making

accusations. I'm up to here with these shenanigans. Get out of here. You're bothering my wife and you're bothering me.''

"It was my intention to bother you," I told him. "Just remember, you might be better off talking to me than to INS. If you change your mind, call me.''

Twelve

AFTER LEAVING MABUHAY TRAVEL I DROVE WEST to Serramonte Boulevard. My earlier search through the Bay Area criss-cross directories had revealed that the phone number Edward Villegas had given Alex matched an address on Serramonte, a restaurant called the Manila Galleon. I'd called the number several times over the past few days, getting no answer, even during the hours a restaurant would be open. Villegas's number didn't match the one listed for the restaurant itself. It must be a private line. Tucked between a drugstore and a discount shoe outlet, the Manila Galleon featured Filipino and American food, and it seemed to have a brisk lunchtime trade.

I spent the next couple of hours plowing through business records, first at the San Mateo County Courthouse, then at its San Francisco counterpart. According to the files on business names, the Manila Galleon was owned by Kaibigan Inc., with an address on Townsend Street in San Francisco. I filled several pages in my notebook as I wrote down the names of various businesses, large and small, owned by Kaibigan Inc. in San Francisco and San Mateo counties. I'd have to wait until I got back to Oakland to see if Kaibigan Inc.'s reach extended to the East Bay. As I researched the company, I encountered three names, all of them familiar. The first was Hector Guzman, the local real estate tycoon and Marcos sympathizer. Both Pete Pascal and Alex had brought up his name. The second name was Salvador Agoncillo, at a Balboa Street address in San Francisco's Richmond district. Nina's brother, I thought. At the fiesta last Saturday Nina told Alex's aunts that she was living with her brother Sal until her wedding to Kaibigan Inc.'s third partner, Enrique Navarro.

The Navarro import business was located at the same Townsend Street address as Kaibigan Inc. I headed for San Francisco's warehouse district south of Market Street. Pacific Rim Imports was midway between Second and Third, not far from the Southern Pacific depot, a two-story redbrick building located in the shadow of the Bay Bridge. I didn't see the black Jaguar Rick Navarro had been driving last week, but a boxy silver Mercedes was parked in front of the building. I pulled into a slot next to it.

A small closed door to my left looked like an afterthought next to the oversize door in front of me. On wheels, the door had been rolled to the right, opening onto a high-ceilinged warehouse with a central aisle. I stepped past a cable dangling from a steel beam in the ceiling and looked around. On either side of me I saw sturdy wooden shelves about twenty feet high, counting eight sets of shelves on either side. The shelves were about six feet wide, with an equal amount of space between them, crowded with merchandise, the higher shelves accessible by movable metal staircases or forklifts that maneuvered on the concrete floor of the warehouse. I started up the center aisle. It was about thirty feet on either side of the aisle to the warehouse's outer walls, banked with rattan bookcases, chairs, and other furniture. At the rear of the building I spotted a narrow staircase with a wooden handrail, just to the left of the center aisle and, above it, a second-story glass window looking out at the main floor. In one of the side aisles I encountered two men in coveralls unloading big, brightly painted ceramic elephants from a crate stamped BANGKOK. I asked where I could find Rick Navarro, and they pointed to the glass window above our heads.

The stairs rose above a corridor leading to a communal bathroom, a rear exit, and a door with a huge padlock, presumably the resting place of more valuable merchandise. I climbed to a small landing outside Rick Navarro's office. The door was open.

Rick stood near the long window, his shirtsleeves rolled up, contemplating a carved board resting on a big easel. The polished dark wood, about three feet by six feet, was covered with relief figures of men and women in a tropical setting, a turtle crawling out of the stylized surf.

"What is it?" I asked as he touched the carved rim of the board. He looked up and saw me in the open doorway, but he didn't look surprised to see this particular visitor.

"A storyboard, from Palau in the western Caroline Islands. It's a legend about turtles and fertility." He smiled and walked toward me, holding out his hand. "Miss Howard, a pleasure to see you again. Are you interested in the art of the Pacific Islands?"

"I don't know much about it."

"This is a small sample," Rick Navarro said. A sweep of his left hand drew my attention to the walls of his office. "I have some wonderful pieces."

A smaller storyboard hung on the back wall of the office, to my left, opposite the window. Next to it I saw a pair of closed sliding doors. In the space above the doors, carved wooden masks alternated with fans intricately woven of rattan and colored fibers, some decorated with shells. To my right, next to the door, stood a white and gold ceramic elephant about three feet high, more elaborately painted than the ones I'd seen downstairs. On its flattened back it held an areca palm in a sturdy clay pot, its fronds fanning out over my head from a sturdy stem, evidently getting enough sun from the skylight in the middle of the ceiling. Beyond it the wall held a series of gold-painted wooden carvings. Opposite me, hanging on the wall between his desk and the sliding doors, I saw a glass case containing a small red and yellow feather cape of the type worn by Hawaiian royalty. I had seen a larger version at the Bishop Museum in Honolulu. I walked over to inspect the feather cape, then I turned to check out Rick's desk.

It stood almost in the middle of the room, facing the door. Behind the desk, within easy reach on a credenza against the wall, stood an array of the high-tech equipment required of any modern businessman—dual disk drive computer, monitor, laser printer, compact copier, and fax machine. The monitor screen was blank. I surveyed the desk surface, seeing only a pale blue file folder, unlabeled, and a round rattan mat next to the phone. A collection of shells and coral rested on the desk's right corner. The left corner held a five by seven photograph in a gold frame, showing Nina Agoncillo with her long dark hair piled atop her head, a smile curving her lips.

"Please, have a seat." Rick gestured toward a chair at the front of his desk. "May I offer you some coffee?" I declined and took the seat he'd indicated. He opened the sliding doors on the back wall, revealing three black filing cabinets with locks, a good-size safe, and a small sink-and-counter arrangement built over a mini-refrigerator. A coffee maker stood on the counter. He poured coffee into a gold-rimmed china cup with a matching saucer, then carried it to his desk, setting it on the rattan mat as he settled into his brown leather chair. He smiled at me across his desk. "Is there a reason you came to see me?"

"Kaibigan Inc.," I said. "You're one of the principals."

"Yes, I am." He frowned in mock seriousness. "Don't tell me Kaibigan has come up in one of your cases."

I shrugged. "Possibly. I encountered the name Kaibigan Inc., then I discovered your name in connection with Kaibigan. I assume Salvador Agoncillo is Nina's brother. What about Hector Guzman?"

"Hector is an old friend of my father's. Just as Salvador is a new friend. *Kaibigan* is Tagalog for 'friend.' "

I digested this for a moment. "Kaibigan owns a restaurant in Daly City called the Manila Galleon. It's on Serramonte Boulevard."

He looked blank. "Is it? I can't recall visiting that one. Kaibigan owns several restaurants here in the Bay Area."

"What is your role in Kaibigan?"

"We're investors, businessmen. That's all I can tell you."

"Or all you're willing to tell me."

He brought his hands up in a dismissive gesture, softened

by his smile. ''Miss Howard, surely you understand that a businessman doesn't reveal information about his business, just as a private investigator doesn't reveal information about her clients. What is your interest, Miss Howard?''

I avoided his question and asked one of my own. ''Do you know a man named Edward Villegas?'' Did I see a flicker of recognition in his eyes? Or was it a trick of the light? Maybe I'd imagined it, so brief I couldn't be certain.

He shook his head. ''Villegas? No, I'm afraid not. It's a fairly common name, though.''

''What about Dolores Cruz?''

This time he shook his head more firmly, with more emphasis. ''Again, a common name. But I don't know her. Who are these people? Why are you asking about them?''

I didn't answer. Instead, I changed the subject. ''Your father is a very powerful man. He seems to have a finger in every slice of the economic pie, in the Philippines and elsewhere. He's doing a lot of business in the United States.''

Navarro's face tensed at the mention of his father. ''Yes, we are. We're always looking for investment opportunities. This is the era of the Pacific rim, Miss Howard. Hence the name of our business.''

''I understand he's planning to run for president of the Philippines. There are a lot of people queued up for a crack at that job. Do you think he has a chance to win?''

''Of course he does.'' His words were hard and challenging, at odds with his bright smile. ''We're ready for some sensible, businesslike government, something that has been sadly lacking in the Philippines. My father has been outside the political sphere, it's true, but that means he can offer some new ideas. That gives him an edge, as far as I'm concerned. People like Laurel and Enrile are holdovers from the past.''

''Like Hector Guzman,'' I added, interrupting his spiel.

He frowned. ''What do you mean?''

''Your other partner, Hector Guzman. Another holdover, and one of your father's biggest financial supporters. I hear Guzman's tight with the pro-Marcos camp. As an outside observer, it seems to me the Filipino-American community spends a lot of time arguing about what goes on back in the Philippines. If someone drops a rock in Manila, you can feel the ripples all the way to California.''

"That's all in the past," he said, dismissing with a wave the ongoing political turmoil in his native land. "You've been talking politics with Alex Tongco. He has a more negative outlook than some of us. How did you meet Alex, by the way?"

I could sidestep questions as well as he could. "We ran into one another. He invited me to the fiesta. Did you know Alex's uncle, Lito Manibusan?"

"No, but Nina has spoken of him. He taught history at Hayward. A colleague of your father's?"

"How did you know my father teaches at Cal State?"

"Felice mentioned it after our initial meeting last week."

"Dr. Manibusan and my father were friends. He was from Pampanga Province, same as your father. Were you born there?"

"Yes, on the plantation near San Fernando."

"The one operated by your brother Jun."

He nodded. "You seem to know a good deal about my family, Miss Howard." That was because the late Dr. Manibusan had such a large file on Maximiliano Navarro. Again I wondered if the late professor had more than a scholar's interest in Maximiliano Navarro's political ambitions and economic clout.

I was ready to ask Rick Navarro more questions, but I was forestalled by the arrival of Nina Agoncillo and another woman. They appeared at the door of Rick's office, dressed in low-heeled shoes and summery pastel dresses, weighted with shopping bags from Neiman-Marcus, I. Magnin, and Nordstrom, which they dropped to the floor just inside the office. They'd been chatting in English, and it was the first time I'd seen Nina look animated.

Rick's face changed when he saw Nina, the affable yet careful businessman replaced by genuine pleasure as he looked at her. He rose, swiftly crossed the room, and took her hand. "Nina, you remember Miss Howard from the fiesta." Nina's smile cooled a bit as she nodded. "And this," Rick continued, turning to the other woman, "is my stepmother, Antonia Navarro."

Mrs. Maximiliano Navarro was about fifty, a sleekly attractive woman with black hair in a chignon and lots of makeup. Not quite an Imelda clone, but she looked as though she'd be at home at a campaign rally or a society reception. She had lots of rings on her hands, diamonds and rubies that pressed against my flesh as she greeted me with a polite handshake. "Isn't Max here?" she asked Rick.

"He's not back from lunch yet, but he should be here soon."

"I knew we should have gone back to the house." Antonia Navarro sighed as she surveyed the shopping bags with a bemused smile. "We're exhausted. And we sent the cab away."

"I'll take you home," Rick said. "Miss Howard was just leaving."

Ms. Howard was being rushed out the door, whether she liked it or not. Rick Navarro went to the sliding doors and pushed them to the other side, retrieving his jacket from a hanger. He rolled down his sleeves, fastened the cuffs, and put on the jacket, smiling at me. "It was nice seeing you again," he told me. I was quite sure he didn't mean it.

Rick looped the handles of several of the shopping bags over his arm. Nina and Antonia picked up the rest. I followed them out to the landing, where Rick locked the office door. The four of us went down the stairs and started up the center aisle of the warehouse. As we reached the wide front doors, two old men came into view, followed closely by two young men in suits and sunglasses. The younger pair reminded me of a matched set of bookends, large and bulky. They also looked as though they had shoulder holsters under their jackets and blank eyes behind their shades.

I was more interested in the first pair of men. Both, dressed in pastel barongs, showed time's passage in silvered hair and wrinkled brown skin, but one looked diminished by age, bent and gnarled by the years. The other looked as vital as an old tomcat who had fought all the other toms in the neighborhood for his hard-won supremacy and was still capable of winning a scrap. I recognized him from the photographs in Dr. Manibusan's file. Maximiliano Navarro himself.

The two older men stood at the warehouse door, talking in low-voiced Tagalog. Max Navarro's right hand held something that looked like a small white envelope. He pressed it into the other man's hand, and the friend took it and folded it in half, tucking it into the back pocket of his loose-fitting tan pants. As we approached the two men, Max Navarro's eyes moved away from his friend and glanced quickly at Nina, Antonia, and me before settling finally on his son.

"Enrique. A cab for Efren." Without a word Rick moved to a wall phone just inside the front door and did his father's bidding. Navarro smiled as he introduced the old man to his wife and his future daughter-in-law. "My dear, this is my cousin Efren. We fought together in the war. Efren, my wife, Antonia, and Enrique's fiancée, Nina Agoncillo."

The old man bowed over Antonia's hand and murmured a few words in Tagalog, then moved politely into the background. Max Navarro turned to me and smiled, white teeth even in his broad face, and I was struck by the force of his personality.

"I don't believe we have met," he said.

I started to answer, but Rick was suddenly there beside us, a paler copy of his father. "This is Jeri Howard. A private investigator." He said the words quickly, as though he were warning his father to guard his tongue.

"A private investigator," the elder Navarro repeated, enveloping my hand with both of his. His palms were firm and smooth, and his brown eyes twinkled with humor. "Now, this is a strange occupation for a beautiful young woman."

I'm not particularly beautiful, and some days I don't feel young either. But Max Navarro's charm was hard to resist, and I could understand why he'd come as far as he had and landed on his feet. I suspect that charm was only part of the package, though. Based on what I knew about him, I had no doubt the sparkle and the smile masked sheer ruthlessness.

"Perhaps," I said. "But then, your own daughter is a photographer."

"A fancy on her part," he said, dismissing Felice's aspirations with a shrug. "Someday she'll settle down. So we indulge her." Until she comes to her senses, he implied, and becomes a proper wife and mother. "What are you investigating, my dear?"

"I'm making inquiries about the death of a man named Lito Manibusan," I said. "A history professor. He was from your home province, Pampanga."

Max Navarro looked thoughtful as he released my hand. I was going to ask him a question about his political aspirations, when Rick interrupted. "The cab is here," he said, appearing at his father's elbow.

The elder Navarro turned from me and walked his friend to a Yellow Cab waiting at the curb, its motor running, helping Efren into the vehicle. Then Max handed a couple of bills to the driver, a bearded and turbaned Sikh. As the cab drove off, Max Navarro stood at the curb, flanked by his bodyguards.

Rick had unlocked the silver Mercedes and was stowing the women's shopping bags in the trunk. Antonia Navarro opened the door and slid onto one of the leather-upholstered seats. I found Nina Agoncillo standing to one side, a compact in her hand as she patted powder onto her perfect nose.

"Congratulations on your engagement."

"Thank you," she said politely, snapping the compact shut. "Maybe I've got it right this time. Rick treats me like a queen." She tilted her chin upward with a tight smile that didn't reach her eyes and pushed a strand of hair away from her face with her left hand. The diamond engagement ring on the third finger winked and flashed, demanding notice.

"How did you meet Rick?"

"My brother introduced us. They have some business ventures together. How did you meet Alex?"

"By chance. I enjoy his company."

"Don't be fooled by my ex-husband's charm, Miss Howard. It masks a lot of things."

"How long were you and Alex married?"

"Too long." A corrosive bitterness colored Nina's words. Part of me understood. It hadn't been that long since my own divorce. "Six years," Nina was saying. "Six years of being a navy wife, having to move just when I got settled into a new area. Of course, I should have thought of that before I married him. But it's easy to get seduced by a fancy uniform and a good line."

She sounded as though she was angry with herself for getting seduced at all. I had to admit she was right in that respect. Alex did have a good line and a full battery of charm. "I'm sure Rick has his drawbacks," I pointed out, looking at her fiancé, who had joined his father at the curb.

"At least he doesn't move every two years. Or have a girl in every port." With these words, Nina's anger came to the surface, black and sharp and untempered. "Alex was never faithful to me. Not during the whole time we were married. I never looked at another man. And don't think I didn't have the opportunity."

I was sure she had. She was a beautiful woman. She had probably played the role of a good and faithful wife according to the expectations of culture and society. Alex's betrayal and the breakup of her marriage still hurt.

"A girl in every port," she repeated, giving the words a savage twist. "That's what people always say about sailors. I don't think they meant anything to him. After a while I didn't mind that he was sleeping with women while he was away. It was what he did while he was at home that I minded. Felice was the last straw."

"Felice Navarro?" Not a surprise, really. I had seen the way Felice looked at Alex Saturday afternoon at the fiesta.

"Rick's sister," Nina said with a sour smile. "Little Felice. She was Alex's last affair. That's why I left him."

Thirteen

DOLORES CRUZ WASN'T AT HER DESK AT THE OAKland branch of Mabuhay Travel. That was fine with me. I wanted to talk with Belinda, her officemate. As I walked in, the slender black woman looked me up and down through the lenses of her oversize glasses, remembering me from my last visit.

"Trip to the Philippines, right? Ms. Cruz isn't here. May I help you?"

"Does Dolly spend a lot of time in the office?"

"Why do you want to know?" Belinda asked, suddenly wary.

"I'm not really interested in a trip to the Philippines." I handed her one of my cards. "But I'm interested in Dolores Cruz. When I was in here last week, it seemed to me that you two don't see eye to eye."

She inspected my card carefully, looking at it over the rims of her glasses. Then she tucked it inside her top desk drawer. "Private investigator, huh? Might have known. That bitch is trouble."

I looked at the clock. It was past three. "Is she out to lunch?"

Brenda snorted and shook her head. "She says she's taking a couple of afternoon classes at Cal State Hayward. To improve herself. Believe me, there's plenty of room for improvement."

So Dolly had been hanging around the university before she made her debut in the role of Dr. Manibusan's widow. That certainly made her a candidate for some of the things

123

that had been going on in the History Department, like the woman who'd been seen in my father's office.

"How long has she worked here?"

"Since February. My Valentine's Day surprise. It's been the longest three months of my life, and I've about had it up to here." Belinda made a sharp horizontal gesture at the top of her head, indicating that her bullshit threshold had indeed been reached. She pushed back her chair and stood up. "You want some coffee? It's decaf."

I'd already had plenty of coffee, but if the java would lubricate the conversation, I was game for another cup. Belinda was already out of her chair, pouring us a couple of mugs from the pot at the back of the office. "You take anything in it?" she asked.

"No," I said, taking the mug she offered. "I gather Dolly's a pain in the butt."

"Lord, you have no idea. She really grinds my gears." Resentment sharpened in Belinda's words as she resumed her seat. "I'm supposed to be the office manager. I'm supposed to have some say about hiring and firing. God knows I've been here a long time, and I work hard. I've complained to Arthur, but he tells me to give Dolly time. But I know what it's all about. Those Filipinos stick together."

"You mean Perlita Randall."

"You better believe it." Belinda grimaced as she took a swallow of coffee. "Dolly is Perlita's sister. That's why she gets away with the stuff she does."

"Like what?"

"We're supposed to be open from ten to six, but Dolly comes and goes as she pleases. In addition to being down at Cal State a couple of afternoons a week—she says—Dolly takes long lunches. She goes shopping, or runs errands, and spends a lot of time on the phone." Belinda was really warming to the subject now, and her anger came boiling out, as hot as the coffee in our mugs. "That woman doesn't do a lick of work. I don't think she knows how. It's like she's never held a job before, like she doesn't understand about regular hours and customer service. I'm the one who keeps this office going. I'm carrying the load, and let me tell you, I'm getting tired of it.''

"Why don't you move on? If you've got experience, you should be able to find work at another travel agency.''

"The pay's good,'' Belinda admitted. "In fact, I just got a big raise. And I live around the corner. I can walk to work in ten minutes. My kids' school is nearby, so they check in on their way home. I guess I got more reasons to stay than I do to leave.''

"The Randalls must be paying Dolly well. That's a new car she's driving, and she lives at the Parkside Towers.''

"She's just house-sitting,'' Belinda said with a laugh. "Arthur's brother owns that condo and that T-bird. He's in the military overseas, but he's coming back this summer, so Dolly will have to shape up and make it on her own. I don't think she can. She acts like a woman who's used to having other people take care of her. But Arthur and Perlita will get tired of carrying her.'' She shrugged and sipped coffee, a cagey little smile playing on her lips. "I figure I can outlast Dolly. She's gonna screw up bad sooner or later. Probably sooner. The fact that you're here asking questions about her is proof of that.''

Family obligation, then, had provided Dolly with a job, a place to live, and the use of a car, even if it jeopardized the goodwill of an employee like Belinda. But it sounded like the obligation was wearing thin. That wasn't the only thing worrying the Randalls. I recalled my earlier visit to the Daly City branch of Mabuhay Travel, colored by Perlita's anxiety and Arthur's premature assumption that I was an immigration agent.

I left the travel agency and headed across town to my office. As I took the messages off my answering machine, the door opened. My visitor was about my age, maybe a bit younger, a sleek, pale blonde with the kind of frosty cheerleader perfection I used to hate when I was in high school. Her ice blue suit matched her eyes and her chilly manner. She reached into her shoulder bag, took out a slim leather wallet, and flashed an ID at me.

"Special Agent Patricia Campbell." A neutral voice, bland and controlled. "Immigration and Naturalization Service. You're Jeri Howard?"

I nodded and sat down at my desk without a word. The ball was in her court, so I let her bat it around some more. After a moment she took one of the chairs facing my desk and crossed one slender leg over another.

"What do you know about Dolores Cruz?" she asked, hands folded lightly on her knee.

"Not much. Why?"

Investigators like to ask questions but they don't like to answer them. Ms. Campbell was no exception. To be fair, I'm the same. But she was a damned cold character and I thought it would be interesting to see if she had any sparks beneath her exterior.

"Look, Jeri . . . May I call you Jeri?"

"Be my guest, Pat."

She hated being called Pat. It made her nostrils flare for a second. But she maintained her cool demeanor.

"I'm interested in Ms. Cruz," she said. "Evidently you are, too."

"What has Dolores Cruz done to attract the attention of the Immigration and Naturalization Service? Besides the obvious?" She didn't respond. "Look, if you won't answer my questions, why do you expect me to answer yours?"

"I'm on official business."

"I'm on business, too. I have a client."

We glared at each other, stuck in mutual standoff mode. INS agents don't have that much clout compared to those from the FBI or DEA. Still, I had nothing to lose by cooperating, up to a point. Why antagonize Immigration when I might instead be able to use it as an ally? Maybe Special Agent Campbell would be more amenable to that sort of arrangement than Sergeant Gonsalves of the Oakland Police Department.

"If Dolly is illegal, why don't you just haul her in?" I answered my own question, ticking off the possibilities on my fingers. "Maybe she's not illegal. But that wouldn't explain why you're here. So, she's illegal but she's a small fish and you'd like to catch a bigger fish. Jump right in if you want to confirm any of this.''

She stared a hole through me, a frown on her face. I didn't think a complete lack of humor was a prerequisite for government service. I wanted to grab her by the shoulders, shake her, and yell, "Lighten up!" Then she surprised me by cracking a smile. At least I think it was a smile. One corner of her mouth curved upward.

''I received an anonymous tip about Dolores Cruz,'' she said. And I bet I knew who had picked up the phone. I'd just finished talking with her. "I started a routine investigation and I spotted you. Several times. I ran a trace on your license plate and a check on your name. Imagine my surprise when I discovered you're a private investigator.''

I very nearly laughed at the thought of someone doing to me what I so often did to others. Now that we'd gotten past the "I'm a federal agent" introduction, Patricia Campbell sounded reasonable. It was certainly an improvement over Sergeant Gonsalves and his macho posturing.

''So Dolly *is* illegal,'' I said.

The INS agent nodded. ''Dolores Cruz entered the United States in late December, right after Christmas, on a tourist visa, and she stayed. Happens all the time. Normally we'd pick her up, send her back to the Philippines, and slap her employer with sanctions. But there's a ring operating in the Bay Area, providing forged documents to illegals, mostly Asians. I'm sure Dolores Cruz got her papers from them. Also, her sister and brother-in-law operate a travel agency. We find that very often travel agencies are involved in document fraud, so we're taking a look at the Randalls, too. The point is, Jeri, I'd like to bust this ring. I've been after them for over a year. So I won't get in the middle of your investigation if you won't screw up mine. Why are you interested in Dolores Cruz?''

I debated for a moment before answering. ''My case may also involve some forged documents,'' I said, thinking of the purported marriage certificate. ''Dolly claims she's the widow of a Cal State Hayward professor. He was Filipino-American, a naturalized citizen, and he was murdered last January in San Francisco. The case is unsolved. Dolly says she and the professor were married last August while he was on a research trip to the Philippines. She has what she claims is a marriage certificate, but so far no one's been able to get a good look at it. What do you know about Dolly?''

"Just that she's Perlita Randall's sister. Do you think she had something to do with the professor's murder?''

"I don't think she killed him, if that's what you mean. But she may know who did. Does the name Eduardo Villegas mean anything to you? Otherwise known as Eddie the Knife?''

She shook her head. "No. Why?''

"According to one of my contacts at OPD, Villegas is connected to an Asian crime syndicate here in the Bay Area. They're currently up to something at the Port of Oakland. As for Eddie, I think he's somehow involved in the Manibusan case. I wonder if his organization's activities include production and sale of bogus green cards.''

Patricia Campbell raised one blond eyebrow. "Thanks for the tip. I'll talk to the Oakland police.''

"Ask for Sergeant Gonsalves in Theft. He's the guy with a permanent frown and the winning personality. Maybe he'll be nicer to you since you have a badge, but I doubt it.''

"Thanks for that tip, too.'' The INS agent smiled and consulted her watch. She stood up, extracting a business card from her handbag. "Keep in touch, Jeri, and I'll do the same.''

After Patricia Campbell left, I switched on my computer and wrote detailed notes of my visits to the Daly City and Oakland branches of Mabuhay Travel, and my encounter with Rick Navarro and his father. It took me over an hour, and I read through the notes, editing them and adding my impressions, mentally mapping out tomorrow's course of action. While I printed out the notes, I dug Felice Navarro's card out of my bag and called her. She picked up the phone on the first ring and her voice turned enthusiastic when I identified myself.

"I'm so glad you called. I really do want to photograph you for my series. I have a woman cop and a woman fire-fighter, so a private investigator would be a great addition."

"I'd like to talk with you," I said, not committing myself to anything but conversation. "What's your schedule tomorrow morning?"

We set up a ten A.M. appointment. As I hung up the phone, my stomach growled at me, reminding me that I'd had no lunch again today, and it was nearly seven. I put the notes into the Cal State Hayward folder and locked the filing cabinet. The phone rang and I reached for it.

"Jeri," my father crowed. "I found it. I found the envelope Lito sent me."

"Where? What's in it?" I perched on the edge of my desk. Maybe now we'd get some answers.

"It had fallen behind a filing cabinet in my office. We were moving some things this afternoon to make room for another bookcase, and there it was. Jeri, it's postmarked San Francisco, the day after Lito was murdered. It's got that note from Lito, some photocopies of documents, and a microcassette. I've got a recorder, but I haven't listened to it yet. I wanted to wait until you were here."

"You're at the university? I'll be right down."

"No, wait. I'm about to go into my seven o'clock graduate seminar. I'll be finished at nine. You've still got my extra key. Meet me at home. I should be there by nine-thirty."

I agreed, though I was eager to get my hands on that damned envelope. I closed up the office and headed for the Jade Villa and a meal of pot stickers and mu shu pork. Then I stopped at my apartment to feed Abigail. She greeted me with her tail up, hungry-cat meows at full volume. I side-stepped the yellow mouse, which she'd dropped in the middle of the living room floor, and headed for the kitchen to dish up cat food. At a quarter to nine I left for Castro Valley. Dad had a light on a timer, so the living room of his town house was bathed in light from a hanging lamp. I was pleased to see that he'd changed the locks on the sliding glass doors leading to the patio. Someone had given him some home-made chocolate chip cookies, so I helped myself to a couple and poured a glass of milk to go with them. I settled onto the sofa to wait for my father, using the remote to switch on the television and scan the channels. He hadn't shown up by nine-thirty, but that didn't surprise me. He was probably talking to some students after class. I hit the kitchen for another round of cookies.

By the time the ten o'clock news started on Channel 2 I was getting concerned. My anxiety grew all the way through sports and weather. When the phone rang, I grabbed it before his answering machine could pick up the call. I heard Isabel Kovaleski's voice on the other end of the wire.

"Jeri," she said, "your father's hurt."

Fourteen

"I WAS PUSHED," DAD SAID.

He sat on a bench just outside the emergency room at St. Rose Hospital, giving his statement to a couple of uniformed Hayward cops. I stood next to him, hands stuck into my pockets, the frown on my face mirrored by Isabel Kovaleski's. Cal State security chief Elaine Martini waited on the opposite side of the corridor, looming like a bad habit one couldn't quite break.

"I parked my car in that small staff lot on the west side of Meiklejohn Hall, near the loading dock," Dad said, rubbing his eyes. His glasses were broken. Without them his face looked old, tired, and vulnerable. "The lot is on the lower level. Ordinarily I would have taken the elevator down to the basement and gone out that door to the parking lot. But after class several of my students had questions, so I walked with them out the north door, the one facing the library. We talked for a few minutes, then split up. I turned to my left and walked down the wheelchair ramp toward the outdoor staircase leading down to that lower-level parking lot. I thought I heard footsteps behind me, but that's not unusual. A lot of classes break at nine. Just as I reached the top step someone rushed at me, pulled my briefcase out of my hand, and shoved. I went flying. All I could think of was trying to cover my face and head."

He had tumbled down the long flight of stairs, flinging his arms up to protect his head from hitting the steps or the metal handrail. At the bottom he landed heavily on his left side, sprawled on the concrete walk, conscious but stunned. Dr. Kovaleski found him a few minutes later.

The ambulance summoned by the campus patrolmen brought Dad to the nearest hospital, where a battery of X rays revealed no broken bones. But he was scraped, bruised, had a sprained wrist, and favored his left ankle when he walked slowly to the bench where he now sat.

"Contents of the briefcase?" one of the cops asked. "Keys? Money? Any valuables?"

Dad looked at me. "An envelope containing some papers and a microcassette. A couple of books. And research papers I had just collected from my seminar students. I hope they kept copies."

The Hayward officers dutifully wrote down everything for their report, but I could tell that as far as they were concerned, the incident was just the latest in the series of assaults plaguing the campus this quarter. But I didn't think so. Judging from the look on Dad's face, neither did he. His assailant had been after Dr. Manibusan's envelope. Someone must have overheard my father when he'd called to tell me he'd located the envelope. Right now the words replaying in my head were those of Belinda at the travel agency, telling me Dolores Cruz was taking a class at Cal State Hayward. That gave Dolly the opportunity as well as the motive. But she wasn't the only player in this game. What about Eddie the Knife Villegas? He, too, wanted something from the late professor's files. Surely it must be the envelope.

Elaine Martini was watching me as though she'd caught the look that passed between my father and me when he mentioned the envelope and could now see wheels turning inside my skull. The police officers departed. Dad stood and attempted to put on his jacket. He winced at the effort and gave up. Isabel took his jacket, and we walked toward the door, but Chief Martini separated me from them as deftly as a sheep dog cutting a ewe out of the flock.

"What's so important about that envelope?" I didn't answer right away. "I'll bet we find Dr. Howard's briefcase ditched on campus tomorrow," she continued, folding her arms across her chest. "Everything will be in it—the books, the research papers—except that envelope your father mentioned. The one with the microcassette. Am I right?"

"You don't miss much."

"It's my job not to miss much."

"Dr. Manibusan mailed the envelope to Dad. I have a feeling he mailed it right before he was murdered. Unfortunately Dad couldn't find it until today. It had fallen behind a filing cabinet. He called me right before his seven o'clock class to tell me. Someone must have overheard him."

"So this is no random mugging," she said, raising one black eyebrow. "Do you think the woman who's claiming to be Dr. Manibusan's widow is responsible?"

"Maybe. According to one of her coworkers, she's taking some classes at Cal State."

Elaine Martini shook her head. "She's not registered under the name Dolores Cruz or Dolores Manibusan. Never has been. However, I did run a check on the license plate of that Thunderbird she's driving. My people have ticketed it twice, the last time on the day the unidentified woman was spotted in your father's office. What do you suppose is on that cassette?"

"It could be anything, from notes on Dr. Manibusan's latest research project to information on why he was killed—and who killed him."

She was silent for a moment while we speculated on the possibilities contained in the envelope. Then she frowned. "I've been trying to decide whether there's a conflict of interest here."

"Not the way I look at it. We're both working for the university."

"But your father is involved," she pointed out, "through no fault of his own. Now he's a target. Don't let personal feelings get in the way of your judgment. It's the worst mistake you could make."

She was right, I thought as I joined Dad and Dr. Kovaleski outside the hospital. I'm always like a bloodhound when I catch the scent, never letting go until I solve whatever puzzle is before me. But it certainly felt different and dangerous to have my own father caught in the middle. First he'd gone through the shock of finding Dr. Manibusan's body. Then his home had been violated, and now his person. All the way from Oakland to the hospital I had gripped the wheel of my car in fury. If I was going to solve this case, I had to douse that fury with the cold water of reason and think logically.

I drove my father home, repeating Isabel's admonition that he needn't go to work tomorrow. I settled him into bed, phone and pain pills within reach, and headed back to Oakland, telling him I'd check in by phone the next morning. My sleep was restless, punctuated by dreams and by Abigail's piercing cries as she stalked and killed the yellow yarn mouse. Thursday's breakfast was interrupted as well, by a phone call.

"Would you kindly explain what happened to your father?"

"Hello, Mother." I masked a sigh as I reached for my coffee. "How did you find out?"

"Your father called your brother, who called me." Ah, the family grapevine, I thought. The news would be all over Monterey by now. "I hope you haven't involved him in one of your cases," Mother was saying, her voice radiating her usual disapproval of my choice of profession.

It was more the other way around, but I didn't elaborate. I managed to calm her concerns about my father, then I called Dad to see how he was feeling. Sore and bruised, he said. His ankle felt better, but the sprained wrist was giving him some pain. He'd canceled his classes for the day, but he hoped to go to work tomorrow.

"There's no need to play hero and tough it out," I said. "They can run the university without you for a couple of days. You stay home and get some rest."

"You sound like your mother." The irony was that he was right. I was a good deal like my mother, which was probably why we didn't get along. Dad grumbled about the inactivity of taking it easy. I thought about calling Isabel Kovaleski and making an end run around him to get him to stay home for the rest of the week, but admitted to myself it was probably a lost cause. Dad was a grown-up. I couldn't very well tie him to the bed if he wanted to go to work.

Felice Navarro lived and worked in a tiny brown-shingled house on a side street just off College Avenue in the Rockridge area, where Oakland gave way to Berkeley. As I drove along College, I saw another car pulling away from the curb and quickly claimed the space. It was ten in the morning, and shops along the avenue were just opening. I smelled freshly ground coffee as I passed an espresso place, then my nose caught the pungent scent of onions from the bagel bakery farther down the street, and my mouth watered.

Now I spotted a wooden sign on a post at the head of the walk, a painted square attached to an upside down L, reading NAVARRO PHOTOGRAPHY. Instead of grass, the postage-stamp-size front yard held ground cover, a mass of sweet-smelling jasmine, tiny white flowers dotting the dark green foliage that threatened to engulf the front walk. Bright orange California poppies flamed next to the house. I mounted the shallow steps of the front porch and rang the bell. A moment later Felice opened the door, wearing a red sweat suit so bright, it hurt my eyes. She carried a blue ceramic mug decorated with a pink duck.

"Come in," she said, saluting me with the duck. "Would you like some coffee?"

"Yes, thanks."

I followed her through the living room. It had been turned into a portrait studio, minimally furnished with a silvery backdrop spread in front of the wall to my right and portable lights on either side of the room's centerpiece, a camera on a tripod. On my left as we walked toward the kitchen were framed color photographs, representative shots showing how Felice made her living. The largest was a portrait of a bride and groom in traditional church-wedding attire, gazing into each other's eyes. It was flanked by portraits, one of a middle-aged couple, the other a family consisting of husband and wife my own age surrounded by four small children, all grinning cheerfully at the camera.

Felice's kitchen was small, bright, and crowded, with cream-colored tile and pots of pink and purple African violets on the windowsills. A variety of mugs hung from a wooden rack on the wall next to the sink. Felice chose one with a black-and-white cow on it and filled it with coffee from a pot sitting next to her microwave oven. She handed me the mug and led the way out onto an enclosed back porch that ran the full length of the house.

The porch served as her living and dining area, a small round table with two chairs at this end, a series of shelves with television and stereo at the other end. Morning sun spilled in the windows, sparkling the dust and streaks on the panes, caressing the velvety petals of another row of African violets. A back door opened out to a tiny yard with a redwood deck, shaded by a magnolia tree. A rattan sofa and a matching chair with bright floral cushions were grouped in the middle, an end table between them. The rectangular coffee table in front of the sofa was stacked haphazardly with photography books and magazines, all threatening to tumble to the floor.

On this wall I saw the photographs taken by Felice the artist, stark black and white, in contrast to the portraits in the living-room-turned-studio. My eye was drawn to a shot taken on Telegraph Avenue in Berkeley, looking toward the university, the camera lens capturing students, panhandlers, and street merchants jostling for space on the crowded sidewalks. Another photo showed a homeless man peering warily from the cardboard box where he'd spent the night. And here was a juggler with her face painted like a clown, long hair tossed by a breeze, four balls suspended in midair.

"These are good," I said. "I like them."

"Thanks." Felice reached for the knob of the open door leading from the back porch to her bedroom, its small space taken up by an unmade double bed and a low dresser. She closed the door on the disarray. "The front bedroom's even tinier. I turned it into my darkroom. And there's hardly any closet space. But I really got a good deal on the house."

"With housing prices what they are these days, it's an accomplishment for any single person to buy a house." I sat down in the rattan chair. Felice pushed a couple of throw pillows to one side and sat cross-legged on the sofa.

"My brother helped me with the down payment. He might as well—he's got lots of money." Her voice held the edge I had heard the first time I met her, the first time she mentioned her brother. I wondered about Felice's relationship with Rick. She seemed at times to resent him, but maybe that sharp tone was indicative of the kind of rough, bantering affection I shared with my own brother.

"Your father's money. Aren't you entitled to some of it as well?"

The edge in her voice sharpened like the blade of a knife. "I don't want anything from my father." Felice must have been immune to her father's charm, or at least less susceptible to it than the rest of the world.

"I met him yesterday at Pacific Rim Imports."

"Max? Yes, he's here on one of his periodic inspection tours. He comes every four months or so, to make sure Rick is running things properly. As though Rick needed anyone looking over his shoulder. He and my father are cut from the same bolt of cloth."

"Will you see your father while he's here?"

"If Max wants to make the trip to Oakland, I'll see him," she said, sipping her coffee. "But I won't be summoned to the house in Pacific Heights to be quizzed and criticized."

"What have you done that warrants criticizing?"

Felice laughed. "I've been disappointing my father since I was old enough to walk. Each time Max visits the Bay Area, he wants to know why I'm not married to the right sort of Filipino husband, having babies like a good Filipino wife."

"I thought Filipino women were more independent than women in other parts of Asia."

"Only up to a point. Then all that Catholic patriarchal

stuff gets in the way. I got thrown out of several of the best convent schools in Manila by the time I was eighteen. So Max decided it was time I got married. He selected the bridegroom, the son of some rich old man who owns gold mines in Benquet. Might as well extend the family fortune while marrying off the rebellious daughter. Of course I refused to go through with it. I finished school in Manila and went to the university instead. My father has been angry with me ever since. He wrote me off. I don't exist to him, except as a disappointment. My brothers are doing what is expected of them. Jun lets the peasants grow his sugar cane on the plantation and he and his wife have produced lots of grandchildren. Rick runs the import business and he'll probably take over the rest."

I pointed the conversation back toward Felice herself. "How did you end up here in the Bay Area?"

A moment passed before she answered. When she did, her voice was subdued. "I got married after all. To an American."

That surprised me. She wore no wedding ring, just the chunky topaz on her right hand. "I thought you were single."

"I am now. Divorced last year. Damaged goods."

"Only if you believe it. Was your father upset because of your divorce?"

"Oh, he's a great believer in the sanctity of marriage," she said bitterly. "Divorce is a disgrace, but he always had a little *querida* on the side, all the time my mother was ill, probably before. After Mama died, I thought he might even marry the last one. So did she. He kept her in a fancy apartment in Manila. But Max is going to run for president, so he needs the right kind of wife, not his mistress, who's getting a little shopworn. Instead, he found someone with lots of social connections and plenty of political clout. Did you meet my new stepmother? Dear Antonia. She's a senator's widow, an ambassador's daughter, and her brother is a general. Her family owns a lot of land in Nueva Ecija Province. She'll look very presentable in Malacañang Palace."

Vitriol blackened Felice's words each time she spoke of her father. I knew from reading Lito Manibusan's file on Max Navarro that the first Mrs. Navarro had been an invalid for a long time, suffering from cancer before she committed suicide several years ago. That, combined with Max's treatment of his daughter, was evidently a festering sore. I aimed the conversation away from Maximiliano Navarro, curious about Felice's husband. This was the first I'd heard of him.

"His name's Neal. Neal Patterson." Felice shrugged, twisting the topaz ring on her finger. "We still see each other now and then. He's a navy flyer, a navigator. Right now he's stationed at Moffett Field, over on the peninsula. But I think he's got orders to San Diego very soon."

"How did you meet him? How long were you married?"

"We met in Baguio four years ago. That's a resort up in the mountains. I'd been working as a photographer in Manila. Lots of weddings and confirmations." She rolled her eyes. "Boring, but it pays the bills. I went up to Baguio for a long weekend to shoot some mountain scenery and see if I could get some interesting pictures of the sort of people who go to Baguio. Neal was there on a few days' leave from his duty station at Cubi Point, near Subic Naval Base. We hit it off, we dated for a while, and then we eloped. If you can call it that, with all the red tape involved when a Filipino national marries an American. Then Neal got orders to the Bay Area. We lived in Mountain View until we split up, about eighteen months ago."

"Why did you split up?"

"A lot of reasons," she said with a lopsided smile. "Maybe we shouldn't have gotten married in the first place."

I could sympathize with that statement. I'd used it myself several times when Sid and I divorced. "Your father didn't approve of your marriage."

"My father doesn't approve of anything I do. When it comes to marriage, he believes like should marry like," Felice said, staring at the dusty windows and not at me.

"Maybe there's some truth to that. At least he was polite about it."

Which meant someone else wasn't. I hazarded a guess. "Neal's parents?"

"His father. He called me a Flip, a gook, right to my face." She repeated the epithets calmly enough, but I knew they still had the power to hurt. Her voice turned weary. "Old men. Damn them all. They think they own the world."

She got up and walked to the kitchen, pouring herself another mug of coffee. I followed her, and she waved the coffeepot at me. "There's another cup here. Want to finish it off?" I nodded and held out my mug. Felice poured the rest of the coffee into it. "I don't know why I'm talking about all this," she said, shaking her head as if to rid herself of the cobwebs. "We were going to talk about me taking pictures of you."

"I didn't really come over here to discuss photography, Felice." I watched her face over the rim of the cup as I took a sip of coffee. "I want to ask you some questions."

Felice's eyebrows went up, and she smiled uncertainly. "You've been doing all right so far."

"It has to do with a case I'm working on."

"Of course," she said. She dumped the spent coffee grounds into the garbage, unplugged the coffee maker, and rinsed the pot in the sink. "It must be a case. You're a private investigator. Why else would you be asking all these questions? What does your case have to do with my family?"

"I'm not sure. I have a lot of threads that seem to be tangled together, but I don't know if they're connected. I was doing some background work and I came across Kaibigan Inc. Rick is one of the principals, along with Hector Guzman and Salvador Agoncillo, Nina's brother."

Felice stood in the middle of her kitchen, coffee mug held with both hands. "I don't know anything about any corporation. I thought all my brother did was run the import business for my father. I've met Sal, of course, and Hector Guzman. I don't like Guzman. He's an odious old man with a fat middle and skinny arms and legs. He reminds me of a spider. He's funneling a lot of money into Max's campaign.''

''How long have your brother and Nina Agoncillo been engaged?''

Felice picked up her mug and stepped past me, returning to the flowered sofa on the back porch. ''I didn't know they were engaged until she showed up at the fiesta, flashing her big diamond. Rick's been after her for a long time, ever since Sal introduced them. Nina and Alex were still together when Rick started pursuing her, but things hadn't been good between them for a while. They separated last year, and Nina filed for divorce.'' She didn't say anything for a moment, then her dark eyes stared directly into mine. ''How did you meet Alex? Is he one of those threads you were talking about?''

''One of the threads is Alex's uncle. Lito Manibusan. He was a history professor at Cal State. Did you ever meet him?''

Felice nodded. ''Once. He was a delightful man, so courtly. He was interesting, too, knowledgeable about Filipino history, about lots of things. Alex was very fond of Lito and really upset over his death. It came at a bad time for him.''

''You mean Alex's divorce from Nina.''

''Alex and I . . .'' She stopped and stared across the room, out the dusty window. ''We had a relationship.''

''I know. I saw the way you looked at him at the fiesta. And Nina mentioned it.''

She leaned down and picked up her coffee mug. ''Nina blames me,'' she said defensively, ''but their marriage was over. She was already making eyes at Rick by the time I became involved with Alex. So, which came first, chicken or egg?'' I didn't respond. I had no answer. ''Are there any other loose threads you want to ask me about?''

''Do you know a woman named Dolores Cruz? She's Filipina, in her thirties, and she has a scar on her chin, right here.'' I traced the line on my own jaw.

Felice looked at me with curiosity in her brown eyes. "Is this someone you've met recently?"

"Yes. I'm trying to figure out who she is."

She shook her head slowly. "I don't know anyone named Cruz."

Fifteen

DOLLY WAS AT HER DESK AT MABUHAY TRAVEL, though she didn't appear to be laboring hard. The Oakland *Tribune* was spread out on the desk and her cigarettes and coffee were within reach. At the other desk Belinda sat with phone propped between chin and ear, both hands moving across her computer keyboard, eyes scanning a screen full of airline fare information. She glanced up as I walked in the front door and her eyes widened behind the big glasses.

"Ready to book that flight to Manila?" Dolly asked pleasantly, closing the newspaper. She remembered me as last week's customer who was interested in a trip to the Philippines. But things had moved well past that pose, and it was time to lay the cards on the table—in this case my business card. I took one from my purse and tossed it onto Dolly's desk.

"I've decided against it, Ms. Cruz. Or is it Mrs. Manibusan?"

Dolly picked up the card, read it, and set it down quickly, as though it were hot to the touch. Her face turned wary and she hesitated before answering. Then she shook a cigarette from the pack at her elbow and flicked on her lighter.

"A private investigator. The university hired you," she said, her voice even. She tilted her head upward in a gesture of bravado and blew a stream of smoke at me. "Well, let them. I was married to Lito Manibusan. I can prove it."

"You'll have to do more than wave a piece of paper under Dr. Kovaleski's nose. That marriage certificate is bogus. I think you bought it from the same place you bought your

143

green card. Besides, the rest of Dr. Manibusan's family never heard of you.''

''That's not surprising.'' Dolly blinked her long-lashed eyes and rearranged her face into a mask of sadness and regret. Her voice was reasonable, sincere. ''Lito and I were sweethearts long ago, before he married Sara. We met again in Manila, last summer, while he was there doing research, and resumed our relationship. I know it was impulsive to get married. Not like Lito at all. But we were married. I have a marriage certificate.''

How did she know the name of the professor's late wife, and about his last trip to the Philippines? She sounded convincing, but I wasn't convinced. Not after that attack on my father and the theft of the envelope.

''So convenient that the professor is dead and can't confirm your story,'' I said, my voice harsh. ''Odd that he didn't list you as a beneficiary on his pension plan, or change his will. It makes me wonder whether you had something to do with his murder.''

She gasped. Her face flushed, and the thin scar stood out along her jawline. ''Are you out of your mind? I didn't kill him.''

''Maybe you know who did.'' That was purely guesswork on my part, but I watched Dolly's eyes as she composed herself. I was sure that she knew who was responsible for the professor's death.

By now Dolly's officemate had finished her phone conversation and was hanging on every word, without any pretense of minding her own business. The phone began to peal and Dolly skewered her coworker with a glare. ''Why don't you answer that, Belinda?''

Belinda hissed something undiscernible as she reached for the phone. I fired another question at Dolly. ''Where were you last night?''

''What business is it of yours?''

''I understand you're taking a class at Cal State. Although the university doesn't have any record that you actually registered. For the sake of argument, let's say you were there late yesterday afternoon. A professor was assaulted last night and his briefcase stolen. Last week his house was burglarized. And the week before, a woman matching your description was seen prowling around his office.''

''And you accuse me?'' Dolly turned haughty, exhaling a stream of smoke into my face. ''First of murder, then these lesser crimes. You're crazy. I think you'd better leave.''

''For now,'' I said as the front door opened and an older couple walked in. Belinda was still on the phone, so they approached Dolly's desk. ''You're playing out of your league, Dolly. The time will come when you want to talk with me.''

Skepticism veiled her eyes as she pounced on the customers, eager for any reason not to talk to me. I heard her go into her spiel as I left the travel agency. When I arrived at my own office, Dr. Manibusan's file boxes greeted me, a silent wall of cardboard and paper reminding me of last night's attack on Dad, its objective the professor's envelope.

There was only one message on my answering machine. Elaine Martini's voice sounded dry and emotionless, telling me a custodian found Dad's briefcase ditched in one of the stalls in a second floor women's rest room at Meiklejohn Hall. Just as she had predicted, everything was there—except the envelope. She wanted me to call her. I tapped my notepad with the pencil. The women's rest room. Dad's assailant was a woman, I thought, wanting it to be Dolly. But it could just as easily have been a man who'd dodged into the first available refuge after attacking my father.

I made myself a pot of coffee, hauled several boxes down from the stack, and set to work, sitting cross-legged on the floor as I pulled folders from cartons. That's how I found Dr. Manibusan's calendar about an hour later. It was stuck between two files. As I pulled them from a box, it fell to the floor, last year's Sierra Club engagement calendar, six by nine inches, one page per week, spiral-bound with a photograph of wildflowers on the cover.

My coffee was cold, so I replenished it before carrying the calendar to my desk. I sat down, opening it randomly to the third week in August. There, in Manibusan's now-recognizable scrawl, was the time and number of his flight to Manila. I turned the pages forward to the first week in September and saw a similar notation for the return flight.

Too bad I didn't have this year's calendar. Maybe I'd find enlightenment or the name of his killer written on that Friday in January where Dr. Manibusan was murdered. But things are never that easy.

I turned to the front of last year's calendar and leafed through the pages, scanning each week in turn. It reminded me of Dad's own calendar, always open on his desk at Cal State. In a litany of the ordinary, Dr. Manibusan had recorded the routine of his life—dental appointments, student consultations, faculty meetings, reminders to pick up his cleaning and have his car serviced.

On the page for the last week in July I found the name Cardiff written at the top, with the name Beddoes alongside it. A double-pointed arrow had been drawn between the two names. The professor had underscored the names twice, with such force that his ballpoint pen went through the page, making a mark on the next week's calendar. Something else had been penciled in the top margin of that page, a list of telephone numbers and names. They were nursing registries in San Francisco and the East Bay.

I got up and located the correspondence folder I'd found during my Sunday-night foray into Dr. Manibusan's files, the one that contained Dr. Manibusan's letters to and from the army inquiring about Lieutenant O. M. Cardiff, and the professor's note to himself to check hospitals and associations. Evidently he had. I looked at the army's letter, at the date of Cardiff's discharge in 1946. An army nurse, circa World War II. Logical enough, I thought. Alex had told me that his uncle was particularly interested in World War II history, and in my search through his files I'd found an extensive array of information on the subject. Okay, so Dr. Manibusan had been researching an article. But there were lots of World War II veterans out there. What was so important about this particular nurse that the professor had made such an effort to locate Cardiff? Had he ever found her?

I turned the calendar pages forward, scanning August, September, and October. A week before his departure for Manila, Dr. Manibusan had been busy. He'd covered the calendar page with his black scrawl, canceling his research trip to the central valley and his reservations in a Fresno motel, rescheduling interview appointments in farming communities like Madera and Turlock. After this flurry of activity there were no entries until after his return from the Philippines. Then the calendar pages detailed the start of fall-quarter classes at Cal State—meetings, conferences, working the History Department table at registration. September and October showed more routine, with weekend trips to the central valley for research interviews. I saw a note indicating that the professor took his nephew Alex to dinner for Alex's birthday in October. So he's a Scorpio, I thought. I might have known.

I flipped the calendar pages to the next month. On a Wednesday in November, right before Thanksgiving, Dr. Manibusan had jotted the name "Potter." Under it he'd written the names of two central California towns, Paso Robles and San Luis Obispo. The following week, on Tuesday, was the word "Sacramento," circled and underscored. A trip to the state historical library? I wondered. My eye moved up to Sunday's entry, and my interest quickened as I read the note. "E. Villegas, SF, 2 p.m."

Eduardo "Eddie the Knife" Villegas? Had Dr. Manibusan interviewed him for the article he had written about Asian immigrants and crime? It had been published in the winter edition of the history journal my father loaned me. But something about the date bothered me. History quarterlies often have long production deadlines. I made a mental note to contact the journal and find out when the professor had submitted his final copy.

I turned back to the calendar page where the nursing registries were listed. Maybe if I backtracked the professor's movements, I'd find out what he was working on that precipitated his sudden trip to Manila. I picked up the phone and punched in numbers, going down the list, and getting the same reaction at each place. The 1940s were a long time ago, literally a lifetime for people like me, born in the postwar era. Few people were willing to take the time away from current tasks to dig through the past. I found only one registry, in San Francisco, that had files going back further than the fifties. The woman who answered the phone told me the registry had been in operation since the thirties. There were some files in a storeroom, dusty and in need of purging. If I wanted to come to San Francisco, she said cheerfully, I was welcome to dig around the haystack in search of the needle. Just ask for Carrie or Bess.

I wrote down the registry's address and the hours of operation. As I hung up the phone, my office door opened and Alex Tongco walked in, wearing his well-tailored summer khaki uniform, a garrison cap tucked into his belt. Two gold oak leaves shone on each side of his collar, denoting the rank of lieutenant commander, and several rows of ribbons anchored his left breast pocket.

"Had lunch?" he asked cheerfully.

I looked at the clock, surprised to find that it was nearly one. "No. Is that why you popped in?"

"Not entirely. I found out something about Charles Randall. He's navy, a chief warrant officer. He was stationed at port services, but he transferred to Yokosuka, Japan, a year ago. What has all this got to do with Uncle Lito?"

"Probably nothing." I leaned back in my chair, lacing my fingers behind my head. "I don't think Charles Randall is involved in this at all. As I told you earlier, Dolores Cruz is living in his condo here in Oakland and driving his car. Charles Randall's brother Arthur is married to Dolly's sister. The Randalls own the travel agency where Dolly works. So it appears they're taking care of a relative by giving her a job and a place to live. But that doesn't explain where Dolly came from and what she's after."

"Another dead end," Alex said.

"Tell me about Felice Navarro."

Alex's face closed up. "Why do you want to know about Felice?"

"You had an affair with her. Nina told me. And Felice confirmed it."

He stared at me with a tight-lipped frown. "What is this? An interrogation?"

"Merely an inquiry."

"Why were you talking to Nina?"

"I went to see Rick. I got a package deal that included Nina. And Max Navarro. Nina took the opportunity to mention your relationship with Felice."

Alex balled his hands into fists. "I'm sure she told you more than that," he said, turning to look at me. "I was unfaithful. So was she. She started seeing Rick right after her brother introduced them."

"Did you know Nina and Rick were engaged?"

"Not until we ran into them at the fiesta." His mouth quirked into a humorless smile. "Well, Nina's found what she wants—a rich husband who doesn't move every two years."

"And what do you want? Revenge? Was Felice retaliation?"

"Felice was a mistake," he said curtly. "It was a fling. It didn't mean anything."

"It meant something to Felice. She still cares about you." He didn't answer. "Do you hit on every woman you meet?"

"What the hell is that supposed to mean?" Anger flared; then his brown eyes turned stony. "I like you, Jeri. Can't we just enjoy each other's company? I guess not. What you do for a living gets in the way." He took his garrison cap from his belt and put it on. "I'll leave you to your work, Jeri. That's obviously the most important thing to you."

Don't blame me and my job, I thought with irritation, staring at the closed door Alex left in his wake. You're not exactly the knight in shining armor, either. I did like the guy, but I was also wary of him, with good reason. He was touchy, moody, and mercurial. Just like me.

I rose from my chair abruptly and left my office, walking to a deli on Broadway, where I muffled my conflicting feelings with pastrami on rye. When I returned, I called the naval air station at Moffett Field, near San Jose. I was passed from office to office before finally locating the one where Neal Patterson, Felice Navarro's ex-husband, worked. He was out flying, but the woman who answered the phone told me I might find him in the office early tomorrow morning.

This Manibusan case had me tied in knots, and I needed to concentrate on something else for a while. I stuck the professor's calendar in my filing cabinet and spent the next few hours doing legwork all over Oakland and Berkeley. It was after five when I returned. I checked the messages on the answering machine and wrote up my notes. As they were printing, my office door opened and Cassie entered, looking fresh and crisp in a red linen dress. Whenever I wear linen, it wrinkles the minute I put it on, but Cassie managed to look as though she'd just ironed the outfit. For a lawyer who habitually worked late, she also looked unfettered.

"What, no briefcase?" I asked.

She laughed. "I am off the clock after I return a few phone calls. And tomorrow you won't find me here. Eric and I are going up the coast to Mendocino for a few days."

"Oh, yes. When am I going to meet this guy?" Eric was the new fellow in Cassie's life. They'd been dating regularly for the past two months, which meant I hadn't seen as much of my friend as was usual in the past. I hadn't even been introduced, although I knew he was tall, lived in San Francisco, and worked as an accountant for some big corporation in the city.

"Soon," Cassie promised. "We'll get together some evening. Me and Eric, you and . . . ?"

"Nobody at the moment," I said, thinking of Alex. "Why is it I'm always attracted to men who are bad for me?"

Cassie sat down and crossed her legs, dangling one high-heeled pump from her toe. "I think we've had this conversation before. When you decided to leave Sid and get a divorce."

"Many times before. About men I'd just as soon forget."

"Who is he?"

"Somebody I met in connection with a case."

"Jeri, Jeri," Cassie said, shaking her head. "The men you meet in connection with your cases are criminals, cops, or people with something to hide. Not exactly prime material for social interaction."

"Stop talking like a lawyer. So who else am I going to meet? And where? Don't tell me to go to church or the Laundromat or the frozen-food section of my local grocery store. The only men I see there look very married. I've made that mistake before and I don't intend to do it again. Where did you meet Eric?"

Suddenly Cassie looked sheepish. "I deposed him for a lawsuit I was handling." I ragged her about it as she hastened to explain that the lawsuit had settled out of court before Eric called to ask her out.

"The hell with it. I've got more important things to worry about than my love life." I told her what had happened to Dad the night before. After she expressed her dismay and promised to call him, I leaned back in my chair and asked her a question that had been in the back of my mind. "You said you met Felice Navarro through this East Bay women's network. What do you know about her?"

Cassie shrugged. "Not much, really. I think she's divorced, but I don't know if she's seeing anyone. She has a studio in her house over in Rockridge and supports herself with the usual weddings and portraits. She also does some work with street scenes, capturing people going about their business. Felice and a couple of other photographers had a show at a gallery in Berkeley earlier this year. It was called 'Avenues'—shots of Telegraph, Shattuck, University, and San Pablo avenues. I thought it was terrific. I'll be interested to see this series she's doing on women and their jobs. Why all this interest in Felice?"

"She may figure into this case I'm working on. Remember when Dad found his friend's body? Things have gotten weird all of a sudden. I'm having trouble fitting it all together."

"I'm sure you will. I have faith in you." She reached down and stuck her foot back into the shoe. "You hungry? Got plans for dinner?"

"I'm always hungry. And equally reluctant to cook."

Cassie stood and reached for the doorknob. "Let me make those calls, then I'll come and get you." She headed back to her own office. I turned off the computer equipment and put the case notes in the appropriate file. I switched on the answering machine and had my keys out, ready to call it a night. The door opened, but it wasn't Cassie.

He looked far more menacing than he had the day he met Alex Tongco for lunch to discuss the late Dr. Manibusan's files. When he walked into my office, the first thing he looked at was the boxes stacked against the wall. Then he looked at me. His eyes flashed and glittered, like obsidian, or the blade of a knife.

"Eduardo Villegas," I said. "What do you want?"

"You know what I want."

"No, I don't. Why don't you enlighten me?"

He clenched his hands and took a step toward me. I might be able to take him if he wasn't armed, I thought, one hand threading through my keys so metal stuck out between my fingers, the other ready to toss my handbag at his face. But I didn't think anyone called Eddie the Knife would go anywhere without that particular weapon, so easy to conceal. I gauged the distance between us, assessing the situation, keeping an eye on his hands. I was a couple of inches taller and I didn't think he outweighed me by much. But a blade made a difference.

"I want that envelope." He spat the words at me. "I know you've got it."

"How do you know about the envelope?"

"Never mind how I know. Just give it to me and nobody gets hurt."

I shook my head. "I don't have it, Eddie. I never did. It was stolen before I could get my hands on it."

Eddie had an unpleasant laugh. "You expect me to buy that? It was your old man he mailed it to. Now you got all the stuff from the professor's office. It's got to be there."

I gestured toward the stacked boxes. "Be my guest. Look through all of them. You won't find it." I watched his face as he considered my words. So Eddie knew that Dr. Manibusan had mailed that envelope to Dr. Timothy Howard. Villegas, or the person he was working for, assumed that the envelope was with the contents of the professor's office. I tried the truth, but people like Eddie very often have trouble recognizing veracity. "My father found the envelope in his office yesterday. He was mugged last night when he left the university. His briefcase was stolen. The envelope's gone."

Eddie the Knife thought about this for a moment, clenching and unclenching his hands. "Son of a bitch," he said. I guessed he'd decided to believe me, or he didn't want to dig through all those file boxes.

"How do you know about the envelope, Eddie?"

"Never mind how I know about it. If you're lying to me, bitch, I'll cut you so bad—" Eddie said, taking another step toward me.

My office door opened and Cassie stood there in her bright red dress and a smile. "Hi. Ready to go? Or am I interrupting something?"

"Mr. Villegas was just leaving." I gestured toward the door.

He looked from me to Cassie and back again. "For now," he said. It sounded like a promise I'd rather he didn't keep.

Sixteen

EDDIE'S WORDS ALSO ERASED ANY DOUBTS ABOUT the identity of Dad's attacker. It had to be Dolores Cruz. And if Eddie found that out, she was in danger. I called her that evening at Charles Randall's condo to warn her about Eddie the Knife, but when I identified myself, she hung up. I punched in the number again, but this time she let it ring and ring without picking up the receiver. Okay, I thought, if you want to play games, it's your funeral. All the same, I was at Mabuhay Travel Friday morning when Belinda unlocked the front door. Dolly wasn't there yet, but Belinda promised to give her my message.

I drove across the Bay Bridge to San Francisco. The nursing registry I had called the day before was located in a down-at-the-heels Victorian on Oak Street, to the west of the Civic Center. I found a parking place, went inside, and introduced myself to the woman who sat behind the counter, asking for Carrie or Bess.

"Oh, the private investigator," she said cheerfully, and stood up. She was a short woman with black hair, very pregnant, moving toward me with ungainly serenity. "I'm Carrie. I talked to you on the phone. Bess is in the other room. She wants to talk to you."

Carrie knocked on a closed door, then opened it. Bess was an older woman, obviously in charge of the whole shebang, tall with a short helmet of iron gray hair. She wanted to know what I was looking for, eyebrows drawn together in concern about privacy of those long-ago nurses whose files the registry held. I assured her that I was merely trying to locate

154

someone whose name had come up in a case. Besides, the forties were a long time ago and she admitted that the files were considered dead.

Finally Bess took a set of keys from her desk and led me down the hallway and a set of steps to a subterranean storeroom full of old metal filing cabinets. They were in a rough chronological order, starting in 1935. I knew from the letters in Manibusan's files that Lieutenant O. M. Cardiff had left the army in November 1945, with a last known address California Street in the Richmond district, and there was some connection with M. Harold Beddoes in June of 1946. It was, as Carrie said yesterday, needle-in-a-haystack time. There was no reason to think that Cardiff had ever signed on with this particular nurses' registry. I was taking the long shot only because this was the sole place that had records back to the forties.

But she had. It was one of those exhilarating moments when the long shot pays off, when the information falls into my lap. It makes up for all the times I have to slog through files and records without finding a damn thing. I dug through dusty file folders from 1946 on, one hour, then another slipping past before I found her in 1949. Olivia Mary Cardiff Beddoes, a surgical nurse living on Wawona Street in the West Portal area of San Francisco. I sifted through the file. The professor's note about M. Harold Beddoes, June 1946 suddenly made sense. That was when Olivia married Harold. Not long after signing on with the registry, Olivia had found a position at Pacific Presbyterian Hospital in San Francisco.

I wrote down as much information as I could find in the slim file, then went upstairs and thanked Bess and Carrie. I headed for the Civic Center and looked up Olivia and Harold in the 1946 marriage records, feeling a glow as I found them. I hit the birth records next. It took a while, but I discovered that Olivia had a baby in 1952, a boy named Walter. My next stop was Pacific Presbyterian Hospital, where I persuaded someone in the personnel office to look up Olivia Beddoes's file. She'd left the hospital in 1952, several months before her baby was born. At that time the Beddoes family was still living on Wawona Street, but a check of the assessor's record showed that Harold and Olivia Beddoes sold their house in 1959. I copied the name of the real estate company without much hope that the Realtor would have any information on a forwarding address more than thirty years after the sale.

Dead end again, I thought. I drove out to West Portal, but no one answered the door of the stucco house and I didn't want to be late for my appointment with Neal Patterson, Felice Navarro's ex-husband. I'd made an early-morning phone call to his office at Moffett Naval Air Station, and he'd suggested a late lunch. I drove back through the city and onto U.S. 101, heading south along the marshy shore of the Bay until I saw the air station's huge hangers off to my left. I located the coffee shop Patterson had suggested and parked my Toyota in its crowded lot. Inside, I looked for a navy uniform, but because of its proximity to the base, the restaurant was full of them. I stood near the cash register and scanned the room, spotting a sandy-haired man sitting alone at a booth in the back. Our eyes met and he stood up, a six-footer, broad at the shoulders in his khaki uniform.

"Neal Patterson?" I asked as I approached.

"Jeri Howard?"

Identities thus confirmed, we sat down. "I already ordered," he said in a down-home southern drawl. "I don't have a lot of time."

When the waitress appeared at our table, I ordered a chef's salad, then studied him as I drank from my water glass. He had a pleasant, tanned face, with crinkly laugh lines at the eyes and a snub nose between a pair of blue eyes, and he wore a lieutenant's bars on the collar of his uniform. On the phone I'd told him that I was investigating a case that peripherally involved the Navarro family. I was surprised that he had agreed to talk with me on the basis of that brief explanation, but there had been a tinge of something in his voice—regret, perhaps—when he spoke of his ex-wife. Maybe he wanted to talk. That desire for communication, even with a stranger, very often makes a private investigator's task easier.

He went over ground that Felice and I had already traveled, telling me how he and Felice had met and married and broken up, the regret in his voice more evident now that he sat across from me. When I asked about his former father-in-law, he frowned, and echoed Felice's comment that Maximiliano Navarro seldom approved of anything his daughter did. His friendly face darkened. "Of course, my own father's no better," he said.

"Felice told me."

He was quiet as the waitress set our lunches on the table, then he took a bite of his club sandwich and chewed, his eyes troubled. I picked up my fork, searching for the lettuce under the layers of ham and cheese atop my salad bowl.

"My dad's an Alabama redneck," Patterson said, sipping his water. "I don't think the past twenty-five years have had any impact on him. When I brought Felice home from the Philippines, I wanted her to meet my family, so we went to Huntsville. Mom was okay, but my old man acted like a horse's ass. Felice stuck it out for a couple of days, then she hopped the next plane back to San Francisco. That really put a wedge between us. I think it contributed to our breakup." He sighed. "As long as we were out here, it was fine. There's a big Filipino-American community in the Bay Area, and a lot of military men are married to Filipino women."

"Felice seems bitter toward her own father."

Patterson worked on his sandwich for a while before he answered. "Hell, the old man treats her like a checker he can move around on a board. From what I could see, he treats everybody that way. Jun just goes along with it and Rick's cut out of the same cloth. He manipulates right back. Felice rebels. It's the only way she can deal with it. She really is a terrific photographer. You should see her pictures. While we were still in the Philippines, she had a big-deal show at a gallery in Manila. It was shots of marketplaces, street scenes, all of them taken right there in the city. She really catches people's faces."

Patterson stopped for another sip of water before continuing. "Anyway, Felice got a lot of attention as a result of this show, but it really bothered her that her own father couldn't find the time to attend. He treats the photography like some damn hobby, and it's so important to her. She just can't seem to make Max understand. I thought she would've given up long ago, but I guess what it boils down to is, Felice is fonder of the old man than she lets on."

I certainly wouldn't have thought that based on my conversation with her, recalling Felice's bitterness as she spoke of her father. "She seems to be close to Rick."

"Oh, yeah. They bicker back and forth, but that's mostly brother-sister stuff. Rick acts as a buffer between Felice and her father, and he's supportive of her work. I think Felice would do anything for Rick."

"Tell me about her mother, the first Mrs. Navarro."

"She killed herself, you know," Patterson said thoughtfully, "right after Felice and I married. An overdose of sleeping pills. She had cancer and went through all sorts of treatment, but she kept getting worse. I was at Cubi Point, the air station up near Subic, and Felice spent a lot of time at her parents' house in Quezon City, near Manila, just so she could be near her mother. We'd get together on weekends. That's when Mrs. Navarro took those pills. She was alone in the house. Max was off somewhere, on a trip to Taipei. Felice took it real hard. She can't talk about it easily. She blames herself for not being there. She blames her father, too, but he wasn't there much anyway."

"Felice said something about a mistress," I said, playing with my salad, remembering the anger in Felice's voice as she spoke of her father and his *querida*. What happens to mistresses after they're discarded? I wondered. Had I seen anything about the mistress in the professor's extensive file on Max Navarro?

"Max wasn't known as a faithful husband. Everyone knew he had a woman on the side. But it seemed like that was fairly common in his circle. He was fairly discreet about it until his wife died."

"Did you ever meet this mistress?"

"Once," Patterson said, and he flushed to the roots of his sandy hair.

"What happened?"

"She made a pass at me." Patterson looked indignant and sheepish at the same time. "I thought Felice was going to kill her."

"What did Felice do? I think you'd better start at the beginning."

"It's in the past," he protested, flushing again. "I'd just as soon forget it." I fixed him with a steady gaze. He wiped his hands on a napkin and glumly continued his story.

"Right before I was due to leave the Philippines, Max decided to have this obligatory family dinner. Jun and his wife and kids were summoned from the sugar plantation up at San Fernando. Rick was there with his latest girlfriend. Felice didn't want to go, but I persuaded her that we should, since she was moving to the States with me and she might not be back to the islands for a while. Things went downhill the minute we arrived."

"Why?"

"The mistress was there. Max called her Mrs. Rios all evening, really formal, as though none of us knew about the situation. He'd been seen with her in public after Mrs. Navarro died, but this was the first time he'd mixed her in with his family. In fact, she was presiding over the table like the lady of the manor. I couldn't tell how Jun and Rick felt about it, but Jun's wife was definitely offended. And Felice was livid. Her eyes started to flash the minute she saw that woman. It was awkward city from the get-go. Mrs. Rios was quite a bit younger than Max, in her thirties, I guess. She was nervous, trying too hard to be accepted. Maybe that's why she was drinking so much. I thought we'd never get through dinner."

Patterson pushed his plate aside, balled up his napkin, and tossed it onto the remains of his lunch. "Afterward I stepped out into the garden to get some air, and Mrs. Rios joined me. As I said, she'd had a bit too much wine. Next thing I was fending her off. That's when Felice came on the scene.

She didn't make a sound, she just went for Mrs. Rios. Felice hit her, and that topaz ring she always wears caught the other woman on the chin. Opened up quite a cut and got blood on both of them.''

"The chin?" I asked, setting down my fork.

Patterson nodded, tracing a finger down the left side of his jawline. "I got Felice out of there quick. When we got home we had a terrible argument. I've never seen her so angry, until that business with my dad. I couldn't convince her that I didn't have anything to do with that woman's behavior.''

"Does that woman have a name other than Mrs. Rios?" I asked. "Where is she now that Max has married Antonia?"

"Back in the Philippines, I guess," Patterson said. "Her name was Dolores.''

Seventeen

FELICE HAD LIED TO ME ABOUT DOLORES CRUZ. She must have known I was describing her father's former mistress when I mentioned the scar that she herself had put on Dolly's chin. Rick had denied knowing Dolly as well. What else were the Navarro siblings hiding?

It took me the rest of the afternoon to get back to Oakland. I encountered commuter hell on the San Mateo Bridge, a jackknifed tractor-trailer rig that blocked all the eastbound lanes and left me fuming in my ovenlike car for nearly two hours. When I finally drove off the bridge, I was in the thick of Friday afternoon rush hour. Sweaty, tired, and irked, I headed for Mabuhay Travel, where Belinda greeted me with a glare and anger crackling in her voice.

"She isn't here. She hasn't been here all day. Didn't even bother to call in, and me up to my eyeballs in work. I've had it with that woman. I'm gonna call Arthur and Perlita first thing tomorrow morning and tell 'em either she goes or I go."

Where was Dolly? I wondered as I drove to the Parkside Towers. It was nearly five o'clock. She'd been out of reach all day. Had she been doing something with the contents of the envelope I was sure she had? Or had Eddie the Knife Villegas gotten to her?

In the condominium's lobby I encountered O. Barnwell, the same sharp-eyed security guard I'd met last week when I was pretending to be a prospective buyer. He didn't recognize me as he looked me over and asked my business. When I asked to see Ms. Cruz in 803, he picked up a house phone on his counter and punched in four digits. He let it ring for a moment, then hung up. "I'm sorry. There's no answer."

I stalled, tapping my fingers on the counter. "I just missed her at work, and I understand she was coming right home. Can you check the parking garage for her car? It's a white Thunderbird."

The guard looked at me as if I'd thrown a stink bomb into his pristine lobby. "If you have business with Ms. Cruz, you'll have to wait. Or call her later."

I made a show of waiting while the guard kept an eye on me, with my rumpled hair, my sweat-stained, wrinkled clothes, and my barely contained impatience, as though he were assessing my potential as a housebreaker. Minutes crawled by on the clock above the mailboxes while the guard answered the phone and spoke with residents who collected their mail.

Just before six he was distracted when a slender, fiftyish woman in designer sweats got off the elevator and strode up to his post, carrying several sheets of paper. "Oliver," she said, "here's the guest list for the party tonight."

He called her Mrs. Beaumont, and the two of them bent their heads over the list while she told him the caterer was due any minute and the photographer after that. The guests should start arriving at eight. As Mrs. Beaumont headed for the elevator, Barnwell and I traded looks and I knew he would have liked to have me out of his lobby before the higher-toned clientele arrived. I was as antsy as he was. Cooling my heels in the lobby of the Parkside Towers was not my idea of a productive evening. But I had to talk with Dolly.

She still hadn't appeared fifteen minutes later, when the caterer arrived and he and his assistants hauled their gear upstairs. Finally, at six-thirty, the door leading to the parking garage opened and Dolly came through it, wearing white pumps and another of her tropical-print dresses, this one a swirl of pink and turquoise. She held a white straw clutch in one hand. Car keys jingled from the other as she punched the elevator button. She was smiling to herself, pink lipstick in a smug, self-satisfied curve, a cat who had feasted on several canaries.

"Oh, Ms. Cruz," the guard said, "this lady is—"

Dolly glanced at us, and the smile segued into a frown. "What are you doing here?"

"We need to talk, Dolly." I took a step toward her, and she stepped back, holding the straw purse up to her bosom as though to keep me at bay.

The guard put up a restraining hand. "If Ms. Cruz doesn't want to see you, you'll have to leave."

"I have nothing to say to you," she said, tilting her head up dramatically as she swept a strand of black hair away from her face.

"Are you sure about that, Mrs. Rios?" Her hard brown eyes narrowed. I pushed past the guard and got between Dolly and the elevator door. "I know you were Max Navarro's mistress. I know how you got that scar on your chin." Behind me the elevator door opened and Dolly made a move to escape, but I blocked her way and the door closed again.

"My name is Dolores Cr—" She caught herself as she punched the elevator button. The doors opened again. "Dolores Manibusan. I don't know what you're talking about. You're crazy. Leave me alone."

"I'm going to call the cops," Barnwell threatened. The guard was older than me, but he was lean and in good shape. His hand clamped down on my left shoulder. I shook it off. Dolly took advantage of this diversion to dart past me into the sanctuary of the elevator. "She's a crazy woman," Dolly told the guard, eyes wide with drama. "She's been following me all over town, harassing me."

The doors started to close, and I reached out and hit the rubber bumper on one side, making them open automatically. "I know you've got that envelope. You pushed my father down the stairs and grabbed his briefcase. Somebody else knows you have it, too. A guy named Eddie the Knife, and he's dangerous." She didn't react, so I fired another salvo. "You know who killed Dr. Manibusan. How else would you know about the envelope?"

She shrank back against the far wall of the elevator, her eyes widening in alarm. The guard grabbed both my arms and yanked me away from the elevator, repeating his threat to call the police. By then the elevator doors had closed and Dolly was on her way to the safety of the eighth-floor condo. I freed myself from the guard's grasp, stepping away from him toward the front door, my hands raised.

"It's okay," I said, my voice calm and conciliatory. "I'm leaving. I'm out of here." He made no further move toward me, but he glared as I backed away from him, out the double glass doors.

All that meant was that I wouldn't try to see Dolly by going in the front door. I walked back to my car, assessing the situation. Mrs. Beaumont's party guests were due at eight, according to what I'd overheard. By then it would be dusk, darkening the areas around the building. Besides, maybe I'd get lucky and the guard would be replaced by another. Even if that wasn't the case, he'd be distracted by a constant stream of arrivals. I went home and exchanged my light-colored clothes for something dark, fed myself and Abigail, and waited.

The bright May day took its time turning into night. The blue sky had turned navy, but it was bright with stars and a moon that was three-quarters full. At nine I returned to the Parkside Towers. I left my car nearby on Seventeenth Street and rounded the corner onto Lakeside. To my left the Necklace of Lights twinkled above the dark water of Lake Merritt, adding their reflection to the other lights of Oakland's nighttime electric show. When I reached Dolly's building, I glanced up and located the balcony of her eighth-floor unit. A light shone in the living room. The party was at the opposite end of the building, on the same floor. It was well under way. People spilled out onto the balcony, and laughter and the buzz of talk carried on the slight breeze that ruffled the trees.

Luck was not with me as far as the security guard was concerned. Barnwell still guarded the entrance to his domain. As I walked slowly past the building, a man and a woman went up the walk, the woman carrying a package wrapped in silver paper. In the lobby they stopped and the guard checked the list of partygoers, then waved them through to the elevators.

I kept walking. A couple of buildings past the Parkside Towers, I turned around and walked back to where the driveway led to the Parkside Towers garage. I walked along the asphalt, sheltered by a stand of rhododendrons along the side of the building next door. Then I waited.

Ten minutes later a Porsche turned off the street and came up the drive. The driver inserted his card into the electronic gadget outside the metal grid door, which slowly lifted. The Porsche drove into the garage, but the driver stopped just inside the entrance to make sure the door dropped back into place. Any other time I would have applauded such caution, but tonight it was damned inconvenient.

I waited another fifteen minutes or so, hoping that someone wouldn't see me lurking in the bushes and call the cops. The party on the eighth floor was cooking, judging from the sounds of merriment echoing off the sides of buildings. Finally another car came up the drive, this time a BMW whose driver didn't bother to wait until the garage door closed. Moving quickly, I slipped under the lowering metal grid and darted for the rear of the garage, hugging the dark edges not illuminated by the electric bulbs on the garage roof. The BMW parked in a space to my left, and a prosperous-looking couple in their forties got out. The man opened the trunk, handed the woman a sack of groceries, and reached in for another sack.

Someone had left a cardboard carton on the concrete floor next to the Dumpster. I picked it up and tossed it into the Dumpster, making sufficient noise to turn the heads of the man and woman who still stood at the rear of the BMW. They noted my presence at the Dumpster, then turned back to their groceries. As the man shut the car's trunk, I walked toward the door that led to the lobby, slowing my gait to let them get there first. The man opened the door to the lobby, holding it so the woman and I could enter.

Both elevator doors and the door leading to the garage were in full view of the guard. Two men in suits had arrived to join the party, one with a package, and the other with a bottle of champagne. They stood in front of the counter as Barnwell checked the list Mrs. Beaumont had given him. He didn't find their names, and I heard him tell the two men he'd have to call upstairs before he could let them in. He picked up the phone. I hoped the elevator would open before the guard turned his head our way. I drew back as far as I could, letting my parking-garage companions block the guard's line of sight.

We clustered in front of the elevators, which were taking their own sweet time getting to the first floor. The car on the right, closest to the guard, seemed to be stuck on nine, and the car on the left was on five. Finally the car on five descended. I stood poised, ready to get in, out of the sight of the guard. When the door opened, I moved forward, then stopped. An older woman with three suitcases piled on a metal luggage carrier struggled out of the elevator. One wheel of the carrier got stuck in the gap between elevator and floor, and the top suitcase began to slip off the pile.

"Here, let me help you with that," said the man, the one who had opened the door from the parking garage. Just then Barnwell hung up the phone, giving the two partygoers sanction to pass. The right-hand elevator descended from the ninth floor and the bell dinged as the doors opened. With exquisitely bad timing Barnwell looked up at the group waiting to board the elevator. He recognized me. "Hey," he said as the doors closed.

The BMW couple pressed the button for the seventh floor and the two men bound for the party pressed eight. We glanced at each other, then away, following elevator etiquette. At seven the BMW couple got out. On eight I left the elevator with the party guests, who turned left and headed for the open door of Mrs. Beaumont's condo. People had spilled out into the hallway, talking and laughing, with glasses and plates in their hands. I moved quickly down the opposite end of the corridor, headed for Dolly's unit. I heard one of the elevators hum in its shaft. Was the guard on his way up to the eighth floor to apprehend me? I hoped he hadn't called Dolly—or the cops.

Dolly's front door was locked. I knocked. No answer. I pulled out my picks. I was working on the lock when a voice behind me almost made me drop them.

"Jeez, honey, did you get locked out?"

I palmed the picks and turned to see a young man with curly brown hair and a round face reddened by booze. He had a glass in his hand and sprayed me with whiskey when he talked.

"No. Everything's fine." I kept my voice even.

"Hey, you're cute." He blinked at me like an owl. "You know the Beaumonts in 809? They're having a party. Come on, lemme buy you a drink."

Son of a bitch, I thought. The elevator door *ding*ed and opened. I expected to see the guard step off the car and point an accusing finger at me. But it was a gray-haired couple who headed for the Beaumonts' open door without a glance in my direction.

I smiled at the drunk. "Whatever you're drinking is fine," I said. The words were sufficient to send him walking unsteadily down the hall. I quickly turned back to the door and opened it in a few tense seconds.

Dolly's condo was dark. I knew I'd seen a light on in the unit while I was on the street. But that was some time ago. Maybe she left while I was hanging around outside the parking garage, trying to get into the building. I tried to remember if I had seen the white Thunderbird anywhere in the garage, and came up blank. I couldn't risk turning on the light, though.

I slipped inside, pulling the door shut, and stood in the darkness, listening. I sifted out the noise from the party down the hall and concentrated on the sounds coming from the area in front of me. The door leading to the balcony must be open. I could hear the whoosh of traffic eight floors down on Lakeside Drive. The wail of a siren ricocheted off the buildings around Lake Merritt.

My eyes adjusted to the darkness, and I made out an open doorway to my right, leading to the kitchen. On my left I sensed open space, a dining area. The living room was beyond it. I could see pale, gauzy curtains framing the big glass door that led to the balcony. Illuminated by moonlight, the curtains swayed in a breeze. I moved slowly, cautiously, toward the living room, listening, trying to sense whether there was another presence in the condo. I didn't feel Dolly's energy, though she could have been there, hiding from me, alerted by the security guard.

I stumbled against a floor lamp, rattling it, and I put my hand out to steady it. Then I sensed something flying toward me, moving so fast I was powerless to stop it. As I turned, it crashed into my head with great force, and pain flashed through me like a white light. I gasped and pitched forward, carrying the lamp to the floor with me, landing clumsily on my stomach. I moaned and slowly rolled to one side, each movement an effort. I felt slow and awkward, tangled in the lamp cord like a fly in a spiderweb. I kicked the lamp away and raised my hands to shield my face, to ward off further blows.

But the anticipated blows didn't come. Instead, I heard someone moving quickly in the dark living room. Then a hand touched mine. It felt odd, not like a hand at all, but it must have been, because it was moving. I couldn't place the texture, and when I tried to think about it, my head throbbed and ached. The other presence wrapped my hand around something cold and hard and cylindrical. Then I thought I heard the door open and close, and there didn't seem to be anyone else in the room but me.

I drifted, thinking about how easy it would be to go to sleep. I was tired, but the floor was hard, even if it was carpeted. Don't pass out, I told myself sternly. Get up. I know it hurts to move, but you have to get up now.

I rolled to my right, my hand still holding the cold, hard thing that felt like metal. My left hand encountered a table, and I used it for leverage as I pulled myself to my feet. I felt cold and shaky as I reached up to touch the place at the back of my head that was the source of all this pain. It was wet and slick. I sniffed the wetness on my fingers, smelled blood, and my stomach reeled, threatening to disgorge its contents.

I reached for the floor lamp and set it upright, running my hand up its base until I found the switch. I turned it on. Its pleated shade was askew, shading the bulb. In the diffused glow I looked at the blood on my fingers and the brass candlestick I held in my right hand. I don't remember picking up this candlestick, I thought, feeling its heft and looking with detachment at the etching on its base.

Just then the light went on, hurting my eyes as it illuminated the living room with sudden harshness. I wasn't alone after all. Dolly Cruz was there. But she was lying on the floor, on her side, facing me, her brown eyes open and unseeing. One of her white pumps was still on a foot, the other some distance away. Crimson smeared the bodice of her summery dress, marring the pink and turquoise pattern. The same red stain pooled on the carpet under her head. Blood splattered the sofa cushions and the white wall beyond and speckled the surface of the table I'd used to pull myself upright.

I tore my eyes from Dolly's body and looked up at the boozy man from the party. He stood in the dining room, his right hand still on the light switch and two glasses balanced precariously in his left. The pink flush had drained from his face and he looked as sick as I felt.

"Oh, jeez," he said in a quavery voice.

Eighteen

AT LEAST I WASN'T IN THE SMALLEST INTERVIEW room. That windowless cubicle, graffiti scratched into the blue and white walls, was reserved for suspects, its claustrophobic confines designed to make a person think about the reason for being there. The fact that I wasn't in the smallest room was a good sign.

I was in the larger interview room, reserved for witnesses and family members. It had the same utilitarian metal table and chairs found throughout the Oakland police administration building. They didn't spend a lot on decor here. This interview room had two pictures on the wall, neither of them particularly cheery, or restful to my bleary eyes. The circles under my eyes were so heavy, I could feel them. I reached up and touched the spot on my head where the doctor at Kaiser Hospital had taken three stitches to close the wound. It itched, and my head still hurt despite the pain pills.

The room had once been an office with a window that looked out onto OPD's Homicide Section, with its metal desks standing sturdily on institutional beige linoleum and case files crowding the bookcases along the walls. Now the venetian blinds were closed and I was alone with my pounding head and the unbidden memory of Dolly Cruz's corpse.

The door opened. I glimpsed the lieutenant's office across the narrow hallway as the homicide team came back into the interview room where they'd been questioning me. Sergeant Harris was the lead investigator, firing questions at me in his gruff voice while both he and Sergeant Griffin took notes. I knew both of them by reputation, if not personally. Sid thought they were savvy, professional, and thorough. They were certainly giving me and my story a thorough going-over, trying to cull out every detail, every nuance. They kept questioning me, then going outside to discuss my answers. I knew they were looking for discrepancies in my statement. After all, I'd had a very public confrontation with the victim several hours before her demise. I had sneaked into her building, eluding the pursuit of the security guard, and the un-nerved partygoer had seen me breaking into Dolly's condo sometime before he returned with the drinks to find me standing over the victim's recently bludgeoned body, the murder weapon in my hand.

As Griffin and Harris started another round of questions, Dolly's corpse rose to haunt me again. If I'd beaten her with the force to do that to her head, I'd have been splattered with blood, just like the sofa, the table, and the wall. The only blood on me was that on my head and my hand, where I'd touched the candlestick. I knew it, and so did the two detectives. I wondered if the police had found any signs of cleanup in the bathroom or the kitchen, like wet and bloody towels. But they wouldn't tell me. I'd have to find out another way.

"You didn't hear anybody behind you before you got hit?" Harris asked again, for what seemed like the fourth time. Fatigue etched his dark brown face. His broad shoulders strained his suit coat and he'd loosened his tie.

I shook my head, which was a mistake, and winced as the throbbing increased in intensity. "I didn't see anything. I didn't hear anything. I just have an impression of something flying through the air, coming at me. After it hit me, I fell on the floor and tried to roll over. Then I felt the hand touch me."

"You said it didn't feel like a hand." Griffin spoke in a level voice, looking at me with a gray, unblinking gaze.

"It didn't feel like flesh." I rubbed my forehead, trying to recall the texture 'of the thing that touched me briefly. "Rubber gloves, maybe. The kind you keep under the sink for cleaning."

Griffin scribbled a few more notes, poker-faced below his

pale hair. He hadn't said much since arriving at the Kaiser emergency room, where the uniformed officer had taken me for treatment. After that Griffin had escorted me downtown and left me in the interview room while he waited for Harris to return from the scene of Dolly's murder. Since that time they'd been in and out as we traversed the same ground over and over again. A glance at my watch confirmed that it was well past midnight. I wondered how long I'd been there. I couldn't be exactly sure when I'd found Dolly's body. I sensed that although I hadn't lost consciousness after being hit in the head, some undetermined amount of time had passed before I'd dragged myself to my feet.

I heard a familiar voice out in the corridor, then someone knocked. Harris opened the door. He loosened his tie as he spoke to someone I couldn't see. Then he turned to me, a question mark in his voice. "Sid wants to talk with you."

I nodded. "It's okay."

Griffin and Harris left the room and Sid appeared in the doorway, his suit rumpled and his face tired, as though both of them had had a long day. He pulled the door shut behind him and put his hands on his hips. He didn't say anything for a moment, just stood there and looked at me with his yellow cat's eyes.

"Did they Mirandize you?"

"No. Which means they don't think I'm a suspect."

"You're not out of here yet," he warned.

"If I killed her, where's the blood? I have a feeling they found some towels and maybe even some rubber gloves in the bathroom. Am I right?"

Sid's face remained maddeningly blank. He wasn't going to tell me anything, and I wouldn't have any access to the police report while the case was under investigation. "What the hell were you doing there, Jeri?" he growled. I folded my arms across my chest and propped my feet up on a chair. He sighed and rolled his eyes upward. "I know, you're working on a case. I just hope you don't get yourself killed one of these days."

So did I.

* * *

It was past two when I stripped off my clothes, leaving them in a heap on my bathroom floor. I turned on the water as hot as I could bear it and stood under the shower with a cake of lemon-scented soap in my hand, heedless of the drought, heedless of the time, wanting only to scrub myself clean of the sight of Dolly Cruz's body and the smell of her blood.

I breathed the tart perfume of the soap and relished the steam and lather that enveloped me and made me feel clean again. With gentle, careful hands I washed the blood out of my own hair, avoiding the stitches as best I could. It was impossible to wash away what had happened that night, though. I had told the two homicide investigators about Dolores Cruz's claim to be Dr. Manibusan's widow and that I had been hired to locate Alex Tongco, the professor's next of kin. Beyond that I didn't say anything about the missing envelope and its contents. I did, however, mention that Eddie the Knife Villegas had contacted Dr. Manibusan's nephew, wanting access to the professor's papers, telling Griffin and Harris that their colleague in Theft, the ever-charming Sergeant Gonsalves, knew about Eddie. As far as I was concerned, Eddie was right up there when it came to qualifying as a murder suspect. I wanted Homicide to give him all the due consideration they were giving me. But Eddie's M.O. was a blade, not a blunt instrument.

By the time Griffin and Harris had finished their probing, my eyes felt like two bags of cement weighing me down and the painkillers were making me woozy. I barely sounded lucid, let alone credible. But they didn't Mirandize me, at least not then. Sid took me back to where I'd left my car, and I drove home, glad to see my apartment and my querulous cat. I fed her and knocked back some more pain pills before making a beeline for the bathroom.

Now I turned off the water and wrapped myself in an oversize towel, carefully patting my head dry. Then I fell into bed, oblivious. The stitches still itched when I woke up, but the pain had lessened. It was almost noon. The phone on my bedside table was ringing, but I didn't answer. I didn't feel like talking to anyone. Abigail was curled into a tight fur ball on my left side, her nose tucked under her forepaws. The phone stopped ringing. I stared at the bedroom ceiling and stroked her silky fur. She commenced a rumbling purr that seemed to vibrate the bed.

If she wasn't hungry, I certainly was. I got up, sticking my arms into my robe as I shuffled to the kitchen. Abigail ran ahead of me and chirruped while I dished up cat food. Two mugs of coffee and some raisin toast took away the sharp edge of hunger. The phone rang again while I was getting dressed. I put on slacks and a T-shirt, then picked up the clothes I'd discarded on the bathroom floor. They had blood on them, whether mine or Dolly's I couldn't be sure. I stared at them, then walked through the apartment to the back door. Outside, I stuffed the clothes into the trash can.

I finished the coffee and a few more pieces of toast, then headed for my office, stopping at the corner to buy an Oakland *Tribune*. Dolly's murder made page three, but the story was small and sketchy. Her death was overshadowed by page-one headlines about another in a series of freeway shootings along Interstate 580. Sid was working on that one, which explained why he'd been at Homicide so late last night. I dropped my eyes to the below-the-fold story on the Cruz murder. I read quickly through the few inches of black type, looking for my name. It was there, noting only that Oakland private investigator Jeri Howard had been at the scene and was being questioned by police.

It was Saturday, and my Franklin Street building was deserted. In my office the answering machine's red light blinked rapidly, indicating lots of messages. I rewound the tape and listened, ignoring repeat calls from a couple of reporters. Dad had called several times. Had he heard the news? That might explain the ringing phone I hadn't answered at home. There were calls from Elaine Martini at Cal State, urgency in her voice as she left both her security office number and her home number. I wagered the Oakland cops had called her to verify that I was working for the university. For how long? I wondered. It was one thing to look into Dolly Cruz's claim that she was the professor's widow, but murder changed everything.

I reached Dad at home. Tension thinned his voice. "Thank God you're all right. Sid called me this morning. He said the Cruz woman was murdered, and you were there. He told me not to worry. How can I not worry about a thing like that?"

I guess Sid figured it was better for my father to hear it from him than from some other source, but I had to spend the next few minutes reassuring Dad. I don't think I succeeded. He had called my brother in Sonoma in between calls to me, so after I disconnected I punched in Brian's number.

"Are you sure you don't want to go into teaching?" he asked when he answered the phone. "I think it's slightly less dangerous than being a private eye. I'm glad you called. Dad was frantic when he couldn't get you on the phone."

"I was home, but dead to the world." I stopped. "Bad choice of words. I suppose I should call Mother."

"I'll do it. You've got enough on your mind without sparring with Mom about a more appropriate line of work." Which just about summed up my current relationship with my female parent. "Better she hears it from one of us than from some reporter. If she hasn't already." Brian paused. "This is fairly serious, right?"

"An accurate assessment, baby brother. I'll be in touch."

I hung up the phone and sat for a moment, contemplating my options. Last night—or, more accurately, early this morning—Sid promised he would try to get a line on the whereabouts of Eddie the Knife Villegas. At least my ex-husband was fairly certain I wasn't guilty of murder. God knows he'd lived with me long enough to formulate the opinion that I wasn't capable of cold-blooded murder. But as a homicide sergeant he also didn't want to tread on the toes of Detectives Griffin and Harris. After all, it was their case. And Sid had enough to deal with, considering his own case load. He warned me to stay out of their way and let them do their jobs.

But I couldn't very well sit there with my teeth in my mouth, waiting for someone else to produce results. I'm an experienced investigator, and it's not my nature to let others take the lead. Besides, I had a lot of unanswered questions of my own. There was more to this than the death of Dolores Cruz. She had started this chain of events herself, when she showed up at the university, claiming to be the professor's widow, with expectations that didn't include her own brutal murder. But surely she knew there was risk involved. I was certain she had more to tell about Dr. Manibusan's murder. If only she'd lived long enough to talk.

That phone number on Eddie's bogus business cards, the restaurant called the Manila Galleon, was a logical place to start looking for Eddie, but I had another reason to drive across the Bay Bridge. Now Dolly couldn't tell me what she had been up to, but maybe she had confided in Perlita Randall. It wasn't a particularly good time to interview the sister of the deceased, but there's never a good time for the kinds of questions I was going to ask.

When I got to the Daly City branch of Mabuhay Travel, it was closed, the door locked and shades pulled. I had copied the Randalls' home address from the Dun & Bradstreet report. Back in my car, I checked the address on a Daly City map. It was near the Westlake Shopping Center, off John Daly Boulevard. I found the house, but it looked closed up, too, and no one answered the doorbell. I walked to the house next door, where a neighbor told me there'd been a death in the family. Perlita Randall was at a nearby Catholic church, praying for the soul of her sister.

I drove to the Manila Galleon on Serramonte Boulevard and went inside, my eyes adjusting from the bright May sunlight to the interior gloom. There was no one at the cashier's counter. It was early afternoon and the lunchtime crowd had thinned, leaving the dining room half empty. I saw a few occupied tables and a busboy clearing the rest. I peered into the bar and spotted several men on stools, knocking back a few and talking to the bartender in Tagalog. Footsteps made me turn. A young Filipino-American woman in her twenties, wearing a black-and-white uniform, approached me from the dining room.

"May I help you?" she asked.

"I'm looking for a friend. He said he'd meet me here. Eddie Villegas."

She frowned and looked at me with wide brown eyes, as though she didn't quite believe me. "He's not here."

I looked at my watch and scowled. "I don't understand. He said one o'clock, and I'm late. He should be here."

"Well, he was earlier," she said, "but he left. He didn't say anything to me about expecting a visitor." From the way she said it and the downward curve of her wide mouth, I realized she was jealous of any female attention Eddie might attract. "Why do you ask?"

"Ask," not "ax," I thought automatically. It would be a long time before I'd stop listening for that particular mispronunciation. "It's business," I told her, making my voice rough with impatience. "This is very important. Do you know where I can find him?"

She shrugged. "On weekends he visits his grandfather in the city. They play pinochle. Or so he says."

"Where does his grandfather live?"

"I don't know. Efren Villegas. He's in the book."

My ears pricked like Abigail's when she spots a bird, and it was all I could do not to purr. Efren Villegas. I had heard the name before, the day I visited Rick Navarro at Pacific Rim Imports, when Maximiliano Navarro ordered his son to call a cab for his cousin Efren. I reached back, recalling the scene. Max had passed an envelope to the bent old man who seemed so obsequious in the presence of his more powerful and important relative. And Max had introduced the old man to Antonia and Nina, saying he and Efren had fought together as partisans in World War II.

I thanked the young woman and headed for the public telephones near the rest rooms, checking the phone directory for San Francisco and Daly City. No luck there. I found no listing for Efren Villegas, but lots of initial E's. I went through a handful of change and got nothing but an empty coin purse.

My next option was the cab company. It had been a Yellow Cab, and I remember the driver wore a turban. A Sikh. It took a couple of twenties to pry out the information. Yes, the cab company dispatcher told me, they had a Sikh driving for them. His name was Roshan Singh, and he'd picked up a south-of-Market fare last Monday. Unfortunately, he wasn't driving today and the dispatcher couldn't or wouldn't tell me where he'd delivered his fare. I did get Singh's phone number, though there was no answer when I called. He was due back at work Monday.

Before I drove back to the East Bay, I called the Randalls' Daly City number but got no answer. I'd have to save my visit to Perlita for another day. Back in Oakland, I detoured past the Parkside Towers. I wanted to talk to the security guard who had tried to throw me out of the lobby yesterday, if he'd talk to me. But someone else was on duty at the highrise. I wasn't batting a thousand this afternoon, but at least I had another lead, about Efren Villegas.

I unlocked my office and headed for my filing cabinet, where I'd stashed Dr. Manibusan's calendar. I turned the pages to the entry where he'd written "E. Villegas, 2 p.m., SF." When I found the calendar earlier in the week, I had assumed the professor met with Eddie Villegas for his article about immigrants and crime. I'd focused my attention on Eddie, who had contacted Alex, trying to get Dr. Manibusan's files. But the professor must have talked to Efren Villegas, not his grandson. About his wartime experiences, perhaps. It made sense, given Dr. Manibusan's interest in that era. I thought about the elusive army nurse named Olivia Mary Cardiff. The circle kept coming back to World War II.

The phone rang and I reached for it before the machine could pick up the call. It was Sid. "Got some bad news for you, Jeri," he said. "Eddie Villegas was at a party last night in Daly City. Lots of witnesses who can swear he never got to this side of the Bay, at least not during the time Dolores Cruz was killed."

"So I guess he's not much of a suspect for Dolly's murder.

Wasn't his M.O. anyway. Thanks for checking, Sid. I know you're busy with this freeway shooting.''

"Yeah, I am." Weariness showed through the gruffness in his voice. "So try and stay out of trouble, okay? I got enough to worry about already, and I can't afford to bail you out of jail.''

After we hung up I felt deflated. Somewhere in the back of my mind I'd been sure Eddie the Knife had murdered Dolly, though logically I knew that was too easy. Still, I had discovered that the Villegas family was connected to the Navarros, linked by more than blood. Cousins, I thought, recalling what Alex had told me about *compadrazgo*, the Filipino kinship system.

I looked at the clock on the wall. Nearly six, and I hadn't eaten since I'd decimated half a loaf of pumpernickel-raisin at noon. I decided to get some comfort food at Nan Yang, my favorite Burmese restaurant down in Oakland's Chinatown. I locked up my office and set off on foot, walking down Franklin Street to Eighth, my mind empty of all thoughts except what I was going to have for dinner. I turned left on Eighth, heading toward Webster. Just as I reached the intersection, the light turned red and I waited with a cluster of people who reflected the ethnic diversity of this part of town. To my right was a Hmong woman in her native dress, head wrapped in a colorful turban, and in front of me two middle-aged women speaking Chinese. The young people on my left looked Filipino, and so did the man on the opposite side of the street.

It was Alex Tongco, striding briskly across Eighth, wearing jeans and a polo shirt. I called out to him, but there was no way he could hear me over the Webster Street traffic. As the light changed and the walk signal flashed on, I saw Alex push open the door of a restaurant called the Lantern. I sidestepped the people in front of me and hurried across the street. If Alex was having dinner, I'd join him. After all that had happened in the last twenty-four hours, I could have used the company.

Inside the Lantern I told the waiter I was looking for a

friend. I stood in the doorway of the dining room and looked at the crowded tables, finally spotting Alex at a table near the back. But he had someone with him, an older man. Scratch that idea, I thought, ready to turn and leave the restaurant. Then a waiter stepped up to the table and both men turned so that I could see their faces.

I stood there, startled, as people eddied past me. For the second time that day I had entered a restaurant and found something unexpected. Alex's companion looked familiar. In fact, he looked like a man I'd met before. But it couldn't be. That man was dead. My father had found his body, attended his funeral, mourned his passing.

I moved through the dining room, staring at the man's profile, at the thick black hair threaded with silver. As the waiter stepped away from the table I took his place. "Hello, Alex."

Alex looked up at me, startled and then alarmed. "Jeri! What are you doing here?"

I looked from Alex to the older man who sat opposite him. "Aren't you going to introduce me to your uncle?"

Nineteen

ALEX'S MOUTH TIGHTENED AS HIS DINNER COMpanion stood. He was in his sixties, gray liberally salting his short black hair. As I approached the table, I thought he looked small and thin. I thought something else, too, but both my initial impressions were wrong. When he moved, I saw the rock-hard muscles on the wiry frame. He tilted his head to one side as he surveyed me with a spark of humor in his dark brown eyes. He knew what thought had passed through my head, as though he had seen it flicker to life and then die, and he was amused by it.

"Yes, Alex," he said, his voice clipped, his English slightly accented. "By all means, introduce us."

Alex got to his feet, slow to speak. "Jeri Howard, my uncle, Javier Manibusan."

"I thought so."

"But not at first," Javier said. He smiled as he took my hand in both of his. "The resemblance to my late brother is quite strong." He pulled out a third chair and signaled the waiter. "Please join us for dinner. We've just ordered."

I took the seat he indicated, waving away the menu the waiter offered as I asked him to add kung pao chicken to the food already ordered. When he departed, I glanced at Alex, still tight around the lips, and at Javier, who was enjoying his nephew's discomfort. Javier picked up the teapot and filled our cups.

"I'm a private investigator," I said. "Alex may have neglected to mention me. Alex leaves out a lot."

"My nephew does not care to broadcast his association

with me." Javier's dark eyes twinkled as a smile curved his lips. "I'm the black sheep of the family."

Alex kept his voice low so as not to attract the attention of other diners. "Do you realize what would happen to my security clearance if the navy found out about you?" From the look on his face I guessed that Javier's politics had moved from organizing sugar plantation workers to something more radical. At the fiesta I'd asked Alex if his uncle might be in the hills, toting a gun. I thought he'd been joking when he said he wouldn't be surprised. Now I wasn't so sure. Javier certainly looked fit enough to be a guerrilla, but given his age, I suspected his involvement was more of a leadership nature.

"You've explained it to me many times," Javier said, "though the internal workings of the United States Navy hold little interest for me. My only concern is that they remove their sailors from my country and turn the bases over to their rightful owners, the Philippine people. Of which you are one."

"I'm an American citizen. And I've worked damned hard to get where I am." Anger and pride burned in Alex's eyes. "In school here in the States, when I was fresh off the boat and the kids called me names and mocked my accent. And in the navy, where Filipinos were always stewards until after the war, because the brass didn't think we were smart enough to do anything but serve food. But I showed them. I came up through the ranks, from enlisted to officer, in spite of the prejudice and the attitudes and the bastards who called me Flip or slant-eye or gook."

"Why do you stay in an organization and a country where people denigrate you?" Javier retorted.

"It's no different in the civilian world. And it's no different in the Philippines, Uncle, where people from Manila look down at the peasants from the provinces, and the Muslims fight the Catholics. There will always be people calling other people ugly names."

Javier launched into a diatribe about the legacy of imperialism, and Alex struck the table with the flat of his hand.

The cutlery and glasses rattled. Several heads turned at the sound. "I'm in the navy because I want to be there. I'm proud of my accomplishments. It took me eighteen years to get my gold oak leaves, and I can go higher. Dammit, I can't risk letting you deep-six my career."

"Why do you see me, then?" Javier asked with a shrug, his mouth turning up at the corners. I realized he was amused by this verbal skirmish. "So we can have the same argument to spice our dinner? If you are so assimilated, why don't you disassociate yourself from me entirely? Or turn me in? But you can't do that. I'll tell you why. *Compadrazgo,* kinship. *Utang na loob,* honor. The ties of family and culture are too strong. You are a Filipino, no matter how Americanized you let yourself become."

Alex growled deep in his throat. I suspected they had been fighting this war of words for a long time, each without convincing the other. This particular battle was being conducted for my benefit, to delineate where each man stood. I looked from the navy officer, who fought his own internal conflict between duty and kin, to the ex-seminarian, who had found his religion in politics. I didn't see any chance that they would ever find a middle ground. But they were family, so they met to eat and argue.

Conversation stopped as the waiter returned with a plate of pot stickers. He set these in the middle of the table and left again. I picked up my chopsticks and speared one of the dumplings, turning to Javier. "Judging from what I've heard, I think you have something to do with the New People's Army." Alex winced at the words but didn't say anything.

"I am part of the revolution that has been evolving in my country for the past hundred years," Javier said, "loyal to the Philippines, opposed to those in power."

"Are you in the States illegally?"

"I don't think I'll answer that. I'll let your imagination run riot." Javier matched my smile with one of his own. He claimed one of the pot stickers and drizzled a spoonful of hot mustard over it before picking it up with his chopsticks. "Alex has mentioned you, Miss Howard. He tells me that several things have happened that may be related to my brother's murder. Until he told me this, I believed Lito to be the victim of a random street crime, killed for the contents of his wallet. Now I think it is something more.''

"I agree. I think it was personal. I need to find out why Dr. Manibusan was in San Francisco that night. I believe that information will lead me to whoever killed him. Why would your brother have an extensive file on Maximiliano Navarro?''

"*Pusa* the cat? I, too, have a large file on Max Navarro.'' Javier moved the pot stickers to one side as the waiter brought the rest of our dinner, making room for additional platters. "I consider him to be a dangerous man.''

"Why?''

"His first loyalty is to himself, a common malady among men in power.'' Javier spooned rice onto his plate and passed the bowl to me. "He switched his support from Marcos to Corazon Aquino only when it became clear that Marcos was about to fall. Now that the army has mounted several coup attempts against Cory, Navarro has decided to back another horse—himself. He's getting money from all the old Marcos connections, in the Philippines and here in the States. He wants to be a member of the oligarchy, and he'd make a bargain with the devil himself to do it.''

I paused, chopsticks poised over my plate. "The oligarchy?''

"The old men,'' Alex said as he helped himself to prawns and snow peas.

"Not just old men. The old families.'' Javier warmed to the subject while the food cooled on his plate. "For more than a century, all the power and wealth in the Philippines has been concentrated in the landowning families, about sixty of them. Cory's family, the Cojuangcos, are one such family. So, for that matter, are the Aquinos. And the Navarros aspire to be another. That is why Max chose his new bride, because of her family. Marcos diluted the power of the oligarchs, but now that he's gone, they've reestablished their hold. Nothing has changed. In some parts of the country these landowners act like feudal lords and they treat the people like chattel. The Navarro sugar plantation is an example. Max's eldest son, Jun, runs it like a private fiefdom. The conditions among the workers are appalling. But Jun and his hired guns have them cowed. He has a private army of vigilantes to terrorize the peasants.''

"Or protect them from your cronies," Alex challenged his uncle, pointing at him with his chopsticks.

Javier chuckled. "You know, Miss Howard, if you ask a dozen Filipinos for an opinion, you will get more than twelve answers.''

"I know that whatever happens in the Philippines reverberates all the way across the Pacific to the Bay Area. That much has become clear to me, if nothing else." I took another helping of kung pao chicken. "So Max Navarro wants to be one of the people who runs things, but he didn't originally come from a wealthy family.''

Javier shook his head. "No. But both his wives have been from the oligarchy. Navarro's grandfather was *mestizo*, like mine, a small farmer who lived outside of San Fernando. He and Max's father, Rufino, bought more land in the twenties and thirties, taking advantage of conditions that widened the gulf between the wealthy and the poor. Rufino Navarro became a very rich man before the war. He got even richer during the war.''

"How?" I asked.

"He collaborated with the Japanese," Javier said. "Most of the wealthy landowners did. They wanted to preserve their own power. It didn't matter to them who was in charge, imperial Japan or imperial America. Nothing happened to them afterward. MacArthur was more interested in rooting out suspected Communists than prosecuting collaborators. So the oligarchy remained in power and the people suffered. As they continue to do.''

"There's some link between Max Navarro and your brother," I told Javier. "So far I haven't made that connection. I just have a lot of threads that don't tie together. One of them is a man named Efren Villegas, evidently Max's cousin, who fought with Max Navarro in World War Two.''

Javier shook his head. ''I have my doubts about Navarro's war record.''

''You think he made it up out of whole cloth, like Marcos?''

''Perhaps. After all this time, who knows?'' The older man shrugged. ''Some of the resistance fighters were committed, organized, disciplined, like the Huks. The rest were a jumble of factions fighting each other as well as the Japanese. Who can say? The country was in chaos after liberation. Manila and other cities in ruins, and the rural areas a wasteland, people unable to feed themselves or grow crops. Maybe Max was a partisan, maybe not. World War Two was a long time ago, Miss Howard. Any historian, like Lito, can tell you that the truth is often obscured by time. And embroidered by those who participate in events. Look at how long Marcos was able to convince us, Filipinos and Americans alike, that he was a decorated war hero despite much evidence to the contrary. A lot of the partisans who fought the Japanese were motivated by things other than patriotism. In many cases they were settling old scores under cover of wartime.''

History is written by the winners. My father the history professor often quoted that statement, but I didn't recall who said it first. Dad was usually referring to the American Indians and the Old West, but the words would fit the situation in the Philippines as well as any other.

''As for this Villegas cousin,'' Javier was saying, ''I've never heard of him. But with our tradition of *compadrazgo*, we have many cousins.''

''Efren's grandson Eddie is the one who was trying to get Alex to give him the professor's papers. Just like Dolores Cruz, pretending to be Dr. Manibusan's widow, trying to get that envelope.''

''Can Miss Cruz be persuaded to explain herself?'' Javier asked.

"Not anymore," I said, pouring another round of tea. "She was murdered last night."

"Good God." Alex looked stunned. He'd been spooning rice onto his plate and now his hand stopped in midair. "Do the police have any suspects?"

"Not so far. They're still making up their minds about me." I rescued the rice bowl, which he was in danger of dropping, as I gave Alex and Javier an overview of the previous night's events. "I think Dolores Cruz knew who killed Dr. Manibusan. That envelope must contain something that proves it."

"You don't even know if she's the one who took it," Alex broke in, his voice grim. "What about Eddie Villegas, posing as a reporter? How do you know he didn't take the damned envelope?"

"He came to my office and threatened me. He was still looking for the envelope then. I think Dolly got it when she attacked my father earlier in the week."

"So Villegas killed her for it."

"I'd like to think so," I said. "But the police say he was somewhere else last night, with lots of witnesses. And I was standing over Dolly's body with the murder weapon in my hand."

"What's in this mysterious envelope?" Javier asked.

"I've never actually seen it, but Dad says it contains a microcassette and some folded sheets of paper. It's postmarked San Francisco, the day after Dr. Manibusan died." I ladled more kung pao chicken on my rice. "I found out something else. Until last fall, Dolores Cruz was Max Navarro's mistress."

"Dolores Rios," Javier said. "Of course. She was a singer."

"You knew her?"

"Knew of her. She was married to a man named Jimmy Rios, a popular singer. He was killed in a car accident. Then a few years later she took up with Navarro. He kept her in an apartment in Manila, very discreet while his first wife was still alive. After Mrs. Navarro's suicide he appeared in public with Mrs. Rios, as he called her. She disappeared from view several months before Navarro married his second wife. I think the last time Dolores Rios was seen with Max Navarro was in January, when Navarro was over here for that fund-raiser.''

''What fund-raiser?''

''Hector Guzman's fund-raiser,'' Javier said. ''A thousand dollars a plate, or so I hear.''

''Guzman, the real estate tycoon in Daly City? I know he's one of Max's financial backers. He's also in business with Sal Agoncillo and Rick Navarro.''

Javier nodded. ''Guzman's one of the old pro-Marcos crowd. He threw his support behind Navarro a year ago and he hosted a big fund-raising dinner for Navarro at the St. Francis Hotel in San Francisco.''

''I remember.'' Alex frowned as though he was trying to recall something. ''Lito told me about it.''

My interest quickened. ''When in January was this dinner?''

''I'm not sure of the date,'' Alex said. ''But I think it was a couple of weeks into the new year.'' He looked across the table at Javier, who shook his head.

''We can find out. There was a big article in the *Philippine News*. Navarro comes to the States several times a year and he always attracts press coverage, especially since he's made known his political ambitions.''

''Let me know the date as soon as you can.'' What if the fund-raising dinner had been the same night the professor was murdered? After Dad encountered Lito Manibusan in the Sutter-Stockton garage, they had walked together to the corner of Post and Powell. The St. Francis covered that block of San Francisco real estate bordered by Post, Powell, Geary, and Mason. Dr. Manibusan could very well have been going to the hotel. I considered the possibilities, but they still didn't give me any reasons. That link I sought between the history professor and the businessman-turned-candidate so far existed only as Jeri's hunch. Hunches don't prove anything.

The waiter cleared away the empty plates and brought a

small dish of fortune cookies. I broke one open and read the sentence on the strip of paper. "Society prepares the crime— the criminal commits it." I set the fortune aside and turned to Javier. "I'm curious about Dr. Manibusan's trip to the Philippines last August. He was planning to do research here, in the central valley, then suddenly he changed his mind and went to Manila instead. Did you see him while he was there?"

"Lito contacted me through an acquaintance at the University of the Philippines. We had dinner one evening shortly after he arrived."

"Did he say anything about his plans?"

"He'd been to see our sister Concepcion and her husband, Oscar." Javier rubbed his chin thoughtfully. "He visited the Pascals, his late wife's family. He planned to see friends at the university. And he said something about looking through the archives. He also said he had to go to San Fernando and San Ygnacio."

"As I look through the professor's files," I said, "World War Two keeps coming up."

"One of my brother's particular obsessions."

"Why an obsession?"

"Our father's death. The way he died. Lito was very young when it happened. I think it scarred him. He has few memories, so he collected mementos and studied the war."

"What do you remember about the occupation?"

"We were hungry all the time." Javier swallowed a mouthful of tea. "And I was terrified of the Japanese soldiers. We children tried to stay away from them. San Ygnacio was off the main road, just another little village in the cane fields. But it was close enough to the route of the Bataan Death March. We had an old uncle who lived along that road. He tried to give some rice to the American POWs. The Japanese soldiers beheaded him and burned his corpse." Javier's matter-of-fact tone underscored the horror of the long-ago atrocity. "Perhaps the fact that San Ygnacio was such a backwater explains how my father was able to survive as long as he did."

"Why do you say that? What was your father doing that would have brought him to the attention of the Japanese?"

"He was a teacher, educated by the Americans, an important man in the village. He had spoken out for land reform in the thirties, and that brought him under the scrutiny of the big landowners in that part of the province. During the occupation he had to walk a narrow line between appeasement and staying alive. That's a hard choice when soldiers stand with guns pointed at your head. Something my mother once said makes me believe he may have been collecting evidence against those who collaborated with the Japanese. The day he and those other men were killed, they had gone to San Fernando to meet with a priest."

"And on the way home the Japanese stragglers attacked them," I finished, repeating the story that Alex and Pete Pascal had told me.

"I'm not certain of that," Javier said, "and neither was Lito. Nor, I think, was my mother. Before she died, she told Lito and me that my father had been writing things down, but she didn't know what happened to these notes. She thinks that he gave them to the priest. And in the course of his research on the war, Lito had uncovered conflicting reports about partisans and stragglers in that part of Pampanga. It's easy enough to blame the Japanese. They were guilty of so many other atrocities. But who can say what really happened? Who can say who killed my father?"

So Dr. Manibusan's interest in World War II was personal as well as professional. That put a different point on the tack. I understood why the professor wanted to know every detail of his father's wartime death. What if that sudden trip to the Philippines had been precipitated by some new information about the San Ygnacio incident? That might explain why he canceled one research trip here in the States and scheduled another back in the Philippines. It might also explain why he'd made such an effort to find a World War II–era army nurse.

"What if . . ." I said aloud, then stopped as Javier and Alex looked at me curiously. "Those landowners your father antagonized in the thirties, was Rufino Navarro one of them?''

"Quite possibly," Javier said. "The Navarro plantation is to the north of San Ygnacio. Rufino kept increasing his acreage before the war, and Max has added to it since. Now its border stretches past San Ygnacio. Back then it would have been close to the village.''

People kill other people for many reasons. A child to protect a parent? I had only to look at my own response to the attack on my father to magnify the fury I had felt, and I knew the answer. Was it the answer I needed?

I looked across the table at Javier. "You mentioned *compadrazgo* and *utang na loob*. Alex explained *compadrazgo* to me. What does *utang na loob* mean?''

He bestowed on me his enigmatic smile. "*Utang na loob* is a debt of gratitude owed to someone who has done you a favor. It is a solemn obligation, one that supersedes all other debts you owe. A debt of honor, if you will. Or dishonor.''

Twenty

MRS. BEAUMONT DIDN'T SEEM PARTICULARLY EA-
ger to talk with me. Understandable, since the events of Friday night had put such a damper on her anniversary party. I
could sense her hesitation over the phone line, her reluctance
to involve herself further with anything as sordid as murder.
Besides, she didn't know what else she could possibly tell
me that she hadn't already told the police. I used my best
persuasion skills, and she finally relented.

"I have to pick up a few things on Piedmont Avenue,"
she said. "I'll meet you at Just Desserts."

I arrived several minutes before our agreed-on time of
three o'clock, eyeing a wicked-looking chocolate cheesecake
while I waited. I'm definitely a stress eater, and there's nothing like being on the scene of a murder to require lots of
calories with strong black coffee to wash them down.

I had already consumed plenty of coffee that Sunday morning at Dad's place in Castro Valley, where I cooked breakfast
for my father and tried to reassure him that the Oakland
police were not going to arrest me for murder. In between
all of this fatherly-daughterly dialogue, I questioned him
closely about Lito Manibusan, but he didn't remember his
friend talking about the death of his father and the other
villagers at San Ygnacio.

Mrs. Beaumont came through the front door of Just Desserts, wearing a pair of jade green slacks and a crisp flowered
shirt, sandals on her feet, and her gray-blond hair in artful
waves around her narrow face. She carried a slim shoulder
bag and several parcels. I stepped up to greet her.

"Mrs. Beaumont, I'm Jeri Howard."

"I know. I got a good look at you Friday night when the police escorted you out." She sighed and looked past me at the bakery cases. "I'm going to have something fattening."

"I'll join you," I said, succumbing to the cheesecake. We stepped up to the counter halfway down the narrow white-walled shop and ordered, then carried our coffee and plates to one of the tiny black-and-turquoise tables at the back. She set her parcels on an empty chair and looked at me with a mixture of exasperation and curiosity.

"I wanted my twenty-fifth anniversary to be memorable," she declared. "Being interviewed by homicide detectives is not what I had in mind. Especially with so many of Ned's business associates there. We'll be the talk of the office tomorrow."

"It's not my idea of a fun Friday night, either, Mrs. Beaumont. Just for the record, I didn't kill Dolores Cruz."

"I don't suppose you did, or the police would have you in jail. And I wouldn't be talking to you, either. I saw you in the lobby earlier, didn't I, when I came downstairs to give Oliver Barnwell my guest list?" As I confirmed this, she plunged a fork into her carrot cake.

"What can you tell me about Dolores Cruz?"

"What I told the police. Not much. I didn't know the woman. I just knew she was living in Mr. Randall's unit. She kept to herself, though I saw her in the building from time to time."

"How long was she there?"

Mrs. Beaumont thought about this for a moment. "Since February, I think. I knew Mr. Randall slightly, as a neighbor, and last year he mentioned that he had orders to go overseas. He said his brother and sister-in-law were going to take care of renting the condo while he was gone. The first tenant was there less than a year, moved out right before Christmas. The place was empty for a month or so. Then one day in February I saw Ms. Cruz unlocking the front door."

"Did she have visitors, anyone you may have seen more than once?"

She shook her head and took another bite of her carrot cake. "I'm afraid not," she said after washing it down with some coffee. "I'm in and out all the time, and I don't make a habit of keeping tabs on my neighbors. Besides, Ned and I went to Cancún for two weeks in March. When we returned, I was busy with my volunteer work. Then I went to visit my mother in April. I didn't really notice anything out of the ordinary."

"It would help if you'd tell me what happened as you got ready for your party Friday night, after I saw you in the lobby. You may have inadvertently seen something that could be important."

"Well," Mrs. Beaumont said, drawing out the word as she divided Friday night into segments. "The party started at eight. The florist had already been there. After he left I took the guest list down to the guard. That must have been about six or a little before. The catering people came at six-fifteen, on schedule, but the photographer was late."

"How late?" I interrupted.

"Past eight. I know because Ned's business partner and his wife showed up on the dot of eight, and the photographer wasn't there yet. I was a bit irked." She stabbed the cake with her fork. "Between seven and eight I was busy getting dressed and taking care of last-minute details. My son and some of his Stanford classmates arrived about seven-thirty, and I had to shoo them away from the food. The photographer finally got there and took pictures as we broke out the champagne and cut the cake. After that I just lost track of time, but I think almost everyone showed up between eight and nine. I'd like to help you, Ms. Howard, but I was attending to my guests. I didn't realize anything had happened until the police arrived."

"What firms did you use?" Mrs. Beaumont readily provided the names of the catering firm, florist, and photographer, but she balked at identifying any of her guests, pointing out that they'd been questioned by the police. I countered that those guests who had spilled out into the eighth-floor hallway could very well have seen someone entering Dolly's unit.

"They saw you," she retorted. "And if you're a suspect, you probably shouldn't be talking to them."

"The police haven't arrested me. If I were an investigator hired by an attorney defending a murder suspect, I'd be doing the same thing I'm doing now." Since I didn't have a prayer of getting my hands on that police report, I needed some names. Finally Mrs. Beaumont relented and gave me a few names. They were friends of her son, including the sandy-haired young man who found me at the murder scene. I suspected that Beaumont *fils* had been one of those in the hallway and she didn't want him involved further.

Mrs. Beaumont finished her carrot cake and departed with her shopping bags. I demolished the rest of my chocolate cheesecake and coffee, contemplating this whole case, which resembled the frayed end of a rope, with so many unruly strands to be tied together.

Oliver Barnwell was on duty at the Parkside Towers. He glowered at me as I came through the front door. It was he who had called the police Friday night. He had arrived a few steps behind the young man who found me standing over Dolly's body, and I knew he'd given the cops his version of my confrontation with the victim in the lobby of his building, a few hours before her demise.

"I don't have to talk to you," he said.

"I know you don't. But I didn't kill her." His eyes were skeptical as they raked over me, but my investigator's license heightened his interest. "You used to be a cop, right? Here in Oakland?" He confirmed this with an abrupt nod. "Do you think I'd be walking around loose if the OPD thought I was a suspect?"

"It only means they don't have enough to charge you," he pointed out.

"That's true. They don't have enough to charge me because I didn't kill Dolores Cruz. I'd sure as hell like to find out who did. Not only would it get me out of the frying pan, it would help me solve a case.''

He considered this for a moment, then nodded again. ''Okay. What do you want to know?''

I pulled a couple of photographs from my purse, pictures I'd taken out of Dr. Manibusan's file on the Navarro family. ''Have you seen either of these men here, perhaps visiting Ms. Cruz?''

He examined the faces of Rick and Max Navarro, then shook his head. ''No. She didn't have many visitors. Just Mr. Randall and his wife. I knew about them because Mr. Randall's brother owns that unit Ms. Cruz was living in.''

I put the photos back in my purse. Too bad it couldn't have been that easy. ''Let's talk about Friday night. I was here when Mrs. Beaumont brought you that list of people who would be attending the party. She told me most of the guests arrived between eight and nine. Did you check everyone on that list?'' He looked insulted. ''Look, I'm not suggesting that you didn't do your job. I just wondered if the killer got into the building through the front door.''

''I checked the name of everyone who was going to that party. Those that weren't on the list, I called upstairs. But there were a lot of people around that time. Some of them arrived in groups. It's possible,'' he conceded grudgingly, ''someone could have walked in while I was talking to somebody else. But everyone I remember seeing was either a tenant I recognized, or they were dressed fancy for that party.''

''The florist had already delivered the flowers. The catering people came while I was there. Did any of those people leave and return? And Mrs. Beaumont said the photographer was late. What do you remember about that?''

''I don't recall seeing any of the catering staff come through the lobby after they hauled all that stuff upstairs, at least not until the party broke up. They'd have been easy to spot, since they were in uniforms.'' He knotted his bushy gray eyebrows. ''Now, the photographer, she came in about twenty minutes after eight. I know Mrs. Beaumont was antsy about that, because she called down to the desk a little after eight to ask if I'd seen the photographer. So I kept my eye peeled. That's how I know the time.''

"The photographer was a woman?'' I asked. The name Mrs. Beaumont gave me was Espinosa Photography on Seventeenth Street here in Oakland. "Describe her.''

"Pretty young thing with dark hair in a braid.''

"You're sure about the braid?'' I interrupted.

"Yeah, about halfway down her back.''

"Was she tall or short? What was she wearing?''

"She was about your height,'' Barnwell said. I'm five eight, so that eliminated Felice Navarro. Besides, Felice's hair was too short for a braid. "She was wearing one of those long blue-jean skirts, with a blue shirt. She was carrying a camera bag.''

"What color was the camera bag?''

"I don't know. Tan or brown. I didn't get that good a look at it.'' He frowned, and his hands went to his shoulder. "I remember seeing a strap. But now I'm not sure if it was a camera bag, or just a camera.''

The camera bag seemed to be the only point on which Barnwell wavered. We went over Friday's events one more time, but he didn't have much to add to what he'd already told me. When I left, I gave him my card and asked him to call me if he remembered anything else.

Downtown Oakland seemed deserted this Sunday afternoon, quiet except for the occasional diesel roar of an AC Transit bus over on Broadway. In my office Dr. Manibusan's boxes summoned me. I wanted to see if I could find anything in his files concerning the fund-raising dinner Javier had mentioned last night, the one Hector Guzman had hosted for Max Navarro.

As I sorted through the folders, I found the one on World War II collaborators and pulled it out, my interest heightened by the discussion with Javier Manibusan. There were newspaper clippings, photocopies of articles, and references to the Karnow book that Alex had lent me. Benigno Aquino, Sr., father of the murdered Ninoy, had collaborated with the

Japanese, and so had Salvador Laurel's father, Jose Laurel, the latter acting as head of the puppet Philippine government set up by the Japanese invaders. Both men were nationalists, chafing at nearly forty years of American rule, and it was easy to see how they and others could have been seduced by Japanese promises of Filipino independence. But the Japanese were interested only in exploiting the people and resources of the Philippines for the Greater East Asia Co-Prosperity Sphere, and the brutality of the occupation soon turned most Filipinos against them.

I closed the collaborator file and returned it to the carton, looking instead for the folder on Maximiliano Navarro. When I found that one, I looked through it slowly, searching for information on the fund-raiser, something I must have missed on my earlier reading. Finally I spotted a short clipping from the *Philippine News* dated late last December. Max Navarro's name was in the headline and so was Guzman's.

I quickly read the article, feeling a surge of excitement. It mentioned Max Navarro's arrival in San Francisco, on a trip to visit his son Rick and his good friend and financial supporter Hector Guzman, who planned to host a dinner for Navarro on a Friday night in January, the same night Dr. Manibusan was killed. The thousand-dollar-a-plate extravaganza would be held at eight in the evening at the St. Francis Hotel.

I sat back and stared at the wall of my office. Dad and Dr. Manibusan met in the parking garage about a quarter after six that night, and according to the ticket stub found in the professor's car, he had entered the garage at 6:04 P.M. If my theory was correct, the professor had been going to see Max Navarro. It was just that, a theory with nothing to back it up. The crucial question—why—remained unanswered.

The phone rang and I reached for it. "Jeri, it's Alex." He sounded excited. "Javier says that fund-raiser was the same night Lito was killed."

"I know. I just found something in your uncle's files. Alex, would Nina have gone to that dinner with Rick?"

"Why do you want to know?" His voice grew cool, and

I could picture his face closing up the way it did when he didn't want to talk about something.

"I wonder if she saw Dr. Manibusan that night."

"She would have mentioned it," he said brusquely.

"You weren't on the best of terms. Still aren't. Nina knew your uncle, didn't she?"

"Of course. She'd met him many times. Look, Jeri, Nina and I hadn't talked in a long time, but she did send me a note when she heard Lito had been killed. The police were begging for witnesses, anyone who might have seen Lito that night. If she'd seen him, she would have mentioned it."

Unless something—or someone—intervened, I thought. "Maybe, maybe not. I'll ask her."

"You'd be wasting your time," he said, a stubborn note in his voice.

I wasn't so sure. Nina Agoncillo spent a lot of time with Rick Navarro, her future husband. It was a good bet that she had been at the St. Francis the night Lito Manibusan was killed. And if that was the case, I wanted to talk with her.

Twenty-one

AFTER THE SUNDAY AFTERNOON CALM OF OAK-
land, San Francisco was full of clamor and noise. I parked
my Toyota on the seventh floor of the Sutter-Stockton garage,
in the same section where Dad found Lito Manibusan's body.
Outside, I crossed Sutter and walked down the hill toward
Post. I cut diagonally through Union Square, where pigeons
crowded the pavement and panhandlers importuned me for
spare change. Ahead of me loomed the St. Francis Hotel, its
bulk stretching along Powell between Post and Geary. At
Powell I waited for the light to change. A cable car came
trundling up the hill, stuffed inside and out with tourists, its
clanging bell competing with the blaring horns of cars on the
congested city streets and a wailing siren somewhere in the
direction of the Tenderloin.

I entered the hotel through the revolving door, stepping
into the front lobby, and paused near one of the huge porcelain urns on either side of the door. Columns of greenish
black marble rose to an ivory and gold ceiling decorated with
rosettes. A chandelier hung over a round glass-topped par-
quet table in the center of the lobby. The vast floral arrangement of exotic tropical blooms overshadowed the backless
upholstered benches grouped around the table. All four of
the benches were occupied. I heard snatches of languages
ranging from English to Chinese as people streamed past me,
entering and exiting the hotel. To my left a preteen girl in a
lacy yellow dress squirmed on one of the high-backed chairs
against the wall, its seat too high for her short legs. In front
of her, a little blond boy of about six turned cartwheels on

the carpet, its plush length patterned in salmon, pink, and gray-green. The boy fell in mid-spin, blocking the path of a group of German tourists in shorts, T-shirts, and cameras. He was pulled to his feet by a slender silver-haired woman in a stylish red suit.

I wondered what chance I had of finding answers to my questions, of finding someone who had been here that night. I had added the snapshot of Dr. Manibusan to the photos of Max and Rick Navarro I'd shown to the security guard earlier that afternoon. The article in the *Philippine News* told me in which room Hector Guzman's dinner was to be held, but Dr. Manibusan hadn't been invited to that party. Besides, given the time his car entered the garage, I reasoned that the professor had approached the Navarros before they went upstairs to dinner, perhaps in the lobby, or in one of the bars. To my right was a sports bar called Dewey's, a small room crowded with tables, more suited to knocking back a few after work than a quiet drink before a fancy dinner. The bartender merely shook his head at my questions and barely glanced at the photographs.

I crossed the lobby to a shallow set of carpeted steps. They led to a bar called the Compass Rose, where afternoon tea was now being served to the accompaniment of piano, bass, and violin. I mounted the steps and stopped at the velvet rope, next to a large black-and-gold figure of a man in a turban, holding a goblet. This is more like it, I thought, looking around me. The bar had a rich, clubby ambience. I could picture the Navarros here. Fluted columns of oak rose from the floor to a ceiling paneled in dark wood, and a long bar, decorated at intervals with panels of blue and clear glass, stretched in front of the arched windows looking out onto Geary Street. The servers were dressed in red and black and gold clothing with a vaguely Russian look, gliding efficiently between pedestal tables and plush orangy red chairs full of customers.

"May I help you?" Poised at the rope was the hostess, a pretty young woman in a black dress, a mane of blond hair tumbling past her shoulders. I produced my business card and explained my mission. "You should talk to the manager," she said, pointing to a tall black man who stood at the bar, talking with the bartender.

I threaded my way through the tables and approached the manager. He listened to me with a thoughtful expression. "Chloe's the only person here today who might be able to help you," he said. "She usually works Friday nights, but she's filling in for someone today."

Chloe was a slender brunette in black pants and a gold tunic. The next time she came up to the bar to turn in a drink order, the manager introduced us. Her wide brown eyes examined the photographs one by one. Then she looked up at me. "I remember them. All three of them."

"You're sure?" I asked, scarcely believing my luck.

Chloe gave me an amused smile. "I always remember big tippers." She tapped a long rose-colored fingernail on the picture of Max Navarro. "This one in particular. Old Silver-Hair tossed a hundred-dollar bill on the table like he was used to lighting cigars with 'em. Pretty funny, when you consider he didn't order anything."

The bartender set three drinks on her tray and she tossed a "Be right back" over her shoulder as she moved away. I waited impatiently until she returned.

"I need to know what you saw, start to finish."

"It was about seven, maybe before. Four men and a woman."

"Describe the woman." Nina Agoncillo, I wondered, or Dolores Cruz?

"They were all Filipino. The woman was in her thirties, wearing a flashy off-the-shoulder red dress and lots of jewelry. I noticed a little scar right here." Chloe's fingers moved to her own face and traced the now-familiar line of the scar on Dolly's jaw. "They sat over there." I turned to look at a plush gold sofa backed by a reclining figurine. A pale yellow orchid in a basket decorated the black oval table in front of the sofa, which was now occupied by a trio of white-haired ladies having tea. "I take that back," Chloe was saying as she pointed to the photos of Max and Rick Navarro. "These two men and the woman sat. The younger men stood on either side of the sofa. They looked like bodyguards, if you know what I mean.''

I nodded. ''What happened?''

''Gotta deliver these and I'll be right back.'' She whirled off with another loaded drink tray and returned a moment later. ''Sorry. I think I can give you an uninterrupted minute now.'' She kicked off one shoe, flexed her foot, then slipped the shoe back on as she asked the bartender for a club soda. He set it in front of her and she picked it up, taking a long drink before resuming her tale.

''I walked up to take their order. Before I could say anything, this man came up.'' She pointed at the snapshot of Lito Manibusan. ''They started talking in their own language. I didn't understand a word, of course, but I could tell from the tone that the conversation had an edge to it. That's when Old Silver-Hair whipped out the hundred-dollar bill, tossed it on the table, and said they didn't want anything right then. Who am I to argue with a picture of Ben Franklin? But I kept my eye on them. I mean, the bodyguards, the foreign language, it made me curious.''

''Where was the woman?'' I asked.

''Silver-Hair must have told her to go to the powder room. He was the one who seemed to be in charge. Anyway, she got up and left the bar, and she didn't look too pleased about it. The two older men appeared to be arguing. Then all of a sudden this man''—she pointed at Dr. Manibusan's picture—''this man waved a piece of paper in Silver-Hair's face. I got distracted, and the next time I looked over there, Silver-Hair and the others were walking out, and the man who was waving the paper was sitting alone at the table.''

She stopped to drink some club soda. So Max and Rick Navarro had left the bar, taking their bodyguards with them. And the professor remained, to do what?

''I walked to the table to see if he wanted a drink,'' Chloe said. ''He looked like he could use it. He'd taken his handkerchief out of his pocket and he was mopping his face. He smiled and ordered a Coke. When I came back, he was addressing an envelope.''

"How big?" I interrupted.

"Oh, five by seven, brown, already stamped. Next to it were some folded papers and one of those little tape recorders. He popped it open and took out the tape, then he put the papers and the tape in the envelope and sealed it. Then he tucked the recorder into the inside of his suit jacket. While he was paying me for the Coke he asked if there was somewhere he could mail the envelope. I told him there's a letter drop in the first corridor off the lobby, opposite the elevators. He drank the Coke, then he left.''

"What about the woman? Did you see her again?"

Chloe thought for a moment. "I don't think so. No, wait. I did see a woman in a red dress standing at the rope. I'm almost sure it was her, looking for Old Silver-Hair and the rest.''

"Was this before or after the man with the envelope left?''

"I can't be sure.''

I thanked Chloe and walked toward the steps. At the velvet rope I stopped and turned, looking at the gold sofa and the black table in front of it. If Dolores Cruz had been standing here while Dr. Manibusan was still in the Compass Rose, she would have had a clear view of the table and the items on it. That could explain how Dolly knew about the envelope. But how had she known whom it was addressed to, or where to look for Dr. Manibusan's personal effects? She must have intercepted him before he mailed the envelope.

I went down the carpeted steps and crossed the lobby to the corridor that led to the hotel's Post Street entrance. Shops and ticket booths lined the hallway. The gold letter box was right where Chloe said it was, opposite a bank of elevators, its slot wide enough to accommodate the professor's envelope. The eye-level notice told me that mail dropped at this site during the evening was collected at 9:30 A.M. the following day. That accounted for the envelope's being postmarked the day after Dr. Manibusan's murder.

After retrieving my car from the garage, I drove west, out

to the avenues of the Richmond district. At the fiesta I'd overheard Nina Agoncillo telling Alex's aunts that she was living with her brother until her summer wedding to Rick Navarro. I knew where Sal Agoncillo lived from the business records on Kaibigan. The house was on Balboa Street, a few blocks north of Golden Gate Park, a pleasant residential neighborhood full of big old houses. It was late afternoon. Maybe I could catch Nina without Rick dancing in attendance.

A short, dark-haired woman in jeans and a knit shirt answered the Agoncillo front door. Nina's sister-in-law, I guessed. She told me Nina was home and left me standing on the porch for a few minutes. The door opened again, and Nina stood on the other side of the screen. Her black hair was down, cascading over her shoulders. She wore a silky dress the color of orange sherbet, and a frown.

"What do you want?"

"Just to talk. May I come in?"

"No." She glanced over her shoulder, and I saw her sister-in-law in the background. "I can't imagine what we would have to talk about."

"We could talk about what it feels like to be marrying into a rich, powerful family like the Navarros. Do you really think Max Navarro has a chance to be elected president of the Philippines?"

Nina tossed a few words over her shoulder. "It's all right, Teresa." She opened the screen door and stepped out onto the porch, folding her arms across the bodice of her dress. "Did you really come here to talk about politics?"

"Politics is a subject that keeps coming up. Your brother, for example, and Hector Guzman, now they're in the pro-Marcos camp."

She gave me a look that said I didn't understand the first thing about it. "Not necessarily pro-Marcos. Those days are gone. It's just that my brother believes that the present administration is doing nothing to solve the problems in the Philippines, and it's time for a change."

"Alex disagrees with you," I commented.

"I'd rather not talk about Alex, if you don't mind."

"Suit yourself. I'm more interested in Rick Navarro. You seem to go everywhere with him."

"Not everywhere. But we do spend a lot of time together. After all, we are engaged. In fact," she said, consulting a thin gold watch on her left wrist, "we're going out tonight. He's picking me up soon and I'm not quite ready. So I don't have much time to spend with you."

"Did you accompany Rick to that fund-raising dinner that Hector Guzman gave for Max? It was a Friday night in January."

"At the St. Francis?" She shrugged. "No, I went there with my brother and his wife. What has that got to do with anything?"

"I'm just trying to get an idea who was there. So you met them there, Rick and Max and Dolores." She looked surprised at my mention of that last name. "You knew Dolores, of course. Mrs. Rios."

"Max's friend." Nina's mouth tightened, and her voice cooled a few degrees. "Mistress, really. I gather she and Max had been involved for several years. Not that I approve, but it's none of my business. Having a mistress is common in the Philippines among men of Max's class. But Mrs. Rios is no longer in the picture. Max is married now."

"Yes, and I'm sure Antonia will grace the halls of Malacaañng Palace with a lot more style than Dolly would have—if the Navarros ever get there. Did you like her?"

Nina shrugged. "We had a rather brief acquaintance. That was the first time she accompanied Max on one of his trips to the States, and the last. Frankly, I thought she was rather crude. And she was extremely nosy, the type of person who listens at keyholes."

"Was she nosy that night at the St. Francis? When did you first see her, in the lobby or upstairs?" Nina blinked under my gaze, brown eyes darting away, out to the street, as though she wanted Rick to come rescue her.

"Why are you asking all these questions?" I kept silent,

hoping she would feel compelled to fill that void. ''I saw her in the lobby before we went upstairs.''

''We?''

''Sal, Teresa, and I had just arrived. Sal went to the men's room. Teresa and I waited for him near that big grandfather clock in the lobby, near the window of the jewelry shop. I saw Mrs. Rios coming down the stairs on the other side, from that bar, the Compass Rose. She was alone, and she had a secretive look on her face, as though she'd been spying on someone. Then I saw—'' She stopped abruptly.

''What else did you see, Nina? Or who else?'' She didn't answer. ''Someone you didn't expect to see? Someone you recognized?''

Her brows drew together and she frowned again. ''I saw Alex's uncle, the professor.''

''Dr. Manibusan. What was he doing?''

''He came out of the bar, too, at the same time as Mrs. Rios. In fact, he bumped into her at the bottom of the steps. He dropped something and she picked it up. She was flirting with him as she handed it to him, I could tell.''

''Did you speak to Dr. Manibusan?''

''I waved at him and he walked over to say hello. I hadn't seen him since last summer, and Alex had mentioned that he'd gone to Manila in August to do some research for a book.''

''Was Mrs. Rios listening to your conversation?''

''Of course,'' Nina said, twisting her mouth. ''Her ears pricked like a cat's and she followed him across the lobby, so I introduced them. Evidently he made quite an impression on her, because while he was there she went into her nosy act, trying to pry into his affairs. He answered a few of her questions just to be polite, but he was a very reserved man, and I could tell he didn't like talking with her. Finally he said he had an appointment to keep. After he left, she kept going on and on about what a charming man Dr. Manibusan was. She wanted me to tell her all about him. Was he married? Where did he work? Things like that.''

''And you answered those questions.''

"Just to get her off my back. I told her that he was a widower and that he taught at the university."

Perhaps more than that, I thought. The information Dolly had gained in this encounter had given her enough facts to toss around for verisimilitude when she decided to play her short-lived role of widow. "Did Dr. Manibusan do anything before he left?"

"No," Nina said impatiently. "Well, he mailed a letter near the elevators. A big envelope. He had to fold it and I held the slot open so he could get it through."

"Did you see who it was addressed to?"

"Someone named Howard. He said it was a colleague at the university." I waited to see if she'd make the connection between the names, but she didn't.

"Then where did the professor go?"

"I told you, he left," Nina said, her voice irritated. "He went off toward the side door."

"The Post Street entrance. Where was Rick during all this?"

"I thought he was upstairs, but he was there in the corridor just as the elevator doors opened, he and his friend Eddie. They said they'd forgotten something in the car and they had to go get it."

"Outside?" I asked. "It was raining, wasn't it? Were they wearing their coats?"

"Of course. Rick had on his topcoat. And Eddie was wearing his jacket."

"Which direction did they go?"

"To the left, I think."

"The same direction as the professor," I said. But the entrance to the St. Francis parking garage was located farther back in the hotel's lobby, beyond the corridor where the professor had mailed the envelope. It was quite possible that Rick Navarro had waited in the lobby for Dr. Manibusan, waited to see what the professor's next move would be, waited for Eddie the Knife so the two of them could eliminate the threat the professor posed to Max Navarro. "Was Dr. Manibusan still in the corridor?"

"I have no idea. It was all jumbled up at the same time."

"Was Rick wearing his coat when he joined you at the party? Did you see Eddie Villegas again?"

"No, Rick must have checked his coat. And no, I didn't see Eddie." She looked at her watch. "These are the most ludicrous questions. I don't see what they have to do with anything. I must go now. Rick will be here any minute, and I haven't done my hair."

"Did you know Dr. Manibusan was murdered that night?"

"I didn't find out until Rick and I got back from Hawaii. It was an impulse trip." She smiled at the memory. "He called me the morning after the dinner and suggested we go to Maui, just like that. We stayed for a week."

"So you never told the police you'd seen Dr. Manibusan?"

"Police? Why would I talk to the police?"

I wanted to shake her. "They were looking for witnesses who might have seen the professor the night he was killed. Didn't you tell anyone?"

"I told Rick the night of the party," she said, as if that explained everything. Perhaps it did. She had told Rick about the envelope as well. "It was a mugging, wasn't it? Rick didn't think my seeing Dr. Manibusan was important."

"I'll bet he didn't."

She made a move toward the door, but I halted her with a hand on her arm, shifting direction again, to a more immediate murder. "Were you out with the Navarros last Friday night?"

"Yes. We went to Postrio."

"What time did you get home?"

"Rick dropped me off early, just before nine, I think. I invited him in for coffee, but he said he had to get home." She pulled away from me and looked out to the street, where Rick's black Jaguar had pulled up to the curb. "There he is now," she said, relief in her voice at the prospect of imminent rescue. "You'll have to leave."

Rick Navarro looked less than pleased to see me standing on the Agoncillo front porch. He hurried up the sidewalk and steps, favoring Nina with a brief kiss before demanding, "What do you want?"

I smiled pleasantly. "I got what I came for. By the way, Dolores Cruz was murdered Friday night. You remember Dolly, don't you, Rick? The woman you told me you didn't know."

Twenty-two

MONDAY MORNING, FORTIFIED WITH COFFEE AND a bran muffin, I drove over the Bay Bridge to San Francisco and caught Roshan Singh at the cab company just as he was about to start his shift. He remembered picking up Efren Villegas outside Pacific Rim Imports last Monday, and told me he'd dropped off the old man at the corner of Twenty-fifth and Taraval in San Francisco, in the neighborhood known as the Sunset district.

"I think he lived nearby," Singh told me. "He said something like, 'I can walk from here.' "

"What did he do when he got out of the cab?"

Singh stroked his beard and thought for a moment. "I was pulled up to the curb near a fireplug. He got out and he went into a little grocery near the corner. That's all I remember."

Many of the little groceries in the City are owned by Arab-Americans, and the one on Taraval was no exception. The bespectacled man operating the register told me his name was Ibrahim. I described Efren Villegas as Ibrahim rang up an order for a Korean woman whose two boisterous offspring were threatening to topple a pyramid of oranges in the produce aisle.

"Oh, yeah, Mr. Villegas," he said as he took the woman's money and bagged her groceries. I waited as he made change. The woman and her children departed, reducing the noise level in the store. Ibrahim pushed his glasses up his nose and took a sip from an oversize coffee mug with a lid. "He's a regular, comes in for tobacco, bread, a quart of milk. Sometimes I deliver things to him when he's sick and can't go out.

211

The address? Just around the corner, Santiago Street near Twenty-sixth.''

Efren Villegas lived in a stucco row house, beige with brown shutters, its exterior in need of a paint job. A short driveway led to a garage tucked under the rest of the house and steps climbed to a minuscule porch and the front door. I rang the bell. After a moment I heard a click as someone opened the security peephole and looked out. He took his time making up his mind. Then he opened the door, the old man I'd seen with Max Navarro the past Monday, black eyes squinting at me through the screen door. He wore a pair of baggy brown pants and an equally capacious white short-sleeve shirt open at the neck, and a pair of brown leather slippers on his sockless feet. He said nothing, waiting for me to speak.

"Efren Villegas?" He nodded slowly. I smiled and hoped he didn't remember my being at Pacific Rim Imports as I went into a spiel about being a graduate history student. One of my history professors had told me that Mr. Villegas was a wealth of information about World War II, since he had fought as a partisan against the Japanese. The old man must have been over this route many times before, because he kept nodding.

"Which professor?" Villegas asked when I paused for breath. "From Berkeley or San Francisco State?"

"Dr. Lito Manibusan, at California State University in Hayward. He talked to you last November." I watched his face for any sign of alarm or wariness, but he merely nodded.

"Oh, yes. Filipino like me."

"May I come in?"

Villegas nodded and unlocked the screen door. I didn't see any evidence of a Mrs. Villegas as I walked into the narrow living room. The sofa was brown tweed, the upholstery worn through in several places. Magazines and newspapers were stacked haphazardly on the coffee table, and the TV set with its oversize screen had a layer of dust on top. On a small bookshelf near an overstuffed chair and ottoman I spotted some family photographs, one showing a younger

Mr. Villegas with a plump, round-faced woman. There were a lot of children and grandchildren pictures, but I didn't see any of Eddie.

Mr. Villegas had been having a cup of coffee and a cigarette with his San Francisco *Chronicle*. Cup, ashtray, and newspaper were arrayed on a round table in a dining area at the back. He offered me coffee and I accepted, watching as he went into the small kitchen to pour a cup. The back wall held a square, curtained window that looked down on a small backyard that was mostly vegetable garden. When my host returned with a cup and saucer, I got him talking about his garden first. He was loquacious on the subject of squash and tomatoes and seemed glad of my company and my interest. Having thus primed the pump, I moved the conversation in the direction I wanted.

Villegas was also from Pampanga Province, near the town of Malolos. I listened and took notes as he transported both of us back in time, telling me that he'd been working as a cane cutter on a sugar plantation when the Japanese invaded in December 1941. He smoked cigarette after cigarette from the battered pack next to his ashtray, detailing the cruelties of the Japanese occupation, describing how he'd escaped into the countryside and joined the partisans. What he told me had the ring of truth. It made me wonder about Javier Manibusan's more cynical view of the motivations of the guerrillas who fought the Japanese.

"Dr. Manibusan said you talked about an incident near the town of San Ygnacio," I said at a break in the conversation, "when some villagers were killed by Japanese stragglers."

At the mention of San Ygnacio, Villegas cocked his head to one side and looked at me steadily, without answering, as though he was suspicious of my motives in asking about the incident. He stubbed his cigarette out in the ashtray, then he spoke. "Such things happened often. The Japanese treated us Filipinos very badly."

"But your group was in San Ygnacio that day. That's why the professor asked you about it."

"Yes," Villegas said slowly, almost reluctantly. "We came upon the Japanese and chased them away, but we were too late to save those men. Three men, two of them dead already. We carried the third one into town, but he died."

"How many Japanese soldiers?"

"I don't remember. Six or seven, maybe." Villegas waved his hand. "It happened very fast. We came on them suddenly, and it was dusk."

"Who else was with you?" He looked at me as though he didn't understand my question. "Who commanded your group? Who was in charge of your unit?"

He didn't answer. Instead, he reached for his cigarettes. I sighed inwardly. I'd had enough passive smoke for one day. "My cousin," he began, reaching for his lighter. He didn't have a chance to finish. I heard the rapid thud of steps on the back stairs. The back door swung open, and Eddie the Knife burst into the kitchen, carrying a brown paper sack cradled in his left arm.

"Hey, Gramps, I brought you some groceries." Eddie stopped as he saw me and dropped the sack onto the nearest counter. He crossed the threshold from kitchen to dining room and grabbed my arm, hauling me to my feet. "What the hell are you doing here?"

The old man stood up and pulled Eddie's hand away from me, admonishing Eduardo in Tagalog. Then he stopped talking and stared at me as Eddie fired back in the same language. The younger Villegas stuck his face about three inches from mine. I didn't like the look in his eyes. "You got a lot of nerve coming here. You're dead meat, bitch."

"What are you going to do, Eddie? Knife me right here in front of your grandfather?" My words were full of bravado, but at the moment Eddie didn't look as though he was wrapped too tightly. People like that are dangerous. "I don't think the Navarros would approve, especially Cousin Max."

At the mention of Max Navarro, I saw something flicker in Efren Villegas's eyes. "You were about to tell me the name of your commander in the partisans. Was it your cousin, Max Navarro?"

"Me?" the old man said, shrugging. "I'm just a retired tailor. How would I know such an influential man?"

"I was at Pacific Rim Imports last Monday afternoon when you and Max Navarro returned from lunch. He gave you a white envelope before he introduced you to his new wife, Antonia, and sent you home in a cab. He said you were his cousin, that you fought together in the war."

Suddenly the old man looked frightened and confused as his eyes moved back and forth between me and his grandson. I almost felt sorry for him, and regret at having deceived him, but I had to get some answers. "What was in the envelope? Money? Is Max Navarro paying you for something? Your silence? Or that story you just told me?"

"You talk too much, Gramps," Eddie snarled. The knife came out of his back pocket so fast, I scarcely saw him move. I took a step back as the blade glittered, my eyes on Eddie, my hands reaching for something, anything, to block the expected thrust. But the old man moved quickly for one of his years, interjecting himself and a stream of Tagalog into the confrontation. Eddie hesitated. His grandfather spoke again, pushing away the hand that held the knife.

"Get out," Eddie snapped, his eyes raking over me, propelling me to the front door. "If I ever see you again, I'll kill you."

When I reached my car, I got in and locked the doors. It was hot with the windows rolled up, and my clothes reeked of cigarette smoke, but I felt chilled as I sat there for a moment, oblivious of the smell, my hands tight on the steering wheel, feeling protected by the glass and metal cage of my automobile.

I found out something, I thought, looking up at the Villegas house. But not enough.

Arthur Randall glared at me with undisguised hostility. "What are you, some kind of a ghoul, coming here and bothering us at a time like this?"

A Randall offspring had opened the front door of the family home in Daly City, a teenage boy who had his father's height and breadth along with his mother's brown eyes and black hair. When I identified myself, his father took his place, fiercely barring the door against my intrusion. For the second time that day, I was an unwelcome visitor.

"First you come prowling around our office," Randall was saying, "then you bring Immigration down on our heads. Now the police think you killed my sister-in-law."

"I didn't kill her, Mr. Randall. Are you interested in finding out who did?"

Perlita Randall joined her husband at the door, a diminutive figure in a plain black dress, her eyes reddened and puffy from tears. She looked at me with those eyes for a moment. Then she looked up at her husband. "Let her in, Art."

He started to argue, but she snapped off a phrase in Tagalog and he closed his mouth, giving me a poisonous look as he stepped aside for me to enter. I walked into a tiled foyer with a hallway to my left and a staircase in front of me. I followed Perlita Randall into the spacious living room, my feet sinking into deep, rust-colored carpet. She sat down on a long sofa upholstered in a chintz print that picked up the color of the carpet and the pale green of the wallpaper. On the coffee table in front of her, its wooden surface protected by an oval lace doily, I saw a cup of tea in a saucer and what looked like an oversize album with a brown leather cover, fat with photographs.

I looked around the living room for other pictures, and saw framed, enlarged snapshots on the fireplace mantel, Arthur and Perlita with a trio of teenage sons. All three of the boys, evidently kept home from school, poked their heads in through the kitchen doorway to stare at me. Their father barked a few words at them. The two younger siblings disappeared, but the kid who'd answered the door remained, catching my eye as though he wanted to tell me something. I returned his look, then turned my attention to his parents. Arthur had taken a protective position, standing over Perlita, who sat back on the sofa and put her hands in her lap, waiting for me to speak.

"What was her real name?" I asked.

"Dolores Monica Cruz." Perlita said the name slowly, as though she were tolling a bell. She sighed, and her voice cracked a bit as she continued. "She was my baby sister. There were seven years between us. We were from Olongapo, near Subic, the naval base. My father had a store. My brothers and sisters and I worked there, stocking the shelves and running the cash register. The sailors would come in to buy things. That's how I met my husband." He put a hand on her shoulder. She reached up and patted it.

I smiled and spoke in a quiet voice. "I don't think your sister was content to work in a store."

Perlita shook her head. "No. Dolly liked to sing and dance. She wanted to be famous, to go to Manila and sing in the clubs there. She would sing in the clubs in Olongapo. My father didn't like it. He was afraid of what would become of her." She stopped and took a deep, ragged breath, reaching for her teacup before she continued. Her hand shook a bit and the china cup chinked against the spoon resting on the saucer.

"Then Dolly met Jimmy Rios. He was well known in the Philippines since he made a couple of records. He came to Subic with a USO show that was visiting all the American bases. They needed backup singers, and Dolly went to audition. They hired her, and she went with them for the rest of the tour. When it was over, Dolly and Jimmy got married." Perlita sighed. "So she got to Manila after all."

I pointed at the oversize book on the coffee table. "Pictures of Dolly's career?"

Without a word Perlita picked up the album and handed it to me. It was heavy. I put it on my lap and opened it. A much younger Dolores Cruz stared up at me from a black-and-white publicity still. She must have been eighteen or nineteen when the photograph was taken, a pretty girl, tossing back shoulder-length black hair, her smile fresh and eager. Next to it was a poster for a nightclub in Olongapo, with Dolly's name midway down the list of acts.

I turned the pages slowly. The yellowed newspaper clippings were mostly in Tagalog, but I was able to follow the pattern of Dolly's career by looking at the pictures and publicity handbills. She had done well after marrying Jimmy Rios, touring with him between gigs at clubs in Manila, singing backup vocals on his records. The marriage and partnership flourished for several years. Then, six years ago, Rios was killed in a car accident, and his wife's career took a corresponding dive. She still worked the clubs in Manila, but evidently she wasn't the draw Jimmy had been. Later photographs showed an increasingly sophisticated look in her clothes and makeup. Her face held a shadow of weariness, the weariness we all get when we realize that life doesn't turn out exactly the way we think it should. Nowhere in the book did I see the Dolly Cruz I had encountered two weeks earlier at the university, the woman whose hard eyes held equal parts cunning and calculation as she tried to convince her audience that she was Lito Manibusan's widow.

I closed the cover on Perlita's collection of memories and put it back on the coffee table. "How did she meet Max Navarro?"

Perlita had been sipping her tea while I scanned the album, looking composed. Now she winced as she set the cup aside. "I'm not sure," she said. "We weren't as close, because of the age difference. When Art and I got married, she was still living at home and working in Papa's store. Then the navy transferred us to Pearl Harbor. My mother would write with all the family news, and send me these pictures and things to put into the book. Papa died ten years ago and Mama died the year after Jimmy, so the link was broken."

"Still, you must know something about the time she spent with Navarro. How did she meet him?"

Perlita didn't like to talk about this period of her sister's life; that much was plain. I let the silence stretch. Finally she spoke. "Dolly sang at a party. I think she met him there. They went out together several times. Next thing I heard was that he was paying all her bills, keeping her as his *querida* in a fancy apartment in Manila."

"How did he treat her?"

"How does a rich old man with a dying wife treat a mistress?'' Perlita asked bitterly, then answered her own question. "He kept her out of sight, but he bought her clothes and jewelry. She had a maid and her own car. She was tired and lonely after Jimmy died, having trouble with money. Navarro seduced her with his riches and his power. I think she believed he would marry her when his wife died. What a fool. She was just a shopkeeper's daughter from Olongapo. People like Maximiliano Navarro don't marry people like us. Besides, everyone knew Navarro had mistresses all the time he was married. His poor wife killed herself, but Navarro didn't marry my sister. He just kept her until he was tired of her, then he threw her away. At the very end she knew their relationship was over. She was . . . resigned to it, accepting it. But I know it hurt her. She was very angry when he married that rich widow.''

She stopped as though the effort of talking about this was more than she could handle. "Would you get me some more tea?'' she asked her husband, handing him the cup and saucer. He reluctantly abandoned his protective stance behind the sofa and walked briskly to the kitchen, returning a moment later with a fresh cup, the string and tag of a tea bag dangling over the rim. Perlita dunked the tea bag a couple of times, then fished it out, pressed it into the spoon and wrapped the string around the bag, squeezing out the last drop of moisture.

"How did Dolly know the relationship was over?'' I asked. "Is that why she decided to stay in the States?''

"She could read the signs, I think,'' Perlita said, nodding slowly as she sipped tea from her cup. "She and Navarro had been together for several years, and such things cool after a while. He never brought her to the States with him before, and I know he comes regularly, three or four times a year. We read about his comings and goings in the *Philippine News.*'' She set the cup down on the coffee table.

"This time Dolly came with him. She was excited about it, her first visit to the United States. They spent Christmas in Manila, then flew over a few days before the new year. He has a big house in Pacific Heights, in San Francisco, and

they stayed there. The first week in January Navarro had
some business to conduct in Los Angeles, so Dolly came to
stay with me for a week. She didn't come right out and say
it, but she hinted that it was over. I think she must have been
planning to stay all along, because she brought things with
her in a box made of sandalwood," Perlita said. "She left
the box here at the house. I thought at the time it was care-
lessness, but now I realize she intended to do it."

"What was in the box?"

"Keepsakes, pictures, some jewelry and papers, like her
birth and baptismal certificates."

"And her marriage certificate to Jimmy Rios," I added.
"She left them here for safekeeping."

Perlita nodded. "Yes, that must have been the reason.
Dolly telephoned me and said she would pick up these things
before she left for Manila. But the next time she came, she
had her luggage. She told me it was over between her and
Navarro. She said she was staying in the United States. Just
like that, on a tourist visa. I said, you can't do that, you have
to have a green card. She said that Navarro took care of it."

"Did he indeed?" So Max Navarro had the means to wave
his fingers and produce green cards. That was a piece of
news that would interest the Immigration and Naturalization
Service. Of course, people with lots of money can generally
buy almost anything. The fact that Navarro had set Dolly up
with her bogus documents probably meant that he—and his
son—knew where she was all along.

"How did she seem to be taking the breakup with Navarro?" I asked. "You did say she was angry when he re-
married."

"She seemed fine at first," Perlita said with a shrug.
"Resigned that it was over and determined to stay here and
make a go of it."

My eyes moved from Perlita's troubled face to that of her
husband, who had resumed his post behind her. "You gave
her a job at the travel agency and a place to live."

"Hell, she was family," Arthur Randall said gruffly. The
kind of family you had to tolerate because you married into

it, I suspected. From the way Arthur scowled, I figured he and Dolly hadn't meshed well. His situation had been made even worse because of Dolly's status as an illegal, leaving him open to fines from INS.

"We had a position open over in Oakland, and my brother's condo was vacant. It seemed like a solution. Except Dolly and Belinda didn't get along. They were at each other's throats all the time. And I thought Dolly seemed real tense. Like she was expecting something to happen. I put it down to her being nervous about Immigration. We all were. She'd overstayed her tourist visa and she was carrying a phony green card. I guess she knew I wasn't too pleased about the whole damn situation. But I went along with it, for Perlita's sake." He clamped his mouth shut in a grimace, and I knew he was wishing he hadn't.

"She was troubled by memories." Perlita smoothed a hand over the cover of the brown leather album. "Once, just after she got here, I found her looking through this book. She had such a sad look on her face."

"But she was angry when Navarro got married," I reminded them. Angry enough to plot some sort of revenge that would coincide with Navarro's expected trip to the Bay Area? "When was that? How did Dolly find out?"

"It was in the newspaper," Perlita said. "In April, just a month ago. She was here for dinner and she picked up a copy of the *Philippine News* lying right here on the coffee table. There was a story in the newspaper about Navarro getting married to that senator's widow, and it said she would be coming with him on his next trip to San Francisco. It made Dolly very angry. I thought she was jealous, but after the things she said about him when she decided to stay here, I knew she didn't care for him anymore. It seemed as though she wanted to get even with him."

How would Dolly Cruz, the discarded mistress, get even with Max Navarro, the rich and powerful businessman? After talking with Chloe yesterday at the St. Francis, I was sure she'd seen Dr. Manibusan with that microcassette recorder. Nina Agoncillo told me that Dolly had seen the professor mail the envelope. Maybe Dolly hadn't known what was in the envelope, but she could guess, particularly since she'd been present during the first part of Dr. Manibusan's confrontation with Max Navarro. What had the two men talked about? I was betting their conversation had something to do with the wartime deaths of those civilians at San Ygnacio, the incident that Efren Villegas described when I talked with him this morning. So Dolly waited, until news of Navarro's marriage set her off and triggered her search for Lito Manibusan's papers. But how did I prove this and tie all these disparate strands together?

Twenty-three

OUTSIDE THE RANDALL HOUSE I WAITED IN MY car as five, then ten minutes went by. I wondered if I'd misread the signs. Then a gate at the side of the house opened and the oldest Randall boy came loping out, wearing high-top sneakers and baggy patterned pants, a large skateboard under one arm. He threw it onto the driveway, put one foot on the board and pushed off with the other, his motions fluid as he skated out into the street, heading in the direction of the Westlake Shopping Center. I quickly made a U-turn and followed. When we reached the center he stopped outside a fast-food joint and used one foot to flip the skateboard into his waiting arms. As I pushed through the glass doors, I saw him at the counter. "Yo, Nick," some friends called from a bank of video games. He waved and ordered a double cheeseburger, large fries, and a chocolate shake.

"Let me get that, Nick," I said as he reached for his wallet.

He looked down at me with long-lashed brown eyes, a fifteen-year-old heartbreaker. "Yeah, okay, sure," he said, and grinned.

I ordered a diet soft drink and gave the girl at the counter a twenty. Nick tucked his skateboard under his arm, picked up the tray with one hand, and followed as I led him to a table in the corner. Once seated, he set upon his food as though he hadn't eaten in days, possibly weeks.

"You wanted to talk," I prompted him, swirling the ice in my cup.

"You're a private eye, huh?" I nodded. He was fascinated by my profession, and I answered several questions about that before he asked the big one. "You gonna try and find out who killed Aunt Dolly?"

"I'd like to."

"I hope you do. It's really bothering Mom." He put down his burger and reached for the fries.

"What can you tell me?"

"Aunt Dolly was here last Thursday night, the day before, you know . . ." He swirled a french fry through a glob of ketchup and popped it into his mouth. "She came over for dinner. Afterward I overheard her on the phone."

"Eavesdropping?"

He blushed. "I picked up the extension in the kitchen 'cuz I wanted to call this girl, you know. Aunt Dolly was on the phone in the bedroom."

"What did she say?" I waited for him to answer, but he was sucking noisily on the straw in his chocolate shake.

"She and this guy were talking in Tagalog," he continued. "I don't understand a lot of it. We speak English at home."

"Did they mention any names?"

He wrinkled his young forehead for a moment. "Yeah. She called him Enrique."

"Thank you, Nick." I saluted him with my soda.

"What for?"

"Never mind. Could you tell what they were talking about?"

Nick looked appropriately conspiratorial as he leaned toward me. "Aunt Dolly wanted some money, and this guy was jerking her around. I was gonna hang up the extension, but when I heard that, I kept listening."

I smiled. It seemed Dolly's nephew shared her nosiness. "What did Dolly have to exchange for this money?"

"She said she had a letter he was looking for. This Enrique wasn't interested at first, but she said something I'm not sure I heard right, about blood on his cuff. Or maybe it was his sleeve." Nick looked perplexed and shook his head. "See, could be I didn't understand that 'cuz they were talking in Tagalog.''

"But they did arrange to meet?''

"Yeah. I heard them talking about the lobby of the Hyatt, and I heard Aunt Dolly say something about Friday night. Then my mom came into the kitchen and I hung up the phone real quick.''

While Nick polished off the rest of his cheeseburger and fries, I considered this information. Nina Agoncillo told me that Rick and Eddie Villegas had left the St. Francis the night of the fund-raising dinner, evidently on the heels of Dr. Manibusan. Rick had been wearing his topcoat, but he didn't have it on the next time she saw him. She assumed he had checked it, but what if he'd ditched it? Because it had blood on it? I had a hunch Eddie the Knife actually killed the professor, but I recalled Inspector Cobb's theory that there were two assailants, one who held Dr. Manibusan's arms while the other stabbed him. Perhaps both men had searched the professor's body. Was that how Rick Navarro wound up with blood on his cuff? A splash of evidence that Dolly Cruz saw and filed away for future use?

If, as Perlita Randall told me, Max Navarro had provided Dolly with a green card so she could stay in the United States, it made sense to assume that the old man and Rick, his agent, knew where to find her. No doubt they knew all about Dolly's sister and brother-in-law, and the travel agency. Navarro may even have paid Dolly off, settling a sum of money on her as a consolation prize for being the discarded mistress. She wasn't considered a danger until she made a move against Max. The woman scorned had sharp teeth, and she intended to bite, but someone had killed her first.

Rick knew Dolly had the envelope, and that she'd guessed he had something to do with Dr. Manibusan's murder. So he'd agreed to meet her last Friday night. Given the jeopardy that Dolly's blackmail scheme had put her in, it didn't make sense that she would arrange to meet Rick Navarro at the place where she lived. Meeting him in the lobby of the Hyatt with witnesses all around was certainly safer. Which Hyatt?

There were two in downtown San Francisco and one in Oakland. But Dolly had been killed at the condo before she could meet Rick.

The Navarros had gone out to dinner that night, to Postrio, one of the City's trendy and expensive restaurants. Plenty of witnesses would attest to their presence. But yesterday Nina told me Rick had left her at home after dinner, around nine, refusing her invitation to come in for coffee. He would have had time, I thought, to cross the Bay Bridge to Oakland. Dolly was killed about nine-thirty. Had he somehow gained entrance to the Parkside Towers? The guard didn't remember seeing him. Unless the guard was mistaken.

Nick had reached the bottom of his chocolate shake, slurping up the last few drops through the straw. I offered to buy him another, but he shook his head. "Why didn't you tell your folks about listening in on your aunt Dolly's phone call? Or the police?"

"I bet I'd catch hell for eavesdropping," he said. "Besides, I wasn't sure if it was important. Is it a good clue?" He looked gratified as I confirmed this. "When the cops came to the house, I thought maybe it was one of those street things, like a mugging, or somebody was trying to rob Aunt Dolly or something like that. But Dad kept saying it was you that killed her, 'cuz you were there. But I don't believe you killed her."

"Thanks. I think I know who did. I hope I can prove it. What else can you tell me about your aunt?"

"Aunt Dolly, she was okay. Sometimes she was hard to get along with, you know. She could really get Dad going." He grinned. I'll just bet she could, I thought. "My folks were real nervous because Aunt Dolly was an illegal alien." He pronounced each syllable carefully, the term foreign to his own experience.

"You knew about that?"

"Shoot, yeah." Nick tossed his dark head and tried to look worldly and sophisticated. The effect was spoiled by his attempt to balance the red-and-white plastic straw, which he'd pulled from the cup, on the knuckles of his right hand.

"Dad was afraid *La Migra* was gonna come down on him. The green card was s'posed to be a big secret, but Aunt Dolly didn't treat it like one. She acted like it was a big joke. Laughed about it and said something about having the last word."

"Having the last word about what?" I asked, thinking of Dolly's relationship with Max Navarro.

Nick shrugged with teenage insouciance. "I dunno." Then he stopped playing with the straw and tilted his head to one side. "Wait a minute, I got that wrong. It was a place. She tore an ad out of the *Philippine News*, about a month ago."

"A place," I repeated, turning what Nick just told me over in my mind. The Last Word was a good name for a bar. Something else tugged at my mind. "Thanks, Nick. You've been a big help."

He blushed and looked at me from under his long dark lashes. "Yeah, well, I hate to see my mom so upset, crying all the time, you know. Like I said, Aunt Dolly was okay. But it was like she was mad at life," Nick said with a flash of insight. "She wanted to get back at it. Guess it got her instead."

That was a damned good guess, I thought as Nick and I parted outside the fast-food joint. He tossed his skateboard onto the pavement and set off, one sneakered foot providing the power. I walked to a nearby pay phone and leafed through the directory. There was a reason the phrase "the last word" sounded familiar. It was located on Mission Boulevard, a scant three blocks from the Daly City branch of Mabuhay Travel, a storefront word-processing service and copy shop with a sign in the window advising that a notary public was also available. I had passed it several times on my way to the travel agency. Dolly Cruz must have seen it, too, as well as the ad Nick mentioned. I suspected it provided other unadvertised services.

I pushed open the front door. A sign on the counter in front of me advertised business cards and stationery. Behind the counter I saw a bank of photocopying machines along the wall to my left, one of them thumping out copies with a noisy rhythm. The right side of the room held a couple of desks, some computer equipment and printers, and several filing cabinets.

Directly in front of me a young woman in tight blue jeans and a peach-colored T-shirt was perched on a stool, bent over a drafting table. She had long black hair piled untidily on top of her head, and a pair of long gold earrings dangled from her lobes like a spray of sparklers. Her face was screwed up with concentration as she worked on a poster, doing calligraphy with several different color pens. She looked up long enough to toss a smile at me and say, "Be with you in a minute."

"No hurry," I told her.

The copy machine stopped thumping. In the sudden silence I heard a radio somewhere, playing a bouncy dance tune. An older woman wearing thick-soled shoes and a shirtwaist dress plodded from the back of the shop to the copy machine. I don't think she saw me. As she picked up a stack of copies, she called over her shoulder, "So what happened, Carmen? You going to tell me, or do I drag it out of you?"

The woman at the drafting table set aside her calligraphy pen and hopped off the stool, pushing a strand of hair away from her face. The earrings swayed and glinted in the light. "Well, I thought he was gonna ax me out," she said in her high, clear voice, "but he got cold feet at the last minute."

At the copy machine the older woman laughed. "You'll just have to warm him up."

Carmen grinned as she approached the counter. "I don't think Eddie would like that."

"I'm going to deliver these." The older woman disappeared through the back door.

Now Carmen gave me a dazzling smile and her full attention. "I'm sorry to keep you waiting. May I help you?"

"You certainly may." I stepped behind the counter and walked to the drafting table, examining her handiwork. "Let's start by talking about that phone call you made a couple of weeks ago, to the History Department at Cal State Hayward. The one where you asked for Dr. Howard's home address. Did Eddie Villegas put you up to it?''

Carmen's mouth had opened, ready to protest my incursion to her side of the counter. Now it rounded into a startled O as I let fly another salvo. "You're good with the calligraphy. It's a real talent. Do your skills extend beyond posters? How about forgery? Green cards, visas, birth certificates, maybe even a marriage certificate?''

"I don't know what you're talking about," she stammered. Her hands fluttered, and she folded her arms across her chest.

"Sure you do." I rounded on her, with nothing to back up my suppositions except Carmen's eyes, which held the look of a wild thing caught in a trap, afraid of me—and afraid of others. "Dolores Cruz came in here about a month ago and asked you to duplicate a marriage certificate." Carmen clamped her mouth shut and shook her head rapidly from side to side. I leaned over her. She backed away until she could go no farther, hemmed in by computer equipment. "Talk to me, Carmen. This is serious. Dolores Cruz was killed Friday night. You could be an accessory to murder."

That word had the desired effect. Carmen's mouth flew open in protest as she grabbed a laser printer for support. "Murder? I don't know anything about a murder. She axed me to do the certificate, so I did. That's all."

"But you told Eddie Villegas about it. Eddie's a suspect."

Her hands went to her temples and she shook her head, fingers catching in the dangling earrings. "Oh, no. He couldn't have killed anyone Friday night. He was with me, at a party."

"Why did you tell him about Dolores Cruz?"

She looked at me for a moment, brows arched over her dark eyes, full of fear as she sought a way out of the snare. Confession is good for the soul—Carmen's, anyway. "I just mentioned it in passing. Because the name on the original certificate was Jimmy Rios. He was a big pop star back in the Philippines before he got killed in that car accident. I've still got a few of his records." She took a deep breath and plunged on. "When I said something about it to Eddie, he started axing me questions about her, like what she looked like, did she have a scar on her chin. I never noticed the scar till he axed me about it."

"What else did he want to know?"

"The stuff she wanted me to put on the marriage certificate. The name. It was Manibusan, I think. He said to let him know when she picked it up. Then a week later he axed me to make that phone call. I don't know why. I just did it as a favor to Eddie."

"And when I leave, you're going to call Eddie, aren't you?"

Carmen's earrings flew as she shook her head. "I won't, I swear. I'm not gonna tell anybody. I don't want to be involved in this."

I didn't believe her. She would be on the phone to Villegas as soon as I walked out that door.

It was past two when I got back to my office. I ignored my growling stomach and dug out the list I'd compiled a week ago, of businesses in San Francisco and San Mateo counties owned by Rick Navarro, Hector Guzman, and Sal Agoncillo, doing business as Kaibigan Inc. I found The Last Word, as I was sure I would. Dolly should have gone somewhere else for her forged marriage certificate, though I guessed she'd heard about The Last Word on some sort of illegal alien grapevine. Instead, she'd become further entangled in the Navarro net that led to her death. First Max Navarro provided Dolly with a green card, right out of thin air, and now I could link his son to a business where at least one document had been forged. At times it's quite true that where there is smoke, there's also fire. I'd let the feds sniff out this blaze. I picked up the phone and called Special Agent Campbell at the San Francisco office of the Immigration and Naturalization Service, giving her a terse rundown of what I'd learned.

That done, I left my office and walked to Espinosa Photography. The address Mrs. Beaumont had given me was on Seventeenth Street near Webster, a few blocks from my Franklin Street office. It was a small studio with wedding pictures and family portraits on the walls. The guard at the Parkside Towers had described Carla Espinosa fairly well. She was attractive, about my height, and she wore her dark brown hair in a braid that fell midway down the back of her plaid cotton dress.

She had been examining contact prints at a chest-level worktable when I interrupted her. Now she pulled up a chair and sat down, crossing one leg over the other and resting her hands on one knee, with her long fingers laced together. "It's about that murder over by the lake Friday night, isn't it? The police questioned me Saturday. What can I tell you?"

I leaned one elbow on the worktable. "I need to know what you were wearing and what time you arrived at the Parkside Towers."

"I got there about a quarter after eight," she said, tugging thoughtfully at the strand of wooden beads around her neck. "I remember, because I checked the clock in my car when I parked. I was late. Mrs. Beaumont was upset with me, but it couldn't be helped. I was delayed finishing another job up in Richmond. I came straight to Oakland from there. I was wearing a denim skirt, blue shirt, and flats. I had been planning to wear something spiffier, but I didn't have time to go home and change. Everyone at the party was so decked out, I felt a bit grubby."

"What kind of camera bag do you carry?"

"That one," she said, pointing to a scruffed brown leather square that had seen many years of service.

"You had it with you Friday night?"

"Yes. I always carry it."

I walked back to my office, stopping at a deli on Franklin, where I picked up a pastrami on rye and a couple of kosher dills. I turned things over in my head, feeling that I must have missed something. As I spread my lunch out on my desk, I played the messages on my answering machine. There was one from Oliver Barnwell, the guard at the Parkside Towers, asking me to call him. I picked up the phone and punched in the number.

"I was talking to one of my men," he said when I identified myself. "He was on the desk Saturday. He says a Filipino man showed up about noon, asking to see Ms. Cruz. Beat a hasty retreat when my man told him she was dead. I told the cops, and now I'm telling you."

"Description?" I asked.

"Young, stocky, had an accent. Sharp dresser." Rick Navarro, I thought. "Something else I wanted to tell you," Barnwell continued in his crisp voice. "I've been mulling it over, and I think the photographer was carrying just a camera, not a camera bag. You thought that was important, so I wanted to let you know."

Now I was perplexed. Carla Espinosa had just verified that she'd carried her camera bag up to the Beaumont party. Now the guard wasn't sure. Of course, he hadn't been certain when I spoke with him yesterday. Had he seen more than one person with cameras? Some of the guests? That was a possibility. I thanked Barnwell for his information and broke the connection. Then I picked up the phone again.

"You again," Mrs. Beaumont said when I called her. She sounded more resigned than exasperated. "Well, of course people brought cameras to the party. It was a celebration. Flashes were going off everywhere. Now, is there anything else, Ms. Howard?"

Something prodded at me as I opened the window to get some air circulating in my office. I stood for a moment, looking out at the girders of the half-constructed high-rise to the west. I turned from the window and grabbed a bottle of mineral water from the refrigerator. Setting it on my desk, I went to the filing cabinet and pulled out Dr. Manibusan's calendar, turning to that week last November where he'd made the notes about his appointment with Efren Villegas, where he had written "Sacramento" and "Potter—Paso Robles, San Luis Obispo." I had a collection of California phone directories on my bookshelf, not all of them current. I found a number of Potters in the two central California cities and began making calls.

It was a time-consuming process, netting me busy signals and phones that rang without being answered. In between calls I ate my pastrami and crunched bites of pickle, my fingers reeking of brine. I wished I had Dr. Manibusan's telephone bills for the last year, I thought as what remained of the afternoon moved toward evening. Those bills would have shown calls to the cities the professor had noted on his calendar. But I couldn't dig through the rest of the cartons, looking for them. I didn't have the luxury of time.

Just after six I found Mrs. Sally Potter at home in San Luis Obispo. "I do remember him," she said after I introduced myself and mentioned Dr. Manibusan. "He was trying to find some old neighbors of ours, Harold and Olivia Beddoes. We lived next door to them in San Francisco, way back in the fifties."

"Did they move to Sacramento?"

"Yes, in 1959. We exchanged letters and Christmas cards for a while. Then I lost track of them, I'm afraid."

"Do you have an address?"

"Yes, I dug it out for Dr. Manibusan." She set the phone down and went to find the old address book. "Vintage 1964, I think," Mrs. Potter told me. "But Harold Beddoes was self-employed. A painting contractor."

Probably long since retired, I thought. But maybe not. My Sacramento phone directory was just a year old. I looked under Painting Contractors in the Yellow Pages and found "Beddoes and Son." But it was now past working hours and I got the firm's answering machine. In the residential listings I found several prospects that could be Harold or Walter, or so their initials led me to believe. I picked up the phone again. The next hour was a replay of the search that had netted me Mrs. Potter. Wrong numbers, no answers, disconnect recordings—I got them all and I still hadn't found the right Beddoes.

It was like playing the slots at Reno and getting two cherries instead of the required three. I took a breather at seven-thirty, ready to call it a night and go home. But I decided to give it another half hour and reached for the phone.

Six calls later the cherries lined up.

Twenty-four

IF I THOUGHT THE BAY AREA HAD BEEN HOT THESE past few weeks, it was nothing compared to the central valley. The temperature inside my Toyota rose steadily as I drove northeast on Interstate 80, and opening the vents only admitted a rush of asphalt-heated air from the freeway. I stopped in Fairfield for the biggest container of iced tea I could buy, with plenty of ice. I reached for it constantly as I continued on through Vacaville and Davis, my clothes damp with sweat by the time I reached the outskirts of California's capital. The next time I bought a car, I vowed, it would have air-conditioning. I certainly spent enough time on the road to justify it.

The boy who had answered the phone the night before told me Olivia Cardiff Beddoes was his grandmother and that she lived with the family. But she was out to dinner with her son and daughter-in-law. I told him I was a private investigator who needed to speak to his grandmother most urgently. This impressed him enough to give me the family's address.

They lived south of central Sacramento, off Florin Road, in a pleasant, middle-class neighborhood with big lawns shaded by oak trees. I had left the Bay Area before seven, getting a jump on the morning rush-hour traffic, so it was about nine when I rang the bell at the front of the ranch-style home. I guessed that the children in the household had gone to school, but a Honda sedan was parked in the double driveway, next to a Chevy van with BEDDOES AND SON painted on the door.

Walter Beddoes answered the door, a tall man in tan coveralls, entering middle age, his blond hair receding and a worried expression in his blue eyes. He was considerably upset that his son had given out the family address over the phone, and both he and his wife had stayed home from work to greet me. Mrs. Beddoes, a head shorter than her husband, with a round pleasant face and dark hair above her blue linen suit, joined him as he peered at my investigator's license.

Beddoes had a frown on his squarish face as I told him why I was there. "I remember the professor," he said. "Seemed like a nice guy. He drove up here to see Mom last November. She's been interviewed a lot about her war experiences. I don't know that she likes to talk about it over and over again."

"This is really important, or I wouldn't have driven all the way up here from Oakland. I think your mother may have some information that would help solve the professor's murder."

The word "murder" got their attention. Beddoes and his wife exchanged glances. "He was very excited after he talked to her," Mrs. Beddoes said. "Something she told him triggered that. I guess if it's important . . ."

They opened the screen door and admitted me to their living room, leading the way through the kitchen and a sliding screen door that led to a covered patio with an oval table and matching chairs in white metal. A large rectangular barbecue grill stood on the far side of the patio, protected by a clear plastic cover. Walter Beddoes pointed me in the direction of his mother.

Olivia Mary Cardiff Beddoes, formerly of the United States Army Nurse Corps, sat at the far end of the patio on a cushioned chaise longue, a hardbound book open on her lap. Her morning coffee sat on a table at her elbow, next to a stack of books. She wore pale green cotton slacks with a matching shirt. A wide-brimmed straw hat covered her white hair. She looked up as I approached, her blue eyes bright and sharp behind a pair of thick-lensed glasses.

"You must be the private eye," she said cheerfully, pushing back the brim of her hat. Her voice had a pleasant crackle, still strong, like her personality. Her blue eyes surveyed me from a face like fine old parchment, shot through with tiny wrinkles.

"I wondered how long it would take you to clear the security checkpoint at the front door. My son's being protective. Though what he thinks he's protecting me from that I haven't already seen—" She shook her head. "Grab a chair, Miss Howard."

"Please call me Jeri." I pulled the chair close enough to examine the titles of the books on the table. They were all library edition mysteries, ranging from Marcia Muller to Susan Dunlap. She stuck a tasseled bookmark between the pages of the novel she was reading, closed it, and rested her hands on the book's plastic-encased dust jacket. I saw that it was Dick Francis's latest. I gestured at the book. "He's one of my favorites."

"Mine, too. And I *love* detective novels. Never thought I'd meet a real-life private eye. I'll bet you've got some stories to tell. But you didn't drive up here from Oakland to talk about yourself, Jeri."

"No, I didn't. I came to talk about Lito Manibusan." I told her about the professor's murder, how my own father found the body that night in January, and described how my search through the professor's files led me to this vital old woman. "I know you were an army nurse in the Philippines during World War Two, Mrs. Beddoes. Why did the professor come all the way to Sacramento to talk with you?"

She picked up her coffee cup and took a sip before she answered. "I was a prisoner of war."

"I thought it was something like that. It must have been terrible."

"I survived," she said, her old blue eyes suddenly steely. "A lot of people didn't."

As she set the coffee cup back on the table, the book slid off her lap, forgotten. I picked it up as she began to talk. She told her story in her own way, simply, as she had no doubt told it many times before, her spare words all the more powerful for the images they evoked.

"I grew up on a farm outside of Ford, Kansas. That's in the western part of the state, near Dodge City. I got a scholarship to nursing school in Wichita. When I graduated in 1938, there weren't any jobs. We were coming out of the Depression. Besides, I wanted to get out of Kansas. I'd been there all my life. So I joined the army. And where did they send me? Fort Bliss, down by El Paso. Desert and dust storms and heat. I might as well have stayed in Kansas." She chuckled.

"After that the Philippines sounded like a tropical paradise. And it was, Jeri, it was." Her smile became dreamy as she reached back into memory. "I arrived in the Philippines in January of 1941. I loved it. Manila was exciting, alive, a whirlwind of fun. When I think of Manila before the war, I remember balmy nights on the veranda at the Army and Navy Club, the scent of frangipani and bougainvillea, and Benny Goodman tunes floating on the breeze." She laughed at the memory. Then the smile left her face.

"Well, it was fun while it lasted. I was stationed at the post hospital on Corregidor. A friend and I had gone to Manila that first weekend in December. It was the Feast of the Immaculate Conception, I recall. The Japanese hit early the morning of December 8, about the same time they attacked Pearl Harbor and Guam. We were on the other side of the International Date Line, of course. Everyone knew it was coming, sooner or later. We should have been better prepared." She stopped and reached for her coffee. "I won't go into excruciating detail about things you can read in books. MacArthur declared Manila an open city and the American forces fell back to Bataan and Corregidor. The Japanese kept coming, relentless, attacking, bombing the island, finally wearing down our defenses. Corregidor surrendered on May 6, 1942, a month after Bataan."

Olivia Beddoes looked at me grimly over her coffee cup. "They sent the nurses to Santo Tomas, an old university on the north side of Manila. The Japanese turned it into a big POW camp, mostly civilians. We had a structure, an organization. I guess that's what kept us going for three years.

We were on short rations and we damn near starved to death. I remember the Filipinos throwing food to us over the walls, even when they didn't have much themselves. The Japanese shot those they caught. It was bad. But it wasn't as bad as Bataan.'' She didn't say anything for a long time. The word *Bataan* conjured up the Death March and its cost in human lives.

"We were liberated by the First Cav on February 3, 1945. The battle for Manila went on for another month. You've heard the term *scorched earth*? Well, the Manila I knew before the war was obliterated. God, what those poor civilians went through.'' She shook her head. "But you wanted to know what Dr. Manibusan and I talked about. And I'm getting to it.

"A couple of months after Manila was liberated, the army sent me home. Before I left I went up to Pampanga Province. It was a pilgrimage, I guess. Before the war I was engaged to a young army lieutenant. His name was Bill. I knew his unit had been at Bataan, but I didn't know what happened to him. After I got out of Santo Tomas I asked around. Finally I talked to someone who knew Bill. He died on the Death March, near the town of Lubao, in Pampanga. I had to go pay my respects, you see, before I left the Philippines for good.'' She closed her eyes for a moment, as though reliving that other lifetime had drained her strength. Then the blue eyes opened and she continued.

"What I did was very dangerous and foolhardy. The war was over in Europe, but not in the Philippines. The Japanese were still fighting on Luzon. But it was something I had to do. I found a couple of soldiers who had to make a run up to Clark Field. Lubao's just a little way off the main road, southeast of the provincial capital, San Fernando. They agreed to take me to Lubao. I found a church and lit a candle for Bill, even though I'm not Catholic. It helped.

"It was late afternoon. The soldiers were in a hurry to get to Clark. While they were waiting for me they'd found out about this shortcut up through the cane fields. So we took this road north. It was more like a track, really. The jeep broke down outside a little village called San Ygnacio."

"Dr. Manibusan's village," I said.

"Yes," Olivia Beddoes said. "He remembered the Americans in the jeep. He told me that's why he started looking for me. The people were wonderful. They fed us, though they had very little to offer, and several of the men helped the soldiers work on the jeep. Around dusk we heard shots. The people were afraid of Japanese stragglers. They said some Japanese had been seen west of there, just the week before. The two soldiers I was with went to investigate. They came back with some Filipino partisans and a wounded man. I did what I could, but he died before morning." Her hands, folded in her lap, now tightened into fists.

"What happened? Or do you know?"

"I know what I heard. My Tagalog was pretty good in those days. The leader of the partisans said several villagers had been ambushed by Japanese stragglers. Two men were killed outright. The third was the man I tried to save. His name was Carlos. I remember that because his wife was there, crying and saying his name over and over again."

"Something else made you remember," I said, "something Dr. Manibusan wanted to know."

She nodded. "Yes. Two things, really. During the night Carlos drifted in and out of consciousness, sometimes alert enough to hear what was being said. He kept saying something to his wife about a priest and an American. I don't know what he meant by that, because when the village priest showed up, Carlos pushed him away. Then, while the men were talking and I was treating his wounds, he kept trying to speak. Finally he reached up, grabbed the front of my shirt, and pulled me close so I could hear."

"What did he say?"

The Tagalog words rolled off her tongue as though etched permanently in her memory. *"Taong sinungaling. Mamamatay tao. Kolaborador."* I looked at her, waiting for a translation. "Liar. Killer. Collaborator."

I could guess what the dying man meant by those words.

The explanation he heard swirling around him was a lie told by those responsible for his death, who may have worked in collusion with the enemy. They were not merely words in a dictionary, but pejoratives that carried the stain of betrayal.

"If the attackers weren't Japanese, who were they?" I recalled Javier Manibusan's speculations about the San Ygnacio incident and his brother Lito's obsession with the manner of their father's death.

"I don't know. I wondered about those partisans. They were a rough-looking bunch. Some of those guerrillas were less interested in fighting the Japanese than they were in fighting each other and grabbing what they could get. All I know is somebody in that room was lying, Jeri. I'll never forget the look on that dying man's face as he hissed those words. The two soldiers and I argued about it the rest of the way to Clark. I thought maybe we hadn't gotten the whole story, but they were quite willing to accept the story about Japanese stragglers. They didn't hear what that man said, but I did. They didn't want to report the incident because of our unofficial side trip. I reported it anyway. I don't know if anything ever came of it, but Dr. Manibusan had a photocopy of my report."

"Did he?" That might explain one of the documents in the missing envelope. "I think the dying man was Carlos Manibusan, the professor's father," I told her.

She sighed heavily. "I remember several children hovering in the doorway. I wonder if one of them was Lito Manibusan."

"What was going on when Carlos spoke to you?"

"The leader of the partisans was talking. He was a young man. I noticed that because he was so much younger than the men he was leading."

"Can you describe him?"

"Short and stocky, with a squarish face and short black hair. He was dressed in fatigues, carrying a rifle. He looked tough and sure of himself. He took charge of things and didn't kowtow to anyone."

"Did anyone refer to him by name?"

"Dr. Manibusan asked me the same question," Olivia Beddoes said, "so the answer must be important. There were a lot of people in the room, all of them talking at once, it seemed. But one of the partisans called his leader by a nickname. Filipinos are very fond of nicknames. He called him *Pusa*. It means cat."

An appropriate nickname, I thought, for someone who always seemed to land on his feet, exactly the words Alex had used at the fiesta when we talked about Maximiliano Navarro. *Pusa*, the cat, who still had a commanding presence, though his short and stocky body had thickened and the black hair above his square face was now silver.

Twenty-five

MEN IN POWER DO NOT GIVE UP POWER EASILY. But they can be made to feel uncomfortable. I hoped I was having that effect on Maximiliano Navarro. But he gave no sign of discomfort as we strolled through the garden of the white stucco house on Vallejo Street in San Francisco's Pacific Heights. He seemed confident, affable, and mildly amused at my presumption in ringing his doorbell in the middle of this bright May afternoon. He must have been curious, though, or I wouldn't have gotten past the series of taciturn men in sunglasses and suits who guarded the door and seemed to accompany him everywhere. The same two men I'd seen with him last week at Pacific Rim Imports now shadowed our steps as Navarro and I walked along a flagstone path to the back of the garden, where a stone fence marked the perimeter of Navarro's property. We looked out at the view, a spectacular vista of the tree-covered Presidio and the Golden Gate Bridge beyond.

"You haven't said why you came, Miss Howard," he said, the afternoon sun glinting off his silver hair as he fingered the glossy leaves of a jade tree planted along the path.

"I came to offer my condolences on the death of a friend."

He raised his eyebrows, a polite question in his eyes and on his lips. "Which friend?"

"Dolores Cruz Rios."

"Ah." His blunt fingers found a dead twig on the jade tree and snapped it off. "Mrs. Rios and I had not been friends for quite some time. How did she die?"

"She was murdered."

243

"How regrettable." He didn't look like a man who regretted anything.

"She was killed Friday night. Where were you Friday night, Mr. Navarro?"

He laughed. "Surely you don't think I had anything to do with her death."

"Not directly. I'm just curious. I'll bet you were somewhere in public, with lots of witnesses."

"I was having dinner at Postrio, with my wife, my son, and his fiancée. And of course my staff was present." He indicated the bodyguards who stood on either side of us. "Does that satisfy your curiosity?"

"To a point. Let's talk about another Friday night, earlier this year, in January. Your friend Hector Guzman threw a party for you at the St. Francis Hotel. He invited a roomful of his rich friends so that you could discuss your burning desire to be president of the Philippines. The soiree was set to begin at eight o'clock. You and Rick and Dolly arrived at the hotel about seven. You went into the Compass Rose bar for a drink. But you were interrupted by Dr. Lito Manibusan."

Navarro left off his inspection of the jade tree and turned to me with emotionless black eyes. "I don't know anyone named Manibusan."

"I believe you met his father many years ago." I shot Navarro a hard look, wanting to see some kind of emotion in his eyes, but they remained blank. "Dr. Manibusan was a history professor at Cal State Hayward. He approached you after your party entered the Compass Rose bar. You and Rick and the professor sat and the bodyguards stood. Then you told Dolly to make herself scarce. You didn't order any drinks, but you and Dr. Manibusan had a rather heated conversation in Tagalog."

"Oh, was that his name?" Navarro said, not missing a beat. "Some man did accost us in the bar, but I don't recall his name. Why is this significant?"

"Dr. Manibusan was murdered shortly after he talked with you."

"Really? How distressing. The world is certainly a violent place, San Francisco as well as Manila."

He was really good at this, but then, he'd had years of practice. I fired a question at him. "What did you and the professor talk about?"

"He had some questions about my war record."

"He wanted to talk about the murders of three men outside the village of San Ygnacio in Pampanga Province in the spring of 1945." As I inched further and further out on this particular limb, I hoped that the subject would generate some sort of reaction from Navarro. But so far he remained impervious to the implied threat in my words, his square, pugnacious face untroubled by me or ghosts of the far or recent past.

He tilted his head to one side, and his face assumed a thoughtful mien. "I am from Pampanga Province. And my partisans fought the Japanese all over that area."

"Yes, I know. Dr. Manibusan had an extensive file on you. I've read it. And he had a personal interest in what happened in San Ygnacio. One of those men was his father."

"The one I'm supposed to have met?" Navarro asked, arching an eyebrow.

"Because you were there. You and your cousin Efren Villegas. I think Dr. Manibusan accused you of killing those men in San Ygnacio for personal reasons."

"I have killed no one," Navarro protested, raising his hands as if to ward off a blow. "Except during war, of course."

"*Taong sinungaling. Mamamatay tao. Kolaborador,*" I repeated, hoping I said the Tagalog words correctly. They had a sting to them, no matter how mangled my pronunciation. So did their English equivalents. "Liar. Killer. Collaborator. Your father was accused of collaborating with the Japanese during the war."

"Those charges were never proved," he protested.

"Maybe that's because the evidence was eliminated. Someone called you by those names a long time ago in a room in San Ygnacio. Lito Manibusan may even have seen you, though he was just a child at the time. He didn't know who you were then, just that you had a nickname. It's the same one you've carried ever since the war. *Pusa.* The cat. Cats are renowned for having nine lives, Mr. Navarro. But even cats run out of luck eventually.''

The bodyguards gave no indication they had heard anything. They might have been constructed of the same material as the stone fence before us. Navarro finally reacted, turning to give me a hard look, revealing the iron fist he so frequently muffled in a velvet glove. ''These are wild accusations you are making, Miss Howard. I wonder where on earth you came up with this ridiculous story.''

''It's the professor's story. And he had proof, some documents he waved under your nose. Something that threatens to torpedo your political aspirations. So Lito Manibusan was stabbed to death on the seventh floor of the Sutter-Stockton garage shortly after he talked with you.'' I jerked my chin in the direction of the veranda. Rick Navarro had just stepped through the back door of the house.

''You sent Rick and Eddie Villegas after him to get those documents. But they didn't succeed. The professor stuck everything in an envelope and mailed it before he left the hotel. And while Rick and Eddie were searching Dr. Manibusan, they found that empty microcassette recorder. The professor taped your conversation in the bar, Mr. Navarro. And I have a feeling you slipped up and said something incriminating.''

Max Navarro's silvery eyebrows drew together as he scowled, but his glare was not directed at me. It focused on Rick, walking rapidly toward us. Odd, I thought, looking from father to son. Something passed between them, swift as lightning, then was gone before I had time to interpret it.

''What are you doing here, bothering my father?'' Rick demanded, his voice sharp. Nothing indicated he'd heard me accuse him of murder.

''I think your father can take care of himself. He has for years. Anyone who gets in his way winds up dead, like those men in San Ygnacio. I know you and Eddie went after Dr. Manibusan that night. Nina saw you. So did Dolores

Cruz. And when you joined the party, Dolly saw blood on your cuff. She was holding that over your head as well as the envelope. You're responsible for Dolly's murder, Rick. I don't care how many people saw you at Postrio the night she was killed.''

"You cannot prove any of these ravings," Navarro said, dismissing me with a swift, cutting gesture. He barked a command at his bodyguards, and they moved to flank me. I was being thrown out. I had succeeded in making Max uncomfortable. But he was right. I couldn't prove any of it. Not until I got my hands on the contents of Dr. Manibusan's envelope.

As the two men with bulges under their arms deposited me in front of the Navarros' Pacific Heights palace, I thought about the look that had passed between Max and his son. Max was sure Rick had the envelope, certain that he had nothing to worry about. But I'd been watching Rick's face while I fired accusations at his father, and I had seen anxiety and a hint of desperation. Rick hadn't found the envelope either. Dolly had hidden the treasure well. It was still out there for the taking.

"I don't know what you think you're going to find," Belinda grumbled. "The cops have already been here."

After getting tossed out of Max Navarro's house, I sped back to my side of the bay, coming directly to the Oakland branch of Mabuhay Travel. Belinda and I were the only ones there at the moment, and she was periodically fielding phone calls. "Did they search the place?"

"Well, they looked around, but they didn't take the joint apart, if that's what you mean."

When I gave my statement to Griffin and Harris after Dolly's death, I didn't tell them about the envelope, so they wouldn't be looking for it either at the condo or at the travel agency. I told Belinda what I was searching for and she looked skeptical. "A brown envelope? We get dozens of brown envelopes every day. Besides, how do you know she didn't keep it at the condo?"

"Because whoever killed her was looking for it, and I don't think he found it there. I figure she hid it somewhere else. Next logical place—work."

"I'll help you," she said grudgingly, "but I've got work to do. And I close the office at six."

The clock Belinda indicated hung like a pointed reminder next to a poster of a Philippine beach, and it read a quarter to four. I set to work, going through Dolly's desk while Belinda looked through filing cabinets. She made slow progress, though. The phone kept ringing and she had to leave the cabinets and spend some time with a couple who wanted to go to Hong Kong.

Dolly's desk was full of the sort of debris that collects in drawers—paper clips, boxes of staples and file labels, scissors, letter opener, rubber bands, pencils, and pens with missing caps. There wasn't much that was personal. One drawer on the side of the desk held work-related files, and behind those I found a glossy fashion magazine and a month-old copy of the *Philippine News*. Another drawer yielded a couple of unpaid parking tickets on Charles Randall's white Thunderbird. The top drawer rattled with loose pencils and pens, rolling unchecked amid paper clips and rubber bands and bits of paper. I pulled out some of the papers. Yellow Post-it notes, pink phone-message slips, and some pasteboard bits. Only two were identifiable, half of a ticket from the Grand Lake Theatre, the movie palace down the street, and a parking stub from the Oakland Airport, dated last week.

"Nothing here," I said, turning from the desk.

"Likewise," Belinda said. She pulled out the bottom drawer of one of the filing cabinets and quickly rifled through the contents.

"Did she keep any personal items here at all?"

"We both kept some stuff on the shelf in the bathroom, like cosmetics, a hairbrush, toothpaste, and a toothbrush. Mine's in a straw basket, but Dolly kept hers in a red-and-yellow bag." Belinda straightened and stretched as the phone summoned her. "And there's a mug and some coffee back in the supply room. I drink decaf, but Dolly liked that heavy-duty stuff from Peet's.''

The bathroom was a cubicle on the right side of the hall-way near the travel agency's back entrance. I pushed open the door and switched on the light, surveying the amenities, which were basic. Stool and sink were the standard white porcelain, and the only other furnishing was the shelf that Belinda mentioned. I spotted Belinda's basket and the toiletry bag. The shelf also held several rolls of toilet paper, a box of facial tissues, and some cleaning supplies. I took the tissue box apart, my fingers searching for something that might have been tucked between the layers, then conducted a similar inspection of the toilet paper, finding nothing. The cleaning supplies didn't have anything hidden in them either.

I gave Belinda's basket a cursory inspection, then opened Dolly's bag of toiletries. There was nothing stuck in the lining, nor was there anything in the case but the items Belinda had mentioned. I dumped everything back into the bag and moved across the hallway to the supply room. There I found a small refrigerator next to a table that held a beat-up toaster oven, a drip coffee maker, and a roll of paper towels. Two mugs, rinsed out, sat with tops down on a neatly folded dish-towel. I opened the refrigerator and saw the remains of some-one's lunch and a quart of milk, slightly sour. Belinda's decaffeinated coffee was in a jar neatly labeled with her name. Next to it I saw a dark brown one-pound bag of Peet's 101 Blend, the industrial-strength stuff that takes paint off walls and sterilizes your coffee cup. Could Dolly have tucked the envelope or its contents into the bag? I reached for the coffee with one hand and the paper towels with the other.

''What are you doing? You're making a mess, that's what you're doing.'' Belinda folded her arms and looked exasperated as I scooped ground coffee out of the bag onto the paper towels I had spread out on the table. The supply room was redolent with the aroma. ''Just what do you expect to find?''

''At the moment I'm not doing anything but getting coffee under my fingernails.'' The bag was now half empty, and I probed the rest of the way with my fingers. If Dolly had stashed that microcassette in the coffee, surely she would have protected it by putting it in a plastic bag. But I didn't feel anything like plastic or paper. I touched the bottom of the bag. Then my finger encountered something metal.

"More towels." I waved at the roll, and Belinda tore off several sheets, spread them on the table, and stepped back as I dumped the rest of the coffee out of the bag. Then I lifted my prize up to the light, holding it by the numbered plastic end as I blew coffee dust off the metal surface.

Belinda looked at the object in my hand and shook her head in wonderment. "Of all the crazy places to hide something. It's a locker key. Like at the bus station."

"Or the airport," I said, remembering the parking stub in Dolly's desk.

Twenty-six

"SLOW DOWN," I TOLD ALEX AS I HUNCHED OVER my computer. "I didn't catch all of that." I raised one hand and brushed my damp hair off my forehead, then took a hit from my bottle of mineral water. Despite the open window, my office felt like a steam bath. The sun was melting in the west, over the buildings along the Oakland waterfront. I pulled the tail of my cotton shirt from the waistband of my slacks, fanning myself with the material. I hoped the evening fog was coming through the Golden Gate, its cooling mercy heading for the East Bay.

Alex switched off the recorder and reached for his beer bottle. After taking a long swallow, he ran the bottle over his face, then set it on the floor. He had one leg hitched over the arm of the chair in front of my desk and managed to look far cooler than I did. Maybe it was because he had unbuttoned his shirt halfway down his chest and was fanning himself with an empty file folder.

"Ready?" he asked. I nodded, shifting in my chair. He tossed the folder onto my desk, held the microcassette recorder up to his ear, and hit the play button. From where I sat I could hear nothing but the hum of my computer equipment, but earlier when I had played the tape the sound of voices speaking in Tagalog was discernible, even through the background noise of the Compass Rose bar.

"I think this is Rick Navarro talking," Alex said. "No, it's Max. Damn, they sound so much alike." He repeated the Tagalog words, then slowly translated them into English, pausing frequently as my fingers flew over the keyboard, transcribing the tape.

I had called Alex from the Oakland Airport after I found the locker where Dolly Cruz hid the envelope. She had stuffed it into a red and yellow cosmetic bag similar to the one at her office. I felt like a knight who had finally located the Holy Grail after a long and arduous quest. I stood in front of that locker, grinning, barely hearing the airline announcements being broadcast over the loudspeaker. Elation and exhilaration made my fingers tingle as I unzipped the bag and pulled out the envelope, its black handwritten address bearing Dad's name. Superimposed over a row of brightly colored stamps on the upper right-hand corner was a cancellation stamp dated the day after Lito's Manibusan's murder. Inside, I found half a dozen folded papers and the tiny cassette.

The documents were photocopies and two of them were in English. The first was Olivia Cardiff Beddoes's report of the incident in San Ygnacio. As I read through the second document, I understood what she hadn't that night long ago, when a dying Carlos Manibusan said something about an American and a priest. The sheets were dated May 1945 and signed by a U.S. Army intelligence officer stationed in San Fernando, Pampanga Province, the Philippines. In it, the officer detailed his interview with three men from San Ygnacio who had been accompanied to his office by a priest from San Fernando, Father Agustin. One of the men was Carlos Manibusan.

The men from San Ygnacio gave statements to the officer, evidence against a landowner named Rufino Navarro, who had collaborated with the Japanese during the war, specific incidents and dates that Carlos Manibusan had written in a notebook. He was reluctant to part with his notebook, but the officer told him the information must be verified. After much discussion, Father Agustin promised to return the notebook to San Ygnacio, and Carlos Manibusan gave it to the officer.

I suspected the army officer had not kept his end of the bargain, and that the information against Rufino Navarro had never been confirmed. But the priest kept his promise, though Carlos was dead by the time his notebook was returned. The third photocopied document was handwritten Tagalog. I'd seen that writing, faded blue on yellowed sheets, bound in an odd-shaped black notebook. It was tucked into a clear plastic bag, mingled in with Dr. Manibusan's World War II files. Perhaps Carlos Manibusan's widow had kept it all those years, finally giving it to her son, the professor. Its pages may have started as a schoolboy's exercises, but they ended as a record. He'd been murdered for the evidence it contained, just as his son had been murdered for further evidence of the same crimes. The irony in both cases was that the killer had not obtained what he sought.

As Alex translated the pages in Carlos's notebook, the story of Rufino Navarro's collaboration took shape, coming to vivid life when added to the voices on the tape Lito recorded the night of his own murder. The professor had waved these photocopies under the nose of the man responsible for his father's death.

"Son of a bitch, Jeri," Alex said, stopping the recorder. "You were right. Max tripped himself. He admitted it."

We had been listening to the tape over and over again for more than an hour. The conversation we transcribed revealed that the silver-haired, silver-tongued cat first denied Dr. Manibusan's accusation. Then, finally, inadvertently, he revealed his knowledge of the notebook's existence. The professor seized on that rent in the fabric of Max Navarro's story, tearing an even larger hole.

The transcript, the documents, and the notebook itself were full of dynamite, the kind of ammunition that could torpedo Maximiliano Navarro's ambitions to run for president. I was as cynical as the next person about politics, whether in the United States or the Philippines. After all, Marcos himself had been tried for murder back in the 1930s, and his war record, too, had been subject to question. But maybe the climate had changed. Maybe even the most jaded citizen would have second thoughts about voting for

Max Navarro, particularly if he could be linked to a more current murder in the Bay Area.

Alex shook his head. "Not a chance. It'll be business as usual. Max will weasel out of this."

"Maybe not. If we put this stuff into the right hands," I said, thinking of Javier as my printer spat out two copies of the transcript. "I like to think there's some justice in the world, even if it comes from unexpected places."

"I suppose that's why you do what you do." He came up behind me and put his arms around my waist. The sun was down now and a breeze finally found its way into my third-story window. It felt good, and so did Alex's embrace. "I'm coming with you," he said.

I shook my head. "No, you're not. I do a solo, Alex. I can take care of myself, and I don't want you involved in this."

"I'm a decorated veteran of the finest navy in the world. You're telling me I'd be in the way?"

"I'm the private investigator. And yes, you would."

I took the pages out of the printer and locked one copy in my filing cabinet, along with the rest of the evidence.

"Will you at least take a gun?"

"I'm better with my wits."

"But Max has all those bodyguards."

"I'm not going after Max, not directly. Rick is the weak link in this chain. My guess is that Max told Rick to tidy up this particular mess, and Rick blew it. Rick is running scared, and that means he can be had."

"It also means he can be dangerous," Alex pointed out.

I headed across the Bay Bridge with his admonition to be careful riding with me, the second copy of the transcript tucked into my purse. I had to choose my moment to talk with Rick, away from his father. It was a good bet that Nina Agoncillo would know where her fiancé was, even though she might not be willing to tell me directly, after the grilling I'd given her Sunday night. Before leaving my office I had called Salvador Agoncillo's house, pretending to be a friend of his sister's. Nina's sister-in-law answered the phone and, with a little prompting, told me Nina was having dinner with the Navarros.

When I reached San Francisco, I cut across town, my Toyota laboring up to the top of Vallejo Street. I parked across the street from the tall stucco mansion and waited. A yellow-gold light burned in the front window, diffused by the fog that lay like a shroud on the streets of Pacific Heights. Headlights loomed through the mist as a car approached the nearby intersection, then turned, heading down the steep slope toward the marina. Finally, about a quarter past ten I saw another set of headlights, this time in the driveway of the Navarro house. The car turned right onto Vallejo. It was Rick Navarro at the wheel of his sleek black Jaguar with Nina Agoncillo in the passenger seat.

I turned the ignition key on my Toyota and followed him as he turned right on Divisadero and right again on Jackson, heading west all the way to Arguello Boulevard. A left turn pointed the Jaguar south, toward Golden Gate Park. He was taking Nina home, I guessed, keeping an eye on my speed and the traffic as I tried to stay half a block behind the Jaguar, which purred along with more power than my four-cylinder basic transportation. At Geary Boulevard I sped through a yellow light as it turned red, not wanting to lose Rick. He turned right onto Balboa Street and made a quick right turn into the driveway of the Agoncillo home, just past Sixteenth Avenue. I parked on the same side of the street, a couple of houses this side of the Agoncillos.

Rick walked Nina to the front door. The porch light illuminated them as they spent several interminable minutes lip to lip, her arms wrapped around him under his jacket, his hands stroking first her shoulders, then down the sides of her dress and circling her waist. I waited until Nina went into the house and opened my car door, ready to nail Rick before he got back into the Jag. Then I hesitated as a San Francisco patrol car drove by slowly, making its rounds. The cop on the passenger side gave me the eye, wondering what I was doing sitting in a parked car in his neighborhood. By the time the patrol car passed, Rick Navarro was behind the wheel of his expensive Jaguar. The engine roared to life and he backed it out of the driveway. But he didn't retrace his route. Instead, he took Park Presidio Boulevard to Geary, a major east-west thoroughfare, and turned right. He was headed downtown rather than home, and that suited my purpose just as well.

I followed the Jag east toward the glittering skyscrapers, managing to keep Rick in sight despite the number of traffic lights. When he reached the Civic Center area, he headed for the South of Market district. He pulled the Jag into his parking space in front of Pacific Rim Imports on Townsend Street. I drove by slowly but kept going. This part of Townsend was deserted, and I didn't want to be noticed, at least not now. Ahead of me I saw the lights of a bar just past the corner of Townsend and Second, smeared around the edges by the fog, which was thicker down here on the city's waterfront. I parked close to the intersection and quickly made my way back to the brick facade of Pacific Rim. By now Rick had disappeared through the single door to the left of the big double doors that had been open the day I visited the warehouse.

I pulled a set of picks from my purse and checked the street for any watchers, but by now the ends of the block in either direction were obscured by fog. The door was locked, but it was just the spring lock rather than the dead bolt, so it was easy to gain access. I slipped inside, cringing first as the door creaked, then again as it shut with a click that seemed to reverberate around the walls of the warehouse. The center bank of fluorescent lights on the high ceiling were on, illuminating the main aisle between the tall wooden shelves. The light was on in the second-floor office at the back of the building. I could see part of Rick's office through the glass window that looked down on the warehouse, but Rick was nowhere in sight.

I walked quickly up the center aisle, then up the stairs, my hand reaching into my purse for the transcript. Slapping the papers onto his desk might be a trifle dramatic, I thought, but effective. As I stepped onto the landing, Rick heard me.

"Eddie?" he called. "Is that you?"

He was expecting Eddie the Knife, and soon. I didn't like that prospect, especially after seeing the crazy look in Eddie's eyes the day I visited his grandfather, as he threatened to kill me the next time he saw me. He was unpredictable and dangerous and his presence would change the equation. I was beginning to wish I'd brought my gun. Or even Alex.

It was too late for any of that now.

Twenty-seven

RICK'S OFFICE LOOKED THE SAME AS IT HAD WHEN I first visited it the previous week, with the big carved storyboard on its easel and the masks and fans decorating the walls. Rick was seated behind his big desk in the center of the room, in shirtsleeves, his jacket visible in the closet on the back wall. He faced the door in anticipation of Eddie's arrival. Now his eyes widened in his square face as he saw me walk through the door. I tossed the folded sheets of paper onto the desk. They slid across the smooth bare surface and came to rest at the base of the gold-framed photograph of Nina Agoncillo.

Rick tore his eyes away from me and stared at the papers. Then he reached for them as though he couldn't quite get his hands or arms to work. He unfolded the sheets and glanced at the pages, the paper crackling in his fingers. His eyes narrowed and his mouth tightened as he read.

"I think the transcript is fairly accurate, even though it's a translation. You can be the judge of that. After all, you were there."

"Where's the tape?" he asked, his voice rough. "And the documents?"

"The same place as the notebook. Locked away." I moved away from the door, taking a few steps to my right, glancing through the glass window down to the warehouse. I didn't want to be surprised by Eddie Villegas.

"I thought you had the envelope until this afternoon, when I was talking with your father. He's sure you have it, maybe because you told him everything was under control. Then I

258

saw the look on your face and I realized you didn't. It has a certain symmetry, doesn't it? Max and Efren Villegas murdered Carlos Manibusan to destroy evidence of Rufino's collaboration with the Japanese. And you and Eddie Villegas murdered Lito Manibusan to cover both crimes. But none of you will get away with it. The proof's still out there. All those ghosts are pointing fingers at you."

Rick refolded the papers and shoved them away. Then he sat back in his brown leather chair, his arms folded across his chest, chin down. I kept my eyes on his hands as I laid it out for him.

"Nina was very informative. Both she and Dolores Cruz were in the corridor near the elevators that night, and they both saw you and Eddie leaving the St. Francis right behind the professor. You followed Dr. Manibusan to the garage, you held him while Eddie stabbed him, then you searched his body. That's how you got blood on your cuff. Dolly saw it when you returned to the party."

Rick looked startled at my words, wondering how I knew. It was third-hand hearsay, but maybe the weight of what I knew and guessed would force an admission from him. "When you searched the professor's body, looking for the papers, you found that empty microcassette recorder. You knew the professor taped everything that was said in the bar. The documents were gone. But you had no idea what Dr. Manibusan did with them, until Nina mentioned that she'd seen Alex's uncle that night."

"Nina has nothing to do with this," he said heavily.

"Not directly. But she saw Dr. Manibusan mail the envelope. With a little prompting, she even told you who it was addressed to. Then you told her it wasn't important and whisked her off to Hawaii so she wouldn't talk to the police. From the newspaper accounts of the murder, you knew my father found the body and you connected his name with the name on the envelope. He didn't know what it contained, so you figured you could let it ride for a while. But you didn't figure Dolly Cruz into that equation." I shook my head, watching his brooding face. His eyes met mine, then quickly flicked away.

"Dolly decided that being paid off with a green card wasn't enough to salve her ego after being booted out of your father's bed to make room for the new and more socially presentable Mrs. Max Navarro," I continued.

"Hell hath no fury, and Dolly was no exception. She decided to enact a little revenge of her own and make some money in the process. She must have guessed how you got that bloodstain on your cuff. After all, she saw part of the confrontation in the bar, and she may have seen the professor with the recorder after you and your father left. She certainly saw the address on the envelope when she bumped into the professor in the lobby. That's how she knew where to look. Eventually she found it and started putting the screws to you and your father. She waited until your father was due to arrive on one of his regular inspection visits because you're particularly vulnerable when Max is around. He expects you to handle everything without mistakes and he doesn't tolerate failure well, does he?"

Rick's lips tightened, and he shifted in his chair. I figured I'd correctly summed up one aspect of his relationship with his father. "Dolly put on the pressure and you sent Eddie Villegas looking for the envelope, first at the university, then at my father's town house. But Dolly got there first, and she hid the evidence. That's why you didn't find it when you killed her."

"I didn't kill her," he said, bringing his head up to glare at me. He unfolded his arms and put his hands palmsdown on the desk, as though he were going to propel himself out of his chair. "I was out to dinner Friday night. With witnesses."

"You arranged to meet Dolly at the Hyatt on Friday. But you had no intention of keeping that appointment. Nina says you left the restaurant before nine o'clock and took her directly home. That gave you plenty of time to drive to Oakland and slip into the building with all the party guests."

"I tell you, I didn't kill her," Rick snarled. "We were

supposed to meet at the Hyatt in San Francisco, the one at the foot of Market Street. Ten o'clock. I waited. She didn't show. I went to the condo the next day. That's how I found out she was dead.''

I heard a door slam, the noise echoing around the warehouse. I glanced over my shoulder and saw Eddie the Knife moving quickly up the center aisle, headed for the stairs. When I turned back to face Rick Navarro, he was on his feet, one hand in a side drawer of his desk. He pulled out a gun and pointed it at me.

I shook my head and rearranged my face into a calm facade, masking the disquiet I felt at looking down the barrel of his gun. ''That solves nothing.''

''It buys me some time.'' He moved to his right, around the end of the desk, in front of the glass case that held the Hawaiian feathered cape.

Eddie thumped up the stairs and appeared in the doorway, eyes moving swiftly from Rick and the gun to me, assessing the situation.

''She's got everything,'' Rick told him.

Eddie's glare was full of venom. ''I told you I'd kill you. I should have done it that day you busted in on my grandfather.'' He looked over at Rick. ''What do we do now?''

''We're going to take a ride over to Oakland, to Miss Howard's office. After we get what we want, you can do whatever you like with her.''

Eddie grinned. He liked that idea. His right hand moved to his back pocket and he pulled out the knife. With a click the blade jumped out and glittered in the light. ''Come along, bitch,'' he said, waving it at me.

''What makes you think it's in my office?''

''I think you can be persuaded to tell us where it is,'' Rick said, glancing at the knife Eddie held.

''And what if I made more than one copy?'' I gestured at the papers on Rick's desk.

''And gave them to whoever translated the tape?'' Rick smiled contemptuously. ''Alex Tongco, perhaps? I'll take care of him later.''

"You always seem to be taking care of things for your father," I taunted him, "though lately you don't do it very well. Is that your function in life? How does it feel, being the cat's paw?"

I touched a nerve, for now Rick's face darkened with anger. "Get her out of here," he told Eddie. "We'll take your car."

Eddie beckoned with his knife. I walked slowly toward him, watching Rick as he turned and pulled his jacket from its hanger in the closet. He set the gun down on his desk in order to put it on. As I passed the white and gold ceramic elephant near the doorway where Eddie stood, my left hand shot out and seized the areca palm around its thick stem, heaving it up so that I wielded plant and pot like a mace. I swung the clay pot directly at Eddie and felt a satisfying thud as it caught him between the chest and neck. He fell onto the landing, knife clattering out of his hand.

By the time Rick grabbed the gun from the desk, I had leapt over Eddie's prone figure. Rick fired at me, the slug slamming into the wall as I took the stairs two at a time. As I reached the central aisle of the import warehouse, Rick was on the stairs, shouting to Eddie, who was back on his feet and swearing. I darted to my right, into one of the middle aisles, dodging behind a forklift. The shelves next to me held stacks of woven baskets, and I peered through them, glimpsing Rick and Eddie as they conferred at the bottom of the stairs. The fluorescent lights glinted off the dull metal of Rick's gun and showed me the blade of Eddie's knife. They split up, each heading toward the outer wall of the warehouse, hoping to circle me before I could get to the door or the phone on the wall near the double front doors, the one Rick had used to call a cab for Efren Villegas.

I backed away from the shelf and stumbled against the forklift. Someone had left a coffee mug on the seat, and now I swore under my breath as I caught it before it could fall. I held it in my hand for a second, then I moved quickly to the center aisle and threw the mug toward the stairs. It shattered on the concrete floor.

I heard running feet in two directions, converging on the spot where I'd thrown the mug. Through the baskets I saw Eddie Villegas in the aisle next to mine. I whirled and ran toward the outer wall, listening to their voices as they shouted in Tagalog. Someone ran down the center aisle toward the front doors. It was dark in this part of the warehouse, and I banged my shin against a wooden crate left in the middle of the passageway.

I peered down each aisle, getting past two with no sign of either of my pursuers. When I peered into the third, I saw one of the movable metal staircases, and, beyond it, Rick Navarro at the opposite side of the building. He shouted to Eddie. I heard steps to my left as Rick ran toward the center aisle. Eddie rounded the corner, the knife in his hand making a vicious circle like the head of a snake. The shelf in front of me held stone carvings and brass trays of varying sizes. I grabbed a tray, using it as a shield as Eddie struck, his knife glancing off the metal surface.

Rick shoved his way past the metal staircase, gun in hand, but he didn't fire. He needed me alive, so I could lead him to the evidence he was trying so hard to destroy. Eddie had no such compunctions. He wanted to kill me. He struck at me again, and again I deflected the knife with the tray. Then I seized a stone carving and hurled it at him as I reached for another. He dodged the first, but the second hit him on the chest and he staggered backward. Rick had circled in back of me and now he grabbed my shoulder. I turned and hit his right arm with the brass tray I still held, stamping on his foot as I grabbed for the gun. He twisted it out of my grasp.

I ran toward the center aisle, but before I could get there, Eddie appeared at the end. I detoured up the tall metal stairs and clambered onto the top shelf some twenty feet above the concrete floor. I looked around. The broad wooden shelf was cluttered with the painted elephants I had seen the workmen unloading the other day. They were about two feet high, in green and blue and yellow ceramic with gold and silver accents glimmering in the light from the fixtures above. I picked up one, deciding it was heavy enough to do some damage.

Eddie was halfway up the metal stairs when I hurled the elephant over the edge. His arms went up reflexively as he tried to cover his head. The elephant caught him on the shoulder and knocked him all the way to the floor. When I looked down at his motionless figure lying amid the chunks of broken ceramic, I wondered if I'd killed him.

I didn't have long to entertain the thought. Rick Navarro had reconsidered using his gun. I ducked out of range as he brought it up and fired at me, then I shoved a few more elephants over the side and he retreated toward the outer wall. How was I going to get down from this perch? I gauged the distance from this shelf to the next. There were two shelves between me and the front door of the warehouse, between me and the phone. I saw the cable I'd seen on my first visit to the warehouse hanging from the ceiling just beyond that last shelf. Maybe I could slide down it to the floor. Of course, I still had to neutralize Rick.

I launched myself across the space and gained the top of the next shelf, knocking several big woven baskets to the floor and alerting Rick that I was on the move. "You're not going to get out of here," he called from the aisle below.

"I wouldn't bet on it." I looked at the next shelf. Carved wooden boxes, stacked neatly together in rows about three feet high. I didn't see any toe room at all, at least not on this end of the shelf. I made my way slowly down the shelf that held the baskets, looking for a foothold in the boxes on the next shelf.

"I swear to you I haven't killed anyone. You can't prove that I did."

"Tell me another story, Rick."

"Maybe we can make some kind of arrangement. Why don't you come down here and we'll talk about it."

"With you holding a gun? Don't make me laugh." As long as he was talking, I could guess where he was. Of course, he was doing the same, following my progress as I rustled through the baskets. He was quiet for a moment, then I heard a different series of sounds. I couldn't place them at first, then I realized he was rolling another metal staircase into position at the end of the shelf, where I stood. Baskets didn't provide as much cover as brass trays. I saw bare wood at the end of the shelf that held the wooden boxes and jumped for it just as Rick's head and shoulders appeared at the top, and he fired.

I knelt behind the inadequate shelter of the boxes. On my left I spotted the cable dangling from one of the overhead supports, tantalizing me as it led down the floor in front of that telephone. I could have reached it if I climbed over the rows of wooden boxes that paved the shelf. I raised my head just enough to see Rick, still crouched at the top of the staircase, waiting for me to break cover. I had to get the boxes out of my way, and I had to move fast.

I quickly shoved boxes over the edge of the shelf, clearing a path toward the cable. Rick heard the clatter as wood rained down on the aisle below. His head disappeared from view as he ducked down the stairs to the center aisle. I seized the cable and swung out over empty air, sliding down, scraping skin off my palms. I landed hard on the concrete floor below, the force of my descent dropping me to my knees. I leapt to my feet, reaching for anything I could use as a weapon. I spotted a crowbar leaning against an unopened crate as Rick rounded the corner from the center aisle, his gun raised.

I brought the crowbar down on his right arm. He cried out as the gun slipped from his grasp. I followed the first blow with a second across his kneecaps. He dropped to the floor, screaming in pain. I picked up the gun and leveled it at him as I reached for the phone.

"Don't move. Don't even think about it."

Twenty-eight

I HAD A LOT OF TIME TO THINK DOWN AT THE HALL of Justice. After I took him out with the crowbar, Rick Navarro needed medical treatment, so the police hauled him off in an ambulance, along with Eddie Villegas, still breathing in spite of the elephant. I spent the next couple of hours laying out the details to Inspector Cobb and his partner, who were chary of my involvement but glad to finally move Lito Manibusan's murder out of the unsolved column. At two in the morning they put me in the custody of two more officers. The three of us took a swift surrealistic trip over the Bay Bridge in an unmarked police car to collect the tape, the documents, and Carlos Manibusan's notebook.

They finally let me go at a quarter to seven that morning. I saw Maximiliano Navarro as I was leaving. He was grim-faced as he walked quickly through the front door of the Hall, his bodyguards on either side. He fixed me with a hard, implacable look that made me think it might be a good idea to postpone any plans I had to visit Manila. I stared right back at him all the same, and the cat blinked. Then he moved on, his bodyguards shouldering a path through a group of reporters, photographers, and TV types toting minicams. They were all shouting questions at him, on the scent of a story, an intriguing one about the arrests of a small-time San Francisco hood and the son of a Philippine presidential candidate charged with the murder of a college professor and the attempted murder of a private investigator.

I drove back to Oakland, toward the sun already risen above the East Bay hills, a golden sunburst like the one on the Philippine flag. My mind struggled past the fatigue that threatened to consume me. Now that one death had been explained, I could consider the other, examining what I knew and what I guessed. There were some things I should have realized before, things that people said that I should have interpreted in a different way. When you look at something so long and so hard, trying to make the pieces fit together, sometimes it's easy to miss that one little piece that fits somewhere else, maybe even in a different puzzle.

The adrenaline rush that had carried me through the events at the import warehouse had disappeared several hours before, plunging me into a pit of exhaustion. More than anything in the world, I wanted to go home and feed my cat, fall into bed, and sleep all day. But I couldn't do that yet. I had one more stop to make.

She was awake despite the early hour. She answered the door, wearing one of the jumpsuits she favored, this one yellow, as bright as the morning sun. The red camera bag and a tripod were stacked near the front door. "You're lucky you caught me," she said. "I'm going up to Sonoma County on a shoot."

"You're not going anywhere, Felice."

Her eyes widened into black pools, but without surprise, as though my presence were somehow inevitable. "Did you want to talk about something?" she asked, words slow as she backed away from the door.

"Let's talk about Dolores Cruz. You really hated her, didn't you? Almost as much as you hate your father."

She turned abruptly, walking toward the back of her house as I shut the door behind me. I followed her into the kitchen, where a pot of coffee sat on the counter, waiting to be poured into a thermos. She went out onto the enclosed back porch and looked around her. I wondered if she was looking for a way out, a way to avoid the words that had to be said. I got between her and the door leading out to her garden, but she made no move to run. It was as though she realized there was no exit, no escape.

"You hated Dolly for ensnaring your father at a time when

your mother was ill and needed him. Then your mother killed herself, and you blamed both of them. It may not be logical, but that's the way you felt. Then Dolly made a pass at your husband at a family dinner one night in Manila. You went after her and put that scar on her chin. But that's not the whole story. Your hate has been festering for a long time.''

She sat down on the flowered cushion of the rattan chair as though weighted with the force of my words.

''Max treated you like part of the furniture, didn't he? Even the fact that you're an accomplished photographer meant nothing to him. He wanted to establish a Navarro dynasty. Your only value to him was as a pawn, a female child to be married off, to form an alliance with another rich family. But you have an independent streak. You refused to marry the man he wanted, and eloped with an American instead. When I was here before, you told me that as far as your father was concerned, you don't exist. They say that negative attention is better than none at all. I guess he'll have to notice you now.''

Felice tilted her head up at me as I stood over her. In her lap her hands clenched and unclenched.

''Murder is as negative as it gets. Before I call the police, I want to sort out some details. Like why you picked this particular time to kill Dolly. You didn't know she was in the United States until I asked you if you knew anyone named Dolores Cruz and so conveniently described her to you, right down to the scar. How did you know where she lived?''

''I knew she had a sister and brother-in-law who ran a travel agency,'' Felice said, her voice a thin reed. ''I made phone calls, I found out where she worked. Then I followed her to that building on Lakeside.''

That made sense, I thought, recalling the words Dolly hurled at me when I confronted her in the lobby the night she was killed. She said I'd been following her, and I had. But when I thought about who else might be following her, my candidates were Rick Navarro and Eddie Villegas, not Felice.

''You must have walked into the building right after the

photographer who came to take pictures of the Beaumont party. You saw her, and that's what gave you the idea. I thought the guard was confused or distracted. He said the photographer was a dark-haired woman, but he wasn't sure whether she was carrying a camera bag or a camera. And I was so certain Rick killed Dolly that I didn't show the guard your picture. What happened after you went upstairs? I imagine Dolly was surprised to see you.''

"It was an accident. I didn't mean to—"

"Yes, you did," I said roughly. "I saw the body, and the blood splattered on the wall. I imagine it took only a couple of blows to kill her, but you kept hitting her with that candlestick over and over again. You must have been covered with blood. So you went into the bathroom and washed yourself off. You took the rubber gloves and a sponge from under the sink and wiped everything you'd touched. I figure you grabbed a coat from Dolly's closet to cover up the bloodstains on your clothes. You were just about to leave, when I walked into that condo. You had your camera. You hit me with it. That flash of light I saw really was a flash. You put the gloves back on and wrapped my hand around that candlestick. I know how, Felice, I just want to know why.''

"I didn't plan it," she cried, anguish and something else on her face. "It just happened.''

"The hell it did. You went there to kill her.''

"The greedy bitch," Felice said. "She poisoned everything she touched, everyone she met.''

I shook my head wearily. Blaming the victim is always a convenient strategy where murder is concerned. But Felice would always hate the woman who had been her father's mistress when her mother committed suicide. "So it's Dolly's fault that you killed her?''

"My father paid her off when he threw her out, with money and a green card so she could stay in the United States. Better if she'd gone back to Manila or whatever cesspool she crawled out of, but she wanted more.''

"How did you know that?''

"When I saw Rick last week, he seemed worried, preoccupied. When I asked him why, he finally told me. He said Dolly had turned up, threatening to make a scandal that would hurt Max. She wanted more money.''

''What else did Rick tell you?''

''Just that there were some important papers in an envelope. Papers that would embarrass Max.''

''You hate your father. Why should you care if Dolly made a scandal?''

''I didn't.'' Felice's mouth twisted. ''When Dolly answered the door, she was surprised to see me. She said she was meeting Rick later. I told her Rick couldn't keep their appointment, and I was there as his emissary. It didn't matter to her. She just wanted money in exchange for the envelope. But I didn't do it to protect Max. I wanted to use it to get back at him. For the way he treated me, the way he treated my mother. I will anyway. Imagine the headlines. Presidential candidate's daughter arrested for murder.''

I didn't tell Felice that her brother was playing out the same role of murder suspect over in San Francisco. She was only half right about Dolores Cruz. Dolly was greedy, but she and Felice both shared the desire to get even with Max Navarro for real or imagined sins, just as Lito Manibusan wanted justice for the death of his father. All three of them had succeeded, though at a cost each had not imagined. Maximiliano Navarro was the sort of man who engendered that kind of passion. Now the headlines Felice spoke of were being written. Max Navarro's chickens were coming home to roost, a whole flock of them.

I reached for the phone for the second time in eight hours, wondering when I would ever get a chance to sleep.

Twenty-nine

"NO MORE NIGHTMARES?" I ASKED MY FATHER AF-
ter he'd fixed dinner for me. We were in the living room of
his town house, cups of coffee in hand. It was the night after
Felice Navarro was arrested for the murder of Dolores Cruz,
and her brother and his accomplice for the murder of Lito
Manibusan. The newspapers and local TV were full of the
story, and I'd been ignoring calls from reporters for the past
thirty-six hours.

He looked at me from his favorite chair, green eyes
shielded by blue-gray plastic. He had a new pair of glasses
to replace those broken last week when Dolly pushed him
down the stairs at Cal State Hayward and stole his briefcase.
This new color made his face look subtly different. His
sprained wrist was still wrapped, but the bruise on his left
side was fading and he could walk without a limp.

"Nightmares," Dad said with a smile, clarifying and
qualifying as professors will. "I had a few bad dreams right
after I found Lito's body, but they went away. Let's just say
that when all of this most recent stuff cropped up, my sleep
was a bit uneasy."

I kicked off my shoes and stretched out my legs on the
sofa, taking a sip of my coffee before setting it on the end
table. My sleep had been troubled, too. I didn't think I'd ever
forget the sight of Dolly's body. The reminder of violent
death also underscored the preciousness of life.

"Max Navarro has a lot of clout," I told him. "On both
sides of the Pacific Ocean. I don't think he'll use it to help
Felice. He doesn't care about her. She didn't wipe Dolly's

condo down as carefully as she thought. The police found her prints in the bathroom. Besides, she's confessed to Dolly's murder. The evidence against Rick Navarro and Eddie Villegas is circumstantial, although Inspector Cobb says the police talked to the staff at the St. Francis who worked the Navarro banquet that night. Turns out a busboy saw Rick Navarro in the men's room, washing blood off his cuff. Cobb's hoping Eddie will turn on Rick, but I don't think that will happen. Not if I understand what's meant by *compadrazgo* and *utang na loob*. Kinship and debts, all tangled together, reaching back years." I picked up my coffee cup. "I guess I'll let SFPD and the D.A. worry about making their case, and take comfort in all the bad press Max is getting."

My father smiled and shifted in his chair. "I had a nice long talk with your mother. I assured her that my aches and pains were diminishing and I even explained that it was I who involved you in a murder case, not the other way around. She'd like it if you'd come to Monterey for a visit. You haven't been down in a while."

"I know," I said, hiding behind the coffee cup. "I'll schedule a weekend soon."

Dad nodded. "So, what about this young man you've been seeing, Lito's nephew Alex? I met him at the funeral, but I don't remember him. Have we got a romance in the offing?"

"Hey, I've already got one mother," I protested, "and she quizzes me plenty." I got to my feet and headed in the direction of the kitchen. "Do you want a refill on coffee?"

He nodded and handed me his cup. In the kitchen, as I poured coffee, I reflected that I was avoiding the question. I didn't know what was going on between Alex and me, except that I was fixing dinner for him on Saturday night. That was a wait-and-see situation. I returned to the living room and handed Dad his cup. Then, on impulse, I leaned forward and kissed him on the top of the head. "What was that for?" he said with a grin.

"General purposes, of a fatherly-daughterly nature."

* * *

Abigail stalked across the living room carpet. She leapt up onto the sofa and deposited the yellow mouse in my lap. Then she sat back and looked pleased with herself.

"Thank you so much," I told her, stroking the top of her head as she purred with a loud rumble. With my other hand I picked up the fuzzy yarn corpse, soggy where the cat had held it in her mouth. Holding it by its tail, I twirled it in the air a couple of times and lobbed it toward the dining room, where Alex and I had finished dinner. I scored a direct hit on Alex, who was en route from kitchen to living room, bearing a glass of wine in each hand.

"You're supposed to yell incoming," he said, handing me one glass as Abigail jumped off the sofa and went thumping after her toy. "What is that thing?"

"Abigail's yellow mouse. She stalks it every night. Then she leaves it at various places in the apartment so I can step on it with my bare feet." I'd almost used the word "kill" to describe what my cat did with her toy, but my recent encounters with the grim reality of death made the word seem trivial when used to describe what happened to an inanimate object.

He sat down, his arm stretched out behind me. We watched as Abigail seized the yellow mouse by the scruff of its neck and headed off in the direction of the bedroom, making deep yowls in her throat.

"Maybe it's the color," he said, watching her go.

"Cats don't see colors. I think it's the texture. Of course, there's catnip inside."

We sat in companionable silence for a moment, sipping wine and ignoring the dinner dishes as we had avoided talking about Dr. Manibusan and the Navarros since Alex arrived a couple of hours earlier bearing a bottle of wine and the flowers that stood in a glass vase in the middle of the table. Instead, we talked about going to Kimball's East in Emeryville to hear some jazz next Saturday night and the upcoming classic movie series at the Paramount Theatre in Oakland.

"I heard the judge denied Rick bail," he said finally, sipping his wine.

"Yes. Max pitched a fit, but the D.A. convinced the judge that Rick would be on the first plane to Manila if he got out of jail. Eddie Villegas has such a track record that the judge just laughed at his lawyer. The case is getting less circumstantial, by the way. I talked to Inspector Cobb this morning. He checked Rick Navarro's fingerprints against that partial print on the battery found at the scene of Lito's murder. And guess what?"

"They match," Alex said. We saluted each other with our wineglasses.

"Rick's attorney is trying to blame it all on Eddie," I continued, "so maybe there is a chance Eddie will give evidence against Rick, which would help. By the time the lawyers plea-bargain, who knows what will happen?"

"I hope they can convict them. Uncle Lito deserves a little justice."

"What about the World War Two deaths in San Ygnacio?" I asked. "How is that playing back in Manila?"

Alex laughed. "I talked to Uncle Javier yesterday. He says the whole thing is a big scandal. The newspapers got hold of the transcript of the tape and printed it. Some of the politicians are even talking about having an investigation. Uncle Lito would have loved it." He stopped and shook his head. "Max Navarro will probably run for president anyway. And a lot of people will vote for him. Am I being cynical?"

"Yes. I'll join you. Greed and power always make me cynical." I raised my glass to my lips.

"What will happen to Felice?" Alex asked.

"Max has disassociated himself from her, as I knew he would, but her ex-husband got her a lawyer. That's probably a plea-bargain situation, too." I glanced at him. "I thought Felice was just a fling that didn't mean anything."

"Felice was a mistake," he said. He drained his wineglass and reached across me to set it on the end table. "I was using her to get back at Rick Navarro for taking my wife away from me. Of course, he wasn't really taking. Nina wanted to leave. And I didn't care enough about the marriage to keep her from going. So I used Felice."

"There's some truth to what you say," I told him, looking into his dark eyes. "You can't take all the blame, though, only part of it. The seeds of what Felice did were planted a long time ago."

"So it's over," Alex said.

"It'll never be over. Not till the old men die. That's what you told me at the fiesta. It's a simplistic statement, and somewhat sexist, but I often feel as though the world is run by old men."

"Trouble is, there are a lot of old men out there. And Max Navarro is no different from the rest of them."

"Trouble is, Alex, that there are always young men like Rick who are eager to take the old men's places. That's what perpetuates the system."

"So what do we do about it?"

"We have to stop being cynical."

"That's what Javier would say. I suppose that's why he keeps working to change things back in the Philippines, even if I don't approve of his methods."

We sat in silence for a moment. Then I finished my wine and set the glass aside. "We haven't solved the problems of the world this evening. We never do, just talking about them. We have to act. I suppose we should concentrate on cleaning up messes that are closer to home. Local politics, for example, or the dinner dishes." I started to get up, but he stopped me.

"Wouldn't you rather sit here and neck?" I looked at him, and his mouth curved in that slow smile I liked.

"Are you still trying to get me into bed?"

"Absolutely," he said. He switched off the table lamp and reached for me.

About the Author

JANET DAWSON is a legal secretary who lives in Alameda, California. She is the author of *Kindred Crimes*, the first book in the Jeri Howard mystery series.

MORE MURDER AND MAYHEM

from
Joyce Christmas